LETHAL LADIES
A Lost Classics Omnibus

LETHAL LADIES

THE LADY VANISHES by Ethel Lina White

LAURA by Vera Caspary

DOUBLEDAY LARGE PRINT HOME LIBRARY EDITION

Garden City, New York

This Large Print Edition, prepared especially for Doubleday Large Print Home Library, contains the complete, unabridged text of the original Publisher's Edition.

This Large Print Book carries the
Seal of Approval of N.A.V.H.

CONTENTS

THE
LADY
VANISHES

CHAPTER ONE
WITHOUT REGRETS

The day before the disaster, Iris Carr had her first premonition of danger. She was used to the protection of a crowd, whom—with unconscious flattery—she called "her friends." An attractive orphan of independent means, she had been surrounded always with clumps of people. They thought for her—or rather, she accepted their opinions, and they shouted for her—since her voice was rather too low in register, for mass social intercourse.

Their constant presence tended to create the illusion that she moved in a large circle, in spite of the fact that the same faces recurred with seasonal regularity. They also made her pleasantly aware of popularity. Her photograph appeared in the pictorial papers through the medium of a photographer's offer of publicity, after the Press announcement of her engagement to one of the crowd.

This was Fame.

Then, shortly afterwards, her engagement was broken, by mutual consent—which was a lawful occasion for the reproduction of another portrait. More Fame. And her mother, who died at her birth, might have wept or smiled at these pitiful flickers of human vanity, arising, like bubbles of marsh-gas, on the darkness below.

When she experienced her first threat of insecurity, Iris was feeling especially well and happy after an unconventional health-holiday. With the triumph of near-pioneers, the crowd had swooped down on a beautiful village of picturesque squalor, tucked away in a remote corner of Europe, and taken possession of it by the act of scrawling their names in the visitors' book.

For nearly a month they had invaded the only hotel, to the delighted demoralisation of the innkeeper and his staff. They scrambled up mountains, swam in the lake, and sunbathed on every available slope. When they were indoors, they filled the bar, shouted against the wireless, and tipped for each trifling service. The proprietor beamed at them over his choked cash-register, and the smiling waiters gave them preferential treatment, to the legitimate annoyance of the other English guests.

To these six persons, Iris appeared just one of her crowd, and a typical semi-Society girl—vain, selfish, and useless. Naturally, they had no knowledge of redeeming points—a generosity which made her accept the bill, as a matter of course, when she lunched with her "friends," and a real compassion for such cases of hardship which were clamped down under her eyes.

But while she was only vaguely conscious of fugitive moments of discontent and self-contempt, she was aware of a fastidious streak, which kept her aloof from any tendency to saturnalia. On this holiday she heard Pan's pipes, but had no experience of the kick of his hairy hind quarters.

Soon the slack convention of the crowd had been relaxed. They grew brown, they drank and were merry, while matrimonial boundaries became pleasantly blurred. Surrounded by a mixed bag of vague married couples, it was a sharp shock to Iris when one of the women—Olga—suddenly developed a belated sense of property, and accused her of stealing a husband.

Besides the unpleasantness of the scene, her sense of justice was outraged. She had merely tolerated a neglected male, who seemed a spare part in the dislocated domestic machine. It was not her fault that he had lost his head.

To make matters worse, at this crisis, she failed to notice any signs of real loyalty among her friends, who had plainly enjoyed the excitement. Therefore, to ease the tension, she decided not to travel back to England with the party, but to stay on for two days longer, alone.

She was still feeling sore, on the following day, when she accompanied the crowd to the little primitive railway station. They had already reacted to the prospect of a return to civilisation. They wore fashionable clothes again, and were roughly sorted into legitimate couples, as a natural sequence to the identification of suitcases and reservations.

The train was going to Trieste, which was definitely on the map. It was packed with tourists, who were also going back to pavements and lamp-posts. Forgetful of hillside and starlight, the crowd responded to the general noise and bustle. It seemed to recapture its old loyalty as it clustered round Iris.

"Sure you won't be bored, darling?"

"Change your mind and hop on."

"You've simply *got* to come."

As the whistle was blown, they tried to pull her into their carriage—just as she was, in shorts and nailed boots, and with a brown glaze of sunburn on her unpowdered face. She fought like a boxing-kangaroo to break free, and only succeeded in jumping down as the platform was beginning to slide past the window.

Laughing and panting from the struggle, she stood and waved after the receding train, until it disappeared round the bend of the gorge.

She felt almost guilty as she realised her relief at parting from her friends. But, although the holiday had been a success, she had drawn her pleasure chiefly from primeval sources—sun, water, and mountain-breeze. Steeped in Nature, she had vaguely resented the human intrusion.

They had all been together too closely and too intimately. At times, she had been conscious of jarring notes—a woman's high thin laugh—the tubby outline of a man's body, poised to dive—a continual flippant appeal to "My God."

It was true that while she had grown critical of her friends she had floated with the current. Like the others, she had raved of marvellous scenery, while she accepted it as a matter of course. It was a natural sequence that, when one travelled off the map, the landscape improved automatically as the standard of sanitation lapsed.

At last she was alone with the mountains and the silence. Below her lay a grass-green lake, sparkling with diamond reflections of the sun. The snowy peaks of distant ranges were silhouetted against a cornflower-blue sky. On a hill rose the dark pile of an ancient castle, with its five turrets pointing upwards, like the outspread fingers of a sinister hand.

Everywhere was a riot of colour. The station garden foamed with exotic flowers—flame and yellow—rising from spiked foliage. Higher up the slope, the small wooden hotel was painted ochre and crimson lake. Against the green wall of the gorge rose the last coil of smoke, like float-ing white feathers.

When it had faded away, Iris felt that the last link had been severed between her and the crowd. Blowing a derisive kiss, she turned away and clattered down the steep stony path. When she reached the glacier-fed river, she lingered on the bridge, to feel the iced air which arose from the greenish-white boil.

As she thought of yesterday's scene, she vowed that she never wanted to see the crowd again. They were connected with an episode which violated her idea of friendship. She had been a little fond of the woman, Olga, who had repaid her loyalty by a crude exhibition of jealousy.

She shrugged away the memory. Here, under the limitless blue, people seemed so small—their passions so paltry. They were merely incidental to the passage from the cradle to the grave. One met them and parted from them, without regrets.

Every minute the gap between her and them was widening. They were steaming away, out of her life. At the thought, she thrilled with a sense of new freedom, as though her spirit were liberated by the silence and solitude.

Yet, before many hours had passed, she would have bartered all the glories of Nature to have called them back again.

CHAPTER TWO
THE THREAT

Some four hours later Iris lay spread-eagled on a slope of the mountain, high above the valley. Ever since she had left the chill twilight of the gorge, at a shrine which marked a union of paths, she had been climbing steadily upwards, by a steep zigzag track.

After she had emerged from the belt of shadow, the sun had beat fiercely through her, but she did not slacken her pace. The fury of her thoughts drove her on, for she could not dislodge Olga from her mind.

The name was like a burr on her brain. *Olga.* Olga had eaten her bread, in the form of toast—for the sake of her figure—and had refused her salt, owing to a dietetic fad. This had made trouble in the kitchen. Olga had used her telephone, and misused her car. Olga had borrowed her fur coat, and had lent her a superfluous husband.

At the memory of Olga's Oscar, Iris put on a sprint.

"As if I'd skid for a man who looks like Mickey Mouse," she raged.

She was out of breath when, at last, she threw herself down on the turf and decided to call it a day. The mountain which had challenged her kept withdrawing as she advanced, so she had to give up her intention to reach the top.

As she lay with her eyes almost closed, listening to the ping of the breeze, her serenity returned. A clump of harebells, standing out against the skyline, seemed hardened and magnified to a metallic belfry, while she, herself, was dwarfed and welded into the earth—part of it, like the pebbles and the roots. In imagination she could almost hear the pumping of a giant heart underneath her head.

The moment passed, for she began to think of Olga again. This time, however, she viewed her from a different standpoint, for the altitude had produced the usual illusion of superiority. She reminded herself that the valley was four thousand feet above sea-level, while she had mounted about five thousand feet.

On the basis of this calculation she could afford to be generous, since she was nine thousand feet taller than her former friend—assuming, of course, that Olga was obliging enough as to remain at sea-level.

She decided to wash out the memory as unworthy of further anger.

"But never again," she said. "After this, I'll never help any one again."

Her voice had the passionate fervour of one who dedicates herself to some service. With the virtuous feeling of having profited by a lesson, for which heavy fees had been paid, she smoked a cigarette before the return journey. The air was so clear that mountains she had never seen before quivered out of invisibility and floated in the sky, in mauve transparencies. Far below she could see an arm of the lake—no longer green, but dimmed by distance to a misted blue.

Reluctantly she rose to her feet. It was time to go.

The descent proved not only monotonous, but painful, for the continual backward jolt of her weight threw a strain on un-exercised muscles. Her calves began to ache and her toes were stubbed on the stony path.

Growing impatient, she decided to desert the zigzag, in favour of a direct short-cut down the face of the mountain. With the lake as a guide to direction, she hurled herself down the slope.

It was a bold venture, but almost immediately she found that the gradient was too steep. As she was going too quickly to stop, her only course was to drop down to a sitting posture and glissade over the slippery turf—trusting to luck.

From that moment things happened quickly. Her pace increased every second, in spite of her efforts to brake with her feet. Patches of blue and green sped past her, as the valley rushed up to meet her, and smashed into the sky. Bumping over the rough ground, she steered towards a belt of trees at the bottom, in the hope that they might save her from a complete spill.

Unfortunately they proved to be rotten from age, and she crashed through them, to land with a bump in the middle of the stony pass.

Her fall had been partially broken, but she felt very sore and shaken as she scrambled to her feet. In spite of her injuries, she did not forget to give the forced laugh which had been drilled into her, at school, as the accompaniment to any game's casualty.

"Rather amusing," she murmured, picking splinters out of her legs.

But she was pleased to notice the shrine, a few yards farther up the track, for this was a definite tribute to her steering. As she was not far from the hotel, she clattered down the gully, thinking of the comforts which awaited her. A long cold drink, a hot bath, dinner in bed. When she caught sight of a gleam of water, at the bend of the gorge, in her eagerness she broke into a limping run.

She rounded the corner and then stopped, staring before her in utter bewilderment. All the familiar landmarks had disappeared, as though some interfering person had passed an india-rubber over the landscape. There were no little wooden houses, no railway station, no pier, no hotel.

With a pang of dismay she realised that she had steered by a faulty compass. This was not their familiar green lake, in which she and her friends had bathed daily. Instead of being deep and ovoid in shape, it was a winding pale-blue mere, with shallow rushy margins.

In the circumstances, there was but one thing to do—retrace her steps back to the shrine and follow the other gully.

It was definitely amusing and she achieved quite a creditable laugh before she began to plod slowly upwards again.

Her mood was too bleak for her to appreciate the savage grandeur of the scenery. It was a scene of stark desolation, riven by landslips and piled high with shattered rocks. There was no crop of vegetation amid the boulders—no chirp of bird. The only sounds were the rattle of loose stones, dislodged by her feet, and the splash of a shrunken torrent, which foamed over its half-dried course, like a tangled white thread.

Used to perpetual company, Iris began to long for faces and voices. In her loneliness, she was even reduced to the flabbiness of self-pity. She reminded herself that, when she returned to England, she would not go home, like others. She would merely go back.

At present she was living at an hotel, for she had sublet her small luxury flat. Although her mode of living was her own choice, at such a time and such a place she felt that she paid a high price for freedom.

Her mood did not last, for, at the top of the pass, she was faced with a call upon her fortitude. Casting about, to pick up her bearings, she made the discovery that the shrine was different from the original landmark where she had struck the mountain zigzag.

This time she did not laugh, for she felt that humour could be carried too far. Instead she was furious with herself. She believed that she knew these mountains, because, with the others, she had clattered up and down the gorges, like a pack of wild goats.

But she had merely followed—while others led. Among the crowd was the inevitable leader—the youth with the map.

Thrown on her own resources, she had not the least idea of her direction. All she could do was to follow the gorge up to its next ramification and trust to luck.

"If I keep on walking, I must get somewhere," she argued. "Besides, no one can get lost who has a tongue."

She had need of her stoicism, for she had grown desperately weary, in addition to the handicap of a sore heel. When, at last, she reached a branch which gave her a choice of roads, she was too distrustful of her own judgement to experiment. Sitting down on a boulder, she waited on the chance of hailing some passer-by.

It was her zero-hour, when her independence appeared only the faculty to sign cheques drawn on money made by others—and her popularity, but a dividend of the same cheques.

"I've been carried all my life," she thought. "And even if some one comes, I'm the world's worst linguist."

The description flattered her, for she had not the slightest claim to the title of linguist. Her ignorance of foreign languages was the result of being finished at Paris and Dresden. During the time she was at school, she mixed exclusively with other English girls, while the natives who taught her acquired excellent English accents.

This was her rendering of the line in the National Anthem—"Send us victorious."

Patriotism did not help her now, for she felt slightly doubtful when a thick-set swarthy man, wearing leather shorts and dirty coloured braces, swung up the pass.

Among Iris' crowd was a youth who was clever at languages. From his knowledge of common roots, he had managed to use German as a kind of liaison language; but he had to draw on his imagination in order to interpret and be understood.

Iris had a vivid recollection of how the crowd used to hoot with derision at his failures, when she called out to the man in English and asked him to direct her to the village.

He stared at her, shrugged, and shook his head.

Her second attempt—in a louder key—met with no better success. The peasant, who seemed in a hurry, was passing on, when Iris barred his way.

She was acutely aware of her own impotence, as though she were some maimed creature, whose tongue had been torn out. But she had to hold his attention, to compel him to understand. Feeling that she had lapsed from the dignity of a rational being, she was forced to make pantomimic gestures, pointing to the alternative routes in turn, while she kept repeating the name of the village.

"He must get that, unless he's an idiot," she thought.

The man seemed to grasp her drift, for he nodded several times. But, instead of indicating any direction, he broke into an unfamiliar jargon.

As Iris listened to the torrent of guttural sounds, her nerve snapped suddenly. She felt cut off from all human intercourse, as though a boundary-line had been wiped out, and—instead of being in Europe—she were stranded in a corner of Asia.

Without money and without a common language, she could wander indefinitely. At that moment she might be headed away from the village and into the wilds. The gorge had many tributary branches, like the windings of an inland sea.

As she grew afraid, the peasant's face began to waver, like the illusion of some bad dream. She noticed that his skin glistened and that he had a slight goitre; but she was definitely conscious of his steamy goatish smell, for he was sweating from his climb.

"I can't understand you," she cried hysterically. "I can't understand one word. Stop. Oh, *stop.* You'll drive me mad."

In his turn the man heard only a string of gibberish. He saw a girl, dressed like a man, who was unattractively skinny—according to the local standard of beauty—with cut dirty knees. She was a foreigner, although he did not know her nationality. Further, she was worked up to a pitch of excitement, and was exceptionally stupid.

She did not seem to grasp that she was telling him less than half the name of the village, whereas three different hamlets had the same prefix. He had explained this to her, and asked for the full word.

Iris could not have supplied it even if she had understood the man. The name of the village was such a tongue-twister that she had never tried to disentangle it, but, like the rest, had called it by its first three syllables.

The position was stalemate. With a final grimace and shrug, the peasant went on his way, leaving Iris alone with the mountains.

They overhung her like a concrete threat. She had bought picture postcards of them and broadcast them with the stereotyped comment—"Marvellous scenery." Once she had even scrawled "This is my room," and marked a peak with a derisive cross.

Now—the mountains were having their revenge. As she cowered under the projecting cliffs, she felt they had but to shake those towering brows, to crush her to powder beneath an avalanche of boulders. They dwarfed her to insignificance. They blotted out her individuality. They extinguished her spirit.

The spell was broken by the sound of English voices. Round the bend of the pass came the honeymoon couple, from the hotel.

This pair of lovers was respected even by the crowd, for the completeness of their reserve and the splendour of their appearance. The man was tall, handsome, and of commanding carriage. His voice was authoritative, and he held his head at an angle which suggested excessive pride. Waiters scampered at his nod, and the innkeeper—probably on the strength of his private sitting-room—called him "Milord."

His wife was almost as tall, with a perfect figure and a flawless face. She wore

beautiful clothes which were entirely un-
suitable for the wilds; but it was obvious
that she dressed thus as a matter of course,
and to please only her husband.

They set their own standard and appeared unconscious of the other visitors,
who accepted them as belonging to a
higher social sphere. It was suspected that
the name "Todhunter," under which they
had registered, was a fiction to preserve
their anonymity.

They passed Iris almost without notice.
The man raised his hat vaguely, but his
glance held no recognition. His wife never
removed her violet eyes from the stony
track, for her heels were perilously high.

She was speaking in a low voice, which
was vehement in spite of its muffled tone.

"No darling. Not another day. Not even
for *you*. We've stayed too—"

Iris lost the rest of the sentence. She
prepared to follow them at a discreet distance, for she had become acutely aware
of her own wrecked appearance.

The arrival of the honeymoon pair had
restored her sense of values. Their presence was proof that the hotel was not far
away, for they never walked any distance.

At the knowledge, the mountains shrank back to camera-subjects, while she was reconstructed, from a lost entity, to a London girl who was critical about the cut of her shorts.

Very soon she recognised the original shrine, whence she had deserted the pass. Limping painfully down the track, presently she caught the gleam of the darkening lake and the lights of the hotel, shining through the green gloom.

She began to think again of a hot bath and dinner as she remembered that she was both tired and hungry.

But although apparently only the physical traces of her adventure remained, actually, her sense of security had been assailed—as if the experience were a threat from the future, to reveal the horror of helplessness, far away from all that was familiar.

CHAPTER THREE

CONVERSATION PIECE

When the honeymoon pair returned to the hotel the four remaining guests were sitting outside on the gravelled square, before the veranda. They were enjoying the restful interlude of "between the lights." It was too dark to write letters, or read—too early to dress for dinner. Empty cups and cake-crumbs on one of the tables showed that they had taken afternoon tea in the open and had not moved since.

It was typical of two of them, the Misses Flood-Porter, to settle. They were not the kind that flitted, being in the fifties and definitely set in their figures and their habits. Both had immaculately waved grey hair, which retained sufficient samples of the original tint to give them the courtesy-title of blondes. They had also, in common, excellent natural complexions and rather fierce expressions.

The delicate skin of the elder—Miss Evelyn—was slightly shrivelled, for she was nearly sixty, while Miss Rose was only just out of the forties. The younger sister was taller and stouter; her voice was louder, her colour deeper. In an otherwise excellent character, was a streak of amiable bully, which made her inclined to scold her partner at contract.

During their visit, they had formed a quartette with the Reverend Kenneth Barnes and his wife. They had travelled out on the same train, and they planned to return to England together. The vicar and his wife had the gift of pleasant companionship, which the Misses Flood-Porter—who were without it—attributed to mutual tastes and prejudices.

The courtyard was furnished with iron chairs and tables, enamelled in brilliant colours, and was decorated with tubs of dusty evergreen shrubs. As Miss Flood-Porter looked round her, she thought of her own delightful home in a Cathedral city.

According to the papers, there had been rain in England, so the garden should look its best, with vivid green grass and lush borders of asters and dahlias.

"I'm looking forward to seeing my garden again," she said.

"Ours," corrected her sister, who was John Blunt.

"And I'm looking forward to a comfortable chair," laughed the vicar. "Ha. Here comes the bridal pair."

In spite of a sympathetic interest in his fellows he did not call out a genial greeting. He had learned from his first—and final—rebuff that they had resented any intrusion on their privacy. So he leaned back, puffing at his pipe, while he watched them mount the steps of the veranda.

"Handsome pair," he said in an approving voice.

"I wonder who they *really* are," remarked Miss Flood-Porter. "The man's face is familiar to me. I know I've seen him somewhere."

"On the pictures, perhaps," suggested her sister.

"Oh, do you go?" broke in Mrs. Barnes eagerly, hoping to claim another taste in common, for she concealed a guilty passion for the cinema.

"Only to see George Arliss and Diana Wynyard," explained Miss Flood-Porter.

"That settles it," said the vicar. "He's certainly not George Arliss, and neither is she Diana."

"All the same, I feel certain there is some mystery about them," persisted Miss Flood-Porter.

"So do I," agreed Mrs. Barnes. "I—I wonder if they are really married."

"Are *you?*" asked her husband quickly.

He laughed gently when his wife flushed to her eyes.

"Sorry to startle you, my dear," he said, "but isn't it simpler to believe that we are all of us what we assume to be? Even parsons and their wives." He knocked the ashes out of his pipe, and rose from his chair. "I think I'll stroll down to the village for a chat with my friends."

"How can he talk to them when he doesn't know their language?" demanded Miss Rose bluntly, when the vicar had gone from the garden.

"Oh, he *makes* them understand," explained his wife proudly. "Sympathy, you know, and common humanity. He'd rub noses with a savage."

"I'm afraid we drove him away by talking scandal," said Miss Flood-Porter.

"It was my fault," declared Mrs. Barnes. "I know people think I'm curious. But, really, I have to force myself to show an interest in my neighbour's affairs. It's my protest against our terrible national shyness."

"But we're proud of that," broke in Miss Rose. "England does not need to advertise."

"Of course not. . . . But we only pass this way once. I have to remind myself that the stranger sitting beside me may be in some trouble and that I might be able to help."

The sisters looked at her with approval. She was a slender woman in the mid-forties, with a pale oval face, dark hair, and a sweet expression. Her large brown eyes were both kind and frank—her manner sincere.

It was impossible to connect her with anything but rigid honesty. They knew that she floundered into awkward explanations, rather than run the risk of giving a false impression.

In her turn, she liked the sisters. They

were of solid worth and sound respectability. One felt that they would serve on juries
with distinction, and do their duty to their
God and their neighbour—while permitting
no direction as to its nature.

They were also leisured people, with a
charming house and garden, well-trained
maids and frozen assets in the bank. Mrs.
Barnes knew this, so, being human, it gave
her a feeling of superiority to reflect that
the one man in their party was her husband.

She could appreciate the sense of ownership, because, up to her fortieth birthday,
she had gone on her yearly holiday in the
company of a huddle of other spinsters.
Since she had left school, she had earned
her living by teaching, until the miracle
happened which gave her—not only a husband—but a son.

Both she and her husband were so
wrapped up in the child that the vicar
sometimes feared that their devotion was
tempting Fate. The night before they set
out on their holiday he proposed a pact.

"Yes," he agreed, looking down at the
sleeping boy in his cot. "He *is* beautiful.
But . . . It is my privilege to read the Com-

mandments to others. Sometimes, I wonder——"

"I know what you mean," interrupted his
wife. "Idolatry."

He nodded.

"I am as guilty as you," he admitted. "So
I mean to discipline myself. In our position,
we have special opportunities to influence
others. We must not grow lop-sided, but
develop every part of our nature. If this
holiday is to do us real good, it *must* be
a complete mental change. . . . My dear,
suppose we agree not to talk exclusively of
Gabriel, while we are away?"

Mrs. Barnes agreed. But her promise did
not prevent her from thinking of him con-
tinually. Although they had left him in the
care of a competent grandmother, she was
foolishly apprehensive about his health.

While she was counting the remaining
hours before her return to her son, and
Miss Flood-Porter smiled in anticipation of
seeing her garden, Miss Rose was pursuing her original train of thought. She always
ploughed a straight furrow, right to its end.

"I can't understand how any one can tell
a lie," she declared. "Unless, perhaps, some
poor devil who's afraid of being sacked.

But—people like *us*. We know a wealthy woman who boasts of making false declarations at the Customs. Sheer dishonesty."

As she spoke, Iris appeared at the gate of the hotel garden. She did her best to skirt the group at the table, but she could not avoid hearing what was said.

"Perhaps I should not judge others," remarked Mrs. Barnes in the clear carrying voice of a form-mistress. "I've never felt the slightest temptation to tell a lie."

"Liar," thought Iris automatically.

She was in a state of utter fatigue, which bordered on collapse. It was only by the exercise of every atom of willpower that she forced herself to reach the hotel. The ordeal had strained her nerves almost to breaking-point. Although she longed for the quiet of her room, she knew she could not mount the stairs without a short rest. Every muscle felt wrenched as she dropped down on an iron chair and closed her eyes.

"If any one speaks to me, I'll scream," she thought.

The Misses Flood-Porter exchanged glances and turned down the corners of their mouths. Even gentle Mrs. Barnes' soft brown eyes held no welcome, for she had been a special victim of the crowd's bad manners and selfishness.

They behaved as though they had bought the hotel and the other guests were inter-lopers, exacting preferential treatment—and getting it—by bribery. This infringe-ment of fair-dealing annoyed the other tourists, as they adhered to the terms of their payment to a travelling agency, which included service.

The crowd monopolised the billiard-table and secured the best chairs. They were always served first at meals; courses gave out, and bath-water ran luke-warm.

Even the vicar found that his charity was strained. He did his best to make al-lowance for the animal spirits of youth, al-though he was aware that several among the party could not be termed juvenile.

Unfortunately, Iris' so-called friends in-cluded two persons who were no testimo-nial for the English nation; and since it was difficult to distinguish one girl in a bathing-brief from another, Mrs. Barnes was of the opinion that they were all doing the same thing—getting drunk and making love.

Her standard of decency was offended by the sunbathing—her nights disturbed by noise. Therefore she was specially grateful for the prospect of two peaceful days, spent amid glorious scenery and in congenial company.

But, apparently, there was not a complete clearance of the crowd; there was a hangover, in this girl—and there might be others. Mrs. Barnes had vaguely remarked Iris, because she was pretty, and had been pursued by a bathing-gentleman with a matronly figure.

As the man was married, his selection was not to her credit. But she seemed to be so exhausted that Mrs. Barnes' kindly heart soon reproached her for lack of sympathy.

"Are you left all alone?" she called, in her brightest tones.

Iris shuddered at the unexpected overture. At that moment the last thing in the world she wanted was mature interest, which, in her experience, masked curiosity.

"Yes," she replied.

"Oh, dear, what a shame. Aren't you lonely?"

"No."

"But you're rather young to be travelling

without friends. Couldn't any of your people come with you?"

"I have none."

"No family at all?"

"No, and no relatives. Aren't I lucky?"

Iris was not near enough to hear the horrified gasp of the Misses Flood-Porter; but Mrs. Barnes' silence told her that her snub had not miscarried. To avoid a further inquisition, she made a supreme effort to rise, for she was stiffening in every joint, and managed to drag herself into the hotel and upstairs to her room.

Mrs. Barnes tried to carry off the incident with a laugh.

"I'm afraid I've blundered again," she said. "She plainly resented me. But it seemed hardly human for us to sit like dummies, and show no interest in her."

"Is she interested in *you?*" demanded Miss Rose. "Or in us? That sort of girl is utterly selfish. She wouldn't raise a finger, or go an inch out of her way, to help any one."

There was only one answer to the question, which Mrs. Barnes was too kind to make. So she remained silent, since she could not tell a lie.

Neither she—nor any one else—could

foretell the course of the next twenty-four hours, when this girl—standing alone against a cloud of witnesses—would endure such anguish of spirit as threatened her sanity, on behalf of a stranger for whom she had no personal feeling.

Or rather—if there was actually such a person as Miss Froy.

CHAPTER FOUR
ENGLAND CALLING

Because she had a square on her palm, which, according to a fortune-teller, signified safety, Iris believed that she lived in a protected area. Although she laughed at the time, she was impressed secretly, because hers was a specially sheltered life.

At this crisis, the stars, as usual, seemed to be fighting for her. The mountains had sent out a preliminary warning. During the evening, too, she received overtures of companionship, which might have delivered her from mental isolation.

Yet she deliberately cut every strand which linked her with safety, out of mistaken loyalty to her friends.

She missed them directly she entered the lounge, which was silent and deserted. As she walked along the corridor, she passed empty bedrooms, with stripped beds and littered floors. Mattresses hung from every window and the small verandas were heaped with pillows.

It was not only company which was lacking, but moral support. The crowd never troubled to change for the evening, unless comfort suggested flannel trousers. On one occasion, it had achieved the triumph of a complaint, when a lady appeared at dinner dressed in her bathing-slip.

The plaintiffs had been the Misses Flood-Porter, who always wore expensive but sober dinner-gowns. Iris remembered the incident, when she had finished her bath. Although slightly ashamed of her deference to public opinion, she fished from a suitcase an unpacked afternoon frock of crinkled crêpe.

The hot soak and rest had refreshed her, but she felt lonely, as she leaned over the balustrade. Her pensive pose and the graceful lines of her dress arrested the attention of the bridegroom—Todhunter, according to the register—as he strolled out of his bedroom.

He had not the least knowledge of her

identity, or that he had acted as a sort of guiding-star to her, in the gorge. He and his wife took their meals in their private sitting-room and never mingled with the crowd. He concluded, therefore, that she was an odd guest whom he had missed in the general scramble.

Approving her with an experienced eye, he stopped.

"Quiet, to-night," he remarked. "Refreshing change after the din of that horrible rabble."

To his surprise, the girl looked coldly at him.

"It *is* quiet," she said. "But I happen to miss my friends."

As she walked downstairs she felt defiantly glad that she had made him realise his blunder. Championship of her friends mattered more than the absence of social sense. But, in spite of her triumph, the incident was vaguely unpleasant.

The crowd had gloried in its unpopularity, which seemed to it a sign of superiority. It frequently remarked in complacent voices, "We're not popular with these people," or "They don't really like us." Under the influence of its mass-hypnotism, Iris wanted no other label. But now that she was alone, it was not quite so amusing to realise that the other guests, who were presumably decent and well-bred, considered her an outsider.

Her mood was bleakly defiant when she entered the restaurant. It was a big bare room, hung with stiff deep-blue wallpaper, patterned with conventional gilt stars. The electric lights were set in clumsy wrought-iron chandeliers, which suggested a Hollywood set for a medieval castle. Scarcely any of the tables were laid, and only one waiter drooped at the door.

In a few days, the hotel would be shut up for the winter. With the departure of the big English party, most of the holiday staff had become superfluous and had already gone back to their homes in the district.

The remaining guests appeared to be unaffected by the air of neglect and desolation inseparable from the end of the season. The Misses Flood-Porter shared a table with the vicar and his wife. They were all in excellent spirits and gave the impression of having come into their own, as they capped each other's jokes, culled from Punch.

Iris pointedly chose a small table in a far corner. She smoked a cigarette while she waited to be served. The others were advanced in their meal and it was a novel sensation for one of the crowd to be in arrears.

Mrs. Barnes, who was too generous to nurse resentment for her snub, looked at her with admiring eyes.

"How pretty that girl looks in a frock," she said.

"*Afternoon frock*," qualified Miss Flood-Porter. "We always make a point of wearing evening dress for dinner, when we're on the Continent."

"If we didn't dress, we should feel we were letting England down," explained the younger sister.

Although Iris spun out her meal to its limit, she was driven back ultimately to the lounge. She was too tired to stroll and it was early for bed. As she looked round her, she could hardly believe that, only the night before, it had been a scene of continental glitter and gaiety—although the latter quality had been imported from England. Now that it was no longer filled with friends, she was shocked to notice its tawdry theatrical finery. The gilt cane chairs were tarnished, the crimson plush upholstery shabby.

A clutter of cigarette stubs and spent matches in the palm pots brought a lump to her throat. They were all that remained of the crowd.

As she sat apart, the vicar—pipe in mouth—watched her with a thoughtful frown. His clear-cut face was both strong and sensitive, and an almost perfect blend of flesh and spirit. He played rough football with the youths of his parish, and, afterwards, took their souls by assault; but he had also a real understanding of the problems of his women-parishioners.

When his wife told him of Iris' wish for solitude, he could enter into her feeling, because, sometimes, he yearned to escape from people and even from his wife. His own inclination was to leave her to the boredom of her own company; yet he was touched by the dark lines under her eyes and her mournful lips.

In the end, he resolved to ease his conscience at the cost of a rebuff. He knew it was coming, because, as he crossed the lounge, she looked up quickly, as though on guard.

"Another," she thought.

From a distance she had admired the spirituality of his expression; but, to-night, he was numbered among her hostile critics.

"Horrible rabble." The words floated into her memory, as he spoke to her.

"If you are travelling back to England alone, would you care to join our party?"

"When are you going?" she asked.

"Day after to-morrow, before they take off the last through train of the season."

"But I'm going to-morrow. Thanks so much."

"Then I'll wish you a pleasant journey."

The vicar smiled faintly at her lightning decision as he crossed to a table and began to address luggage-labels.

His absence was his wife's opportunity. In her wish not to break her promise, she had gone to the other extreme and had not mentioned her baby to her new friends, save for one casual allusion to "our little boy." But, now that the holiday was nearly over, she could not resist the temptation of showing his photograph, which had won a prize in a local baby competition.

With a guilty glance at her husband's

back she drew out of her bag a limp leather case.

"This is my large son," she said, trying to hide her pride.

The Misses Flood-Porter were exclusive animal-lovers and not particularly fond of children. But they said all the correct things with such well-bred conviction that Mrs. Barnes' heart swelled with triumph.

Miss Rose, however, switched off to another subject directly the vicar returned from the writing-table.

"Do you believe in warning dreams, Mr. Barnes?" she asked. "Because, last night, I dreamed of a railway smash."

The question caught Iris' attention and she strained to hear the vicar's reply.

"I'll answer your question," he said, "if you'll first answer mine. What *is* a dream? Is it stifled apprehension——"

"I wonder," said a bright voice in Iris' ear, "I wonder if you would like to see the photograph of my little son, Gabriel?"

Iris realised dimly that Mrs. Barnes—who was keeping up England in limp brown lace—had seated herself beside her and was showing her the photograph of a naked baby.

She made a pretence of looking at it while she tried to listen to the vicar.

"Gabriel," she repeated vaguely.

"Yes, after the Archangel. We named him after him."

"How sweet. Did he send a mug?"

Mrs. Barnes stared incredulously, while her sensitive face grew scarlet. She believed that the girl had been intentionally profane and had insulted her precious little son, to avenge her boredom. Pressing her trembling lips together she rejoined her friends.

Iris was grateful when the humming in her ears ceased. She was unaware of her slip, because she had only caught a fragment of Mrs. Barnes' explanation. Her interest was still held by the talk of presentiments.

"Say what you like," declared Miss Rose, sweeping away the vicar's argument, "I've common sense on my side. They usually try to pack too many passengers into the last good train of the season. I know I'll be precious glad when I'm safely back in England."

A spirit of apprehension quivered in the air at her words.

"But you aren't really afraid of an accident?" cried Mrs. Barnes, clutching Gabriel's photograph tightly.

"Of course not." Miss Flood-Porter answered for her sister. "Only, perhaps we feel we're rather off the beaten track here, and so very far from home. Our trouble is we don't know a word of the language."

"She means," cut in Miss Rose, "we're all right over reservations and coupons, so long as we stick to hotels and trains. But if some accident happened to make us break our journey, or lose a connection, and we were stranded in some small place, we should feel *lost.* Besides it would be awkward about money. We didn't bring any travellers' cheques."

The elder sister appealed to the vicar.

"Do you advise us to take my sister's dream as a warning and travel back tomorrow?"

"No, *don't,*" murmured Iris under her breath.

She waited for the vicar's answer with painful interest, for she was not eager to travel on the same train as these uncongenial people, who might feel it their duty to befriend her.

"You must follow your own inclinations," said the vicar. "But if you do leave prematurely, you will not only give a victory to superstition, but you will deprive yourself of another day in these glorious surroundings."

"And our reservations are for the day after to-morrow," remarked Miss Rose. "We'd better not risk any muddles. . . .

And now, I'm going up to pack for my journey back to dear old England."

To the surprise of every one her domineering voice suddenly blurred with emotion. Miss Flood-Porter waited until she had gone out of the lounge, before she explained.

"Nerves. We had a very trying experience, just before we came away. The doctor ordered a complete change so we came here, instead of Switzerland."

Then the innkeeper came in, and, as a compliment to his guests, fiddled with his radio, until he managed to get London on the long wave. Amid a machine-gun rattle of atmospherics, a familiar mellow voice informed them, "You have just been listening to . . ."

But they had heard nothing.

Miss Flood-Porter saw her garden, silvered by the harvest moon. She wondered whether the chrysanthemum buds, three to a pot, were swelling, and if the blue salvias had escaped the slugs.

Miss Rose, briskly stacking shoes in the bottom of a suitcase, quivered at a recollection. Again she saw a gaping hole in a garden-bed, where overnight had stood a cherished clump of white delphiniums. . . . It was not only the loss of their treasure, but the nerve-racking ignorance of where the enemy would strike next . . .

The Vicar and his wife thought of their baby, asleep in his cot. They must decide whether they should merely peep at him, or risk waking him with a kiss.

Iris remembered her friends in the roaring express, and was suddenly smitten with a wave of home-sickness.

England was calling.

CHAPTER FIVE
THE NIGHT EXPRESS

Iris was awakened that night, as usual, by the express screaming through the darkness. Jumping out of bed, she reached the window in time to see it outline the curve of the lake with a fiery wire. As it rattled below the hotel, the golden streak expanded to a string of lighted windows, which, when it passed, snapped together again like the links of a bracelet.

After it had disappeared round the gorge, she followed its course by its pall of quivering red smoke. In imagination, she saw it shooting through Europe, as though it were an explosive shuttle ripping through the scorched fabric of the map. It caught up cities and threaded them on a gleaming whistling string. Illuminated names flashed before her eyes and were gone—Bucharest, Zagreb, Trieste, Milan, Basle, Calais.

Once again she was flooded with home-hunger, even though her future address were an hotel. Mixed with it was a gust of foreboding—which was a legacy from the mountains.

"Suppose—something—happened, and I never came back."

At that moment she felt that any evil could block the way to her return. A railway crash, illness, or crime were possibilities, which were actually scheduled in other lives. They were happening all round her and at any time a line might give way in the protective square in her palm.

As she lay and tossed, she consoled herself with the reminder that this was the last time she would lie under the lumpy feather bed. Throughout the next two nights she, too, would be rushing through dark landscape, jerked out of every brief spell of sleep by the flash of lights, whenever the express roared through a station.

The thought was with her when she woke, the next morning, to see the silhouette of mountain-peaks iced against the flush of sunrise.

"I'm going home to-day," she told herself exultantly.

The air was raw when she looked out of her window. Mist was rising from the lake which gleamed greenly through yellowed fans of chestnut trees. But in spite of the blue and gold glory of autumn she felt indifferent to its beauty.

She was also detached from the drawbacks of her room, which usually offended her critical taste. Its wooden walls were stained a crude shade of raw sienna, and instead of running water there was a battered washstand which bore a tin can, covered with a thin towel.

In spirit, Iris had already left the hotel. Her journey was begun before she started. When she went down to the restaurant she was barely conscious of the other guests, who, only a few hours before, had inspired her with antipathy.

The Misses Flood-Porter, who were dressed for writing letters in the open, were breakfasting at a table by the window. They did not speak to her, although they would have bowed as a matter of courtesy, had they caught her eye.

Iris did not notice the omission, because

they had gone completely out of her life. She drank her coffee in a silence which was broken by occasional remarks from the sisters, who wondered whether the English weather were kind for a local military wedding.

Her luck held, for she was spared contact with the other guests, who were engrossed by their own affairs. As she passed the bureau, Mrs. Barnes was calling a waiter's attention to a letter in one of the pigeon-holes. Her grey jersey-suit, as well as her packet of sandwiches, advertised an excursion.

The vicar, who was filling his pipe on the veranda, was also in unconventional kit— shorts, sweater, nailed boots, and the local felt hat—adorned with a tiny blue feather— which he had bought as a souvenir of his holiday.

His smile was so happy that Iris thought he looked both festive and good, as though a saint had deserted his shrine, knocking his halo a trifle askew in the process, in order to put a coat of sunburn over his pallid plaster.

Her tolerance faded as she listened to a

dialogue which was destined to affect her own future.

"Is that a letter from home?" called the vicar.

"Yes," replied his wife, after a pause.

"I thought Grandma told us to expect no more letters. . . . What's she writing about?"

"She wants me to do a little shopping for her, on our way through London. Some Margaret Rose silk. The little Princess, you know."

"But you'll be tired. It's not very considerate."

"No." Mrs. Barnes' voice was exceptionally sharp. "It's not. Why didn't she *think?*"

Iris condoned her own ungracious conduct of the preceding night, as she left them to their discussion. She told herself that he was justified in protecting herself from the boredom of domestic trifles.

As she strolled past the front of the hotel, she had to draw back to avoid trespassing on the privacy of the honeymoon pair, whose sitting-room opened on to the veranda. They were breakfasting in the open air, off rolls and fruit. The man was resplendent in a Chinese dressing-gown, while his wife wore an elaborate wrapper over satin pyjamas.

The Todhunters annoyed Iris, because they affected her with vague discontent. She was conscious of the same unacknowledged blank when she watched a love-scene played by two film stars. Theirs was passion—perfectly dressed, discreetly censored and with the better profile presented to the camera.

She felt a responsive thrill when the man looked into his bride's eyes with intense personal interest.

"Has it been perfect?" he asked.

Mrs. Todhunter knew exactly how long to pause before her reply.

"Yes."

It was faultless timing for he understood what she did not say.

"Not perfect, then," he remarked. "But, darling, is anything——"

Iris passed out of earshot, while she was still slightly envious. Her own experience of love had been merely a succession of episodes which led up to the photographic farce of her engagement.

The morning seemed endless, but at length it wore away. She had little to pack, because—following tradition—her friends had taken the bulk of her luggage with them, to save her trouble. An hour or two were killed, or rather drowned, in the lake, but she was too impatient to lie in the sun.

After she had changed for her journey, she went down to the restaurant. The dish of the day was attractively jellied and garnished with sprigs of tarragon, chervil, and chopped eggs; but she suspected that it was composed of poached eels. Turning away, with a shudder, she took possession of a small buttercup-painted table in the gravelled garden, where she lunched on potato soup and tiny grapes.

The sun flickered through the dense roof of chestnuts, but the iron chair was too hard and cold for comfort. Although the express was not due for more than an hour, she decided to wait for it at the railway station, where she could enjoy a view.

She had worked herself up to a fever, so that the act of leaving the hotel seemed to bring her a step nearer to her journey. It gave her acute pleasure to pay her bill and tip the stragglers of the staff. Although she saw none of her fellow-guests, she hurried through the garden like a truant from school, as though she feared she might be detained, at the last minute.

It was strange to wear a sophisticated travelling-suit and high heels again, as she jolted down the rough path, followed by a porter with her baggage. The sensation was not too comfortable after weeks of liberty, but she welcomed it as part of her return to civilisation. When she was seated on the platform, her suitcase at her feet, and the shimmer of the lake below, she was conscious of having reached a peak of enjoyment.

The air was water-clear and held the sting of altitude. As the sun blazed down on her, she felt steeped in warmth and drenched in light. She took off her hat and gazed at the signal post, anticipating the thrill of its drop, followed by the first glimpse of a foreshortened engine at the end of the rails.

There were other people on the platform, for the arrival of the express was the main event of the day. It was too early for the genuine travellers, but groups of loiterers, both visitors and natives, hung round the fruit- and paper-stalls. They were a cheerful company and noisy in many languages.

Iris heard no English until two men came down the road from the village.

They leaned over the palings behind her, to continue an argument. She did not feel sufficient interest, at first, to turn and see their faces, but their voices were so distinctive that, presently, she could visualise them.

The one whom she judged the younger had an eager untidy voice. She felt sure that he possessed an active brain, with a rush of ideas. He spoke too quickly and often stumbled for a word, probably not because his terms were limited, but because he had a choice of too many.

Gradually he won her sympathy, partly because his mind seemed in tune—or rather, in discord—with hers and partly because she disliked the other speaker instinctively. His accent was pedantic and consciously cultured. He spoke deliberately, with an irritating authority, which betrayed his inflexible mind. "Oh, no, my dear Hare." Iris felt it should have been "Watson." "You're abysmally wrong. It has been proved conclusively that there can be no fairer or better system of justice than trial by jury."

"Trial by fatheads," spluttered the younger voice. "You talk of ordinary citizens. No one is ordinary, but a bag of his special prejudices. One woman's got a spite against her sex—one man's cranky on morality. They all damn the prisoner on different issues. And they've all businesses or homes which they want to get back to. They watch the clock and grasp the obvious."

"They are directed by the judge."

"And how much of his direction do they remember? You know how your own mind slips when you're listening to a string of words. Besides, after he's dotted all the i's and crossed the t's for them, they stampede and bring him in the wrong verdict."

"Why should you assume it is wrong? They have formed their own conclusion on the testimony of the witnesses."

"Witnesses." In his heat the young man thumped the railing. "The witness is the most damnable part of the outfit. He may be so stupid as to be putty in the hands of some wily lawyer, or he may be smart and lie away some wretched man's life, just to read about his own wonderful memory and powers of observation and see his photograph in the papers. They're all out for publicity."

The elder man laughed in a superior manner which irritated his companion to the personal touch.

"When I'm accused of bumping you off, professor, I'd rather be tried by a team of judges who'd bring trained legal minds and impartial justice to bear on the facts."

"You're biassed," said the Professor, ". . . Let me try to convince you. The Jury is intelligent in bulk, and can judge character. Certain witnesses are reliable, while others must be viewed with suspicion. For instance, how would you describe that dark woman with the artificial lashes?"

"Attractive."

"Hum. I should call her meretricious and so would any average man of the world. Now, we'll assume that she and that English lady in the Burberry are giving contrary evidence. One of the two must be telling a lie."

"I don't agree. It may depend on the point of view. The man in the street, with his own back garden, is ready to swear to lilac when he sees it; but when he goes to a botanical garden he finds it's labelled syringa."

"The generic name——"

"I know, I know. But if one honest John Citizen swears syringa is white, while another swears it's mauve, you'll grant that there is an opportunity for confusion. Evidence may be like that."

"Haven't you wandered from my point?" asked the conventional voice. "Put those two women, separately, into the witness-box. Now *which* are you going to believe?"

In her turn, Iris compared the hypothetical witnesses. One was a characteristic type of county Englishwoman, with an athletic figure and a pleasant intelligent face. If she strode across the station as though she possessed the right of way, she used it merely as a short cut to her legitimate goal.

On the other hand, the pretty dark woman was an obvious loiterer. Her skin-tight skirt and embroidered peasant blouse might have been the holiday attire of any continental lady; but, in spite of her attractive red lips and expressive eyes, Iris could not help thinking of a gipsy who had just stolen a chicken for the pot.

Against her will, she had to agree with

the professor. Yet she felt almost vexed with the younger man when he ceased to argue, because she had backed the losing side.

"I see your point," he said. "The British waterproof wins every time. But Congo rubber was a bloody business and too wholesale a belief in rubber-proofing may lead to a bloody mix-up. . . . Come and have a drink."

"Thank you, if you will allow me to order it. I wish to avail myself of every opportunity of speaking the language."

"Wish I could forget it. It's a disgusting one—all spitting and sneezing. You lecture on Modern Languages, don't you? Many girl students in your classes?"

"Yes. . . . Unfortunately."

Iris was sorry when they moved away, for she had been idly interested in their argument. The crowd on the platform had increased, although the express was not due for another twenty-five minutes, even if it ran to time. She had now to share her bench with others, while a child squatted on her suitcase.

Although spoiled by circumstances she did not resent the intrusion. The confusion could not touch her because she was held by the moment. The glow of sunshine, the green flicker of trees, the gleam of the lake, all combined to hypnotise her to a condition of stationary bliss.

There was nothing to warn her of the attack. When she least expected it, the blow fell.

Suddenly she felt a violent pain at the back of her neck. Almost before she realised it, the white-capped mountains rocked, the blue sky turned black, and she dropped down into darkness.

CHAPTER SIX
THE WAITING-ROOM

When Iris became conscious, her sight returned, at first, in patches. She saw sections of faces floating in the air. It seemed the same face—sallow-skinned, with black eyes and bad teeth.

Gradually she realised that she was lying on a bench in a dark kind of shed while a ring of women surrounded her. They were of peasant type, with a racial resemblance, accentuated by inter-marriage.

They stared down at her with indifferent apathy, as though she were some street spectacle—a dying animal or a man in a fit. There was no trace of compassion in their blank faces, no glint of curiosity in their dull gaze. In their complete detachment they seemed devoid of the instincts of human humanity.

"Where am I?" she asked wildly.

A woman in a black overall suddenly broke into guttural speech, which conveyed no iota of meaning to Iris. She listened with the same helpless panic which had shaken her yesterday in the gorge. Actually the woman's face was so close that she could see the pits in her skin and the hairs sprouting inside her nostrils; yet their fundamental cleavage was so complete that they might have been standing on different planets.

She wanted some one to lighten her darkness—to raise the veil which baffled her and blinded her. *Something* had happened to her of which she had no knowledge.

Her need was beyond the scope of crude pantomime. Only some lucid explanation could clear the confusion of her senses. In that moment she thought of the people at the hotel, from whom she had practically ran away. Now she felt she would give years of her life to see the strong saintly face of the clergyman looking down at her, or meet the kind eyes of his wife.

In an effort to grip reality she looked

round her. The place was vaguely familiar, with dark wooden walls and a sanded floor, which served as a communal spittoon. A bar of dusty sunlight, slanting through a narrow window, glinted on thick glasses stacked upon a shelf and on a sheaf of fluttering handbills.

She raised her head higher and felt a throb of dull pain, followed by a rush of dizziness. For a moment she thought she was going to be sick; but the next second nausea was overpowered by a shock of memory.

This was the waiting-room at the station. She had lingered here only yesterday, with the crowd, as it gulped down a final drink. Like jolting trucks banging through her brain her thoughts were linked together by the connecting sequence of the railway. She remembered sitting on the platform, in the sunshine, while she waited for a train.

Her heart began to knock violently. She was on her way back to England. Yet she had not the least idea as to what had happened after her black-out, or how long ago it had occurred. The express might have come—and gone—leaving her behind.

In her overwrought state the idea seemed

the ultimate catastrophe. Her head swam again and she had to wait for a mist to clear from her eyes before she could read the figures on her tiny wrist watch.

To her joy she discovered that she had still twenty-five minutes in which to pull herself together before her journey. "What happened to me?" she wondered. "What made me pass out? Was I attacked."

Closing her eyes, she tried desperately to clear her brain. But her last conscious moment held only a memory of blue sky and grass-green lake, viewed as though through a crystal.

Suddenly she remembered her bag and groped to find it. To her dismay it was not beside her, nor could she see it anywhere on the bench. Her suitcase lay on the floor, and her hat had been placed on top of it, as though to prove the limit of her possessions.

"My bag," she screamed, wild-eyed with panic. "Where's my bag?"

It held not only her money and tickets, but her passport. Without it, it was impossible for her to continue her journey. Even if she boarded the train, penniless, she would be turned back at the first frontier.

The thought drove her frantic. She felt sure that these ring women had combined to rob her when she was helpless and at their mercy. When she sprang from the bench they pulled her down again. The blood rushed to her head and she resisted them fiercely. As she struggled she was conscious of a whirl of confusion—of throbbing pain, rising voices, and lights flashing before her eyes. There were breathless panting noises, as an undercurrent to a strange rushing sound, as though an imprisoned fountain had suddenly burst through the ground.

In spite of her efforts, the woman in the black pinafore dragged her down again, while a fat girl, in a bursting bodice, held a glass to her lips. When she refused to swallow they treated her like a child, tilting her chin and pouring the spirit down her throat.

It made her cough and gasp, until her head seemed to be swelling with pain. Terrified by this threat of another attack, she relaxed in helpless misery. Her instinct warned her that, if she grew excited, at any moment, the walls might rock—like the snow-mountains—as a prelude to total extinction.

Next time she might not wake up. Besides, she dared not risk being ill in the village, alone, and so far away from her friends. If she returned to the hotel she could enlist the financial help of the English visitors, while, doubtless, another passport could be procured; but it meant delay.

In addition, these people were all strangers to her, whose holiday was nearly ended. In another day they would be gone, while she might be stranded there, indefinitely, exposed to indifference, and even neglect. The hotel, too, was closing down almost immediately.

"I mustn't be ill," thought Iris. "I must get away at once, while there is still time."

She felt sure that, if she could board the train, the mere knowledge that she was rolling, mile by mile, back to civilisation, would brace her to hold out until she reached some familiar place. She thought of Basle on the milky-jade Rhine, with its excellent hotels where English was spoken and where she could be ill, intelligibly, and with dignity.

Everything hung upon the catching of

this train. The issue at stake made her suddenly desperate to find her bag. She was struggling to rise again, when she became conscious that some one was trying to establish contact with her.

It was an old man in a dirty blouse, with a gnarled elfin face—brown and lined as the scar on a tree-trunk, from which a branch had been lopped. He kept taking off his greasy hat and pointing, first upwards, and then to her head.

All at once she grasped his meaning. He was telling her that while she sat on the platform she had been attacked with sunstroke.

The explanation was a great relief, because she was both frightened and baffled by the mystery of her illness. She rarely ailed and had never fainted before. Besides, it had given her proof, that in spite of her own misgiving, the channels were not entirely blocked, provided the issues were not too involved.

Although she still felt sick with anxiety about her train, she managed to smile faintly at the porter. As though he had been waiting for some sign of encouragement, he thrust his hand into the neck of his dirty blouse and drew out her bag.

With a cry, she snatched it from him. Remembering the crowd on the platform, she had no hope of finding her money; but there was a faint chance that her passport had not been stolen.

She tore at the zipp-fastener with shaking fingers, to find, to her utter amazement, that the contents were intact. Tickets, money, passport—even her receipted hotel-bill, were still there.

She had grossly maligned the native honesty, and she hastened to make amends. Here, at last, was a situation she understood. As usual, some one had come to her rescue, true to the tradition of the protective square in her palm. Her part, which was merely to overpay for services rendered, was easy.

The women received their share of the windfall with stolid faces. Apparently they were too stunned with astonishment to show excitement or gratitude. The old porter, on the other hand, beamed triumphantly and gripped Iris' suitcase, to show that he, too, had grasped the situation.

In spite of her resistance to it, the raw spirit, together with her change of circumstance, had revived Iris considerably. She felt practically restored again and mistress of herself as she showed her ticket to the porter.

The effect on him was electric. He yammered with excitement, as he grabbed her arm and rushed with her to the door. Directly they had passed through it, Iris understood the origin of the curious pervading noise which had helped to complicate her nightmare.

It was the gush of steam escaping from an engine. While she had let the precious minutes slip by, the express had entered the station.

Now it was on the point of departure.

The platform was a scene of wild confusion. Doors were being slammed. People were shouting farewells and crowding before the carriages. An official waved a flag and the whistle shrilled.

They were one minute too late. Iris realised the fact that she was beaten, just as the porter—metaphorically—snatched at the psychological moment, and was swung away with it on its flight. He took advantage of the brief interval between the first jerk of the engine and the revolution of the wheels to charge the crowd, like an aged tiger. There was still strength and agility in his sinewy old frame to enable him to reach the nearest carriage and wrench open the door.

His entrance was disputed by a majestic lady in black. She was a personage to whom—as a peasant—his bones instinctively cringed. On the other hand, his patron had paid him a sum far in excess of what he earned in tips during the whole of a brief season.

Therefore, his patron must have her place. Ducking under the august lady's arm, he hurled Iris' suitcase into the compartment and dragged her inside after it.

The carriage was moving when he scrambled out, to fall in a heap on the platform. He was unhurt, however, for when she looked back to wave her thanks, he grinned at her like a toothless gnome.

Already he was yards behind. The station slid by, and the lake began to lap against the piles of the rough landing-stage. It rippled past the window in a sheet of emerald, ruffled by the breeze and burnished by the sun. As the train swung round the curve of the rails to the cutting in the rocks, Iris looked back for a last view of the village—a fantastic huddle of coloured toy-buildings, perched on the green shelf of the valley.

CHAPTER SEVEN
PASSENGERS

As the train rattled out of the cliff tunnel and emerged in a green tree-choked gorge, Iris glanced at her watch. According to the evidence of its hands, the Trieste express was not yet due at the village station.

"It must have stopped when I crashed," she decided. "Sweet luck. It might have lost me my train."

The reminder made her feel profoundly grateful to be actually on her way back to England. During the past twenty four hours she had experienced more conflicting emotion than in a lifetime of easy circumstance and arrangement. She had known the terrifying helplessness of being friendless, sick and penniless—with every wire cut. And then, at the worst, her luck had turned, as it always did.

From force of contrast the everyday business of transport was turned into a temporary rapture. Railway travel was no longer an infliction, only to be endured by the aid of such palliatives as reservations, flowers, fruit, chocolates, light literature, and a group of friends to shriek encouragement.

As she sat, jammed in an uncomfortable carriage, in train which was not too clean, with little prospect of securing a wagon-lit at Trieste, she felt the thrill of a first journey.

The scenery preserved its barbarous character in rugged magnificence. The train threaded its way past piled-up chunks of disrupted landscape, like a Doré steel-engraving of Dante's Inferno. Waterfalls slashed the walls of granite precipices with silver-veining. Sometimes they passed arid patches, where dark pools, fringed with black-feathered rushes, lay in desolate hollows.

Iris gazed at it through the screen of the window—glad of the protective pane of glass. This grandeur was the wreckage of a world shattered by elemental-force, and reminded her that she had just been bruised by her first contact with reality.

She still shrank from the memory of first facts, even though the nightmare railway station was the thick of the mountain away. Now that it was slipping farther behind the coils of the rails with every passing minute, she could dare to estimate the narrow margin by which she had escaped disaster.

Amid the crowd at the station there must have been a percentage of dishonest characters, ready to take advantage of the providential combination of an unconscious foreigner—who did not count—and an expensive handbag which promised a rich loot. Yet the little gnome-like porter chanced to be the man on the spot.

"Things always do turn out for me," she thought. "But—it must be appalling for some of the others."

It was the first time she had realised the fate of those unfortunates who had no squares in their palms. If there were a railway accident, she knew that she would be in the un-wrecked middle portion of the train, just as inevitably as certain other passengers were doomed to be in the telescoped coaches.

As she shuddered at the thought, she glanced idly at the woman who sat opposite to her. She was a negative type in every respect—middle-aged, with a huddle of small indefinite features, and vague colouring. Some one drew a face and then rubbed it nearly out again. Her curly hair was faded and her skin was bleached to oatmeal.

She was not sufficiently a caricature to suggest a stage spinster. Even her tweed suit and matching hat were not too dowdy, although lacking any distinctive note.

In ordinary circumstances, Iris would not have spared her second glance or thought. To-day, however, she gazed at her with compassion.

"If *she* were in a jam, no one would help her out," she thought.

It was discomforting to reflect that the population of the globe must include a percentage of persons without friends, money, or influence; nonentities who would never be missed, and who would sink without leaving a bubble.

To distract her thoughts, Iris tried to look at the scenery again. But the window was now blocked by passengers, who were unable to find seats, so stood in the corridor. For the first time, therefore, she made a deliberate survey of the other occupants of her compartment.

They were six in number—the proper quota—which she had increased to an illegal seven. Her side was occupied by a family party—two large parents and one small daughter of about twelve.

The father had a shaven head, a little waxed moustache, and several chins. His horn-rimmed glasses and comfortable air gave him the appearance of a prosperous citizen. His wife had an oiled straight black fringe, and bushy eyebrows which looked as though they had been corked. The child wore babyish socks, which did not match her adult expression. Her hair had apparently been set, after a permanent wave, for it was still secured with clips.

They all wore new and fashionable suits, which might have been inspired by a shorthand manual. The father wore stripe—the mother, spots—and the daughter, checks. Iris reflected idly that if they were broken up, and reassembled, in the general scramble, they might convey a message to the world in shorthand.

On the evidence, it would be a motto for the home, for they displayed a united spirit, as they shared a newspaper. The mother scanned the fashions; the little girl read the children's page; and from the closely-printed columns Iris guessed that the head of the family studied finance.

She looked away from them to the opposite side of the carriage. Sitting beside the tweed spinster was a fair pretty girl, who appeared to have modelled herself from the photograph of any blonde film actress. There were the same sleek waves of hair, the large blue eyes—with supplemented lashes, and the butterfly brows. Her cheeks were tinted and her lips painted to geranium bows.

In spite of the delicacy of her features, her beauty was lifeless and standardised. She wore a tight white suit, with high black satin blouse, while her cap, gauntlet-gloves and bag were also black. She sat erect and motionless, holding a rigid pose, as though she were being photographed for a "still."

Although her figure was reduced almost to starvation-point, she encroached on the tweed spinster's corner, in order to leave a respectful gap between herself and the personage had opposed Iris' entrance.

There was no doubt that this majestic lady belonged to the ruling classes. Her bagged eyes were fierce with pride, and her nose was an arrogant beak. Dressed and semi-veiled in heavy black, her enormous bulk occupied nearly half the seat.

To Iris' astonishment, she was regarding her with a fixed stare of hostility. It made her feel both guilty and self-conscious.

"I know I crashed the carriage," she thought. "But *she's got* plenty of room. Wish I could explain, for my own satisfaction."

Leaning forward, she spoke impulsively to the personage.

"Do you speak English?"

Apparently the question was an insult, for the lady closed heavy lids with studied insolence, as though she could not endure a plebeian spectacle.

Iris bit her lip as she glanced at the other passengers. The family party kept their eyes fixed on their paper—the tweed spinster smoothed her skirt, the blonde beauty stared into space. Somehow, Iris received an impression that this well-bred unconsciousness was a tribute of respect to the personage.

"Is she the local equivalent to the sacred black bull?" she wondered angrily. "Can't any one speak until she does? . . . Well, to *me,* she's nothing but a fat woman with horrible kid gloves."

She tried to hold on to her critical attitude, but in vain. An overpowering atmosphere of authority seemed to filtrate from the towering black figure.

Now that her excitement was wearing off, she began to feel the after-effects of her slight sunstroke. Her head ached and back of her neck felt as stiff as though it had been reinforced by an iron rod. The symptoms warned her to be careful. With the threat of illness still hanging over her, she knew she should store up every scrap of nervous force, and not waste her reserves in fanciful dislikes.

Her resolution did not save her from increasing discomfort. The carriage seemed not only stuffy, but oppressive with black widow's personality. Iris felt positive that she was a clotted mass of prejudices—an obstruction in the healthy life-stream of the community. Her type was always a clog on progress.

As her face grew damp, she looked toward the closed windows of the compartment. The corridor-end, where she sat, was too crowded to admit any of the outer air, so she struggled to her feet and caught the other strap.

"Do you mind?" she asked with stressed courtesy, hoping, from her intonation, that the other passengers would grasp the fact that she was asking their permission before letting down the glass.

As she expected, the man of the family party rose and took the strap from her. Instead of finishing the job, however, he glanced respectfully at the personage, as though she were sacrosanct, and then frowned at Iris, shaking his head the while.

Feeling furious at the opposition, Iris returned to her corner.

"I've got to take it," she thought. "Take it on the chin. I'm the outsider here."

It was another novel sensation for the most popular member of the crowd, to be in a minority. Besides having to endure the lack of ventilation, the inability to explain her actions, or express a wish, gave her the stunted sense of being deprived of two faculties—speech and hearing.

Presently the door was opened and a tall man squeezed into the carriage. Although she realised that her feelings had grown super-sensitive, Iris thought she had never seen a more repulsive face. He was pallid as potter's clay, with dead dark eyes, and a black spade beard.

He bowed to the personage and began to talk to her, standing the while. His story was evidently interesting, for Iris noticed that the other passengers, including the child, were all listening with close interest.

As he was speaking, his glasses flashed round the compartment, and finally rested on her. His glance was penetrating, yet impersonal, as though she were a specimen on a microscope-slide. Yet, somehow, she received the impression that she was not a welcome specimen, nor one that he had expected to see.

Stooping so that his lips were on a level with the personage's ear, he asked a low-toned question. She replied in a whisper, so that Iris was reminded of two blowflies buzzing in a bottle.

"Am I imagining things, or do these people really dislike me?" she wondered.

She knew that she was growing obsessed by this impression of a general and secret hostility. It was manifestly absurd, especially as the man with the black spade beard had not seen her before. She had merely inconvenienced some strangers, from whom she was divided by the barrier of language.

Shutting her eyes, she tried to forget the people in the carriage. Yet the presence of the man continued to affect her with discomfort. His white face seemed to break through her closed lids, and float in the air before her.

It was a great relief when the buzzing ceased and she heard him go out of the compartment. Directly he had left, she grew normal again, and was chiefly conscious of a very bad headache. The most important things in life were tea and cigarettes; yet she dared not smoke because of the threat of sickness, while tea seemed a feature of a lost civilisation. The train was now rushing through a deserted country of rock and pine. The nearest reminder of habitation was an occasional castle of great antiquity, and usually in ruins. As she was gazing out at the fantastic scenery, an official poked his head in at the door and shouted something which sounded like blasphemy.

The other passengers listened in apathy, but Iris began to open her bag, in case tickets or passport were required. As she did so, she was amazed to hear a crisp English voice.

The tweed spinster had risen from her seat and was asking her a question.

"Are you coming to the restaurant-car to get tea?"

CHAPTER EIGHT
TEA-INTERVAL

Iris was too stunned with surprise to reply.
She looked incredulously at the sandy,
spiny stretches, flowing past the window,
as though expecting to see them turn to
Swiss chalets, or blue Italian lakes.

"Oh," she gasped, "you're English."

"Of course. I thought I looked typical. . . . Are you coming to tea?"

"Oh, *yes.*"

As Iris followed her guide out of the carriage, she was rather disconcerted to find
that their compartment was at the end of
the corridor. It looked as though her protective square had not insured her against
railway smashes, after all.

"Are we next to the engine?" she asked.

"Oh, no," the tweed lady assured her.
"There are ordinary coaches in between.

It's an extra long train, because of the end of the season rush. They had to pack them in with a shoe-horn."

Apparently she was the type that collected information, for she began to broadcast almost immediately.

"Just glance at the next carriage to ours as you go by—and I'll tell you something."

Although Iris felt no curiosity, she obeyed. Afterwards she was sorry, because she could not forget what she saw.

A rigid figure, covered with rugs, lay stretched on the length of one seat. It was impossible to tell whether it were a man or a woman, for head, eyes and forehead were bandaged, and the features concealed by a criss-cross of plaster strips. Apparently the face had been gashed to mutilation-point.

Iris recoiled in horror, which was increased when she realised that the pallid man with the spade beard was in charge of the invalid. Beside him was a nun, whose expression was so callous that it was difficult to connect her with any act of mercy.

While they chatted together, the patient feebly raised one hand. Although they saw the movement, they ignored it. They might have been porters, responsible for the transport of a bit of lumber, instead of a suffering human being.

The fluttering fingers affected Iris with a rush of acute sympathy. She shrank from the thought that—had the cards fallen otherwise—she, too, might be lying, neglected by some indifferent stranger.

"That nun looks a criminal," she whispered.

"She's not a nun," the tweed lady informed her, "she's a nursing-sister."

"Then I pity her patient. Ghastly to be ill on a journey. And she's not a spectacle. Why can't they pull down the blind?"

"It would be dull for them."

"Poor devil. I suppose it's a man?"

Iris was so foolishly anxious to break the parallel between the motionless figure and herself, that she was disappointed when her companion shook her head.

"No, a woman. They got in at our station, higher up. The doctor was telling the baroness about it. She's just been terribly injured in a motor smash, and there's risk of serious brain injury. So the doctor's rushing her to Trieste, for tricky operation. It's a desperate chance to save her reason and her life."

"Is that man with the black beard a doctor?" asked Iris.

"Yes. Very clever, too."

"Is he? I'd rather have a vet."

The tweed lady, who was leading, did not hear her muttered protest. They had to force their way through the blocked corridors, and had covered about half the distance, when the spinster collided with a tall dark lady in grey, who was standing at the door of a crowded carriage.

"Oh, I'm so sorry," she apologised. "I was just looking out to see if our tea was coming. I gave the order to an attendant."

Iris recognised Mrs. Barnes' voice, and shrank back, for she was not anxious to meet the vicar and his wife.

But her companion gave a cry of delight.

"Oh, you're English, too," she said. "This is my lucky day."

As Mrs. Barnes' soft brown eyes seemed to invite confidence, she added, "I've been in exile for a year."

"Are you on your way home?" asked Mrs. Barnes, with ready sympathy.

"Yes, but I can't believe it. It's far too

good to be true. Shall I send a waiter with your tea?"

"That would be really kind. My husband is such a wretched traveller. Like so many big strong men."

Iris listened impatiently, for her temples were beginning to throb savagely. Now that Mrs. Barnes had managed to introduce her husband's name into the conversation, she knew that her own tea might be held up indefinitely.

"Aren't we blocking the way?" she asked.

Mrs. Barnes recognised her with rather a forced smile, for the Gabriel episode still rankled.

"Surprised to see us?" she asked. "We decided, after all, not to wait for the last through train. And our friends—Miss Flood-Porters, came with us. In fact, we're a full muster, for the honeymooners are here, too."

Iris had struggled a little farther down the surging corridor, when the tweed lady spoke to her over her shoulder.

"What a sweet face your friend has. Like a suffering madonna."

"Oh, no, she's very bright," Iris assured her. "And she's definitely not a friend."

They crossed the last dangerously clanking connecting-way, and entered the restaurant-car, which seemed full already. The Misses Flood-Porter—both wearing well-cut white linen travelling-coats—had secured a table and were drinking tea.

Their formal bow, when Iris squeezed by them, was conditional recognition before the final fade-out.

"We'll speak to you during the journey," it seemed to say, "but at Victoria we become strangers."

As Iris showed no inclination to join them, Miss Rose could not resist the temptation to manage a situation.

"Your friend is trying to attract your attention," she called out.

Iris turned and saw that her companion had discovered the last spare corner—a table wedged against the wall—and was reserving a place for herself. When she joined her, the little lady was looking round her with shining eyes.

"I ordered the tea for your nice friends," she said. "Oh, isn't all this *fun?*"

Her pleasure was so spontaneous and

genuine that Iris could not condemn it as gush. She stared doubtfully at the faded old-gold plush window-curtains, the smutty tablecloth, the glass dish of cherry jam— and then she glanced at her companion.

She received a vague impression of a little puckered face; but there was a sparkle in the faded blue eyes, and an eager note in the voice, which suggested a girl.

Afterwards, when she was trying to collect evidence of what she believed must be an extraordinary conspiracy, it was this discrepancy between a youthful voice and a middle-aged spinster, which made her doubt her own senses. In any case, her recollection was far from clear, for she did not remember looking consciously at her companion again.

The sun was blazing in through the window, so that she shaded her eyes with one hand most of the time she was having tea. But as she listened to the flow of excited chatter, she had the feeling that she was being entertained by some one much younger than herself.

"Why do you like it?" she asked.

"Because it's travel. We're moving. Everything's moving."

Iris also had the impression that the whole scene was flickering like an early motion-picture. The waiters swung down the rocking carriage, balancing trays. Scraps of country flew past the window. Smuts rained down on the flakes of butter and the sticky cakes. Dusty motes quivered in the rays of the sun, and the china shook with every jerk of the engine.

As she tried to drink some tea before it was all shaken over the rim of her cup, she learned that her companion was an English governess—Miss Winifred Froy—and was on her way home for a holiday. It came as a shock of surprise to know that this adult lady actually possessed living parents.

"Pater and Mater say they can talk of nothing else but my return," declared Miss Froy. "They're as excited as children. And so is Sock."

"Sock?" repeated Iris.

"Yes, short for Socrates. The Pater's name for him. He is our dog. He's an Old English sheep-dog—not pure—but *so* appealing. And he's really devoted to me. Mater says he understands that I'm coming home, but not *when. So* the old duffer meets every train. And then the darling comes back, with his tail down, the picture of depression. Pater and Mater are looking forward to seeing his frantic joy the night I *do* come."

"I'd love to see him," murmured Iris.

The old parents' happiness left her unmoved, but she was specially fond of dogs. She got a clear picture of Sock—a shaggy mongrel—absurdly clownish and overgrown, with amber eyes beaming under his wisps, and gambolling like a puppy in the joy of reunion.

Suddenly, Miss Froy broke off, at a recollection.

"Before I forget I want to explain why I did not back you up about the window. No wonder you thought I could not be English. It was stuffy—but I didn't like to interfere, because of the baroness."

"D'you mean the appalling black person?"

"Yes, the baroness. I'm under an obligation to her. There was a muddle about my place in the train. I'd booked second-class, but there wasn't a seat left. So the baroness most kindly paid the difference, so that I could travel first-class, in her carriage."

"Yet she doesn't look kind," murmured Iris.

"Perhaps she is rather overwhelming. But she's a member of the family to which I had the honour of being governess. . . . It's not wise to mention names in public, but I was governess to the very highest in the place. These remote districts are still feudal, and centuries behind us. You can have no idea of the *power* of the—of my late employer. What he says *goes*. And he hasn't got to speak. A nod is enough."

"Degrading," muttered Iris, who resented authority.

"It is," agreed Miss Froy. "But it's in the atmosphere, and after a time one absorbs it and one grows spineless. And that's not English. . . . I feel so reinforced, now I've met you. We must stick together."

Iris made no promise. Her fright had not changed her fundamentally, only weakened her nerve. She had the modern prejudice in favour of youth, and had no intention of being tied to a middle-aged spinster for the rest of the journey.

"Are you going back again?" she asked distantly.

"Yes, but not to the castle. It's rather awkward, but I wanted another twelve months to perfect my accent, so I engaged to teach the children of the——Well, we'll call him the leader of the opposition."

She lowered her voice to a whisper.

"The truth is, there is a small but growing Communist element, which is very opposed to my late employer. In fact, they've accused him of corruption and all sorts of horrors. I don't ask myself if it's true, for it's not my business. I only know he's a marvellous man, with wonderful charm and personality. Blood tells. . . . Shall I tell you something rather indiscreet?"

Iris nodded wearily. She was beginning to feel dazed by the heat and incessant clatter. Her tea had not refreshed her, for most of it had splashed into her saucer. The engine plunged and jolted over the metals with drunken jerks, belching out wreaths of acrid smoke which streamed past the windows.

Miss Froy continued her serial, while Iris listened in bored resignation.

"I was terribly anxious to say 'Good-bye' to the—to my employer, so that I could assure him that my going over to the enemy—so to speak—was not treachery. His valet and secretary both told me that he was away at his hunting-lodge. But somehow I felt that they were putting me off. Anyway, I lay awake until early morning, before it was light, when I heard water splashing in the bathroom. . . . Only one, my dear, for the castle arrangements were primitive, although my bedroom was like a stage royal apartment, all gilding and peacock-blue velvet, with a huge circular mirror let into the ceiling. . . . Well, I crept out, like a mouse, and met him in the corridor. There we were, plain man and woman—I in my dressing-gown, and he in his bathrobe, and with his hair all wet and rough. . . . But he was charming. He actually shook my hand and thanked me for my services."

Miss Froy stopped to butter the last scrap of roll. As she was wiping her sticky fingers, she heaved a sigh of happiness.

"I cannot tell you," she said, "what a relief it was to leave under such pleasant circumstances. I always try to be on good terms with every one. Of course, I'm insignificant, but I can say truthfully that I have not got an enemy in the world."

CHAPTER NINE
COMPATRIOTS

"And now," said Miss Froy, "I supposed we had better go back to our carriage, and make room for others."

The waiter, who was both a judge of character and an opportunist, presented the bill to Iris. Unable to decipher the sprawling numerals, she laid down a note and rose from her seat.

"Aren't you waiting for your change?" asked Miss Froy.

When Iris explained that she was leaving it for a tip, she gasped.

"But it's absurd. Besides, they've already charged their percentage on the bill. . . . As I'm more familiar with the currency, hadn't I better settle up for everything? I'll keep an account, and we can get straight at our journey's end."

The incident was fresh evidence of the smooth working of the protective-square system. Although Iris was travelling alone, a competent courier had presented herself, to rid her of all responsibilities and worries.

"She's decent, although she's a crashing bore," she decided, as she followed Miss Froy down the swaying restaurant-car.

She noticed that the Misses Flood-Porter, who had not finished their leisurely tea, took no notice of herself, but looked exclusively at her companion.

Miss Froy returned Miss Rose's stare with frank interest.

"Those people are English," she whispered to Iris, not knowing that they had met before. "They're part of an England that is passing away. Well-bred privileged people, who live in big houses, and don't spend their income. I'm rather sorry they're dying out."

"Why?" asked Iris.

"Because, although I'm a worker myself, I feel that nice leisured people stand for much that is good. Tradition, charity, national prestige. They may not think you're their equal, but their sense of justice sees that you get equal rights."

Iris said nothing, although she admitted to herself that, while they were at the hotel, the Misses Flood-Porter were more considerate of person and property than her own friends.

When they made their long and shaky pilgrimage through the train, she was amazed by Miss Froy's youthful spirits.

Her laugh rang out whenever she was bumped against other passengers, or was forced, by a lurch of the engine, to clutch a rail.

After they had pushed their way to a clearer passage, she lingered to peep through the windows of the reserved compartments. One of these specially arrested her attention and she invited Iris to share her view.

"Do have a peek," she urged. "There's a glorious couple, just like film stars come to life."

Iris was feeling too jaded to be interested in anything but a railway collision; but as she squeezed her way past Miss Froy, she glanced mechanically through the glass and recognised the bridal pair from the hotel.

Even within the limits of the narrow

coupé, the Todhunters had managed to suggest their special atmosphere of opulence and exclusion. The bride wore the kind of elaborate travelling-costume which is worn only on journeys inside a film studio, and had assembled a drift of luxurious possessions.

"Fancy," thrilled Miss Froy, "they've got hot-house fruit with their tea. Grapes and nectarines. . . . He's looking at her with his soul in his eyes, but I can only see her profile. It's just like a beautiful statue. Oh, lady, please turn your head."

Her wish was granted, for, at that comment, Mrs. Todhunter chanced to glance towards the window. She frowned when she saw Miss Froy and spoke to her husband, who rose instantly and pulled down the blind.

Although she was not implicated, Iris felt ashamed of the incident; but Miss Froy only bubbled with amusement.

"He'll know me again," she said. "He looked at me as if he'd like to annihilate me. Quite natural. I was the World—and he wants to forget the World, because he's in paradise. It must be wonderful to be exclusively in love."

"They may not be married," remarked Iris. "Any one can buy a wedding-ring."

"You mean—guilty love? Oh, no, they're too glorious. What name did they register under?"

"Todhunter."

"Then they *are* married. I'm so glad. If it was an irregular affair, they would have signed 'Brown,' or 'Smith.' It's always done."

As she listened to the gush of words behind her, Iris was again perplexed by the discrepancy between Miss Froy's personality and her appearance. It was as though a dryad were imprisoned within the tree-trunk of a withered spinster.

When they reached the end of the corridor, a morbid impulse made her glance towards the carriage which held the invalid. She caught a glimpse of a rigid form and a face hidden by its mass of adhesions, before she looked quickly away, to avoid the eyes of the doctor.

They frightened her, because of their suggestion of baleful hypnotic force. She knew that they would be powerless to affect her in ordinary circumstances; but she was beginning to feel heady and unreal, as though she were in a dream, where every emotion is intensified.

In all probability this condition was a consequent symptom *of* her sunstroke, and was due, partly, to her struggle to hold out, until she could collapse safely at her journey's end. She was directing her will-power towards one aim only, and therefore draining herself of energy.

As a result she was susceptible to imaginary antagonism. When she caught sight of a blur of faces inside the gloom of her carriage, she shrank back, unwilling to enter.

She received unexpected support from Miss Froy, who seemed to divine her reluctance.

"Don't let's sit mum like charity-children any longer," she whispered. "Even if I am under an obligation to the baroness, I am going to remember that these people are only foreigners. They shan't impress me. We're English."

Although the reminder was patriotism reduced to its lowest term of Jingoism, it braced Iris to enter the compartment with a touch of her old abandon. Precaution forgotten, she lit a cigarette without a glance at the other passengers.

"Have you travelled much?" she asked Miss Froy.

"Only in Europe," was the regretful reply. "Mater doesn't really like me going so far from home, but she holds the theory that the younger generation must not be denied their freedom. Still, I've promised to stick to Europe, although, whenever I'm near a boundary, I just ache to hop over the line to Asia."

"Is your mother very old?"

"No, she's eighty years young. A real sport, with the spirit of the modern girl. Pater is seventy-seven. He never let her know he was younger than she, but it leaked out when he had to retire at sixty-five. Poor Mater was terribly upset. She said, 'You have made me feel a cradle-snatcher.' . . . Oh, I can't believe I'm really going to see them again soon."

As she listened, Iris watched the smoke curling up from her cigarette. Occasionally she saw a vague little puckered face swaying amid the haze, like an unsuccessful attempt at television. Out of gratitude for services rendered—and still to come—she tried to appreciate the old parents, but she grew very bored by the family saga.

She learned that Pater was tall and thin, and looked classical, while Mater was short and stout, but dignified. Apparently Pater had unquenchable ardour and energy, for at the age of seventy he began to learn Hebrew.

"He's made a detailed time-table for every month of his life, up to ninety," explained Miss Froy. "That's what comes of being a schoolmaster. Now, Mater is passionately fond of novels. Love ones, you know. She makes a long bus journey every week to change her library book. But she says she can't imagine them properly unless she makes me the heroine."

"I'm sure you had a marvellous time," said Iris.

Miss Froy resented the attempt to be tactful.

"Have, and had," she declared. "Pater was a parson before he kept a school, and his curates always proposed to me. I expect it is because I have fair curly hair. . . . And I still have the excitement and hope of the eternal quest. I never forget that a little boy is born for every little girl. And even if we haven't met yet, we are both growing old together, and if we're fated to meet, we *shall.*"

Iris thought sceptically of the mature men who refuse to adhere to the calendar, as she listened with rising resentment. She wanted quiet—but Miss Froy's voice went on and on, like the unreeling of an endless talking-picture.

Presently, however, Miss Froy recaptured her interest, for she began to talk of languages.

"I speak ten, including English," she said. "At first, when you're in a strange country, you can't understand one word, and you feel like a puppy thrown into a pond. You flounder and struggle, so unless you want to drown you've simply got to pick it up. By the end of a year you're as fluent as a native. But I always insist on staying a second year, for the sake of idiomatic polish."

"I expect foreigners to speak English," declared Iris.

"When you're off the map they may not, and then you might find yourself in a terrible fix. Shall I tell you a true story?"

Without waiting for encouragement,

Miss Froy spun a yarn which was not cal-
culated to cool Iris' inflamed nerves. It was
all very vague and anonymous, but the actual horror was stark.

A certain woman had been certified as
insane, but owing to a blunder the ambulance went to the wrong house and forcibly
took away an Englishwoman, who did not
understand a word of the language, or of
her destination. In her indignation and horror at finding herself in a private asylum,
she became so vehement and violent that
she was kept, at first, under the influence
of drugs.

When the mistake was found out, the
doctor—who was a most unscrupulous
character, was afraid to admit it. At the
time he was in financial difficulties, and he
feared it might ruin his reputation. So he
planned to detain the Englishwoman until
he could release her as officially cured.

"But she couldn't know she wasn't in for
life," explained Miss Froy, working up the
agony. "The horror of it would probably have
driven her really insane, only a nurse exposed the doctor's plot, out of revenge. . . .
But can you imagine the awful position of
that poor Englishwoman? Trapped, with no

one to make inquiries about her, or even to know she had disappeared, for she was merely a friendless foreigner, staying a night here and a night there, at some Pension. She didn't understand a word—she couldn't explain—"

"Please *stop*," broke in Iris. "I can imagine it all. Vividly. But would you mind if we stopped talking?"

"Oh, certainly. Aren't you well? It's difficult to be sure, with your sunburn, but I thought you looked green, once or twice."

"I'm very fit, thanks. But my head aches a bit. I've just had a touch of sunstroke."

"Sunstroke? When?"

Knowing that Miss Froy's curiosity had to be appeased, Iris gave a brief account of her attack. As she did so, she glanced round the carriage. It was evident, from the blank faces, that—with one exception—the passengers did not understand English.

Iris could not be certain about the baroness. She had the slightly stupid expression of an autocrat who has acquired power through birth, and not enterprise; yet there was a gleam of intelligence in her eyes that betrayed secret interest in the story.

"Oh, you poor soul," cried Miss Froy, who overflowed with sympathy. "Why didn't you stop me chattering before? I'll give you some aspirin."

Although she hated any fuss, it was a relief to Iris when she was able to sit back in her corner, while Miss Froy hunted the contents of her bag.

"I don't think you had better have dinner in the restaurant-car," she decided. "I'll bring you something here, later. Now, swallow these tablets, and then try to get a little nap."

After Iris had closed her eyes, she could still hear Miss Froy fluttering about her, like a fussy little bird, on guard.

It gave her a curious sense of protection, while the carriage was so warm that she soon became pleasantly drowsy.

As the drug began to take effect, her thoughts grew jumbled, while her head kept jerking forward. Presently she lost consciousness of place, as she felt herself moving onwards with the motion of the train, as though she were riding. Sometimes she took a fence, when the seat seemed to leap under her, leaving her suspended in the air.

Clankety-clankety-clank. On and on. She kept moving steadily upwards. Clankety-clankety-clank. Then the rhythm of the train changed, and she seemed to be sliding backwards down a long slope. Click-click-click-click. The wheels rattled over the rails, with a sound of castanets.

She was sinking deeper and deeper, while the carriage vibrated like the throbbing of an airplane. It was bearing her away—sweeping her outside the carriage—to the edge of a drop. . . .

With a violent start she opened her eyes. Her heart was leaping, as though she had actually fallen from a height. At first she wondered where she was; then as she gradually recognised her surroundings, she found that she was staring at the baroness.

In slight confusion she looked away quickly to the opposite seat.

To her surprise, Miss Froy's place was empty.

CHAPTER TEN
THE VACANT SEAT

Iris was ungratefully glad of Miss Froy's absence. Her doze had confused rather than refreshed her, and she felt she could not endure another long installment of family history She wanted peace; and while it was impossible to have quiet amid the roar and rush of the train, she considered herself entitled, at least, to personal privacy.

As regarded the other passengers, she was free from any risk of contact. Not one of them took the slightest notice of her. The baroness slept in her corner—the others sat motionless and silent. Inside the carriage, the atmosphere was warm and airless as a conservatory.

It soothed Iris to a tranquil torpidity. She felt numbed to thought and feeling, as though she were in a semi-trance and incapable of raising a finger, or framing two consecutive words. Patches of green scenery fluttered past the window, like a flock of emerald birds. The baroness' heavy breathing rose and fell with the regularity of a tide.

Iris vaguely dreaded Miss Froy's return, which must destroy the narcotic spell. At any moment, now, she might hear the brisk step in the corridor. Presumably Miss Froy had gone to wash, and had been obliged to wait her turn, owing to the crowd.

Hoping for the best, Iris closed her eyes again. At first she was apprehensive whenever any one passed by the window, but each false alarm increased her sense of security. Miss Froy ceased to be a menace and shrank to a mere name. The octogenarian parents went back to their rightful place inside some old photograph-album. Even Sock—that shaggy absurd mongrel, whom Iris had grown to like—was blurred to an appealing memory.

Clankety-clankety-clank. The sound of breathing swelled to the surge of a heavy sea, sucking at the rocks. Muted by the thunder of the train, it boomed in unison with the throb of the engine. Clankety-clankety-clank.

Suddenly the baroness' snores arose to an elephantine trumpet which jerked Iris awake. She started up in her seat—tense with apprehension and with every faculty keyed up. The shock had vibrated some seventh sense which made her expectant of disaster, as she glanced swiftly at Miss Froy's place.

It was still empty.

She was surprised by her pang of disappointment. Not long ago she had been praying for Miss Froy's return to be delayed; but now she felt lonely and eager to welcome her.

"I expect I'll soon be cursing her again," she admitted to herself. "But, anyway, she is human."

She glanced at the blonde beauty, who was beginning to remind her of a wax model in a shop window. Not a flat wave of her honey-gold hair was out of place. Even her eyes had the transparency of blue wax.

Chilled by the contrast to the vital little spinster, Iris looked at her watch. The late hour, which told her that she had slept longer than she had suspected, also made her feel rather worried about Miss Froy's prolonged absence.

"She's had enough time to take a bath," she thought. "I—I hope nothing's wrong."

The idea was so disturbing that she exerted all her common sense to dislodge it.

"Absurd," she told herself. "What *could* happen to her? It's not night, when she might open the wrong door by mistake, and step out of the train in the dark. Besides, she's an experienced traveller—not a helpless fool like myself. And she knows about a hundred languages."

A smile flickered over her lips as she remembered one of the little spinster's confidences.

"Languages give me a sense of power. If an international crisis arose in a railway carriage, and there were no interpreters, I could step into the breach and, perhaps, alter the destinies of the world."

The recollection suggested an explanation for Miss Froy's untenanted seat. Probably she was indulging her social instincts by talking to congenial strangers. She was not divided from them by any barrier of language. Moreover, she was in holiday mood and wanted to tell every one that she was going home.

"I'll give her another half-hour," decided Iris. "She must be back by then."

As she looked out of the window, the clouded sky of late afternoon filled her with melancholy. The train had been gradually descending from the heights, and was now steaming through a lush green valley. Mauve crocuses cropped up amid thick pastures, which were darkened by moisture. The scene was definitely autumnal and made her realise that summer was over.

The time slipped away too quickly, because she dreaded reaching the limit which she had appointed. If Miss Froy did not return she would have to make a decision, and she did not know what to do. Of course, as she reminded herself, it was not really her business at all; but her uneasiness grew with the passing of each five minutes of grace.

Presently there was a stir among the other passengers. The little girl began to whine fretfully, while the father appeared to reason with her. Iris guessed that she had complained of sleepiness, and had been persuaded to take a nap, when she saw the mother's preparations to keep her daughter's trim appearance intact.

After the black patent belt and the organdie collar had been removed, she drew out a net and arranged it carefully over the little girl's permanent wave. The blonde beauty showed her first signs of animation as she watched the process, but her interest died when the matron pulled off her child's buckled shoes and replaced them with a pair of shabby bedroom-slippers.

Finally she pointed to Miss Froy's vacant place.

Iris felt a rush of disproportionate resentment when she saw the little girl sitting in the spinster's seat. She wished she could protest by signs, but was too self-conscious to risk making an exhibition of herself.

"When she comes back, Miss Froy will soon turn her out," she thought.

Upon reflection, however, she was not so sure of direct action. When she remembered the friendly spirit Miss Froy displayed towards every one, she felt certain that she had already established a pleasant understanding with her fellow passengers.

The little girl was so heavy with sleep

that she closed her eyes directly she curled up in her corner. The parents looked at each other and smiled. They caught the blonde beauty's attention, and she, too, nodded with polite appreciation. Only Iris remained outside the circle.

She knew that she was unjustly prejudiced, since she was the real interloper, yet she hated this calm appropriation of Miss Froy's place. It was as though the other passengers were taking unfair advantage of her absence—since she could not turn out a sleeping child.

Or even as though they were acting on some secret intelligence.

They were behaving as though they knew she was not coming back. In a panic, Iris looked at her watch, to find, to her dismay, that the half-hour had slipped away.

The lapse of time was registered outside the window. The overcast sky had grown darker and the first mists were beginning to collect in the corners of the green saturated fields. Instead of crocuses, she saw the pallid fungoid growths of toadstools or mushrooms.

As the sadness of twilight stole over her, Iris began to hunger for company. She wanted cheerful voices, lights, laughter; but although she thought wistfully of the crowd, she was even more anxious to see a little lined face and hear the high rushing voice.

Now that she was gone, she seemed indefinite as a dream. Iris could not reconstruct any clear picture of her, or understand why she should leave such a blank.

"What was she *like?*" she wondered.

At that moment she chanced to look up at the rack. To her surprise, Miss Froy's suitcase was no longer there.

In spite of logic, her nerves began to flutter at this new development. While she told herself that it was obvious that Miss Froy had moved to another compartment, the circumstances did not fit in. To begin with, the train was so overcrowded that it would be difficult to find an empty unreserved place.

On the other hand, Miss Froy had mentioned some muddle about her seat. It was barely possible that it had proved available, after all.

"No," decided Iris, "the baroness had already paid the difference for her to travel first. And I'm sure she wouldn't leave me without a word of explanation. She talked of bringing me dinner. Besides, I owe her for my tea. I'm simply bound to find her."

She looked at the other passengers, who might hold the key to the mystery. Too distracted now to care about appearances, she made an effort to communicate with them. Feeling that "English" was the word which should have lightened their darkness, she started in German.

"Wo ist die dame *English?*"

They shook their heads and shrugged, to show that they did not understand. So she made a second attempt.

"Où est la dame *English?*"

As no sign of intelligence dawned on their faces, she spoke to them in her own language.

"Where is the English lady?"

The effort was hopeless. She could not reach them, and they showed no wish to touch her. As they stared at her, she was chilled by their indifference, as though she were outside the pale of civilised obligations.

Feeling suddenly desperate, she pointed to Miss Froy's seat, and then arched her brows in exaggerated inquiry. This time she succeeded in arousing an emotion, for the man and his wife exchange amused glances, while the blonde's lip curled with disdain. Then, as though she scented entertainment, the little girl opened her black eyes and broke into a snigger, which she suppressed instantly at a warning glance from her father.

Stung by their ridicule, Iris glared at them, as she crossed to the baroness and shook her arm.

"Wake up, please," she entreated.

She heard a smothered gasp from the other passengers, as though she had committed some act of sacrilege. But she was too overwrought to remember to apologise, when the baroness raised her lids and stared at her with outraged majesty.

"Where is Miss Froy?" asked Iris.

"Miss Froy?" repeated the baroness. "I do not know any one who has that name."

Iris pointed to the seat which was occupied by the little girl.

"She sat *there,*" she said.

The baroness shook her head.

"You make a mistake," she declared. "No English lady has sat there ever."

Iris' head began to reel.

"But she *did,*" she insisted. "I talked to her. And we went and had tea together. You must remember."

"There is nothing to remember." The baroness spoke with slow emphasis. "I do not understand what you mean at all. I tell you this. . . . There has been no English lady, here, in this carriage, never, at any time, except you. You are the only English lady here."

CHAPTER ELEVEN
NEEDLE IN A HAYSTACK

Iris opened her lips only to close them
again. She had the helpless feeling of being shouted down by some terrific blast of
sound. The baroness had made a statement which was an outrage on the evidence of her senses; but it was backed up
by the force of an over-powering authority.

As she held the girl's eye, challenging
her denial, Iris looked at the leaden eyelids,
the deep lines graven from nose to chin—
the heavy obstinate chin. The lips were
drawn down in a grimace which reminded
her of a mask of the Muse of Tragedy.

She realised that further protest was
useless. The baroness would flatten down
any attempt at opposition with relentless
pressure. The most she could do was to

acknowledge defeat with a shrug which disdained further argument.

Her composure was only bluff for she felt utterly bewildered as she sank back in her seat. She was scarcely conscious of slides of twilight scenery streaming past the window, or of the other passengers. A village shot out of the shadows and vanished again in the dimness. She caught the flash of a huddle of dark roofs and the white streak of a little river, which boiled under a hooded bridge.

The next second the church tower and wooden houses were left behind as the express rocked on its way back to England. It lurched and shrieked as though in unison with the tangle of Iris' thoughts.

"No Miss Froy? Absurd. The woman must be mad. Does she take me for a fool? . . . But why does she say it? *Why?*"

It was this lack of motive which worried her most. Miss Froy was such a harmless little soul that there could be no reason for her suppression. She was on friendly terms with every one.

Yet the fact remained that she had disappeared, for Iris was positive now that she would not come back to the carriage.

In a sudden fit of nerves she sprang to her feet.

"She must be somewhere on the train," she argued. "I'll find her."

She would not admit it, but her own confidence was flawed by the difficulty of finding a reason for Miss Froy's absence. She had taken Iris under her wing, so that it was entirely out of line with her character as a kindly little busybody for her to withdraw in such an abrupt and final manner.

"Does she think I might be sickening from some infectious disease?" she wondered. "After all, she's so terribly keen to get back to her old parents and the dog, that she wouldn't dare run risks of being held up. Naturally she would sacrifice me."

Her progress down the train was a most unpleasant experience. It had been difficult when Miss Froy acted the part of a fussy little tug and had cleared a passage for her. Now that more passengers had grown tired of sitting in cramped compartments and had emerged to stretch, or smoke, the corridor was as closely packed with tourists as a melon with seeds.

Iris did not know how to ask them to step aside and she did not like to push.

Moreover, the fact that she was attractive did not escape the notice of some of the men. Each time a swerve of the express caused her to lurch against some susceptible stranger, he usually believed that she was making overtures.

Although she grew hot with annoyance her chief emotion was one of futility. She had no hope of finding Miss Froy in such confusion. Whenever she passed each fresh compartment to peer inside she always saw the same blur of faces.

Because she was beginning to run a temperature, these faces appeared as bleared and distorted as creations of a nightmare. It was a relief when she worked her way down the train, in an unavailing search, to see the vicar and his wife in one of the crowded carriages.

They were sitting opposite each other. Mr. Barnes had closed his eyes and his face was set. In spite of his sunburn it was plain that he was far from well and was exerting his will-power to subdue his symptoms.

His wife watched him with strained attention. She looked wan and miserable, as though—in imagination—she was sharing his every pang of train-sickness.

She did not smile when Iris struggled inside and spoke to her.

"Sorry to bother you but I'm looking for my friend."

"Oh, yes?"

There was the familiar forced brightness in Mrs. Barnes' voice but her eyes were tragic.

"You remember her?" prompted Iris. "She sent the waiter with your tea."

The vicar came to life.

"It was kind indeed," he said. "Will you give her my special thanks?"

"When I find her," promised Iris. "She went out of the carriage some time ago—and she hasn't come back."

"I haven't noticed her pass the window," said Mrs. Barnes. "Perhaps she went to wash. Anyway, she couldn't possibly be lost."

Iris could see that she was concentrating on her husband and had no interest in some unknown woman.

"Can I find her for you?" offered the vicar manfully, struggling to his feet.

"Certainly not." His wife's voice was

sharp. "Don't be absurd, Kenneth. You don't know what she looks like."

"That's true. I should be more hindrance than help."

The vicar sank back gratefully and looked up at Iris with a forced smile.

"Isn't it humiliating to be such a wretched traveller?" he asked

"I wouldn't talk," advised his wife.

Iris took the hint and went out of the compartment. She, too, considered the vicar's weakness was a major misfortune. He was not only a man of high principle but she was sure that he possessed imagination and sympathy; yet she was unable to appeal to him for help because nature had laid him low.

Because she was beginning to fear that she faced failure she grew more frantic with determination to find Miss Froy. If she failed she was loaded with a heavy responsibility.

Of all the people in the train she— alone—seemed conscious of the disappearance of a missing passenger.

She shrank from the prospect of trying to arouse these callous strangers from their apathy. As she clung to rails and was buffeted by the impacts of other tourists pushing their way past her, she hated them all. In her strung-up condition she could not realise that these people might experience her own sensations were they suddenly placed in a crowded London Tube or New York Subway and jostled by seemingly hostile and indifferent strangers.

When she reached the reserved portion of the train, the blind was still pulled down over the Todhunters' window, but she recognised the Misses Flood-Porter in one of the reserved coupés. They sat on different sides of the tiny compartment—each with her feet stretched out on the seat. The elder lady wore horn-rimmed glasses and was reading a Tauchnitz, while Miss Rose smoked a cigarette.

They looked very content with life and although kind-hearted, the sight of others standing in the corridors subtly enhanced their appreciation of their own comfort.

"Smug," thought Iris bitterly.

They made her realise her own position. She reminded herself that her place, too, was in a reserved compartment, instead of fighting her way into the privacy of strange people.

"Why am I taking it?" she wondered as

she met the unfriendly glance of the ladies. Miss Rose's was perceptibly more frigid as though she were practising gradations, in preparation for the cut direct, at Victoria Station.

At last she had combed the train with the exception of the restaurant-car. Now that tea was finished it was invaded by men who wanted to drink and smoke in comfort.

As she lingered at the entrance to make sure that Miss Froy was not inside seeking her soul-mate of whom she had spoken, a hopeful young man touched Iris' arm. He said something unintelligible which she translated as an invitation to refreshment, and leered into her face.

Furious at the liberty she shook him off and was on the point of turning away, when, amid the rumble of masculine voices, she distinguished the distinctive vowels of an Oxford accent.

She was trying to locate it when she caught sight of the spade-bearded doctor. His bald, domed head, seen through the murk of smoke, reminded her of a moon rising through the mist. His face was blanched and bony—his dead eyes were magnified by his thick glasses.

As they picked her out with an impersonal gaze, she felt as though she had been pinned down and classified as a type.

Suddenly—for no reason at all—she thought of the doctor in Miss Froy's tale of horror.

CHAPTER TWELVE
WITNESSES

Although she was conscious of the interest she aroused, Iris was too overwrought to care. Raising her voice she made a general appeal.

"Please. Is there any one English here?"

The spectacle of a pretty girl in distress made a young man leap to his feet. He was of rather untidy appearance with a pleasant ordinary face and audacious hazel eyes.

"Can I be of use?" he asked quickly.

The voice was familiar to Iris. She had heard it at the railway station, just before her sunstroke. This was the young man who had been opposed to trial by jury. He looked exactly as she had pictured him; he had even a rebellious tuft of hair, of the kind that lies down under treatment, as meekly as a trained hound, but which springs up again, immediately the brush is put away.

In other circumstances she would have been attracted to him instinctively; but in this crisis he seemed to lack ballast.

"Gets fresh with barmaids and cheeks traffic-cops," she reflected swiftly.

"Well?" prompted the young man.

To her dismay Iris found it difficult to control her voice or collect her thoughts when she tried to explain the situation.

"It's all rather complicated," she said shakily. "I'm in a jam. At least, it's nothing to do with me. But I'm sure there's some horrible mistake and I can't speak a word of this miserable language."

"That's all right," said the young man encouragingly. "I speak the lingo. Just put me wise to the trouble."

While Iris still hesitated, doubtful of her choice of champion, a tall, thin man rose reluctantly from his seat, as though chivalry were a painful duty. In this case his academic appearance was not misleading, for directly he spoke Iris recognised the characteristic voice of the professor of modern languages.

"May I offer my services as an inter-preter?" he asked formally.

"He's no good," broke in the young man. "He only knows grammar. But I can swear in the vernacular and we may need a spot of profanity."

Iris checked her laugh for she realised that she was on the verge of hysteria.

"An Englishwoman has disappeared from the train," she told the professor. "She's a *real* person, but the baroness says——"

Her voice suddenly failed as she noticed that the doctor was looking at her with fixed attention. The professor's glacial eye also reminded her that she was making an exhibition of herself.

"Could you pull yourself together to make a coherent statement?" he asked.

The chill in his voice was tonic for it braced her to compress the actual situation into a few words. This time she was careful to make no allusion to the baroness but confined herself to Miss Froy's non-re-turn to the carriage.

To her relief the professor appeared to be impressed for he rubbed his long chin gravely.

"You said—an *English* lady?" he asked.

"Yes," replied Iris eagerly. "Miss Froy. She's a governess."

"Ah, yes. . . . Now, are you absolutely certain that she is nowhere on the train?"

"Positive. I've looked everywhere."

"H'm. She would not be likely to leave her reserved seat for an inadequate reason. At what time precisely did she leave the compartment?"

"I don't know. I was asleep. When I woke up she wasn't there."

"Then the first step is to interview the other passengers. If the lady does not return by that time, I may consider calling the guard and asking for an official examination of the train."

The young man winked at Iris, to direct her attention to the fact that the professor was in his element.

"Gaudy chance for you to rub up the lingo, professor," he said.

The remark reminded Iris that while the professor's acquaintance with the language would be academic, the young man probably possessed a more colloquial knowledge. This was important, since she was beginning to think that the confusion over Miss Froy sprang from the baroness' imperfect command of English. Her accent was good, but if she could not understand all that was said she would never admit ignorance.

Determined to leave nothing to chance, Iris appealed to the frivolous youth.

"Will you come, too, and swear for us?" she asked.

"Like a bird," he replied. "A parrot, I mean, of course. Lead on, professor."

Iris' spirits rose as they made their way back through the train. Although she was still worried about Miss Froy, her companion infused her with a sense of comradeship.

"My name's 'Hare,' " he told her. "Much too long for you to remember. Better call me Maximilian—or, if you prefer it, Max. What's yours?"

"Iris Carr."

"Mrs.?"

"Miss."

"Good. I'm an engineer, out here. I'm building a dam up in some mountains."

"What fun. I'm nothing."

Full of confidence in the support of her compatriots, Iris felt exultant as they neared her carriage. Tourists—seated on their suitcases—blocked the way and children chased each other, regardless of adult toes. As a pioneer Hare was better than Miss Froy. While she hooted to warn others of their approach, he rammed a clear passage, like an ice-plough.

The professor stood aside to allow Iris to enter the compartment first. She noticed immediately that the spade-bearded doctor was seated beside the baroness and was talking to her in low rapid tones. He must have left the restaurant-car in a hurry.

The fact made her feel slightly uneasy.

"He's one jump ahead of me," she thought.

The family party shared a bag of nectarines and took no notice of her, while the blonde was absorbed in rebuilding the curves of her geranium lips. The baroness sat unmoved as a huge black granite statue.

There was a glint in Iris' eyes when she made her announcement.

"Two English gentlemen have come to make some inquiries about Miss Froy."

The baroness reared up her head and glared at her, but made no comment. It was impossible to tell whether the announcement were a shock.

"Will you kindly allow me to enter?" asked the professor.

In order to make more room for the investigation, Iris went out into the corridor. From where she stood she could see the invalid's carriage and the nursing-sister who sat at the window. In spite of her preoccupation, she noticed that the woman's face was not repulsive but merely stolid.

"Am I exaggerating everything?" she wondered nervously. "Perhaps, after all, I'm not reliable."

In spite of her pity for the wretched patient it was a real relief when the original nurse, with the callous expression, appeared at the door. The fog of mystery, together with the throb of her temples, combined to make her feel uncertain of herself.

She smiled when Hare spoke to her.

"I'm going to listen-in," he told her. "The professor's bound to be a don at theory, but he might slip up in practice, so I'll check up for you."

Iris looked over his shoulder as she tried to follow the proceedings. The professor seemed to carry out his investigation with thoroughness, patience and personal dignity. Although he bowed to the baroness with respect, before he explained the situation, he conveyed an impression of his own importance.

The personage inclined her head and then appeared to address a general question to her fellow passengers. Iris noticed how her proud gaze swept each face and that her voice had a ring of authority.

Following her lead the professor interrogated every person in turn—only to receive the inevitable shake of the head which appeared the language of the country. Remembering her own experience Iris whispered to Hare.

"Can't they understand him?"

He replied by a nod which told her that he was listening closely and did not wish to be disturbed. Thrown on her own resources she made her own notes and was amused to remark that—in spite of being accustomed to teach mixed classes—the professor was scared of the ladies, including the little girl.

Very soon he confined his questions to the business man who answered with slow deliberation. He was obviously trying to be helpful to a foreigner, who might have difficulty in understanding him. In the end he produced his card and gave it to the professor, who read it, and then returned it with a bow of thanks.

In spite of the general atmosphere of politeness Iris grew impatient and tugged Hare's arm.

"Is he finding out anything about Miss Froy?" she asked.

She was unpleasantly surprised by his grave face.

"Oh, it's rather involved," he told her. "All about where is the pen of the aunt of my gardener?"

Her confidence began to cloud as she grew conscious of an unfriendly atmosphere. The baroness did not remove her eyes from her face during her short speech, to which the professor listened with marked respect. At its end she made a sign to the doctor, as though ordering him to support her statement.

Hitherto he had been a silent witness of the scene. His white impassive face and dead eyes made him resemble one newly-returned from the grave, to attend a repeat performance of the revue of life—to its eternal damnation.

But as he began to talk at his patron's bidding he grew vital and even vehement, for he used his hands to emphasise his words.

When he had finished speaking the professor turned to Iris.

"You appear to have made an extraordinary mistake," he said. "No one in this carriage knows anything about the lady you *say is* missing."

Iris stared at him incredulously.

"Are you telling me I invented her?" she asked angrily.

"I hardly know what to think."

"Then I'll tell you. All these people are telling lies."

Even as she spoke Iris realised the absurdity of her charge. It was altogether too wholesale. No rational person could believe that the passengers would unite to bear false witness. The family party in particular looked solid and respectable, while the father was probably the equivalent to her own lawyer.

The professor was of the same opinion, for his manner grew stiffer.

"The people whom you accuse of being liars are citizens of good standing," he said, "and are known personally to the baroness, who vouches for their integrity. The gentleman is not only a well-known banker in the district, but is also the baroness' banker. The young lady"—he glanced warily at the blonde—"is the daughter of her agent."

"I can't help that," protested Iris. "All I know is that I'm owing Miss Froy for my tea. She paid for me."

"We can check up on that," interrupted Hare. "If she paid, you'll be so much to the good. Just count up your loose cash."

Iris shook her head.

"I don't know how much I had," she confessed. "I'm hopeless about money. I'm always getting R.D. cheques."

Although the professor's mouth turned down at the admission, he intervened in proof of his sense of fair play.

"If you had tea together," he said, "the waiter should remember your companion. I'll interview him next, if you will give me a description of the lady."

Iris had been dreading this moment because of her clouded recollection of

Miss Froy. She knew that she had barely glanced at her the whole time they were together. During tea she had been half-blinded by the sun, and when they returned to the carriage she had kept her eyes closed on account of her headache. On their way to and from the restaurant-car, she had always been either in front or behind her companion.

"I can't tell you much," she faltered. "You see, there's nothing much about her to catch hold of. She's middle-aged, and ordinary—and rather colourless."

"Tall or short? Fat or thin? Fair or dark?" prompted Hare.

"Medium. But she said she had fair curly hair."

"'Said'?" repeated the professor. "Didn't you notice it for yourself?"

"No. But I think it looked faded. I remember she had blue eyes, though."

"Not very enlightening, I'm afraid," remarked the professor.

"What did she wear?" asked Hare suddenly.

"Tweed. Oatmeal, flecked with brown. Swagger coat, finger-length, with patch pockets and stitched cuffs and scarf. The ends of the scarf were fastened with small blue-bone buttons and she wore a natural tussore shirt-blouse, stitched with blue—a different shade—with a small blue hand-kerchief in the breast-pocket. I'm afraid I didn't notice details much. Her hat was made of the same material, with a stitched brim and a Récamier crown, with a funny bright-blue feather stuck through the band."

"Stop," commanded Hare. "Now that you've remembered the hat, can't you make another effort and put a face under it?"

He was so delighted with the result of his experiment that his dejection was ludicrous when Iris shook her head in the old provoking manner.

"No, I can't remember any face. You see, I had such a frantic headache."

"Exactly," commented the professor dryly. "Cause and effect, I'm afraid. The doctor has been telling us that you had a slight sunstroke."

As though awaiting his cue the doctor—who had been listening intently—spoke to Iris.

"That blow of the sun explains all," he

said, speaking in English, with slow emphasis. "It has given you a delirium. You
saw some one who is not there. Afterwards, you went to sleep, and you dream.
Then, presently, you awake and you are
much better. So you saw Miss Froy no
more. . . . She is nothing but a delirium—a
dream."

CHAPTER THIRTEEN
A DREAM WITHIN A DREAM

At first Iris was too surprised to protest. She had the bewildered sensation of being the one sane person in a mad world. Her astonishment turned to indignation when the professor caught Hare's eye and gave a nod of mutual understanding.

Then he spoke to Iris in a formal voice.

"I think we may accept that as final. If I had known the circumstances I should not have intervened. I hope you will soon feel better."

"We'd better clear and let Miss Carr get some quiet," suggested Hare, with a doubtful grin.

Iris felt as though she were being smothered with featherbed opposition. Controlling her anger she forced herself to speak calmly.

"I'm afraid it's not so simple as that. As far as I'm concerned the matter's by no means ended. Why should you imagine I'm telling a lie?"

"I do not," the professor assured her. "I am convinced it is your mistake. But, since you've raised the point of fairness, you must admit that the weight of evidence is against you. I have to be fair. . . . Can you explain why six persons should lie?"

Iris had a sudden flash of intuition.

"I can't," she said, "unless one person started the lie, and the others are backing her up. In that case it's only her word against mine. And as I'm English and you're English and this concerns an English-woman, it's your duty to believe me."

As she spoke Iris challenged the baroness in an accusing stare. Although the personage heard the charge with complete composure, the professor coughed in protest.

"You mustn't confuse patriotism with prejudice," he said. "Besides your insinuation is absurd. What motive would the baroness have for telling a lie?"

Iris' brain began to swim.

"I don't know," she said weakly. "It's all

such a mystery. No one could want to injure Miss Froy. She's too insignificant. Besides, she was proud of having no enemies. And she told me herself that the baroness had geen kind."

"What have I done?" asked the baroness blandly.

"She said that there was a muddle about her place and you paid the excess-fare for her to travel in here."

"That was charming of me. I'm gratified to hear of my generosity. Unfortunately I know nothing of it. But the ticket-collector should be able to refresh my memory."

The professor turned to Iris dutifully.

"What am I to do?" he asked. "You are making things rather difficult by persisting in this attitude. But, if you insist, I will question the man."

"I'll dig him out," offered Hare.

Iris knew that he wanted a chance to escape. She felt that his sympathies were with her while he withheld his faith.

After he had gone the professor began to talk to the baroness and the doctor, presumably for the sake of further practice. Suspicious of every glance and inflection, Iris believed that he was explaining the delicacy of his position and stressing the absurdity of the charge, for the baroness looked almost as benevolent as a sated tigress that kills just for the sport.

She was glad when Hare—his rebellious tuft sticking out like a feather—battled his way down the corridor, followed by the ticket-collector. He was a sturdy young man, in a very tight uniform and he reminded Iris of a toy soldier, with two blobs of crimson-colour on his broad cheeks and a tiny black waxed moustache.

As he entered the baroness spoke to him sharply and then waved to the professor to continue.

By this time Iris' nerve was shattered; she was so sure that the ticket-collector would prove another victim to mass-hypnotism that she was prepared when Hare made a grimace.

"He's telling the old, old story," he said.

"Of course he is." Iris tried to laugh. "I expect he was one of her peasants. He looks bucolic. She seems to own the lot—including you and the professor."

"Now, don't get het up," he urged. "I know just what you are feeling, because

I've been through this myself. I'll tell you about it, if I can dislodge this young lady."

The little girl, who had been making precocious eyes at Hare, responded to his invitation to move with shrugs and pouts of protest. All the same she reluctantly went back to her original place, while he squeezed into the corner originally occupied by the elusive spinster.

"Cheer up," he said. "Unless your Miss Froy was invisible, other people in the train must have seen her."

"I know," nodded Iris. "But I can't think. My brain's too sticky."

The professor, who was just leaving the compartment, caught the drift of Hare's argument, for he turned back to speak to Iris.

"If you can produce some definite proof of this lady's existence, I'm still open to conviction. But I sincerely hope that you will not expose us and yourself to further ridicule."

Iris felt too limp for defiance.

"Thank you," she said meekly. "Where shall I find you?"

"In the reserved portion."

"We're sharing a bunny-hutch," supplemented Hare. "Didn't you know we're rich? We started a prosperity chain."

"I hate that man," burst out Iris when the professor had gone.

"Oh, no," protested Hare, "he's not a bad old fossil. You've got him scared stiff because you're young and attractive."

Then the grin faded from his lips.

"I want to bore you with a true story," he said. "Some years ago, I was playing in an international at Twickenham. Just before the match both teams were presented to the Prince of Wales and he shook hands with all of us. Well, after I'd scored the winning try—I had to slip that in—I got kicked on the head in a scrum and passed out. Later on, when I was fairly comfortable in a private ward at the hospital, the nurse came in, all of a flutter, and said there was a special visitor to see me."

"The Prince?" asked Iris, trying to force an intelligent interest.

"The same. Of course, he didn't stay more than a minute. Just smiled at me and said he hoped I'd soon be all right and he was sorry about my accident. I was so steamed up I thought I wouldn't sleep a wink, but I dropped off the instant he had gone. Next morning the nurses said, 'Weren't you pleased to see your captain?' "

"Captain?"

"Yes, the captain of the team. It was definitely not the Prince. . . . And yet I saw him as plainly as I see you. He shook hands with me and said something nice about my try. He was *real.* And that's what a spot of head trouble can do to the best of us."

Iris set her lips obstinately.

"I thought you believed in me," she said. "But you're like the rest. Please go away."

"I will, because I'm sure you ought to keep quiet. Try and get some sleep."

"No. I've got to think this out. If I let myself believe all of you, I should be afraid I was getting mental. And I'm not. I'm *not.*"

"Now take it easy."

"What a soothing nurse you'd make. You only want a silly cap. Listen." Iris dropped her voice. "I'm extra in the dark, because I couldn't understand these questions. Do you really know the language?"

"Better than English now. And it was so elementary that even the professor couldn't slip up. Sorry—but there are no holes anywhere. . . . But you look all in. Let me get you a life-saver."

"No. Miss Froy promised she'd get me something and I prefer to wait for her."

Her defiant eyes told Hare that she was nailing her colours to the mast. Since he regarded Miss Froy as a kind of ghost, he did not think that Iris would derive benefit from anything she might bring, so he resolved to renew his offer later. Meanwhile he could serve her best by leaving her alone.

Just as he was going he remembered something and beckoned Iris into the corridor.

"There was just one bit I didn't tumble to," he confessed. "The baroness spoke to the ticket chap in a dialect which was Chinese to me."

"Then that proves they came from the same district," cried Iris triumphantly.

"Hum. But as we don't know what she said it's not too helpful. Salaams. See you later."

After Hare had gone Iris crouched in her corner, rocking with the vibration of the train. It was clattering through a succession of short tunnels and the air was full of sound, as though a giant roller were flattening out the sky. The noise worried her acutely. She had scarcely eaten all day and was beginning to feel exhausted. But although she was unused to being ill, and was consequently frightened, she was far more alarmed by the jangling of her brain.

She started violently when a nursing-sister appeared in the doorway and beckoned to the doctor. She hardly noticed the relief of his absence, because her thoughts raced in a confused circle round the central incident of the black-out.

"I was on the platform, one second— and the next second I went out. Where did I go? Was the waking up in the waiting-room, and all those women, and the funny little old porter—*real?* Of course they were, or I should not be on the train. . . .

"But I met Miss Froy *afterwards.* They say she's only my dream. So, if she's a dream, it means that I've dreamed the waiting-room and the train and that I'm not on the train at all. I'm not awake yet. . . . If it was true, it would be enough to drive any one mad."

She resolutely fought back the rising tide of hysteria.

"But it's absurd. I am awake and I'm

here in this train. *So I did* meet Miss Froy. . . . Only I'm up against some mystery and I have to fight a pack of lies. All right, then, *I will.*"

At this stage her concern was for herself, rather than for Miss Froy. She had been spoiled since her birth, so it was natural for her to be selfish; and because that self was a gay and charming entity, the world had united to keep her fixed at her special angle.

But now her ego was getting involved with the fate of an obscure and unattractive spinster. Once again she began to review the incidents of their meeting. And then, suddenly, her clouded brain cleared and a sealed cell in her memory became unblocked.

The baroness looked at her as she sprang from her seat.

"Is madame worse?" she asked.

"Better, thanks," replied Iris. "And I'm going to test some English memories, just for a change. I'm going to talk to some English visitors from my hotel who saw me with Miss Froy."

CHAPTER FOURTEEN
FRESH EVIDENCE

Now that she was about to establish Miss Froy's existence, Iris began to wonder what had become of her. When she remembered her exhaustive search of the train it seemed positive that she could not be there. But it was also impossible for her to be anywhere else.

The corridors and carriages were thronged with tourists, so that she could not open a door or window to jump out, without attracting immediate attention. It was equally certain that no one could make a parcel of her and dump her on the permanent way, without becoming an object of general interest.

There was no place for her to hide—nor could Iris conceive any motive for such a course. In short, she was protected from any form of injury—accidental or intentional—by the presence of a cloud of witnesses.

In despair Iris shelved the problem.

"She can't be proved missing until it's proved that she was there in the first place," she argued. "That's my job. After that, the others must carry on."

As she remembered the professor's standard for reliable evidence she felt she could understand a showman's pride in his exhibits. Her witnesses must satisfy the most exacting taste—being British to the core.

The baroness looked at her when she opened her bag and drew out her pocket-mirror and lipstick. Although her detachment was complete and her face void of expression, she somehow conveyed an impression of secret activity, as though she were spinning mental threads.

"She's pitting her brain against mine," thought Iris, in a sudden flurry. "I must get in first."

Directly she began to hurry she went to pieces again. Her hands shook so that she painted her mouth with a streak of vivid red—more suggestive of crushed fruit than the crimson blossom after which the tint was named. Unable to find her comb she gave up the attempt and dashed out into the corridor.

Men stared at her and women muttered complaints as she pushed them aside without apology. As a matter of fact she was hardly conscious of them, except as so many obstacles in her way. After so much delay, every wasted moment was a personal reproach. In her excitement she could only see—a long way off—the blurred figure of a little spinster.

She must hurry to reach it. But faces kept coming in between her and her goal— faces that grinned or scowled—the faces of strangers. They melted away like a mist, only to give place to other faces. There was a flash of eyes and teeth—a jam of bodies. She thrust and struggled, while her cheeks burned and a wave of hair fell across her cheeks.

When at last she won through to the clearer stretch of corridor, the sight of the professor—smoking, while he looked through the window—reminded her of the conventions. She felt ashamed of her haste and she spoke breathlessly.

"Do I look like a jigsaw? It was that devastating crowd. They wouldn't let me through."

The professor did not smile, for in spite of a picturesque attraction, her wild hair and brilliant colour produced a wanton effect which did not appeal to him. Neither did Mr. Todhunter approve her, as he criticised her through the open door of his coupé.

Although he claimed to be a judge of feminine charm, he was of the type that prefers a lily-pond to a waterfall. He never lingered before an unframed picture, for he exacted the correct setting for beauty. Abandon was only permissible in a negligée and definitely bad form on a train journey. Although he had often seen Iris, when she looked like a member of an undress beauty chorus, he had never noticed her until the evening when she wore a becoming frock.

"Who's the girl?" asked the bride as she flicked over the pages of a pictorial paper.

He lowered his voice.

"One of the mob from the hotel."

"Help."

In the next coupé Miss Rose Flood-

Porter raised her head from the soft leather cushion without which she never travelled. Her movement roused her sister from her doze, and she, too, strained to listen.

Unconscious of her audience Iris spoke to the professor in a high excited voice.

"Your marvellous witnesses have let you down. They were all telling lies. The six of them."

He looked at her burning cheeks with cold concern.

"Is your head worse?" he asked.

"Thanks, I'm perfectly fit. . . . And I can prove Miss Froy was with me, because the English visitors from my hotel saw her, too. We'll get in touch with the English Consul when we reach Trieste and he'll hold up the train for a thorough examination. Oh, you'll see."

Iris thrilled at the prospect of her triumph. At that moment she seemed to see the Union Jack fluttering overhead and hear the strains of the National Anthem.

The professor smiled with dreary patience.

"I'm waiting to be convinced," he reminded her.

"Then you shall be." Iris swung round to

find herself facing Mr. Todhunter. "You'll help me find Miss Froy, won't you?" she asked confidently.

He smiled down indulgently at her but he did not reply at once. It was the pause of deliberation and was characteristic of his profession.

"I shall be delighted to co-operate with you," he told her. "But—who is Miss Froy?"

"An English governess who is missing from the train. You must remember her. She peeped in at your window and you jumped up and drew down the blind."

"That is exactly what I should have done in the circumstances. Only, in this case, the special circumstances did not arise. No lady did me the honour to linger by my window."

His words were so unexpected that Iris caught her breath, as though she were falling through space.

"Didn't you *see* her?" she gasped.

"No."

"But your wife called your attention to her. You were both annoyed."

The beautiful Mrs. Todhunter, who had been listening, broke in with none of her habitual languor.

"We are not a peep-show and no one looked in. . . . Do you mind if we shut the door? I want to rest before dinner."

The professor turned to Iris with forced kindness.

"You're tired," he said. "Let me take you back to your carriage."

"No." Iris shook off his hand. "I won't let the matter rest. There are others. These ladies——"

Dashing into the next coupé where the Misses Flood-Porter now sat upright in dignity, she appealed to them.

"You'll help me find Miss Froy, won't you? She's *English.*"

"May I explain?" interposed the professor as the ladies looked to him for enlightenment.

Iris could hardly control her impatience as she listened to the cultured drawl. Her eyes were fixed on the solid fresh faces of the sisters. Then Miss Rose spoke.

"I have no recollection of your companion. Some one may have been with you, but I was not wearing my glasses."

"Neither was I," remarked Miss Flood-Porter. "So you can understand that we shall not be able to help you. It would be against our principles to identify some one of whom we were not sure."

"Most unfair," commented Miss Rose. "So, please, don't refer to us. If you do, we must refuse to interfere."

Iris could hardly believe her ears.

"But isn't it against your principles not to raise a finger to help an Englishwoman who may be in danger?" she asked hotly.

"Danger?" echoed Miss Rose derisively. "What could happen to her on a crowded train? Besides, there are plenty of other people who are probably more observant than ourselves. After all, there is no reason why we should be penalised because we are English."

Iris was too bewildered by the unexpected collapse of her hopes, to speak. She felt she had been betrayed by her compatriots. They might boast of wearing evening dress for the honour of their country, but they had let down England. The Union Jack lay shredded in tatters and the triumphant strains of the National Anthem died down to the screech of a tin whistle.

She hated them all so fiercely that when the vicar's wife put her head round the door she could only glare at her.

Mrs. Barnes gave a general smile as she explained her presence.

"My husband is sleeping now, so I thought I'd run in for a chat. When we travel, I'm first in command, which is a new experience for me and only comes once a year."

She spoke eagerly as though to justify her husband's weakness. Then she turned to Iris, who was following the professor from the coupé.

"Don't let me drive you away."

"Nothing could keep me." Iris spoke with bitter hopelessness. "Of course, you didn't see Miss Froy?"

"Was that the little lady in tweed, with a blue feather in her hat?" asked Mrs. Barnes. "Why, *of course,* I remember her, and her kindness. We were so grateful for the tea."

CHAPTER FIFTEEN
TRANSFORMATION SCENE

Her relief was so overwhelming that Iris felt on the verge of tears as she turned to the professor.

"Are you convinced now?" she asked shakily.

The professor glanced at the vicar's wife with almost an apologetic air, for the lady was a familiar type which he admired and approved, when it was safely married to some one else.

"The question is unnecessary," he said. "It was simply a matter of getting corroborative evidence. I'm sorry to have doubted your word in the first place. It was due to the unfortunate circumstances of your sunstroke."

"Well, what are you going to do?" insisted Iris.

Having made one blunder, the professor was not inclined to be precipitate.

"I think I had better consult Hare," he said. "He is an expert linguist and has quite a fair brain, although he may appear irresponsible at times."

"Let's find him at once," urged Iris.

In spite of her haste she stopped to speak impulsively to the vicar's wife.

"Thank you so very much. You don't know what this means to me."

"I'm glad—but why are you thanking me?" asked Mrs. Barnes, in surprise.

Leaving Miss Rose to explain Iris followed the professor. Hare was frankly incredulous when they ran him to earth in the restaurant car.

"Bless my soul," he explained, "Miss Froy popping up again? There's something about that good woman that keeps me guessing. I don't mind admitting that I never really believed in the old dear. But what's happened to her?"

The professor took off his glasses to polish them. Without them his eyes appeared weak, rather than cold, while the painful red ridges on either side of his nose aroused Iris' compassion. She felt quite friendly towards him, now that they were united in a common cause—the restitution of Miss Froy.

"The Misses Flood-Porter didn't want to be drawn in," she declared. "That was clear. But why did those six foreigners all tell lies about her?"

"It must be some misunderstanding," said the professor nervously. "Perhaps I——"

"No, you didn't," cut in Hare. "You were a clinking interpreter, professor. You didn't slip up on a thing."

Iris liked him for the ready good nature which prompted him to reassure the professor because she was sure that he considered him privately a pompous bore.

"We'll have to play the good old game of 'Spot the lady,' " went on Hare. "My own idea is, she's disguised as the doctor. That black beard is so obvious that she's making it too easy. . . . Or she may be pulling the train, dressed up as a ladylike engine. I'd put nothing past Miss Froy."

Iris did not laugh.

"You're not amusing," she said, "be- cause you seem to forget that, besides being a real person, she is still missing. We must *do* something."

"Admittedly," agreed the professor. "But it's a perplexing problem, and I do not care to act without careful consideration."

"He means he wants to smoke," explained Hare. "All right, professor. I'll take care of Miss Carr, while you squeeze out some brain-juice."

He grinned across the ash-dusted table at Iris, when the professor had gone.

"Have I got it right?" he asked. "Is this Miss Froy a complete stranger to you?"

"Of course."

"Yet you're nearly going crackers over her. You must be the most unselfish person alive. Really, it's almost unnatural."

"But I'm not," admitted Iris truthfully. "It's rather the other way round. That's the amusing part. I can't understand myself a bit."

"Well, how did it start?"

"In the usual way. She was very kind to me—helpful, and all that, so that at first, I missed her because she wasn't at the back of me any more. And then, when every one declared I dreamed her, it all turned to a horrible nightmare. It was like trying to explain that every one was out of step but myself."

"Hopeless. But why had you to prove that she was there?"

"Oh, can't you understand? If I didn't, I could never feel that anything, or any one, was *real* again?"

"I shouldn't fly off the handle," remarked Hare stolidly. "I should know it was a post-symptom of brain injury, and therefore perfectly logical."

"But you can't compare your own experience with mine," protested Iris. "You saw a real person and mistook him for the Prince. But I was supposed to have talked to the thin air, while the thin air answered back. . . . I can't tell you what a *relief* it was when Mrs. Barnes remembered her."

She smiled with happiness as she looked out of the window. Now that she was safely anchored to a rational world again, after spinning amid mists of fantasy, the gloomy surroundings had no power to depress her. The afternoon had drawn in early, so that the period of twilight was protracted and it added the final touch of melancholy to the small town through which the express was slowly steaming.

Whenever they crossed a street, Iris could see mean shops, with pitifully shrunken wares—cobbled roads—and glimpses of a soupy swollen river through the gaps between the buildings. The houses—clinging to the rocky hillside, like tufts of lichen on a roof—seemed semi-obliterated by time and weather. Long ago, wood and plaster had been painted grey, but the rain had washed and the sun had peeled some of the walls to a dirty white. Every aspect betrayed poverty and desolation.

"What a horrible place," shuddered Iris, as they passed tall rusty iron gates which enclosed a dock-grown garden. "I wonder who can live here, besides suicides."

"Miss Froy," suggested Hare.

He expected an outburst, but Iris was not listening to him.

"When do we reach Trieste?" she asked.

"Twenty-two-ten."

"And it's five to six now. We mustn't waste any more time. *We must* find her. . . . It sounds exactly like some sloppy picture, but her people are expecting her home. They're old and rather pathetic. And the fool of a dog meets every train."

She stopped—aghast at the sound of

her choked voice. To her surprise she found that she was actually affected by the thought of the parents' suspense. As emotion was treason to the tradition of the crowd, she felt ashamed of her weakness.

"I'll have that drink, after all," she declared, blinking the moisture from her eyes. "I feel all mushy—and that's absurd. Old people aren't nearly as pathetic as young ones. They're nearly through—and we've got it all to come."

"You do want a drink," agreed Hare. "I'll dig out a waiter."

As he was rising Iris pulled him back.

"Don't go now," she whispered. "There's that horrible doctor."

The spade-bearded gentleman seemed to be searching for some one; and directly his glasses flashed over the young couple his quest was finished. He crossed directly to their table and bowed to Iris.

"Your friend has returned to the carriage," he said.

"Miss Froy?" Iris forgot her repulsion in her excitement. "How marvellous. Where was she?"

He spread his hands and shrugged.

"All the time she was so near. In the next carriage, talking with my nurses."

"Yes," declared Iris, laughing, "that's just where she would be. The first place I ought to have looked in, and didn't."

"Hum." Hare rubbed his chin doubtfully. "It's all very rum. Sure it's the right one?"

"She is the lady who accompanied madame to the restaurant-car," replied the doctor. "A little short lady—not young, but not very old, with a blue feather in her hat."

"That's Miss Froy," cried Iris.

"But why was there all the mystery?" persisted Hare. "No one knowing a thing about her—and all that."

"Ah, that was because we did not understand madame."

The doctor shrugged deprecatingly. "She talked so fast and she talked of an English lady. Now the lady is German, may be, or Austrian—I do not know—but she is not English."

Iris nodded to Hare.

"I made the same mistake, myself, at first," she told him. "She looks anything and she speaks every language. Come on and you shall check up on her."

The journey along the train was growing

so familiar that Iris felt she could make it blindfolded. As she passed by the Barnes' compartment she peeped inside. The vicar looked grimly heroic, with folded arms and knotted brow, while his wife showed visible signs of strain. Her eyes were sunken in black circles, but she smiled bravely at Iris.

"Still looking for your friend?" she asked.

"No," called Iris. "She's found."

"Oh, thank God."

"I didn't like that holy woman," Iris confided to Hare as they struggled on again, "but her stock has simply soared with me. She's really kind."

When they reached the reserved coupés, Iris insisted on collecting the professor, to whom she told her news.

"I want you to come, too, and meet my Miss Froy," she said. "She'll be thrilled when she hears of the sensation she's made."

"A desire to attract attention seems a feminine characteristic," observed the professor acidly.

Iris only laughed with excitement as her heart gave a sudden bound.

"There she is," she cried. "There she is, at the end of the corridor."

Once again she was overwhelmed by the derided human element as she saw the familiar flat figure in the light tweed suit.

"Miss Froy," she cried huskily.

The lady turned so that Iris saw her face. At the sight she recoiled with a cry of horror.

"That's not Miss Froy," she said.

CHAPTER SIXTEEN
THE STAR WITNESS

As Iris stared at the face of a stranger, she was plunged back into the inky darkness of the tunnel. She believed that she had emerged into the daylight and her heart was still singing for the joy of deliverance. But she had been deceived by a ray of sunshine striking through a shaft in the roof.

The horror persisted. Blackness was behind her and before—deadening her faculties and confusing her senses. She felt that she was trapped in a nightmare which would go on for ever, unless she could struggle free.

Miss Froy. She must hold on to Miss Froy. At that moment she suddenly remembered her elusive face distinctly in its strange mixture of maturity and arrested youth, with blue saucer eyes and small features all scratched and faded faintly by time.

An impostor stood before her, wearing Miss Froy's oatmeal tweed suit. The face under the familiar hat was sallow—the black eyes expressionless. It looked wooden, as though it could not weep, and had never smiled.

Breaking out of her nightmare, Iris challenged her.

"You are not Miss Froy."

"No," replied the woman in English, "I have not heard that name ever before. I am Frau Kummer, as I told you, when we had our tea together."

"That's a lie. I never had tea with you. You're a complete stranger to me."

"A stranger, certainly, such as one meets on a journey. But we talked together. Only a little because your poor head ached."

"Ah!"

The significance of the doctor's exclamation was deliberately stressed. It made Iris quiver with apprehension, even while it put her on her guard.

"I mustn't let them get me down," she thought. Then she turned desperately to the professor.

"This is not Miss Froy," she said vehemently.

"The lady has told us that herself," remarked the professor impatiently. "In fact, with the exception of yourself, no one appears to have heard the somewhat uncommon name of 'Froy.' "

It was obvious that he believed that Miss Froy lived at the sign of The Unicorn, in the congenial company of Mrs. Harris and the Spanish prisoner.

"But she's wearing her clothes," persisted Iris, trying to keep her voice from quivering. "Why? *Why?* What's become of Miss Froy? It's some conspiracy—and I'm afraid. . . . She says we had tea together, but we didn't. The waiter knows. Send for him."

To her dismay Hare did not bound off on his mission like a Hermes in nailed boots. Instead, he twisted his lip and looked sheepish.

"Why not call it a day and get some rest?" he suggested in the soothing tone which infuriated Iris.

No one believed her—and the combined force of their incredulity made her doubt herself. The darkness seemed to be closing round her again when she remembered her supporting witness—the vicar's wife.

"Mrs. Barnes," she said faintly.

"I'll fetch her," offered the professor, who was anxious to put an end to the scene.

Although he was kind-hearted and eminently just—when he knew his bearings— he was prejudiced against Iris, because of an unfortunate incident which marred the close of his last term. One of his most brilliant pupils—a plain, sedate young person, about whose progress he had been almost enthusiastic—had suddenly gone back on him and involved him in a very unpleasant emotional scene.

When she came to his study to wish him good-bye, she had broken down completely, assuring him that she had worked solely to please him, and that she could not face the thought of their parting.

As he had insisted on keeping the door open, from motives of prudence, a version of the affair had been put into circulation, to his intense annoyance. Therefore he cursed his luck in being involved with another hysterical girl, as he passed the coupé occupied by the Misses Flood-Porter.

Through the glass he could see Mrs. Barnes, who had returned to finish her interrupted chat, so he entered.

"More trouble for you, I'm afraid," he warned her. "That very emotional young lady now wants you to identify some one. I wonder if you would mind coming with me to her compartment?"

"Certainly," said Edna Barnes. "Is it the kind little lady in parchment tweed, speckled with brown and a blue feather in her hat?"

"Presumably. I seem to recollect the feather." The professor looked down at her strained brown eyes and added kindly. "You look very pale. Not ill, I hope?"

"Oh, no." Mrs. Barnes' voice was extra cheerful. "It's my husband who is ill. But I'm bearing his pain for him, so that he can sleep."

"Absent treatment?"

"Something of the kind, perhaps. When you're married—if there is a real bond—you share more than an income."

"Well, I call it silly," broke in Miss Rose. "He's far stronger than you are."

The professor, however, looked at her sweet face with additional respect.

"I don't like to worry you with this matter," he said. "In my opinion, the girl is hysterical and wants to be in the limelight. She says now that the lady is not the original one, who, according to her—is still missing."

"We'll hope she is the right one, for your sake," remarked Miss Flood-Porter placidly. "If not, she'll keep you hanging about at Trieste, and you'll miss your connection to Milan."

Mrs. Barnes pressed her hand over her eyes.

"Oh, I hope not," she cried. "My husband wants to get this wretched journey over. Still, one has to do one's duty—whatever the cost."

"But it's so futile," declared Miss Rose. "From your description, this missing governess is no chicken and an experienced traveller. She's either lying low and has given the girl the slip for some good reason of her own, or else it's all moonshine."

"Indubitably the latter," remarked the professor, as he accompanied Mrs. Barnes out into the corridor.

Here they met the vicar who had come in search of his wife.

"This *is* my husband," cried Mrs. Barnes, her face lighting up. "Did you think I'd deserted you, Ken?"

While they lingered to chat, Iris sat awaiting the return of Hare with the waiter. She had no real hope of the issue, since she had begun to regard all the officials as being tools of the baroness. A mysterious power was operating on a wholesale scale, to her own confusion. In proof of this, opposite to her was the horrible changeling who wore Miss Froy's clothing. Yet the incident was inexplicable, since she could find no motive for such a clumsy subterfuge.

Every detail of the woman's figure corresponded so exactly with her recollection of Miss Froy, as she stared at the familiar blue bone buttons, that the first real doubt began to sap her confidence. She asked herself whether she were, in reality, the victim of some hallucination. Hare's story about the prince proved that it was no uncommon experience.

She was feeling so limp that it seemed almost the easiest way out of her troubles. After all, she would have her work cut out to fight the constant threat of overhanging illness, without the additional worry of a problematical Miss Froy.

"I shall soon know," she thought, as Hare returned with a waiter in tow.

"You said the chap with the fair hair," he said to Iris. "I've bagged the only blond in the whole collection. By the way, he is proud of speaking English."

Iris remembered the youth directly she saw the straw-coloured plastered hair and slanting forehead. He wore glasses, and looked more like a student or clerk.

"Do you really understand English?" she asked.

"Certainly, madame," he replied eagerly. "I have my certificates, both for grammar and the conversational test."

"Well, do you remember waiting on me at tea? Have you a reliable memory for faces?"

"Yes, madame."

"Then I want you to look at this lady—" Iris pointed to Kummer and added, "Don't look at her clothes, but look at her face. Now tell me—is that the lady who was having tea with me?"

The waiter hesitated slightly, while his

pale eyes grew momentarily blank. Then he nodded with decision.

"Yes, madame."

"You're *sure?*"

"Yes, madame, I am positive sure."

As Iris made no comment, Hare tipped the youth and sent him away. Although the interview had corresponded with his own forecast, he felt acutely uncomfortable. He glanced uneasily at the baroness and the doctor, but their faces only registered enforced patience, as they waited for the end of the infliction.

Suddenly a muffled cry rang out from the next carriage. Instantly, the doctor sprang up from his seat and hurried back to his patient.

The sound was so unhuman and inarticulate, with its dulled yet frantic reiteration of "M-m-m-m," that Iris was reminded of some maimed animal, protesting against suffering it could not understand. She had forgotten about the poor broken body—trussed and helpless in the next carriage—lying in complete dependence on two callous women.

The recollection caused all her latent distrust of the doctor to flare up again. She asked herself what awaited the patient at her journey's end? Did she guess that she was being hurried to some operation—doomed to failure, yet recommended solely as an experiment, to satisfy scientific curiosity?

Iris had still sufficient sense to know that she was indulging in neurotic and morbid speculation, so she hurriedly smashed up the sequence of her thoughts. As a characteristic voice told her of the approach of the professor, she tilted her chin defiantly.

"Mrs. Barnes remembered Miss Froy when all the rest pretended to forget her," she said to Hare. "I know she couldn't tell a lie. So I don't care two hoots for all the rest. I'm banking on *her.*"

Edna Barnes advanced, her arm linked within that of her husband, as though for support. As a matter of fact, he was really leaning on her, for the shaking of the train made him feel rather giddy. Although still resolute, his face showed something of the strain of a knight approaching the end of his vigil.

"I understand you want us to identify a friend of yours," he said to Iris, taking command of the situation as a matter of course.

Then he looked down at his wife.

"Edna, my dear," he asked, "is this the lady?"

Unlike the waiter, Mrs. Barnes did not hesitate. Her recognition was instantaneous.

"Yes," she said.

The vicar came forward with outstretched hand.

"I am glad of this opportunity to thank you for your kindness," he said.

Miss Kummer stolidly accepted the tribute paid to Miss Froy. Or—was she really Miss Froy? Iris felt a frantic beating, as though of wings inside her head, as she slipped down into a roaring darkness.

CHAPTER SEVENTEEN
THERE WAS NO MISS FROY

The immediate effect of Iris' faint was to steady her nerves. When she recovered consciousness, to find someone forcing her head down below the level of her knees, she felt thoroughly ashamed of her weakness. There was not a trace of hysteria in her voice as she apologised.

"Sorry to be such a crashing bore. I'm quite all right now."

"Don't you think you had better lie down?" asked Mr. Barnes. "I'm sure the Miss Flood-Porters would be only too glad to lend you their reserved compartment."

Iris was by no means so sure that the ladies measured up to the vicar's own standard of charity; yet she felt a great need of some quiet place, where she could straighten out the tangle in her brain.

"I want to talk to you," she said to Hare, leaving him to do the rest.

As she anticipated, he jumped at the opportunity.

"Sorry to eject you, professor," he said, "but our bunny-hutch is booked for the next half-hour."

"Delighted," murmured the professor grimly.

After swallowing some brandy from the vicar's flask, Iris staggered up from her seat. Her knees felt shaky and her temples were still cold; but the brief period of unconsciousness had relieved the pressure on her heart, so that she was actually better.

As she and Hare—linked together, to the general inconvenience—lurched down the corridor, she noticed that the lights were now turned on. This arbitrary change from day to night, seemed to mark a distinct stage in the journey. Time was speeding up with the train. The rushing landscape was dark as a blurred charcoal-drawing, while a sprinkle of lights showed that they had reached a civilised zone, of which the wretched little town was the first outpost.

Now that the outside world was shut

out, the express seemed hotter and smok-
ier. At first the confined space of the coupé
affected Iris with a sense of claustrophobia.

"Open the window wide," she gasped.

"There's plenty of air coming in through
the top," grumbled Hare, as he obeyed.
"You'll be so smothered in smuts that your
own mother wouldn't know you."

"I haven't one," said Iris, suddenly feeling very sorry for herself. "But I'm not here
to be pathetic. There's something too real
and serious at stake. . . . I want to remind
you of something you said this morning at
the railway station. You were having an argument with the professor, and I overheard
it. You said trial by jury was unfair, because
it depended on the evidence of witnesses."

"I did," said Hare. "And I stick to every
word."

"And then," went on Iris, "the professor
talked about reliable evidence, and he
compared two women. One was English
and country—the sort that collect fir-cones
and things when she goes for a walk. The
other had bought her eyelashes and was
dark."

"I remember *her.* Pretty woman, like a juicy black cherry."

"But the professor damned her. . . . And that's exactly what has happened now. I'm damned as a tainted witness, while he is prejudiced in favour of all those British matrons and Sunday school teachers."

"That's only because they're plain Janes, while you've quite a different face—and thank heaven for it."

Hare's attempt to soothe Iris was a failure, for she flared up.

"I hate my face. It's silly and it means nothing. Besides, why should I be judged on face value if it goes against me? It's not fair. You said it wasn't fair. You told the professor it would lead to a bloody mix-up. . . . You can't blow hot and cold. Unless you're a weather-cock, you've simply got to stand by me."

"All right, I'll stand by. What do you want me to do?"

Iris laid her hot palms on the sticky old-gold plush seat and leaned forward, so that her eyes looked into his.

"I say there *is* a Miss Froy," she told him. "You've got to believe me. But my head feels like a three-ring circus, and I've grown confused. Will you go over it with me, so that I can get it clear?"

"I'd like to hear your version," Hare told her.

He smoked thoughtfully as she went over the story of her meeting with the alleged Miss Froy, up to the time of her disappearance.

"Well, you've got one definite fact," he told her. "What the—the lady told you about the big boss is right. I can make an accurate guess as to her employer. At this moment a certain noble Johnny is in the local limelight over charges of bribery, tampering with contracts, and funny little things like that. The latest is he's accused of bumping off the editor of the revolutionary rag which brought the charges."

He picked up a flimsy yellow sheet of badly printed newspaper.

"It's in the stop press," he explained, "but as he was at his hunting-lodge at the time, the final sensation's squashed. However, nobody will bother. It's quite true about the feudal system being in force in these remote districts."

"But it proves me right," cried Iris in great excitement. "How could I know all about her employer, unless Miss Froy told me? And there's something else. When I told Miss Froy about my sunstroke the baroness was listening. She couldn't know about it in any other way. So Miss Froy was there in the carriage with me."

She looked so radiant that Hare hated to crush her confidence.

"I'm afraid," he said, "that it only proves that Miss Kummer was there. She told you about her employer, and perhaps a spot of family history when you were having tea with her. Later on, you mentioned your sunstroke to her. . . . If you remember, when you came on the train, directly after your sunstroke, you were under the impression that all the other passengers were foreigners. Then you dozed and woke up all confused, and suddenly, Miss Froy, an Englishwoman, comes to life."

"But she had blue eyes and giggled like a schoolgirl," protested Iris. "Besides, there were her old parents and the dog. I couldn't have made them up."

"Why not? Don't you ever dream?"

Dejectedly, Iris conceded the point.

"I suppose so. Yes, you must be right."

"I must remind you," continued Hare,

"that Kummer was positively identified by the parson as the lady who sent them their tea. Now, I'm the last person to be biased, because all my uncles and fathers are parsons, and I've met them at breakfast—but the church does imply a definite standard. We insist on parsons having a higher moral code than our own and we try them pretty hard; but you must admit they don't often let us down."

"No," murmured Iris.

"Besides that parson has such a clinking face. Like God's good man."

"But he never saw Miss Froy," Iris reminded him. "He was speaking for his wife."

Hare burst out laughing.

"You have me there," he said. "Well, that shows how we can slip up. He took the stage so naturally, that he got us all thinking he was the witness."

"If you're wrong over one thing, you can be wrong over another," suggested Iris hopefully.

"True. Let's go into it again. You suggest that the baroness got rid of Miss Froy—never mind how—and that the other passengers, being local people and in awe of the family, would back her up. So far, you are right. They would."

"Only it seems such a clumsy plot," said Iris. "Dressing up some one quite different and passing her off as Miss Froy."

"But that bit was an eleventh hour twist," explained Hare. "Remember, you upset their apple-cart, barging in at the last minute. When you made a fuss about Miss Froy, they denied her existence, at first. You were just a despised foreigner, so they thought they could get away with it. But when you said that other English people had seen her, they had to produce some one—and trust to luck that your friends had never heard of Pelman."

He was talking of Miss Froy as though he took her existence for granted. It was such a novelty, that, in her relief, Iris' thoughts slipped off in another direction.

"Can't you get that bit of hair to lie down?" she asked.

"No," he replied, "neither by kindness nor threats. It's my secret sorrow. Thank you. That's the first bit of interest you've shown in me."

"Miss Froy is bringing us together, isn't she? You see, you believe in her too."

"Well, I wouldn't go quite so far. But I promised to believe in you—false lashes and all—against the Flood-Porter Burberry. In that case, we must accept a plot, inspired by the all-highest, and carried out by his relative, the baroness—in connection with the doctor, to bump off Miss Froy. . . . So, naturally, that wipes out all the native evidence—train-staff and all."

"You are really rather marvellous," Iris told him.

"Wait before you hand out bouquets. We pass on to that English crowd. The Misses Flood-Porter seem typical John Bulls. What are they like?"

"They've been to the right school and know the best people."

"Are they decent?"

"Yes."

"Then they'd do the decent thing. I'm afraid that is one up against Miss Froy. . . . Now we'll pass the honeymoon couple—who are presumably not normal—and come to the vicar's wife. What about her?"

"I don't know."

"Remember, you're on oath, and I'm believing you."

"Well,"—Iris hesitated—"I don't think she could tell a lie."

"And I'm positive she wouldn't. I mix with publicans and sinners and know very little about saints. But, to me, she looks like a real good woman. Besides, she supported you the first time. That shows she has no axe to grind. She said Miss Kummer was the lady who accompanied you to tea. Don't you think we must believe her?"

"I suppose so. . . . Yes."

"Well, then, the weight of evidence is against Miss Froy. But since I've declared my distrust of evidence—however convincing it may sound—I'm going to wash out the lot. To my mind, the whole point is—motive."

Iris saw Miss Froy fading away as Hare went on with his inquisition.

"I understand Miss Froy was quite small beer. Would she be mixed up in any plot?"

"No," replied Iris. "She was against the Red element."

"And neither young nor pretty? So she wasn't kidnapped by the order of the high hat?"

"Don't be absurd."

"Any enemies?"

"No, she boasted of being friends with every one."

"Hum. It's hardly a motive for murder, but was the family annoyed because she was going to teach in the opposition camp?"

"No. She told me how her employer shook hands with her when he said 'Good-bye,' and thanked her for her services."

"Well—is it clear to you now? Unless you can show me a real motive for a high life conspiracy against a poor but honest gov-erness, I'm afraid there's an end of Miss Froy. Do you agree?"

There was a long pause while Iris tried to battle against the current that was sweep-ing Miss Froy away. She told herself that so many people, with diverse interests, could not combine to lie. Besides, as Hare had said, what was the motive?

It was useless to struggle any longer and she let herself be swung out with the tide.

"You must be right," she said. "One can't go against *facts*. . . . Yet, she was so real. And her old parents and the dog were real, too."

She had the feeling that she had just slain something fresh and joyous—that fluttered and fought for life—as she added, "You've won. There is no Miss Froy."

CHAPTER EIGHTEEN
THE SURPRISE

Mrs. Froy would have been furious had she known that any one doubted her reality.

While Iris was sighing for the passing of a pleasant ghost, she was at home in the depths of the country, and entertaining friends in her drawing-room.

It was a small room with diamond-paned windows—hung with creepers—which made it rather dark; but in spite of the shabby carpet, it was a gracious place, where odd period chairs fraternised with homely wickerwork, and a beautiful red lacquer cabinet lent the colour which the faded chintz could not supply.

Pots of fine golden chrysanthemums, grown by Mr. Froy, screened the empty iron grate. The guests might have preferred a fire, for there was that slight chill—often associated with old country houses—suggestive of stone flags. Yet the sun could be seen, through the curtain of greenery, shining on the flower-beds outside; for, although the electric lamps were gleaming in the express, the daylight still lingered farther north.

Mrs. Froy was short and stout, with grey hair and great dignity. In addition to having a dominant personality, to-day she felt extra full of vitality. It was born of her excitement at the thought that her daughter was actually on her way home.

The postcard was on the marble mantelshelf, propped up against the massive presentation clock. On its back was printed a crudely coloured picture of mountains, with grass-green bases and white tops, posed against a brilliant blue sky. Scribbled across the heavens, in a round unformed handwriting, was the message.

"Home Friday night. Isn't it topping?"

Mrs. Froy showed it to her guests.

"Everything is 'topping' to my daughter," she explained with proud indulgence. "I'm afraid at one time it used to be 'ripping.' "

A visitor looked at the string of conso-

nants printed at the base of the picture—
shied at them—and compromised.

"Is she *there?*" she asked, pointing to
the line.

"Yes." Mrs. Froy reeled off the name rapidly and aggressively. She did it to impress,
for it was only the home-interpretation of
Winnie's address. But, on her return, their
daughter would give them the correct pronunciation, and put them through their
paces while they tried to imitate her own
ferocious gargling.

Then the room would know more of the
laughter on which it had thriven and grown
gracious.

"My daughter is a great traveller," went
on Mrs. Froy. "Here is her latest photograph. Taken at Budapest."

The portrait was not very revealing since
it was expensive. It hinted at the lower half
of a small vague face, and a hat which photographed very well.

"She looks quite cosmopolitan with her
eyes covered by her hat," remarked Mrs.
Froy. "Now, this is the Russian one. . . .
This one was taken at Madrid, on her birthday. . . . Here she is in Athens."

The collection was chiefly a geographical trophy, for while Mrs. Froy was proud of the printing on the mounts, she secretly resented the middle-aged stranger, who—according to her—was not in the least like her daughter.

She ended the parade by stretching to reach a faded portrait in a silver frame, which stood on a shelf. It was taken at Ilfracombe, and showed a young girl with a slim neck and a smiling face, framed by a mass of curling fair hair.

"This is my favourite," she declared. "Now, this really is Winnie."

It was the girl who had taught in Sunday school, giggled at churchwardens, and refused her father's curates, before she spread adventurous wings and fluttered away.

But she always returned to the nest.

Mrs. Froy looked again at the clock. She tried to picture Winnie in a grand continental express, which stamped proudly all over the map of Europe. The poor girl would have to endure two nights in the train, but she always vowed she loved the experience. Besides, she knew all the little dodges of an experienced traveller, to secure comfort.

Although a gregarious soul, Mrs. Froy began to wonder when her guests would go. There had been a hospitable big tea round the dining-room table, with blackberry pie, and a guest had made a stain on the best tablecloth. Although she had guiltily pushed her plate over it, Mrs. Froy had seen it. And since every minute's delay in rubbing salt into the mark would make its removal more difficult, she had found it difficult to maintain the myopia of a hostess.

Besides she wanted to watch the clock alone, and gloat over the fact that every minute was bringing Winnie's return nearer.

Although her fingers were itching to remove the tablecloth, after she had escorted her visitors to the gate, she did not return immediately to the house. In front of her was the field where she gathered mushrooms every morning. It was vividly green, and the black shadows of the elms were growing longer as the sun dipped lower.

It was rather melancholy and lonely, so that she thought of her husband.

"I wish Theodore would come home."

Apparently he heard her wish for he appeared suddenly at the far end of the meadow—his tall thin black figure striding over the grass, as though he were in competition with the elm-shadows.

Around him capered a dog which had some connection with the breed of Old English sheepdog; but his original line had slipped and he was suppressed in the family tree. During a recent hot spell, his shaggy coat had been clipped, transforming him to a Walt Disney creation.

Sock was the herald and toastmaster of the family. Directly he espied the little dumpy grey lady at the garden gate, he made a bee-line towards her and circled round her, barking excitedly to tell her that the master was coming home.

Having done his duty at her end of the field, he tore back to Mr. Froy with the glad news that the mistress of the house was waiting for him. As he gradually drew them together, both his owners were laughing at his elephantine gambols.

"It must be a great relief to the poor fellow, getting rid of that thatch," said Mr. Froy. "He evidently feels very cool and light now."

"He probably imagines he is a fairy," remarked his wife. "Look at him floating through the air like a puff of thistledown."

"The dear old fool. . . . Won't Winsome laugh?"

"Won't she?"

In imagination, both heard the joyous girlish peal.

"And won't she be thrilled with her room?" went on Mrs. Froy. "Theo, I've a confession. The carpet came when you were out. . . . And I am only human."

Mr. Froy hid his disappointment.

"You mean, you've unpacked it?" he asked. "Well, my dear, I deserved it for running away with Sock, instead of staying and helping you to entertain your visitors."

"Come upstairs and see it. It looks like moss."

They had bought a new carpet for Winifred's bedroom, as a surprise for her return. It represented stringent personal economy, since with a rigid income, any extra purchase meant taking a bite out of the weekly budget.

So he had cut down his allowance of tobacco, and she had given up her rare visits to the cinema. But now that the forty days were over, these good things would have been nothing but ashes and counterfoils.

The carpet remained—a green art-square.

When they reached the bedroom, Mr. Froy looked round him with proud satisfied eyes. It was a typical schoolgirl's bedroom, with primrose washed walls and sepia photogravures of Greuze's beauties—limpid-eyed and framed in dark stained oak. The modern note was there also in photographs of Conrad Veidt and Robert Montgomery, together with school groups and Winnie's hockey-stick.

The faded yellow-rosebud cretonne curtains and bedspread were freshly washed and ironed; a cake of green soap was displayed on the washstand; and two green candles—never to be lit—were stuck into the glass candlesticks before the mirror of the toilet-table.

"We've made it look very nice," said Mr. Froy.

"Yes, but it's not finished yet."

Mrs. Froy pointed to the narrow oak bed, where two lumps at the top and the bottom told of hot water bottles.

"It won't be finished until there's something inside that bed," she said. "I can't believe that in two nights' time I shall be slipping in to kiss her 'Good-night.' "

"Only the first night," advised Mr. Froy. "Remember our daughter is the modern girl. Her generation avoids sentiment."

"Yes, for all her heart, Winnie is modern," agreed his wife. "That is why she gets on so well with every one—high and low. You may depend on it, that even on her journey, by now she has made some useful friends who may be helpful at a pinch. I expect she knows all the best people on the train. And by 'best' I mean it in every sense of the word. . . . I wonder where she is at this moment."

Well for Mrs. Froy that she did not know.

CHAPTER NINETEEN
THE HIDDEN HAND

In the professor's opinion, the Misses Flood-Porter were representative of the best people. At home he had the reputation of being unsociable and self-sufficient; but directly he travelled he developed a distrust of unfamiliar contacts, and a timidity which sought instinctively the security of his own class.

He wanted to hear his own accent reproduced by some one—however uncongenial—who had been to his college, or lunched at his club, or who knew a cousin of one of his acquaintances.

As he smoked in the corridor after his banishment, he glanced rather wistfully at the compartment where the sisters sat. Miss Rose—although his senior—was sufficiently near his age to be a potential danger. But her face dispelled any fears of dormant hysteria. It was slightly underhung and the firm outline of her protruding lip and chin was reassuring.

Although he recoiled automatically when the elder lady caught his eye and invited him to come in with a smiling gesture, he entered and sat down rather stiffly beside Miss Rose.

"Are you being kept out of your reserved carriage by that girl?" asked Miss Rose bluntly.

When the professor explained the situation both sisters were indignant.

"Fainted?" Miss Rose's tone was incredulous. "She was laughing when she passed, arm in arm with that youth. It's all too mysterious for me. Only I sincerely hope she won't stir up a fuss and get us all hung up at Trieste, for nothing."

"It's her dog," explained the elder sister in an aside.

Miss Rose caught her lower lip between her teeth.

"Yes, it's Scottie," she said defiantly. "I'll own up I'm not quite normal over him. But he's so devoted to me—and he pines. The only other person I can trust him to is the butler."

"Strange," remarked the professor. "My own dog has a marked aversion to butlers. Particularly, to my uncle's."

The social temperature rose several degrees, and Miss Rose grew confidential.

"It's like this. Coles—our butler—is due to go on a cruise, directly I come back. It's a new experience for him and he is thrilled. If I'm overdue he will probably stay at home with Scottie, and, of course, I don't want him to lose his holiday. . . . On the other hand, if he went, poor little Scottie would be frantic. He would feel he had lost every friend."

"We have an excellent staff," supplemented Miss Flood-Porter, "but, unfortunately, none of them likes animals."

The professor's long face wrinkled up in a smile which made him resemble a benevolent horse.

"I can enter into your feelings," he told them. "I confess that my own dog makes me lose my sense of proportion. I rarely go abroad, because I cannot take her with me owing to quarantine regulations. But this year a complete change seemed indicated."

The sisters exchanged glances.

"Isn't that strange?" declared Miss Flood-Porter. "That is exactly our own position."

Miss Rose flinched and changed the subject quickly.

"What's your dog?" she asked.

"Sealyham. White."

The professor was sitting bolt upright no longer. Introduced by butlers, and their friendship cemented by the common ownership of dogs, he felt he was in congenial company. So he relaxed to gossip.

"A position of responsibility towards the extraordinary young lady seems to have been thrust upon me," he said. "She appears bent on making things very awkward for every one. I understand she was staying at the same hotel as you. . . . What opinion did you form of her?"

"Don't ask me," said Miss Rose bluntly. "I'm prejudiced. So, perhaps, I shouldn't be fair."

Her sister made the explanation.

"We know nothing about *her,* but she was with a party of near-nudists, who drank all day and night, and were a complete nuisance. The noise was worse than a pneumatic road-drill. And we came so far especially to get perfect rest and quiet."

The professor clicked.

"I quite understand your feelings," he said. "The point is—did she strike you as hysterical?"

"I only know there was a disgraceful scene on the lake yesterday. Two women screaming about a man. She was one."

"I'm not surprised," commented the professor. "At present she is either telling a pack of lies to get into the limelight, or she is suffering from slight delirium as a result of sunstroke. The latter is the charitable view. But it involves responsibility. After all, we are her compatriots."

Miss Rose began to fidget. When she opened her case and drew out a cigarette, her fingers were not quite steady.

"Suppose—she is telling the truth?" she asked. "It's not fair for us to leave the girl behind us at Trieste without any backing. . . . I'm worried stiff not knowing *what* to do."

Had Mrs. Froy been listening, she would have clapped her gouty old hands. At last

Miss Rose's attitude was coming into line with her expectations. The best people would be looking after Winnie. So no harm could possibly come to her. . . . But all the same, "Keep her safe—and bring her home to us."

Unfortunately the professor was proof against the power of prayer. He wrinkled up his face in a sceptical grimace.

"Her story is too unfounded for me to credit it," he said. "But even if the vanished governess were not a myth, I cannot conceive any cause for anxiety on her behalf. Her disappearance must be voluntary, because if she had come to any harm, or met with an accident, it would have been notified at once by an eye-witness."

"Exactly," agreed Miss Flood-Porter. "The train is so crowded that if she knew the ropes, she could play 'hide and seek' indefinitely with the ticket-collector."

"Therefore," summed up the professor, "if she *is* hiding, she must have some strong personal reason for such a course. My own feeling is never to interfere with private issues. It would be extremely tactless and inconsiderate of us to start a general search for her."

Miss Rose drew deeply at her cigarette. "Then you don't think me definitely feeble to put Scottie's interests first?" she asked.

"I should consider that you were letting your dog down if you sacrificed him to such an absolutely preposterous issue," replied the professor.

"That goes for me. Thank you, professor." Miss Rose examined her firm pink hands. "I'm smutty. I'd better wash."

When she had lurched out into the corridor, Miss Flood-Porter spoke to the professor confidentially.

"I couldn't mention it before my sister—she is so sensitive on the subject—but we've just been through a nerve-shattering experience. And I don't see that we did a pennorth of good. . . . Am I boring you?"

"Not in the least."

Miss Flood-Porter began her story of those events which played their part in shaping the conduct of the sisters, and so—indirectly—affected the destiny of a stranger.

"We live in a very quiet neighbourhood, close to the cathedral. It was ruined for every one when a terrible person came to live there. A War profiteer—at least, I call them all that. One day, when he was scorching in his car—drunk, as usual—he knocked down a woman. We saw the accident, and our evidence got him six months' imprisonment, as it was a bad case."

"I congratulate you on your public spirit."

"I'm afraid we, too, were quite pleased with ourselves, until he came out. After that we were marked people. This man—aided by his two boys—persecuted us in every kind of way. Windows were smashed—flower beds raided—horrible things thrown over the garden walls—obscene messages chalked on the gates. We could never catch them in the act, although we appealed to the police and they had a special watch kept on the premises. . . . After a time it got on our nerves. It did not matter where we were, or what we were doing, we were always listening for another crash. It affected my sister most, as she was terrified lest one of her pet animals might be the next victim. Luckily, before it came to that, the man left the town."

Miss Flood-Porter stopped, overcome by the memories she had raised.

It began on the morning when she went out into the garden, to find that her unique white delphiniums had been uprooted during the night.

After that there was the ever-increasing tension—the constant annoyance—the cumulative pecuniary loss—the futility of repairs, when panes of glass were replaced, only to be smashed again. It was like standing at a cross-roads in windy weather and being buffeted by an invisible weathercock, which whirled round again after it had struck its blow. There were flutters of apprehension whenever the fiendish boys scorched by them on their bicycles, grinning with impudent triumph. And the time came when their nerve was worn down, so that their imaginations raced away with them and they grew fearful of worse evils in store.

It ended on the evening when Miss Flood-Porter found her sister Rose in tears. If the Rock of Gibraltar had suddenly shaken like a jelly, she could not have been more aghast.

She looked up to meet the professor's sympathetic eye.

"Can you blame us," she asked, "when I

tell you that, after that, we made a vow never to interfere in anything again—unless it was a case of cruelty to animals or children?"

As Iris passed the window, in token that he was free to return to his own compartment, the professor rose.

"Tell your sister," he advised, "not to worry any more, but to get back to her dog as quickly as possible. No one is going to suffer in any way. In case of any further complications, you can trust me to take charge."

A few minutes later, when Miss Flood-Porter repeated the message, Miss Rose was greatly relieved.

"Now I can go home to Scottie with a *clear* conscience," she said. "Any one must have complete confidence in the professor."

She forgot one important point. The professor was working on the basis that Miss Froy was a fiction of hysteria—while both the sisters had seen her in the flesh.

CHAPTER TWENTY
STRANGERS INTERVENE

After Miss Froy had shrivelled to a never-never, Iris was thrown back on herself again. When her first relief at shelving the riddle had passed, she grew worried by her own sensations. Her knees were shaky, while her head felt light and empty as a blown egg-shell.

Miss Froy would have known that, in addition to the after effects of sunstroke, the girl was exhausted for lack of light nourishment. At this juncture she was a dead loss to Iris, for Hare—with the best intentions—could only offer stimulants.

As she clung to the shaking rail, fighting off recurrent spells of giddiness, Iris told herself that she must forcibly hang out until she reached Basle.

"It would be fatal if I collapsed," she

thought fearfully. "Max is too young to be any good. Some busybody would push me out at the first station, and pack me off to the local hospital."

And anything might happen to her there, as in Miss Froy's terrible story. Or did Miss Kummer tell it to her?

It was an ordeal to stand, but although she had insisted on leaving Hare—when she found that both talking and listening had become a strain—she shrank from the thought of return to her own compartment. It was too near the doctor and too remote from her compatriots. At the far end of the corridor she felt bottled up in enemy territory.

Besides—it was haunted by the ghost of a little tweed spinster, of whom it was not wise to think too long.

The high-pitched conversation of the Misses Flood-Porter—audible through the open door—was a distraction.

"I've written to Captain Parker, to meet us with his car at Victoria, to push us through the customs," said Miss Flood-Porter.

"Hope he'll be there," fussed Miss Rose. "If he fails us, we may lose our connection.

And I've written to cook that dinner is to be ready at seven-thirty to the dot."

"What did you order?"

"Not chicken. Definitely. It will be some time before I can endure one again. I said a nice cutlet of salmon and a small leg of lamb. Peas, if possible. If it is too late for them, French beans and marrow. I left the sweet to cook."

"That sounds very good. I'm longing to eat a plain English dinner again."

"So am I."

There was a short pause before Miss Rose began to worry anew.

"I do hope there'll be no muddle over our wagon-lits at Trieste."

"Oh, my dear," cried her sister, "don't suggest such a thing. I couldn't face the idea of sitting bolt upright all night. Didn't you hear the manager telephone for them?"

"I stood by him while he was doing it. Of course, I could not understand anything. But he assured me positively that they were being reserved for us."

"Well, we must hope for the best. . . . I've been looking through my engagement-book. It's the bishop's last garden party, the day after we get back."

"Oh, we *couldn't* miss that."

Iris' half-smile was bitter as she listened to the characteristic chatter of two inexperienced women-travellers, who felt very far from their beaten track.

"And I expected *them* to risk losing their reservations and spoiling their dinner," she thought. "What a hope."

Once again she flattened herself against the window, as the flaxen-haired waiter came down the corridor. Miss Rose saw him pass for she bounded out after him.

"Stop," she cried in her most imperious tone. "You speak English?"

"Yes, madame."

"Then get me some matches, please. Matches."

"Oh, yes, madame."

"I wonder if he really understood her," thought Iris, who had grown sceptical of every one.

Her doubts were unfounded, for after a brief interval the waiter returned with a box of matches. He used one to light Miss Rose's cigarette and handed her the remainder with a bow.

"The engine-driver is fulfilling his obligations and the express will reach Trieste within the scheduled time," he informed Miss Rose, who remarked, "Oh, definitely good."

He seemed anxious to oblige every one. When Iris in her turn called out to him, he wheeled round smartly as though eager for service.

As he recognised her, however, a change came over his face. His smile faded, his eyes shifted, and he appeared to conquer an impulse to bolt.

All the same he listened obediently as she gave her order.

"I'm not going to the dining-car for dinner." she told him. "I want you to bring me something to my carriage—right at the end of the corridor. A cup of soup or Bovril, or Ovaltine. Nothing solid. You understand?"

"Oh, yes, madame."

He bowed himself away. But he never brought the soup. . . .

Iris forgot her order directly she had given it. A stream of passengers had begun to file steadily past her, crushing her against the side of the corridor. Since every one was heading in the same direction, she glanced at her watch.

The time told her that the first dinner was about to be served.

"Only three hours now to Trieste," she thought gladly—goaded no longer by the thought of wasted minutes.

Where she stood she was very much in the way of the procession, and—since the majority was hungry—she was resented as an obstacle. She met with ruthless treatment, but it was useless to fight her way out against the human current. When she made the attempt she was nearly knocked down, as some of the rougher element began to push.

No one appeared to notice her plight as she tried to get out of the jam. The train was racing at top speed, and she was shaken and bruised as she gripped the rail. Terrified of being crushed, her palms were sticky and her heart leaped with panic.

At last the pressure was relaxed and she breathed more freely, as she waited for the better-behaved passengers to pass. Presently a combination of strokes, dots and dashes, in black and white, told her that the family party—linked together—was on its way to dinner. Free from the restraining presence of the baroness, they talked and laughed, evidently in high spirits at the prospect of their meal.

Although the parents were sufficiently big to inflict some merciless massage as they squeezed past her, Iris was glad to see them, for she argued that they must be in the tail of the procession. Then the blonde slipped by—cool as a dripping icicle—with unshatterable composure and without one ruffled hair.

Although the corridor was practically clear, Iris still lingered, unable to face the prospect of being alone in the carriage with the baroness. To her relief, however, the personage herself came in sight, accompanied by the doctor. Sure of getting a seat in the dining-car—however late her entrance—she had waited for the mob to disperse.

As her vast black figure surged past Iris, a simile floated into the girl's mind. An insect and a relentless foot.

The doctor threw her a keen professional glance which noted each symptom of distress. With a formal bow he passed on his way, and she was able to bump and sway along the corridors, back to the empty carriage.

She had barely seated herself, after an involuntary glance at Miss Froy's empty corner, when Hare hurried in.

"Coming to first dinner?" he asked. "I warn you, the second one will be only the scrapings."

"No," she told him, "the waiter's bringing me some soup here. I've been in a rough-house and I simply couldn't stand the heat."

He looked at her as she wiped her damp brow.

"Gosh, you look all in. Let me get you a spot. No? . . . Well, then, I've just had an intriguing experience. On my way here, a woman's trembling hand was laid on my sleeve and a woman's piteous voice whis-pered, 'Could you do something for me?' I turned and looked into the beautiful eyes of the vicar's wife. Needless to say, I pledged myself to the service of the distressed lady."

"Did she want a hot water bottle for her husband?" asked Iris.

"No, she wanted me to send a telegram for her directly we reached Trieste. But now comes the interesting bit. I'm not to let her husband know or suspect anything. After that, I can't hint at the message."

"Who wants to know it?" asked Iris dully.

"Sorry. I see you really are flat. I won't worry you any more. Chin-chin."

Hare left the compartment, only to pop his head again round the corner of the door.

"There's the ugliest ministering angel I've ever seen in the next carriage," he told her. "But what I really came back for was this. Do you know who 'Gabriel' is?"

"An archangel."

"I see. You're definitely *not* in the know."

As the time passed and no waiter appeared with her soup, Iris came to the conclusion that he was too rushed to remember her order. But she felt too limp to care. All that mattered was the crawling hands of her watch, which drew her imperceptibly nearer to Trieste.

As a matter of fact, the fair waiter possessed a heart of gold, together with a palm which twitched as instinctively as a divining-twig in the direction of a tip. He would have found time to rush in that cup of soup, whatever the demand on his resource. The only drawback was he knew nothing about the order.

Like most of his fellow-countrymen, he had been made a good linguist by the method of interchange between families of different nationalities. As he was ambitious, he felt that one extra language might turn the scale in his favour, when he applied for a job. Accordingly, he learned English from his teacher, who had taught himself the language from a book of phonetic pronunciation.

The waiter, who was an apt pupil, passed his school examination and was able to rattle off strings of English phrases. But the first time he heard the language spoken by a Briton, he was unable to understand it.

Fortunately English tourists were rare and most of their conversation was limited to the needs of their meals. While his ear was growing accustomed, therefore, he managed to keep his job by bluff and by being a good guesser.

Miss Rose's unlighted cigarette gave him the clue that she wanted matches. Moreover her voice was loud and she was brief.

But in Iris, he met his Waterloo. Her low

husky voice and unfamiliar words beat him completely. After his first nerve-racking experience, he could only fall back on the mechanical, "Yes, madame," and rush to take cover.

Before the other passengers returned to the carriage, Iris had another visitor—the professor. He took off his glasses to polish them nervously, while he explained the nature of his mission.

"Hare has been talking to me, and—frankly—he is worried about you. I don't want to alarm you. Of course, you are not ill—that is, not definitely ill—but we are wondering if you are fit to continue the journey alone."

"Of course I am," cried Iris in a panic. "I'm perfectly fit. And I don't want any one to worry on my account."

"Yet, if you should collapse later, it would be decidedly awkward for you and every one. I was discussing it with the doctor, just now, and he came to the rescue with an admirable suggestion."

As he paused, Iris' heart began to flutter with apprehension, for she knew by instinct what the proposal would be.

"The doctor," went on the professor, "is taking a patient to a hospital at Trieste, and he offers to see you safely placed in a recommended nursing-home for the night."

CHAPTER TWENTY-ONE
LIES

As the professor made his proposal, Iris saw the opening of the trap. But he had forgotten the bait: She was a free agent—and nothing could induce her to walk inside.

"I will not go anywhere with that doctor," she said.

"But——"

"I refuse to discuss it."

The professor seemed about to argue, so she decided that it was no time for politeness.

"I can't pretend to be grateful for your interest," she told him. "I consider it interference."

The professor stiffened at the last word.

"I have not the slightest wish to be intrusive," he said. "But Hare was genuinely concerned about you, and he asked me to use my influence."

"No one can influence me to go with that horrible doctor."

"In that case there is no more to be said."

The professor was only too thankful to be rid of his responsibility. Since the girl was bent on antagonising those who held out a helping hand, there would be time for a smoke, while he waited for the second dinner.

Iris did not like the professor's face, but his Harris-tweed back was British and re-assuring. She realised with a pang that she was sending it away.

Acting on impulse she called him back.

"I won't go with that doctor," she said. "He's like death, but—supposing I *should* flop—which is absurd—I'd go with you."

She thought she was making a conces-sion, but at that there were two frightened people in the carriage.

"That is impossible," said the professor sharply, to hide his nervousness. "The cir-cumstances put it out of court. The doctor has made you a kind and helpful offer—which comes best from a medical man."

He opened the door of the trap again, but she shook her head. She would never go inside. Unless—of course—she were tricked.

It was a disquieting reflection, for she was beginning to think that she could trust no one. Even Hare had let her down. While he was, in reality, concerned about her condition, he had been facetious about Mrs. Barnes. According to him, she had asked him to send a telegram to some man called "Gabriel," while her husband was to be kept in the dark.

Since it was impossible to connect the vicar's wife with a clandestine affair, Iris concluded that Hare had been trying to pull the wool over her eyes.

She resented the feebleness of the effort, especially as Mrs. Barnes was connected with a poignant memory. It was she who had driven away Miss Froy and sent her groping back into Limbo.

Iris could not forgive her for that, for she was missing badly the support which only the little governess could give. At this juncture, she knew she would be safe in those experienced hands. She felt terrified, sick, friendless—for she had burned her bridges.

Besides, whenever she thought about the mystery, she felt near the border-line of that world which was filled with shifting shadows—where phantasy usurped reality, and she existed merely in the Red King's dream. Unless she kept a firm grip on herself, her sanity might hang—or crash—on the fact of Miss Froy's existence.

There were others in that trainful of holiday folk who were in a worse plight than herself. One was the invalid in the next carriage. Although she was chiefly unconscious, the flash of every lucid second held the horror of the shock which had stunned her into darkness. And if the moment lasted a fraction too long, there was time for a cloud of awful doubts to arise.

"Where am I? What is going to happen to me? Where are they taking me?"

Luckily, before these questions could be answered, the flare always died down again. So, therefore, she was in better case than Edna Barnes, who was in full possession of her faculties while she endured a protracted martyrdom of mental suffering.

She had been completely happy in anticipation of their last mountain ramble when she saw the letter in the pigeonhole of the bureau. Her mother-in-law's hand-writing gave her a warning pang which broke slightly the shock of the contents of the note.

"I've been wondering what to do for the best," wrote the excellent lady. "I don't want to make you anxious during your long journey, yet, on the other hand, I feel I ought to prepare you for a disappointment. I had hoped to have Gabriel in perfect health for your return, and up to now he's been splendid. But now he has developed a cold in his chest. He is quite comfortable and the doctor says he is going on as well as can be expected. So there is no need for you to worry."

Edna Barnes skimmed the letter in a flash which read between the lines. If her mother-in-law had composed it with a view to alarm her, she could not have succeeded better. All the familiar soothing phrases were there. "No need to worry." "As well as can be expected." "Comfortable"—the hospitable formula for a hopeless case.

A cold on the chest could camouflage bronchitis or even pneumonia; and she had heard that a big strong baby, stricken by these complaints, was sometimes snuffed out after a few hours' illness. Her heart nearly burst as she wondered whether, at that moment, he were already dead.

Then her husband called out to inquire the contents of the letter. The answer had been "Margaret Rose silk."

She had lied with a fierce protective instinct to save him from her own agony. There was no need for two to suffer, if she could bear his pain for him. Screening her torment with her habitual smile, she racked her brains desperately for some reason to leave for England that same day.

Just as the vicar took the packet of sandwiches from her, preparatory to their start, she snatched at the excuse of Miss Rose Flood-Porter's warning dream.

Although he was disappointed, the vicar gave way to her in the matter. The sisters, too, decided to take no chances, when they heard that the vicar's wife had changed her plans owing to superstitious presentiments. As the honeymoon couple had previously decided to go, the exodus from the hotel was complete.

For the first time Edna Barnes was glad that her husband suffered from train-sickness. While he sat with closed eyes and gritted teeth, she had some respite from acting. Her only consolation was knowing that she was on her way home. Therefore, when she was threatened with the prospect of an enforced delay at Trieste, she felt desperate.

She was faced with the first real test of her principles—and her conscience won. Deception to save her husband from unnecessary suffering was a form of the lie magnificent. But now she told herself that the cause of humanity must come before family ties, because it was selfless.

She was prepared to do her duty—whatever the cost—by Miss Froy. But when she was assured by those whose judgement she could trust, that the peril was negligible, her resolution slipped.

The cause was too inadequate to exact such a sacrifice. On the evidence, it was nothing but the trumped-up invention of a hysterical girl to attract notice. But Gabriel was ill. He needed her, and he won.

It was after she had identified Miss Kummer as Miss Froy that she suddenly realised the advantage of a willing young man who could send off a telegram to her mother-in-law. As she doubted whether she could receive the reply without her husband's knowledge—since her name might be bawled out by some official—she asked for the latest bulletin to await her at Calais. The sea-crossing would revive the vicar, while it would not be kind to keep him in the dark until he reached home.

Although her eyes were tragic, she smiled faintly at the thought of his unconsciousness. Like a big baby he was sorry for his aches and pains, but he knew nothing of what he was spared.

"Only a mother knows," she thought.

This was exactly Mrs. Froy's own conviction as she sat in the twilight and hungered for her child's return.

CHAPTER TWENTY-TWO
KILLING TIME

As a rule Mrs. Froy lived on the sunny side of the street. This evening, however, the long black shadows of the elms seemed to have stretched out to reach her mind, for she was unaccountably depressed.

The sun no longer shone greenly through the creepers which muffled the windows, but she was accustomed to gloom. For reasons of economy, the lamp was never lit until the last possible moment. Neither was she influenced by the melancholy of the view from her bedroom, which overlooked a corner of the churchyard.

Having dwelt in rectories for so long, it was second-habit for the Froys to live close to the church. Whenever she looked out at the slanting tombstones of forgotten dead, she had trained herself to picture a spectacular resurrection, when the graves suddenly burst open and their glorified contents shot up into the air like a glittering shower of rockets.

This evening, when the green had all turned grey, she had her first misgivings.

"I wonder if it's healthy for us to sleep so near all those mouldering corpses."

In ordinary circumstances she would have scoffed at her idea; but she could not dislodge the black monkey that sat on her shoulder. Vague misgivings and presentiments kept shaking through her mind.

She told herself that she would be profoundly grateful when Winnie was safely home. Travel must be risky—otherwise railway companies would not issue insurance policies. Suppose Winnie were taken ill on the journey and had to be dumped in some foreign waiting-room.

Anything might happen to her—a smash, or even worse. One read of terrible things which happened to girls travelling alone. Not that Winnie was actually a girl—thank goodness—but she was so young for her age.

At this point Mrs. Froy took herself in charge.

"Only two nights more," she reminded herself. "You ought to be happy as a queen, instead of carrying on like a weeping-willow with a stomach ache. Now, you find out what's at the bottom of all this."

Before long she believed she had worked back to the original cause of her depression. It was the blackberry stain on the best tablecloth, which had not yielded entirely to salt.

"Goose," she said. "It'll boil out in the wash."

Making a face at the tombstones, she stumped out of the room and down the stairs in search of her husband.

Contrary to custom she found him in the parlour sitting in the dark.

"Lazybones, why haven't you lit the lamp?" she asked.

"In a minute." Mr. Froy's voice was unusually lifeless. "I've been brooding. Bad habit. . . . It's an extraordinary thing that Winsome has been away so often, yet this is the first time I've ever felt apprehensive about her safety. These continental trains— I suppose I'm growing old. The ground is pulling me."

Mrs. Froy's heart gave a sudden leap as

she listened. So he, too, had caught the warning whisper.

Without speaking, she struck a match, turned up the wick of the lamp, lit it, and fitted on the chimney. As she waited for the glass to warm through, she looked at her husband's face, visible in the weak glow.

It appeared white, bloodless and bony—the face of a man who should be going to bed in a damp corner under the window, instead of sharing her spring-mattress.

At the sight she exploded with the righteous wrath of a woman who is rough on shadows.

"Never let me hear you talk like that again," she scolded. "You're as bad as Miss Parsons. She's only sixty-six, yet the last time we came back from town together, she grumbled because the bus was full and she had to stand. I said, 'My dear, don't let every one know that you are not accustomed to court circles.' And then I said, 'Take my seat. I'm young.' "

"Did the people in the bus laugh?" asked Mr. Froy appreciatively.

In the circle of mellow lamplight his face had lost its pallor. Before she replied, his wife pounced on the window-cords and rattled the green window-curtains together, shutting out the bogie-twilight.

"Yes," she said, "they simply roared. Then some one started to clap. But when I thought the joke had gone far enough, I stopped it. . . . I *looked* at them."

Although Mrs. Froy was proud of her gifts as a comedian, her sense of dignity was stronger. Her head was held high, as though she were still quelling her audience, as she inquired, "Where is Sock?"

"My dear, I'm afraid he is waiting outside until it is time to meet the train. I do wish I could make the poor fellow understand it's Friday."

"I'll make him," announced Mrs. Froy. "Sock."

The big dog shambled in immediately, for although normally too spoiled to be obedient, he always respected a certain rasp in his mistress's voice.

Mrs. Froy took three biscuits from the tin and laid them in a row on the fender-stool.

"Look, darling," she said. "Mother's got three biscuits for you. This is to-night, but Winnie's not coming to-night. This is to-morrow, but Winnie's not coming to-mor-row. *This* is Friday, and Winnie's coming

Friday and you shall go and meet the train. . . . Remember—*this* one."

Sock looked up at her as though he were straining to understand—his amber eyes beaming with intelligence under his wisps of hair, for his head had not been shorn.

"He understands," declared Mrs. Froy. "I can always talk to animals. Perhaps our vibrations are the same. I know what's in his mind and I can always make him know what is in mine."

She turned back to the fender-stool and picked up the first biscuit.

"This is to-night," she explained. "Well, to-night's over. So you can eat to-night."

Sock entered into the spirit of the game. While he was making a mess of crumbs on the mat, Mrs. Froy spoke to her husband.

"That's an end of to-night for us, too," she said. "And good riddance. I wish you would remember that it's bad form to go half-way to meet troubles which are not coming to your house, and which have no intention of calling on you. . . . What are you grinning at?"

Shaking with laughter, Mr. Froy pointed

to Sock, who was in the act of crunching the last biscuit.

"'He understands,'" he quoted with gentle mockery.

The sight of his face made Mrs. Froy forget her momentary discomfiture. It looked years younger. There was no question now of where he ought to sleep that night.

She patted Sock, kissed his nose and flicked the biscuit crumbs from his coat.

"Yes," she said tartly, "he understands—and better than you do. Don't you see that he is trying to make the time pass quicker?"

CHAPTER TWENTY-THREE
STAKE YOUR COUNTER

At that moment others besides Mrs. Froy were anxious to speed up the march of time. Some were on the express which was being stoked up for its final spurt, to reach Trieste on time.

One of these—Mrs. Todhunter—hid her impatience under a pose of nonchalance. Wherever she went, she attracted notice and she also excited feminine envy by her special atmosphere of romance. Apparently she had everything that a woman could want—beauty, poise, exquisite clothes, and a wealthy, distinguished bridegroom.

In reality she was feverishly eager to get back to her husband.

He was a stout middle-aged building-contractor, named Cecil Parmiter. When at home Mrs. Laura Parmiter lived in a super-

fine new house, with all those modern im-
provements which her husband introduced
into the blocks of flats he built for others—
and with none of their short-comings. She
had a comfortable income, a generous
allowance, competent servants, leisure, a
trusting affectionate husband and two
large children.

She had the additional detail of respectability.

Although she was the social queen of
her set, she was secretly ambitious and
discontented. During the rehearsals of a local pageant, when class-distinctions were
levelled, she met a certain rising barrister—
a visitor to the district, who had been roped
into taking a part. He was a king and she
was a queen—and the royal atmosphere
lent a glamour to their meetings.

He was infatuated—temporarily—by her
statuesque beauty and the facility with
which she could quote passages from
Swinburne and Browning, culled from her
Oxford Book of Verse. After a few meetings
in London, under the seal of the apple, he
swept her away with him on a passionate
adventure.

Although she lost her footing, Mrs.

Laura's brain still functioned. She had a definite ulterior motive for her surrender. During a session of Browning lectures, she had read "The Statue and the Bust" and had imbibed its spirit. She determined, therefore, to risk her counter on a bold fling—the chance of a double divorce.

After the preliminary patch of mud was crossed, she would take her rightful place in Society as the beautiful wife of a distinguished barrister. The world soon forgets—while she was confident that she could compel her husband to admit her moral claim to the children.

She lost. . . . And Browning could have been proud of the spirit in which she took her toss.

The barrister was married to a sour elderly wife; but she possessed both a title and wealth. When Mrs. Laura discovered that he had not the slightest intention of making their adventure a prelude to matrimony, her pride forbade her to show any disappointment.

Perhaps her nonchalance was easier to assume by reason of her own disillusionment. The passionate adventure had not matured according to its promise. It taught her that a professional man did not differ so greatly from a tradesman in essentials and that they looked much the same before shaving and without their collars.

Moreover, the barrister had a handicap from which the builder was immune. He was a hard snorer.

To make matters worse, while he was careless of his own failings, his standard for women was so fastidious that she found it a strain to live up to it. She could never relax, or be natural, without being conscious of his criticism or impatience.

Being practical, she determined to cut short the holiday and get back to her husband while the going was good. Fortunately, she had not burned any bridges. Her husband had bought her return ticket to Turin, and she had told him to expect no mail, since he was going on a sea trip to the Shetlands.

Her plan was to leave the barrister at Turin, where he had joined her on the outward journey, and to stay there, for a night, so that her luggage could display the hotel labels.

The end of it all would be a happy domestic reunion and a better understanding, for—by contrast—she had learnt to appreciate her husband's solidity. Thus one more matrimonial shipwreck had been averted by a trial-venture and a smashed code of morality.

As the Todhunters sat in their coupé, waiting for the second dinner to be served, they were a spectacle which attracted the interest of the tourists who straggled past the window. They must still be known by the name in which they had registered, since the barrister was too cautious to sign his own name.

It was "Brown."

However, his parents had done their best for him, and his title of "Sir Peveril Brown" was sufficiently well-known to be dangerous—in addition to a striking profile which had been reproduced often in the pictorial press.

True to her character of Browning's good loser, Mrs. Laura continued to play her part. Although her acquired drawl was replaced sometimes by her natural accent she still looked choice and aloof as a beautiful princess—remote from the rabble. But her fingers kept tapping the greasy old-

gold plush seat, while she glanced continuously at her watch.

"Still hours and hours," she said impatiently. "It seems as though we'd never
make Trieste—let alone Turin."

"Anxious to drop me?" asked Todhunter
incredulously.

"I'm not thinking of you. . . . But children
get measles—and deserted husbands prove
unfaithful. The world is full of pretty typists."

"In that case, he'd have nothing on you,
if it came to a show-up."

She started at the word.

"Show-up? Don't give me the jitters,"
she cried sharply. "There's no chance of it,
is there?"

He stroked his lip.

"I should say we are reasonably secure,"
he told her. "Still . . . I've handled some
queer cases in my career. One never
knows what will break. It was unfortunate
that there were any English visitors at the
hotel. And you are entirely too beautiful to
remain anonymous."

Mrs. Laura shook off his hand. She
wanted reassurance, not compliments.

"You told me there was no risk," she
said. Forgetting that her original scheme

had been to force her husband to take action, she added bitterly, "What a fool I've been."

"Why are you suddenly so anxious to get back to your husband?" asked Todhunter.

"Well, to be brutally frank, we are all of us out for what we can get. And he can give me more than you can."

"Haven't I given you a memory you'll never forget?"

Mrs. Laura's eyes flashed angrily, and Todhunter laughed. He had grown rather bored by the languid beauty and her synthetic culture; but now that she had suddenly become alive, he was aware of the fact that she was slipping from him.

"I was only teasing you," he said. "Of course, no one will ever know about us. I could risk nothing like that. . . . But we might have been in a jam if I had not thought a jump ahead when that girl asked me about the peeping woman."

"Why," asked Laura, who had only grasped the fact that Todhunter would never go an inch out of his way to champion an unattractive middle-aged woman.

"Why? Because she's disappeared. If I had not repudiated her, I should have to make a statement at Trieste," Todhunter laughed. "Can't you see the headlines? 'Englishwoman lost on Continental express.' Photograph of Mr. Todhunter who was on his honeymoon, when. . . . And thus and thus. It wouldn't be long before the English press got on to my identity. One of the penalties of fame—however limited."

Mrs. Laura did not look as impressed as he wished, for his words had raised a new issue.

Perhaps, after all, the game was not lost, because it was not yet ended. Although Todhunter had no intention of risking a scandal when he lured her away on this trip, she saw a chance to engineer one and so force his hand.

If she went to the professor and assured him of Miss Froy's existence the result was bound to be future complications. There could be no doubt of the professor's probity and public spirit, which would enforce an investigation—whatever the cost to his personal convenience.

Her violet eyes suddenly glittered. As the beautiful bride of the alleged Todhunter, she was an important detail in the picture, and one that reporters would not overlook or suppress. She always made such an appealing photograph.

Afterwards there would be a sensational divorce case, and Sir Peveril—in honour bound—would be obliged to make her the second Lady Brown.

At the thought she drew a deep breath, for the wheel was still spinning.

Her counter was not yet lost.

CHAPTER TWENTY-FOUR
THE WHEEL SPINS

Mrs. Laura sat and looked at the window which held the reflection of the lighted carriage, thrown on panels of rushing darkness. She smiled at her dimly-mirrored face—smoky-dark, with shadowed eyes and triumphant lips. The wheel was still spinning for her.

And since their fates were interlinked it was spinning also for Miss Froy. The little spinster was in a perilous plight, but she was an obstinate optimist. She clung to the hope that everything would come right in the end, and that at long last she would reach home.

Miss Froy loved her home with that intense perverted passion which causes ardent patriots to desert their native lands and makes men faithless to their wives.

Like them, she left what she loved most—
for the joy of the return.

This special absence had been a thrilling experience. During the first six months of exile, she had been excited by the novelty of living in semi-royal surroundings. Everything was so exaggerated and unreal that she had a confused sense of having strayed into some fairy tale. She wandered and lost herself amid a maze of pillared halls and gilded apartments. There seemed to be endless marble stairs—countless galleries—all duplicated in enormous mirrors, so that at least one-half of the castle was illusion.

The scenery, in its breathless beauty, held the same bewildering quality of unreality. In her letters to her family she gave up the attempt to describe blue and purple mountains, whose white crests smashed through the sky—boiling jade rivers—lush green valleys—towering precipices.

"There aren't enough adjectives," she wrote. "But it's all simply topping."

True to schedule, however, when she cracked her seventh month of absence, her rapture suffered its first eclipse and she began to realise the drawbacks of living in a castle. To begin with she got lost no longer, and there were not so many marble staircases, since she had located the mirrors.

There were other unpleasant details, including fleas in the thick carpets and rich upholstery, for the hounds were many and the servants few.

Her vast bedroom, which was like a stage royal apartment, was comfortless and cold, since the enormous coloured porcelain stove—resembling a cathedral altar-piece—was insufficiently stoked.

There were ten courses for dinner—but only one knife and fork, which the diner cleaned with bread.

All the men were handsome and respectful, but none seemed to realise that she was a curly-headed girl whose pet sport was refusing curates.

Before her last five months were up she became so homesick that her longing for a small stone house—backed by an apple orchard, and overlooking a country churchyard—grew to a passion. Sick of the theatrical scenery, she would have exchanged all the mountains and rivers for one corner *of* an English meadow with a clump of elms and a duck-pond.

The night before her return her excitement was so great that she could not sleep, in anticipation of her journey. She could not believe in it, although her luggage was packed and labelled. One suitcase held soiled linen, destined for a real good boil. She did her personal washing in the bathroom, by stealth, since she had seen too many pails emptied into the beautiful green river which was the communal laundry.

As she lay and tossed she heard the faint scream of an engine, muted by distance to an amplified mosquito-ping. It was the night express, which—when farther down the valley—woke up the homesick sleepers in the hotel and whistled their thoughts after it, as though it were a monstrous metallic Pied Piper.

Just as, later, it called to Iris, it now drew the little spinster from her bed. She ran to the window and was in time to see it shoot past the end of the gorge, like a golden rod of light slipping into grooves of darkness.

"To-morrow night I shall be in an express, too," she gloated.

It was a rapture to anticipate her long journey, stage by stage and frontier by frontier, until she reached a small dingy station which was merely a halt built amid empty fields. No one would meet her there, because her father was afraid that blundering Sock, in his ecstasy, might leap at the engine and try to lick its face too.

But they would be waiting for her farther down the lane—and her eyes grew misty at the thought of that meeting. Yet even then she would not reach her journey's end until she ran through a dim white gate and a starlit garden, to see the light streaming through an open door.

"Mater," said Miss Froy, with a lump in her throat.

Then a sudden fear touched her heart.

"I've never been so homesick before," she thought. "Is it a warning? Suppose— suppose something happened—to keep me from getting home."

Something happened—something so monstrous and unexpected that she could not really believe in it. It was an adventure which could only be credited in connection with any one else.

At first she was certain that some one

would soon come to her aid. She told herself it was a fortunate circumstance that she had met the charming English girl. They were compatriots, and she could rely on her with utmost confidence, because—were the situation reversed—she knew she would tear the train apart, wheel by wheel, in order to find her.

But as the time crawled on and nothing happened, doubts began to flock into her mind. She remembered that the girl had a touch of sunstroke and was far from well. She might be worse, or even seriously ill. Besides it would be difficult to try to explain the circumstances when one was ignorant of the language.

There was an even worse possibility. Iris might have tried to intervene and been snatched up, too, in the great machine which had caught her up in one of its revolutions. At the thought, Miss Froy's lip grew beaded from desperation and fear.

Then, suddenly, she felt the braking of the train. Its clatter and roar died down to a grinding slither, and with a mighty jerk the engine stopped.

"They've missed me," she thought triumphantly. "Now they are going to search the train."

And once again she saw the lights of home streaming through the open door.

As she waited in happy expectation she would have been surprised and gratified to know that the beautiful bride—who looked like a film star—was thinking of her.

Although she was only a pawn, she was the central figure in a plot to restore her liberty. At that moment the professor was standing in the corridor just outside Mrs. Laura's coupé. She had only to call to him and Miss Froy's ultimate release would be put in train.

As there was plenty of time before Trieste was reached, she delayed in order to be quite certain of the wisdom of her decision. Once she had applied the match she could not stop the blaze of publicity.

In reality, however, her mind was made up. Although she had discovered the barrister's drawbacks he was the original prize for which she had played. When she was Lady Brown, Sir Peveril would be merely a husband and she knew how to deal with this useful domestic animal. Hitherto she had been humiliated by the knowledge that his programme did not include marriage, and in her anxiety to impress him favourably, she had developed an inferiority complex.

Royal smashing tactics suited her better. Her voice was arrogant as she spoke to the barrister.

"What are we stopping for?" she asked, looking out at a squalid platform, dimly visible in a few flickering lights.

"Frontier," explained the barrister.

"Help. Have we got to get out and go through the Customs?"

"No, we take on the officials here. . . . What's that shockheaded lunatic up to?"

The barrister frowned as Hare raced into the telegraph office, shouting back the while to the guard who was yelling to him. It was evidently a first-class slanging match, but unintelligible to the English passengers who were deprived of its finer points.

As a matter of fact it had struck the bright young man that he could save his own valuable time at Trieste if he took advantage of the halt to send off Mrs. Barnes' telegram to Bath, England. The idea, however, did not make him popular with his compatriots.

"Fool's holding us up," growled the barrister, looking at his watch.

To his surprise Laura was perfectly calm at the menace to their time-table.

"Does it matter?" she drawled. "We shall get there."

"We might lose our connection. We've cut it pretty fine. That reminds me of something. I was wondering whether, in your interests, we had better part before we get into Italy. We might run up against some one we know."

"Personally I should not compare Italy with Piccadilly Circus. Still, it's on the map. What do you want to do?"

"I could take the Trieste-Paris express. Could you manage by yourself at Milan?"

"Perfectly. I shall find some one. Or some one will find me. In any case, I can look after myself."

There was a confident note in her voice—associated with the dismissal of cooks—for the professor had just gone back to his compartment. She rose from her seat, prepared to follow him, when the Customs officials appeared at the end of the corridor.

That check was of vital importance to

Froy. As Laura did not wish to be interrupted, she wanted for the professor's luggage to be examined. In the interval the barrister had sensed a situation which prompted a few leading questions.

"What makes you look so serious?" he asked.

"You forget, this may be serious for me."

"In what way? We're not parting for ever, are we? I can meet you in London."

"How nice."

Now that her pride was no longer a buffer between the natural woman and self-expression, Laura felt mistress of the situation. She held the winning card.

"I'm wondering," she said, "if I can endure the name of 'Brown,' after being Mrs. Parmiter."

"Will the occasion arise?"

"Well, if there's a divorce, you could hardly let me down. It's not done, is it, darling?"

"But, my sweet, there will be no divorce."

"I'm not so sure. I know you made it very plain to me that you would not give your wife the evidence to divorce you. But she'll read about us in the papers—and no woman could stand for that."

"You seem very sure of your publicity. Perhaps you have a better knowledge of the possibilities than I have?"

The barrister glowered at her as though she were a hostile witness, for he had realised the threat which underlay her smiles.

She meant to try to rush a situation.

"I can reassure you on one point," he said coldly. "If your husband brings an action, you may lose your own charming name. But you will not be called upon to make the greater sacrifice. There is already one Lady Brown. . . . My wife will never divorce me."

Laura stared at him incredulously.

"You mean, she'd take it lying down?" she asked.

"Does the posture matter? The point is that we have a complete understanding. It would be against our mutual interests ever to part company. . . . But I think here is no real risk of publicity. Do you?"

He knew he had won and she knew it too. His cool level voice stirred up Laura's smouldering passion.

"If there was," she said, "it seems as if I

was the only one that stood to lose. You boast that your wife won't divorce you. Well, my husband would. And I thank God for it. At least I am married to a real man with decent natural feelings."

The barrister screwed his monocle in his eye in an instinctive effort to preserve his dignity.

"I'm afraid I've disappointed you," he said. "I had no idea that I had led you to hope for anything beyond a pleasant and unconventional holiday."

Before Laura could speak, the Customs officer entered their compartment and was very courteous and obliging over the luggage and passport of the distinguished Englishman and his beautiful bride.

After he had gone the professor appeared again in the corridor—still puffing at his pipe.

Laura shivered at the sight of him because he reminded her of what she had nearly lost by a premature disclosure. Her fine house, her social position, her respectability, and perhaps even her children would all have been swept away for a man who would not marry her.

"Thanks be I sounded him first," she told herself.

Her gain was Miss Froy's loss. The express carried a ghost-passenger, whose passport—although in order—was never examined. An experienced traveller, she realised what had actually happened when the train began to move slowly for the second time.

"Frontier," she thought.

But in the interval between picking up the Customs officials and dropping them again, she swept through a cycle of emotions, as she shot up from midnight to sunshine, and then—through the gradual twilight of suspense, deferred hope and anxiety—sank back again into darkness.

The train rushed on.

CHAPTER TWENTY-FIVE
"STRANGE DISAPPEARANCE"

After the Professor had left her Iris slumped down in her seat and listened to the choppy current of the train's frantic rhythm. The grimed glass was beginning to grow steamy, so that it was difficult to see anything outside the window, except an occasional line of lights when the express flashed through some small station.

Since Miss Froy had been proved non-existent by the laws of logic she felt too flat to be interested in her surroundings. She had not even sufficient spirit to remain angry with the professor for his interference.

"All travellers are selfish," she reflected. "It was those Miss Flood-Porters. They were afraid they might be saddled with me, so they got at the professor. I expect he consulted the doctor about what could be done."

She straightened herself in an effort to relieve the aching of her back. The continual shaking of the train had worn her out, while her neck felt as though it were made of plaster of Paris and would crack in two if she jerked it. At that moment she longed for a comfortable bed where she could rest, far from the incessant rattle and din.

It was the doctor's suggestion—a good night's rest. Yet, although she began to doubt her own wisdom in trying to swim against the current, she remained set in her determination to oppose advice.

Presently Hare entered and sat opposite to her in Miss Kummer's seat.

"Well?" he asked hopefully. "Going to stop off at Trieste?"

"No," replied Iris stiffly.

"But are you sure you're fit to go on?"

"Does it matter to you?"

"No. But, all the same, I'm worried stiff about you."

"Why?"

"Hanged if I know. It's not a habit of mine."

Against her will Iris smiled faintly. She

could not forget Miss Froy. The memory of her was a grumbling undercurrent, like the aching of a stopped tooth. Yet whenever Hare was present he acted in the same manner as a local application that deadened the pain. In spite of her misery there was a queer thrill in being alone with him on the same nightmare journey.

"Cheer up," he said. "You'll soon be home. Back with your colony of friends."

The prospect seemed suddenly distasteful to Iris.

"I don't want to see one of them," she declared petulantly. "I don't want to get back. I've no home. And nothing seems worth while."

"What do you do with yourself?"

"Nothing. . . . Oh, play about."

"With other chaps?"

"Yes. We all do the same things. Silly things. There's not one real person among the lot of us. . . . Sometimes I get terrified. I'm wasting my youth. What's at the end of it all?"

Hare made no attempt to console her or answer her question. He stared out at the darkness with a half-smile playing round his mouth. When he began to talk, it was about himself.

"My life's very different from yours. I never know where I'm going next. But it's always rough. And things happen. Not always pleasant things. . . . Still, if I could take you with me on my next job, you'd get a complete change. You'd go without every comfort a refined home should have—but I'd lay you odds you'd never feel bored again."

"Sounds lovely. . . . Are you proposing to me?"

"No. Just waiting to dodge when you start to throw custard pies at me."

"But lots of men propose to me. And I'd like to go to a rough place."

"Fine. Now I can go into it seriously. Got any money?"

"Some. Just chicken feed."

"Suits me. I've none."

They were scarcely conscious of what they said as they talked at random in the only language they knew—their light words utterly at variance with the yearning in their eyes.

"You know," said Hare, breaking a

pause, "all this is rot. I'm only doing it to take your mind off things."

"You mean—Miss Froy?"

"Yes, confound the woman."

To his surprise Iris changed the subject.

"What sort of brain have you?" she asked.

"Fair to middling, when it's lubricated. It works best on beer."

"Could you write a detective thriller?"

"No. Can't spell."

"But could you solve one?"

"Every time."

"Then suppose you give me a demonstration. You've been very clever in proving Miss Froy could not exist. But—if she did—could you find out what might have happened to her? Or is it too difficult?"

Hare burst out laughing.

"I used to think," he said, "that if ever I liked a girl, I'd be cut out by some beautiful band conductor with waved hair. I'm hanged if I thought I'd have to play second fiddle to an ancient governess. Time's revenge, I suppose. Long ago, I bit one. And she was a good governess. . . . Well, here goes."

He lit his pipe and furrowed his brow

while Iris watched him with intense interest. His face—no longer slack and careless—was hardened into lines of concentration, so that he looked almost a different man. Sometimes he ran his fingers through his hair, when his rebellious tuft flared up rampant and sometimes he chuckled.

Presently he gave a crow of triumph.

"I've got it to fit. Bit of jiggery-pokery in parts, but it hangs together. Now would you like to hear an original story called 'The Strange Disappearance of Miss Froy'?"

Iris winced at the light tone.

"I'd love to," she told him.

"Then you're for it. But, first of all, when you boarded the train, was there one nun next door to you, or two?"

"I only noticed one as we passed the carriage. She had a horrible face."

"Hum. My story demands a second one, later on."

"That's convenient, because there is another one. I met her in the corridor."

"Seen her since?"

"No, but I shouldn't notice one way or another. There's such a jam."

"Good. That proves that no one would be likely to notice whether there was one nun, or two, connected with the invalid out-fit. Especially as it's corked up at the end of the corridor. You see, I've got to play about with these blessed nuns, so they're very important."

"Yes. Go on."

"I haven't started yet. The nun part was preamble. Here really goes. . . . Miss Froy is a spy who's got some information which she's sneaking out of the country. So she's got to be bumped off. And what better way than on a railway journey?"

"You mean—they've thrown her on the rails going through a tunnel?" asked Iris faintly.

"Don't be absurd. And don't look so wan. If they chucked her on the line her body would be found and awkward ques-tions asked. No, she's got to *disappear.* And what I was getting at was this. On a journey, a lot of valuable time will be wasted before it can be proved even that she is missing. At first her people will think she's lost a connection or stopped at Paris for a day or two, to shop. So, by the time they get busy, the trail will be stone cold."

"But they wouldn't know what to do. They're old and helpless."

"Tough luck. You're making my tale positively pathetic. But even if they are influential and know the ropes, when they begin to make inquiries they'd find themselves up against a conspiracy of silence."

"Why, is the whole train in the plot?"

"No, just the baroness, the doctor and the nuns. Of course, there'd be a passive conspiracy of silence, as I mentioned before. None of the passengers, who are local folk, would dare to contradict any statement of the baroness."

"But, don't forget the baroness said something to the ticket collector which you couldn't understand."

"Is this my yarn or yours? But—perhaps you're right. There may be a railway official or two in it. In fact, there must have been some dirty work at the cross-roads over her reserved seat. They had to be sure that she would be in the baroness' compartment, and at the end of the train."

"Next door to the doctor, too. . . . But what's *happened to her?*"

In spite of her resolution to keep cool, Iris clenched her fingers in suspense as she waited.

"Aha," gloated Hare. "That's where my

brain comes in. . . . Miss Froy is lying in the next compartment to this, covered with rugs, and disguised with bandages and trimmings. Her own mother wouldn't know her now."

"How? When?"

"It happened when you obligingly dropped off to sleep. Enter the doctor. He asks Miss Froy if she could render some slight service to his patient. I'm sure I don't know why he should rope her in as he's got a nurse on tap. But she'll go."

"I know she would."

"Well, directly she enters the compartment she gets the surprise of her life. To begin with all the blinds are drawn down and the place is in darkness. She smells a rat, but before she can squeal the three of them set on her."

"The three?"

"Ja, the patient is one of the gang. One of them pinions her, the other throttles her so she can't shout, and the doctor is busy giving her an injection, to make her unconscious."

Iris felt her heart hammer as she pictured the scene.

"It *could* happen," she said.

Hare gave her a delighted beam.

"Wish I had you to listen to my golf-stories. You've got the right reaction to lies. Artistic ones, of course. . . . By the way, one of the nuns is a man. The one with the ugly face."

"I believe she is."

"Don't be so prejudiced. All men aren't ugly. Well, Miss Froy is now down and out, so they're able to bandage her up roughly, and stick a lot of plaster over her face, to disguise her. Then they tie her up, gag her, and lay her out, in the place of the false patient, who was already dressed in uniform, only she was covered with rugs. So she's only to pull off her plaster and stick a veil over her bandaged head, to look the perfect nun. Number two."

"I saw a second one in the corridor," nodded Iris.

"But, by now, you've unearthed some English people who will remember Miss Froy, and you've roped in the parson's wife. As I think I explained before, the conspirators have to produce some one, and trust to bluff. So, down comes the blind again, while the second nun—the one who

posed as the original patient, dresses herself in Miss Froy's clothes."

As Iris remained silent Hare looked
rather depressed.

"Admittedly feeble," he said, "but the
best I can do."

Iris scarcely heard him, for she was
nerving herself to ask a question.

"What will happen to her when they
reach Trieste?"

"Oh, this is the part my readers will
adore," explained Hare. "She'll be put in
an ambulance and taken to some lonely
house, overlooking deep deserted water—
a creek, or arm of the river, or something.
You know the sort of thing—black oily water lapping a derelict quay. Then she'll be
weighted, and all that, and neatly dumped
among the mud and ooze. But I'm not altogether ruthless. I'll let them keep her
drugged to the bitter end. So the old dear'll
know nothing about it. . . . Here. What's
up?"

Iris had sprung to her feet and was tugging at the door.

"Everything you say may be true," she
panted. "We mustn't waste time. We must
do something."

Hare forced her back to her seat.

"Here—you," he said. Already she meant everything to him but he'd completely forgotten her name. "This is simply a yarn I made up for you."

"But I must get to that patient," cried Iris. "It's Miss Froy. I must see for myself."

"Don't be a fool. The patient next door is *real,* and she's been smashed up. If we forced our way into that carriage and started to make any fuss the doctor would order us out. And quite right too."

"Then you won't help me?" asked Iris despairingly.

"Definitely no. I'm sorry to keep harping on it, but I can't forget your sunstroke. And when I remember my own experience and how I mistook my own footer captain——"

"For the Prince of Wales. I know, I know."

"I'm frightfully sorry I led you on. I only told you how things *might* be worked. But I'm just like the old lady who saw a giraffe for the first time. Honestly, 'I *don't believe it.*'"

CHAPTER TWENTY-SIX
SIGNATURE

"Of course," agreed Iris dully, "you were just making it up. What a fool I am."

As she tried to stifle her disappointment some one—farther down the corridor—began to speak in an unnaturally loud voice. The words were unintelligible to her and sounded like an incantation for rain; but Hare's face lit up.

"Some one's got a wireless set," he said springing up. "It's the news. Back in two shakes."

When he returned he told Iris what he had heard.

"Another good murder sensation gone west. The medical evidence on the editor states he was shot about midnight—while the High Hat had left for his hunting lodge directly after dinner. So they can't hang it on him. Pity."

As he spoke something floated across Iris' memory, like one of those spirals of cobweb which are wafted on the air on still autumn mornings. She started up as Hare looked at his watch.

"Nearly time for the second dinner," he told her. "Coming?"

"No. But the others will be coming back."

"What's the odds? Are you frightened of them?"

"Don't be absurd. But they make a little clump, all together, this end. And I—I don't like being so near that doctor."

"Not frightened then. Well, our compartment will be empty while the professor and I are having dinner. I am willing to sub-let it, at a nominal rent, to a good tenant."

After he had gone Iris felt the old limpness stealing over her. A long-drawn howl, as though some damned soul were lamenting, followed by the rattle of machine-gun fire, told her that they were passing through a tunnel. It suggested a gruesome possibility.

Suppose—at that minute—a dead body were being thrown out of the train.

She reminded herself that Hare's story was fiction and managed to drive it from her mind. But another tale—which she had read in a magazine and which was supposed to be authentic—slipped in to take its place.

It was about two ladies who arrived by night at a continental hotel, on their way back from an oriental tour. The daughter carefully noted the number of her mother's room before she went to her own. When she returned some time later, she found no trace of her mother, while the room itself had different furniture and a new wallpaper.

When she made inquiries, the entire staff, from the manager downwards, assured her that she had come to the hotel alone. The mother's name was not in the register. The cab-driver and the porters at the railway terminus all supported the conspiracy.

The mother had been blown out like a match.

Of course there was an explanation. In the daughter's absence the mother had died of plague, contracted in the East. The mere rumour would have kept away millions of visitors from the exhibition about to be held in the city. With such important interests at stake a unit had to be sacrificed.

Iris' hands began to grow clammy as she wondered whether Miss Froy's disappearance might not be a parallel on a very small scale. In her case it would not involve a vast and complicated organisation, or a fantastic conspiracy—merely the collusion of a few interested persons.

And Hare had shown her how it *could* be worked.

She began to try to fit the facts to the theory. To begin with, although the baroness was wealthy, she was sharing a compartment with the proletariat. Why? Because she had decided to take her journey at the last minute and was unable to make a reservation? In that case, the Flood-Porters and the Todhunters could not have secured coupés.

Then was it meanness? Or was it because she wanted a special compartment at the end of the corridor, next to the doctor's carriage, where they would not be seen nor disturbed?

Further—was it chance that the rest of the seats were occupied by local people whose destinies she swayed to a great extent?

The questions hung in the air while a cloud of fresh suspicions quivered into Iris' mind. It was an extraordinary fact that the blinds remained undrawn in the invalid's compartment. She was left on show—so to speak—to declare the goods. Was that to prepare the way for a version of the old strategy—to hide an object in some place where it was visible to every one?

Only—what had poor little Miss Froy done? Hare was right when he declared that he was influenced mainly by the question of motive. As far as Iris could tell she had discharged her duties so faithfully that her august employer had personally thanked for her services rendered.

Suddenly Iris caught her breath with excitement.

"That was why," she whispered.

The personage was supposed to be in his hunting-lodge at the time of the murder. Yet Miss Froy, by tactlessly lying awake, had surprised him coming from the one and only bathroom, where presumably he had been washing before he flitted.

She had destroyed his alibi.

Her knowledge would be a positive danger in view of the fact that she was returning to teach the children of the Red leader. Every one knew that she was a confirmed gossip and rattle. She would be proud of the personage's confidence and advertise it. And, as a British subject—with no axe to grind—her testimony would have weight against a mass of interested evidence.

When the personage shook hands so graciously with her, he was sealing her doom.

Iris pictured the hurried family conference at dawn—the hasty summons to the necessary confederates. Telephones would be humming with secret messages. In view of the urgency, it followed of necessity that Miss Froy's suppression could not be the perfect crime.

She tried to control the gallop of her imagination.

"Maximilian-Max"—she had not forgotten his name, since "Hare was too long"— "spun me a yarn. He was stretching the facts to make them fit in. Perhaps I'm doing the same. It's futile to palpitate about some one who may not exist. After all, as they say, she may be only a delusion. . . . I do wish I could be sure."

Her wish was granted in a dramatic manner. The carriage had grown hot and the steam on the window was turning gradually to beads of moisture, which was beginning to trickle downwards.

Iris followed the slow slide of one of these drops from the top to a grimy corner of uncleaned pane.

Suddenly she gave a start as she noticed a tiny name which had been written on the smoked glass.

Leaning over she was able to decipher the signature.

It was "Winifred Froy."

CHAPTER TWENTY-SEVEN
THE ACID TEST

Iris stared at the name, hardly able to believe that her eyes were not playing her a trick. The tiny neat handwriting was round and unformed as that of a schoolgirl, and suggested the character of the little governess—half-prim adult, and half-arrested youth.

It was proof positive that Miss Froy had sat recently in the corner seat. Iris vaguely remembered that she was knitting when she first entered the carriage. When she scrawled her name on the grimy glass with the point of one of her pins, she was working off some of the gush of her holiday mood.

"*I* was right, after all," thought Iris exultantly.

It was an overwhelming relief to emerge

from the fog of her nightmare. But her exhilaration was blotted out almost immediately by a sense of impending crisis.

She was no longer fighting shadows—but facing actual danger.

A terrible fate awaited Miss Froy. She was the only person on the train who realised the peril. And time was slipping remorselessly away. A glance at her watch showed that it was ten minutes past nine. In less than an hour they would arrive at Trieste.

Trieste now assumed a terrible significance. It was the place of execution.

The train was rushing at tremendous speed, in a drive to make up lost time. It rattled and shrieked as it swung round the curves—shaking the carriages as though it recked nothing of its human load. Iris felt that they were in the grip of an insensate maddened force, which, itself, was a victim to a relentless system.

The driver would be fined for every minute over the scheduled time of arrival.

The sense of urgency made Iris spring up from her seat, only to stagger back again at a sudden wave of faintness. She felt a knocking inside her head and stab-

bing pains behind her eyeballs, as the result of her unguarded movement. With a
vague hope that it might act as an opiate
she lit a cigarette.

A babel of voices in the corridor told her
that the passengers were returning from
dinner. The family party, with the blonde,
came first. They were all in excellent spirits
after their meal and took no notice of Iris,
who glowered at them from her corner. She
resented their passive conspiracy, even
though they were ignorant of any threat to
Miss Froy, and were pleased only to be of
some slight service to the baroness.

They were followed by the woman who
wore Miss Froy's tweed suit and feathered
hat. At the sight of the impostor, Iris' temperature rushed up again as she asked
herself whether this were actually the second nursing-sister whom she had met in
the corridor.

Both had dull black eyes, a sallow skin,
and bad teeth; but the peasants in the railway waiting-room had looked much the
same. As it was impossible to reach any
conclusion, Iris rose and dashed out into
the corridor.

She was strung up to action and intended to storm the next carriage. But blocking her way and almost filling the narrow space was the gigantic black figure of the baroness. As she towered above her, Iris realised that she was bottled up in the danger-zone of the train—away from every one she knew.

She felt suddenly helpless and afraid as she looked away from the grim face to the shrieking darkness rushing past the window. The maniac shrieks of the engine and the frantic shaking of the train increased her sense of nightmare. Once again her knees began to shake and she had a terrible fear that she was going to faint.

Her horror of becoming insensible and so being at their mercy made her fight the dizziness with every ounce of her strength. Licking her dry lips, she managed to speak to the baroness.

"Let me pass, please."

Instead of giving way, the baroness looked at her twitching face.

"You are in pain," she said. "That is not good, for you are young and you travel without friends. I will ask the nurse here for a tablet to relieve your head."

"No, thank you," said Iris firmly. "Please, will you stand on one side?"

The baroness took no notice of her request, or of her refusal. Instead, she shouted some imperative command which brought the callous-faced nurse to the doorway of the invalid's carriage. Iris noticed sub-consciously that the baroness' words did not conform to a conventional request, but were a peremptory order for prompt action.

The glass of the patient's window was also growing steamy from heat, but Iris tried to look inside. The still form laid out on the seat appeared to have no face— only a white blur.

As she asked herself what lay underneath the bandages, the nurse noticed her interest. She pounced forward and gripped the girl's arm, as though to pull her inside.

Iris looked up at the brutal mouth, the dark shading round the lips and the muscular fingers, which were covered with short black hairs.

"It is a man," she thought.

Terror urged her to an elemental action of self-defence. She was scarcely conscious of what she did as she pressed the end of her smouldering cigarette against the back of the woman's hand. Taken by surprise, she relaxed her grip with what sounded like an oath.

In that instant Iris pushed past the baroness and dashed down the corridor, fighting her way against the stream of returning diners. Although they opposed her advance, she was glad of their presence, because they formed a barrier between her and the baroness.

As her terror waned, she began to realise that every one in the train seemed to be laughing at her. The guard openly sneered as he twisted his little black spiked moustache. There was a white flash of teeth and hoots of smothered laughter. The passengers evidently considered her slightly mad and were amused by a funny spectacle.

Their derision made Iris aware of the situation. She felt self-conscious and ashamed as though she were in an unclothed kind of dream.

"Heavens, what have I done?" she asked herself. "That nurse only offered me some aspirin, or something. And I burned her wrist. If they're really on the level, they will think me mad."

Then her terror flared up again at the thought of Miss Froy.

"They won't listen to me. But I must make them understand about her. . . . This train seems a mile long. I'll never get there. . . . Faces. Grinning faces. . . . Miss Froy. I must be in time."

She seemed imprisoned in some horrible nightmare, where her limbs were weighted with lead and refused to obey her will. The passengers blocked her way, so that she appeared to recede two steps where she advanced one. To her distorted imagination, the faces of these strangers were caricatures of humanity—blank, insensible and heartless. While Miss Froy was going to be murdered, no one cared for anything but dinner.

After an age-long struggle through several sections of the train—when the connecting-passages turned to clanking iron concertinas, which tried to catch her and press her to death—she reached the restaurant-car. As she heard the clink of china and the hum of voices, her brainstorm passed and she lingered in the entrance—her returning sense of convention at war with elemental fear and horror.

Soup was being served, and the diners were spooning it up vigorously, for they had been waiting a long time for their meal. In her lucid interval, Iris realised the hopeless prospect of trying to convince hungry men who had only just begun their dinner.

Once again she ran the gauntlet of faces as she reeled down the gangway. Two waiters, whispering to one another, tittered, and she felt sure that they were sneering at her.

The professor, who shared a table with Hare, saw her first, and an expression of apprehension flitted across his long face. He was chatting to the doctor, who had lingered over his coffee and liqueur, since the places for the second dinner were not all filled.

Iris felt chilled by her reception when they all stared at her in silence. Even Hare's eyes held no welcome, as he watched her with a worried frown.

In desperation she appealed to the professor.

"For heaven's sake go on with your soup. Don't stop—but please listen. This is of deadly importance. I know there is a

THE LADY VANISHES 293

Miss Froy. I know there's a conspiracy against her. And I know why."

The professor gave a resigned shrug as he continued drinking his soup. As Iris poured out her incoherent story, she was herself appalled by the weakness of her arguments. Before she finished she despaired of convincing him. He listened in stony silence, and was obviously absorbed by the exact proportion of salt to add to his soup.

At the end of the tale he raised his brows interrogatively as he glanced at the doctor, who broke into some rapid explanation. Watching their faces with anxious eyes, Iris could tell that Hare was disturbed by what was said, for he cut into the conversation.

"That's not her yarn. It's mine. I spun it for a lark, and the poor kid sucked it in. So, if any one's loopy, it's——"

He broke off, suddenly aware of what he had revealed. But Iris was too distraught to notice implications.

"Won't you come now?" she entreated the professor.

He looked at his empty plate which the waiter had placed in readiness for the fish course.

"Can't it wait until after dinner?" he asked wearily.

"Wait? Won't you understand. It's deadly, terribly urgent. When we reach Trieste it will be too late."

Again the professor mutely consulted the doctor, who stared fixedly at Iris as though he were trying to hypnotise her. When at last he spoke, it was in English for her benefit.

"Perhaps we had better come at once to see my patient. I'm sorry that your dinner should be spoiled, professor. But the young lady is in a very highly-strung condition. It may be—safer—to try and reassure her."

Wearing the expression of a martyr to his sense of justice, the professor unfolded himself from his seat. Once again the little procession staggered in single file down the corridors of the reeling train. As they neared the end, Hare turned and spoke to Iris in a fierce whisper.

"Don't be a blasted fool and start anything."

Her heart sank as she realised that his advice was too late. The nursing-sister was already displaying her hand for the benefit of the doctor and the professor. Iris noticed vaguely that she had wound a handkerchief around her wrist as though she wished to conceal it from too close a scrutiny.

Then the doctor turned to her and spoke in soothing-syrupy accents.

"My dear young lady, wasn't it rather—impetuous—to burn my poor nurse? And all because she offered you a harmless tablet to relieve the pain of your head. . . . See, professor, how her face twitches."

Iris shrank as he touched her forehead with a cold forefinger to illustrate his meaning.

Suddenly she remembered that when one is losing a defensive game, the only hope is to attack. Plucking up her courage, she managed to steady her voice.

"I cannot be sorry enough about the burn. It's no excuse to say I was hysterical. But there was some excuse for my being so. There is so much that I cannot understand."

The doctor accepted her challenge.

"Such as—?" he asked.

"Well, the professor tells me you offered to take me to a nursing home at Trieste."

"The offer is still open."

"Yet you are supposed to be rushing a patient to hospital for a dangerous operation. How could you possible bother yourself with a complete stranger? . . . It makes one wonder exactly how serious her injuries are. Or if she has any at all."

The doctor stroked his beard.

"My offer was made merely to relieve the professor of an unwelcome responsibility, which is in my line and not in his. But I am afraid that you exaggerate your own importance. My intention was to give you a seat in the ambulance which took us to the hospital. After we had gone inside with our patient, the driver would follow his instructions and drive you to some recommended nursing home. It was not for professional service—but merely to give you a good night's rest, so that you could continue your journey on the following day."

The proposal sounded so reasonable that Iris could only fall back on her second question.

"Where is the other nurse?"

The doctor paused perceptibly before his reply.

"There is only one nurse."

As she looked at his impassive face, further screened by his black spade-beard, Iris knew instinctively that it was useless to protest. The result would be the same— denials on every side. No one but herself would have seen that second nurse. Just as no one would accept Miss Froy's signature as genuine—supposing that it had not been already destroyed by condensation.

The doctor spoke to the professor.

"I am sorry to detain you further," he said, "but here is a young lady who believes very terrible things. We must try to convince her of her *delusions.*"

He crossed to the shrouded form of his patient and pulled up a corner of one of the rugs, displaying a neat pair of legs.

"Can you identify these stockings or these boots?" he asked.

Iris shook her head as she looked at the thick silk stockings and regulation brown calf single-strap shoes.

"You know I can't," she said. "But you might have better luck if you would raise just one bandage and let me see her face."

The doctor grimaced with horror.

"Ah," he said, "I see you do not understand. I must tell you something that is not pretty. Listen." He touched the swathed forehead with a butterfly flick of his fingertips. "There is no face here at all. *No face.* Only lumps of raw flesh. Perhaps we shall make quite another face, if we are lucky. We shall see."

His fingers moved on and hovered for a second over the bandage which covered the eyes of the figure.

"We await the oculist's verdict on these," he said. "Till then, we dare not expose them to a flicker of light. It may be total blindness, for one eye is but pulp. But science can work marvels."

He smiled at Iris and continued.

"But most terrible of all is the injury to the brain. I will not describe it, for already you look sick. First of all we must attend to that. Afterwards—the rest, if the patient still lives."

"I don't believe you," Iris told him. "It's all lies."

"In that case," said the doctor smoothly, "you can convince yourself. You have only to tear one little strip of plaster from the face, to see. . . . But if you do, I warn you that bleeding will start again and the patient will die instantly from shock. . . . You will be charged with murder and you will be hanged. . . . But since you are so sure of the face which is under these bandages, you will not hesitate. . . . *Will* you tear off this strip?"

Iris felt Hare's fingers closing over her arm, as she hesitated. Her instinct told her that the doctor was putting up a bluff, and that she ought to grasp at even the hundredth chance to save Miss Froy's life.

Yet the doctor had done his work too well. The thought of that mutilated face spouting fountains of blood made her shrink back. Afterwards? The rope—or Broadmoor for life. It was too horrible a prospect to contemplate.

"I—I can't," she whispered.

"Ah," sneered the doctor, "you talk, but you are not so brave."

For the first time it struck Iris that he had never intended to risk his patient. Had he done so, he would have committed professional suicide. Both he and the nurse were on guard, to anticipate her movements.

All the same, he had some ulterior object in view, for he seemed disappointed.

At the time Iris was too sick at heart over

her own cowardice to question further. She realised that she had two enemies in the carriage.

The doctor—and herself.

CHAPTER TWENTY-EIGHT
RAISE YOUR HAND

Iris started from her daze to realise that the professor was talking of dinner.

"If you would hurry back to the dining-car, Hare," he said hopefully, "you might explain to the waiter that we've missed the fish course."

"He'd only say it was 'off,' " Hare told him. "They've got to rush the second dinner through before we make Trieste."

"Tut, tut." The professor clicked. "In that case, we had better return at once. Perhaps you would go on ahead and order extra portions of meat, since we've gone without our fish."

"Not their fault. We walked out on the fish. But I'll see what can be done about it."

Hare checked himself and turned to Iris rather doubtfully.

"Do you mind?" he asked.

She gave an hysterical laugh, for it had just struck her that although the professor was confident of his ability to conduct her investigation, he could not risk his linguistic talent where vital interests were concerned.

"Go back, for pity's sake," she said. "Nothing matters but dinner, does it?"

The professor, whose lean face had brightened at the prospect of food, resented her reproach. Although famished, he felt he must defend his own reputation for meticulous justice.

"Are you being quite fair?" he asked. "We've paid a stiff price for a meal, so we are entitled to claim—at least—a portion of it. And you must admit we have not spared time or convenience in trying to convince you of your mistake."

She shook her head, but she was oppressed by a weight of hopelessness. There seemed nothing more to be done to help Miss Froy. Any attempt at interference would only expose her to the risk of reprisal.

It was not cowardice alone that made

her fear the power of the doctor, but common sense. Since she was the sole person on the train who believed in Miss Froy's existence, it stood to reason that she could be of use to her only if she were a free agent.

Her one chance lay in convincing the professor that there was a real need of further investigation. Although she disliked him, he possessed those qualities which counted in such a crisis. He was pigheaded, coolly humane, and rigidly just. If he were morally certain that he was right, nothing could shake him, and he would plug away at his objective in face of all opposition.

It was bad luck that—at the moment— he was concentrating on his dinner.

Her curdled brain cleared just as he was about to leave the carriage.

"Professor," she said, "if I'm right, when you get back to England you'll read about a missing Englishwoman—Miss Froy. When you do, it will be too late to save her. Won't it haunt you for the rest of your life, that you wouldn't listen to me now?"

"I might regret it," admitted the professor, "only the occasion is not likely to arise."

"But if you'll only do something—a very little thing—later you won't have to be sorry at all. And you won't have to cut short your dinner."

"What is it that you want me to do?"

"Go with the doctor to the Trieste hospital and watch while a bandage or strip of plaster is removed. Just enough to show you that there is genuine injury."

Although the professor was staggered by the suggestion, he considered it slowly with habitual conscientiousness. It encouraged Iris to follow up her advantage with a fresh argument.

"You must admit, I can do nothing. I'm not a lunatic and it might mean manslaughter. Besides, the doctor wouldn't let me. So it boils down to this. His precious test means nothing at all."

At her words, the first distrust of the doctor entered the professor's mind. It was visible in his puckered face and drumming fingers. He always counted the cost before he entertained any project, although it was typical of his high sense of duty that it could not deter him.

In this case the drawbacks were numerous, the chief of which was finance. Although he was no spendthrift, his standard of living at Cambridge was only covered by his salary, and he had to encroach on his capital for holidays. To get a complete mental change he went away at least three times a year, so he had to practise economy.

As the most expensive part of this special trip was the long railway journey, he had booked through one of the cheaper tourist agencies which specialised in cut-prices. Therefore, his ticket would not admit his breaking the journey anywhere.

To make matters more difficult he was short of cash, since his dislike of communal travel had made him yield to the temptation of sharing a coupé with Hare on the return journey.

There was another and more urgent reason why he should not stop at Trieste for the night. Delay involved the sacrifice of a cherished engagement. He had been invited to spend the following week-end with an elderly peer—an intellectual recluse—who lived in a remote corner of Wales. If he reached England on Saturday, instead of Friday, it would be too late.

The doctor watched him closely as he frowned and tapped his cheek-bones.

"Is it not convenient for you to stop at Trieste?" he asked.

"Definitely inconvenient."

"I am sorry. Because, in my own interest, I must beg of you to do what this young lady asks."

"Why?" asked the professor, incensed by this double assault on his week-end.

"Because I am growing convinced that there must be some reason for this poor young lady's distress. It is always 'Miss Froy.' Is that a common name in England, like 'Smith'?"

"It is not familiar to me."

"But she had heard it before—and in connection with some terrible experience. I do not know what has happened. But I think that there really is a lady called 'Miss Froy,' and that some harm has happened to her. I think, too, that this poor young lady knew, but the shock has driven away all memory."

"Absurd," interrupted Iris. "I won't——"

"Shut up," whispered Hare fiercely.

He had listened with close attention, for he was beginning to wonder whether the doctor had not found the true explanation of Iris' delusion. She had been unconscious until just before she managed to catch the train. Although the explanation was sunstroke, it might have been supplied through the agency of some interested person, who wanted to confuse her recollection.

"You will understand," went on the doctor, "that I do not wish to be under any suspicion, if—later—a lady might be declared missing."

"It's a preposterous idea," said the professor. "Besides, the hospital authorities would back you up."

"But how am I to prove that it is this patient I bring to them, and not some substitute? But if you, professor, would accompany me to the hospital and wait for the surgeon's initial examination, there can be no further question. It is your high reputation that I crave for my protection."

The professor smiled bleakly, for he was very hungry. Although he was an excellent bridge player, he had no knowledge of poker. Consequently the doctor's offer seemed to him proof positive that there was not even the flimsiest foundation for Iris' fantastic theory.

"I think you are carrying professional caution too far," he said. "Miss Carr"—unlike Hare, he was used to memorising names—"has declared that she went to the dining-car with one lady whom she called 'Miss Froy'—and that lady has since been identified as a Miss Kummer. . . . She is not well, which accounts for her mistake. . . . In the circumstances, there is no shred of evidence that the real Miss Froy—if there is such a person—is on the train at all."

"Then, in case of future trouble, may I apply to you to support any statement I might make?" asked the doctor.

"Certainly. I will give you my card."

The professor wheeled round and turned dinnerwards.

Hare divined that Iris was on the verge of an explosion.

Hitherto he had managed to restrain her by the warning pressure of his hand on her arm, but she was at the end of her patience.

"Don't throw a scene," he implored. "It's no good. Come back to the coop."

Instead of obeying she raised her voice. "Miss Froy. Can you hear me? Hold up your hand if you can."

CHAPTER TWENTY-NINE
TRIESTE

Miss Froy heard her. She held up her hand.

Although she was blinded by her bandage, she had recognised Iris' voice among a murmur of other sounds. In a confused fashion she realised that people were talking; but their tones were blurred and broken, as though they were far away—giving the impression of an imperfect long-distance call.

She tried to speak to them, but could not because of her gag. Once before she had contrived to move it partially, with frenzied pressure—remembering the while how her father used to tease her about the power of her tongue. She put every ounce of strength into that cry for help, but it was an uncouth incoherent sound, like an animal in pain.

No one heard her—and her captors had wedged the gag tighter, increasing her discomfort. Her arms were bound to her body above the elbows, and her legs were tied together at the ankles by a surgical bandage. The doctor made no attempt to hide it when he exposed her shoes and stockings for identification. He knew that among such a profusion of strappings, one more or less would never be remarked.

However, her hands were free from the wrists, because the supply of bindings had given out, and—in any case—they were powerless to do more than wave feebly. Miss Froy's heart fluttered with joy as she told herself that her clever girl knew that an instantaneous response to her appeal, however slight, would show that the patient recognised her name and was giving proof of identity.

So she spread out her fingers—fanwise—and flapped them in the air in a pathetic S.O.S.

Then once again her mind, which she was unable to control, slid away. It was cobwebbed and smeared from drugs, but every now and again a corner would clear, like the transparent red stains of juice that veins the scum of boiling jam. In these lucid moments a whirl of memories returned, but in the end her mind always went back to that first moment of shock.

It was incredible—monstrous. She had been sitting in her compartment when the doctor had entered and asked if any one would help him raise his patient. He explained that the nurse had gone away for a few minutes and the poor creature in his charge had grown restless, as though she were uncomfortable.

It was second-nature to Miss Froy to respond. She was not only always ready to be of service, but she was also anxious to see the crash casualty at closed quarters, besides learning perhaps more about the accident. It would be something with which to thrill the family when she related her adventures on Friday night.

When they entered the patient's compartment the doctor asked her to raise the head while he lifted the body. It was with specially deep sympathy that she bent over the prostrate form, because she was reminded of the contrast between them.

"She's smashed," she thought, "and I'm well and happy. I'm going home."

Suddenly a long pair of white linen-clad arms shot out and clutched her throat.

The helpless patient was gripping her windpipe in a merciless grip. In that appalling moment she remembered a Grand Guignol horror, when an electrified corpse had strangled the man who had galvanised it to synthetic life. Then the pressure tightened, lights flashed under her eyelids, and she knew no more.

For some time the eclipse had been total. Then, gradually there were infinitesimal rifts in the darkness of her senses. She became conscious that she was trussed, gagged and blinded, while muffled voices discussed her fate.

It was not a cheerful prospect. Although she was ignorant of her crime, she had an inkling of her sentence. It was connected with an ambulance which would meet them at Trieste. But it would take her to no hospital.

Yet in spite of cramp and thirst, of bodily anguish and mental torment, she never gave up hope.

It was said in the family that she followed Aunt Jane. In her lifetime, this Victorian lady had wanted a talking-doll, a tricycle, an operatic career, a husband, a legacy. She got none of these things, but she never discarded a single wish, nor doubted that each would be granted—in the end.

When the end came, she was seventy-seven and a pensioner on family charity; yet she closed her eyes with as lively a faith in the talking-doll as in the legacy which would grant her a leisured life and a dignified death.

Aunt Jane helps to explain why Miss Froy remained tolerably calm in the face of each fresh disappointment. Mercifully, however, her clear moments were of brief duration. Most of the time she was in a drugged dream, when she was for ever trying to get home.

She always managed to reach the gate and saw the lighted garden path with its exaggerated hollows—when a displaced pebble revealed a pit. The turf borders and the pink and purple Chinese asters were unnaturally vivid in the lamplight, while the pungent scent of early chrysanthemums hung on the frosty air.

But although she was so near that she could see the cracked red tile in the passage, she knew that something was wrong, and that she would never reach the door. . . . It was when she was struggling out of one of these tantalising visions, that she heard Iris calling her name and telling her to hold up her hand.

Unfortunately she did not know that there was a bad block in her system of communication. None of the channels were clear, so that her brain did not register the message from her ears until after the doctor—in a state of indignant horror—had literally swept his visitors out into the corridor. Even after that, some time elapsed before her nerve-centres were linked up with the intelligence department, and by then it was too late.

The blinds had all been drawn down, so there was no one besides the nurse to witness the futile signal of her fluttering fingers.

Outside the door the doctor wiped his face in his agitation.

"That was a terrible thing to do," he said, his voice vibrating with passion. "I was wrong to let you in at all. But I never dreamed you would be so imbecile as to try and injure my poor patient."

As Iris shrank involuntarily before his rage, he appealed to the professor.

"You can understand, professor, that absolute quiet is essential for my patient. The grave injury to the head——"

"How can she get quiet on a railway journey?" broke in Iris, as the engine plunged into a tunnel with an ear-splitting yell.

"That is something quite different," explained the doctor. "One can sleep through traffic. It is the slight unaccustomed sound which wakens one from sleep. If she had heard you she might have been called back, while I am doing my utmost—in mercy—to keep her unconscious."

"I quite understand," the professor assured him. "And I regret this has happened." His voice was glacial as he spoke to Iris. "You had better get back to your carriage, Miss Carr."

"Yes, come on," urged Hare.

Iris felt that they were all against her. In sudden defiance she launched a lone offensive.

"Directly we reach Trieste I am going to the British Embassy," she told them.

They were brave words, but her head was swimming and her knees shook so violently that she felt incapable of carrying out her threat. All the same, her intentions filled her with an illusion of power. Then Hare tackled her in his old international form and carried her along the corridors with the impetus of a tidal-bore, while the professor plodded in the rear.

"My only hope is we shall get some sort of a dinner," was his parting remark to the doctor.

Iris was too bewildered by what had happened to resist Hare's high-handed treatment. She could not understand why there had been no response to her cry. It shook her confidence and made her feel that her moral cowardice in failing to expose the mystery patient was justified.

Yet even if she were a genuine accident case, the danger which threatened Miss Froy was not dormant. When she was back in the coupé she presented Hare with an ultimatum.

"Are you with me or against me? Are you stopping at Trieste?"

"No," replied Hare firmly. "Neither are you."

"I see. Then you didn't mean what you said about liking me—and all that."

"I certainly meant—all that."

"Well, if you don't come with me to the Embassy, I'm through with you."

Hare tugged at his collar miserably.

"Can't you realise I'm your only friend?" he asked.

"If you were a friend you'd prove it."

"Wish I could, only I haven't the spunk. As your best friend, I ought to knock you out, so that you'd stay put for the next twenty-four hours, and rest your poor old head."

"Oh, I hate you," stormed Iris. "For heaven's sake, go away."

In the next compartment the Misses Flood-Porter overheard scraps of the dialogue.

"That girl certainly contrives to get some excitement out of a railway journey," remarked the elder sister astringently.

While the young people were quarrelling about her, Miss Froy was lying rigid, with still hands. It had gradually dawned upon her that she had no audience, so her demonstration was wasted. However, she had one crumb of comfort when Iris mentioned appealing to the British Consul. She had heard that cry of defiance through the closed door.

Presently she realised that the hint had not been wasted. There was a low rumbling conference inside the carriage.

"Trieste," remarked a masculine voice. It belonged to the doctor's chauffeur, who was wearing the incongruous uniform of a nursing-sister. "What now?"

"We must waste no time at Trieste," replied the doctor. "We shall have to drive all night, like hell, to get back to protection."

"But—where will you dump the body now?"

The doctor mentioned a place.

"It is on our road," he explained. "The wharf is deserted—and the eels swarm."

"Good. They will be hungry. Very soon there will be no face to tell tales, if it should be found later. . . . Will you dump the clothes and baggage there too?"

"Fool. They would be a certain mark of identification there. No, we take them with us in the car. You will incinerate them without delay directly we get back."

Although her brain was so misty, some

vibration of her senses made Miss Froy aware that they were talking about her. She shuddered instinctively at the thought of black stagnant water, thick with mud and scummed with refuse. She had such a violent dislike to corruption.

But she missed the real implication.

The chauffeur went on to anticipate difficulties.

"What if any one makes inquiries at the Trieste hospitals?"

"We shall explain that the patient died in transit."

"But if they demand to see the corpse?"

"They will see it. There will be no difficulty about that, once we are back. The mortuary will provide me with a female corpse which I will mutilate."

"Hum. I wish I was safely at home. There is still that girl."

"Yes," remarked the doctor, "it is extraordinary how the English will regard themselves as the policemen of the world. Even a girl has the habit. But it is a mistake to think them a stupid nation. That professor has a good brain, and he is no fool. . . . But luckily, he is honourable, and believes that all the world must be honourable, too. He will support all I say."

"Still, I wish I was back," harped the chauffeur.

"The risk is great," his employer reminded him. "So, also, is the reward."

The drone of masculine voices which drummed against Miss Froy's semi-sealed ears—like the hum of a spinning wheel—ceased. The chauffeur thought of the garage he would buy, while the doctor planned to retire from practice.

He did not relish his present commission, but the ruling family claimed his loyalty and self-interest forbade disobedience. Directly the baroness had sent for him, privately, by night, he had evolved the best scheme he could devise on the spur of the moment, to clear an obstacle in the illustrious pathway.

He knew why he had been chosen, for he, himself, would not use a delicate surgical instrument to cut a tarry string. His reputation was smutted because of recent mishaps at the local hospital. His scientific curiosity was keener than his wish to exterminate disease, and he was under suspi-

cion of having prolonged operations un-
duly, and at the expense of life.

From the beginning the venture had
been unlucky, because of the interference
of the English girl. But for her, the little plan
would have worked perfectly, by reason of
its simplicity, and the small number of confederates. He knew that he and his chauffeur would take their lives in their hands
when they scorched homewards through
dangerous passes, rounding dizzy precipices on one wheel, in their effort to race
the express back to their native territory.

But once they were back, every emer-
gency would be forestalled. An adequate
explanation would be forthcoming to any
inquiry. No one would have any awkward
knowledge to disclose and every wire that
connected the dead patient with Miss Froy
would be cut.

"Will you dump the English girl in the
sewer, too?" asked the chauffeur suddenly.

"No," replied the doctor. "Further com-
plication would be dangerous. But when
we reach Trieste she will not be in a position to make further trouble for us."

Miss Froy heard his words and, for the
first time, her optimism failed her. With a

wave of agonised longing she thought of the family at home, for she had sent them her timetable, and she guessed they would be tracing it on the map.

True to her forecast, at that moment they were thinking of her. They had done their best to fight their unusual depression, for they had lighted a fire—composed principally of fir-cones—and had been guilty of an extravagant supper—scrambled eggs.

Sock lay on the rug watching the flames. In spite of the welcome warmth, he was still subdued after his disappointment, for he had rushed off against orders to meet the train, with a hope new-born.

Mr. Froy looked at his wife and noticed that the underlip of her small firm mouth was pendulous and that she sagged in her chair. For the first time he realised that she was his senior, and that he, too, had grown old.

Then he glanced at the clock.

"Winsome's nearly come to the end of her first stage homewards," he told his wife. "She'll soon reach Trieste."

Mrs. Froy passed the information on to the dog.

"Sock, the little mistress is really on her

way home now. Every minute she is coming nearer—nearer—nearer. In another half-
hour she'll be at Trieste."

Trieste.

CHAPTER THIRTY
RECANTATION

The waiter managed to salvage some dinner for the professor and Hare, who ate through the courses in silence. As they were finishing their cheese and biscuits, the doctor entered the dining-car and seated himself at their table.

"I am sorry to disturb you," he said, "but I want a little conference about the young English lady."

The professor stifled an exclamation, for he feared that Iris had broken out in some fresh indiscretion.

"Coffee, please," he said to the waiter. "Black. . . . Well—what is the trouble *now?*"

"As a medical man I find myself faced with a responsibility," explained the doctor. "The lady is in a dangerous mental state."

"What grounds have you for your conclusion?" asked the professor, who never accepted a statement without data.

The doctor shrugged.

"Surely it is obvious to the meanest intelligence that she is suffering from a delusion. She invents some one who is not here. But there are other signs. She is highly excitable—suspicious of every one—inclined to be violent——"

As he noticed Hare's involuntary grimace, he broke off and turned to the younger man.

"Pardon. Is the young lady your affianced?"

"No," grunted Hare.

"But perhaps a lover—or a dear friend? Yet it would not surprise me to hear that she has been very angry recently with you. Has she?"

"I'm not really popular at present," admitted Hare.

"Thank you for the confidence, for it confirms my diagnosis. It is always a sign of mental malady when they turn upon those they love best."

He could tell he had captured Hare's sympathy as he continued.

"There is no real danger if we can take a

precaution. It is essential at this stage that her brain should be rested. If she could have a long sleep, I am confident she will wake up quite well again. But if we let her persist in working herself up into a fever, the mental mischief may be—irreparable."

"I think there is something in that, professor," agreed Hare. "It's exactly what I've been thinking myself."

"What do you propose?" asked the professor cautiously.

"I should suggest," replied the doctor, "that you persuade her to swallow a harmless sedative which I can give you."

"She will object."

"Then it should be given by force."

"Impossible. We cannot control her wishes."

"Then, perhaps, you could trick her into taking it?"

As the professor remained mulishly silent, the doctor half rose from the table.

"I can assure you," he said, "that I have more than enough responsibility of my own to shoulder, with my patient. I only felt it my duty to warn you. We doctors are pledged to the service of humanity—whether we receive fees or no. But now that I have explained the position, I can leave the decision to you. My own conscience is clear."

The doctor was on the point of departing with dignity, when Hare called him back.

"Don't go, doctor. I feel the same as you about this. I've had personal experience of delusions, with concussion." He turned eagerly to the professor. "Can't we wangle it somehow?"

The professor's long upper lip seemed to lengthen in his disapproval.

"I could not be a party to such a course," he said. "It would be gross interference with Miss Carr's personal liberty. She is a free agent."

"Then—you'd prefer to remain 'good form' and see her go bughouse?" asked Hare indignantly.

The professor smiled acidly.

"My own impression is," he told them, "that there is not the slightest danger of that. I have had experience of such cases.

"My work brings me into contact with neurotic young women. To my mind, Miss Carr is merely hysterical."

"Then—what do you propose?" asked Hare.

"I think a salutary shock will probably bring her to her senses."

Reinforced by his meal, the professor felt master of the situation. He finished his coffee and liqueur, flicked a crumb from his waistcoat, and rose in a leisurely manner.

"I will reason with Miss Carr," he said.

He strolled out of the dining-car and lurched along the corridors. As he passed the coupé occupied by the Misses Flood-Porter, he was tempted to resign his mission and join them in a little chat. The ladies looked so composed and immaculate—for they were well in advance of their preparations for arrival at Trieste—that he was hopeful that further conversation would reveal some mutual friend.

Resolute in his self-imposed duty, he entered his carriage and seated himself opposite to Iris. His first glance told him that she had been lighting cigarette after cigarette, only to throw them away, barely smoked. Although her action was merely a sign of nervous tension, he looked with distaste at the litter of spent matches on the floor and seats.

"Will you take some advice offered in a

friendly spirit?" he asked, speaking to her as though she were a fractious child.

"No," replied Iris mutinously. "I want to hear the truth, for a change."

"The truth may be a bit of a shock. But you've asked for it, so you shall have it. . . . The doctor has just told me that, as a result of your sunstroke, you are—very slightly, and only temporarily—deranged."

The professor honestly believed that he was dealing with a neurotic girl who was telling lies from a love of sensation, so he watched her reaction with complacent confidence. When he saw the horror in her eyes, he felt his experiment was justified.

"Do you mean—mad?" she asked in a whisper.

"Oh, dear, no. Nothing to be frightened of. But he is not happy about your safety as you are travelling alone. He may be forced to take steps to ensure it, unless you can manage to keep perfectly quiet."

"What steps?" asked Iris. "Do you mean that nursing home? I should resist. No one can do anything to me against my will."

"In the circumstances, violence would be most unwise. It would only confirm the doctor's fears. But I want to make the position quite clear to you. Listen."

The professor sawed the air with his forefinger and spoke impressively.

"You have only to keep calm and everything will be all right. No one will interfere with you in any way, unless you remind them of your existence. To be brutally frank, you've made yourself a public nuisance. It's got to stop."

The professor was not so unhuman as he seemed. His own unpleasant experience with his infatuated student had prejudiced him against emotion, but he thought he was acting in Iris' interests.

Therefore he could have no idea of the hell of fear into which he plunged her. She was white to her lips as she shrank into the corner of the carriage. She was afraid of him—afraid of every one in the train. Even Hare seemed to have entered into the conspiracy against her. The whole world appeared roped into a league that threatened her sanity.

Lighting yet one more cigarette with shaking fingers, she tried to realise the position. It seemed clear that she had blundered into important issues and that, consequently, she had to be suppressed. The professor had been sent to bribe her with immunity in return for her silence.

Even while she rejected compromise angrily, she had to face the cold truth. She had not a ghost of a chance to fight these influential people. If she persisted in her hopeless quest to find Miss Froy, the doctor would merely pull wires and whisk her away to some nursing home in Trieste.

She remembered Miss Froy's tale of the woman who had been held in a private mental asylum. The same might happen to her. Any opposition on her part would be used as evidence against her sanity. They could keep her imprisoned and under the influence of drugs, until she really crashed under the strain.

It would be some appreciable time before any one missed her. She was not expected in England, for she had not troubled to engage rooms at an hotel. Her friends would believe that she was still abroad. When at last her lawyers or the bank made inquiries, it would be too late. They would trace her to the nursing home, and arrive to find a lunatic.

In her distraught state, she plunged herself into a morass of distorted fears and exaggerated perils. But although her reason was nearly submerged by a tidal wave of panic, one corner of her brain still functioned on common-sense lines.

It convinced her that Miss Froy's rescue was an utterly hopeless proposition.

"Well?" asked the professor patiently, as she tossed away her unsmoked cigarette.

Suddenly Iris thought of the familiar Calais-Dover express—the white cliffs—Victoria Station—with almost frantic longing. She felt homesick for England and the cheery casual crowd of her friends. Before her eyes, in letters of fire, flashed the familiar slogan—"SAFETY FIRST."

"Well?" repeated the professor. "Have you come to your senses?"

Utterly worn out and paralysed with fear, Iris slipped into the trough of lost hopes. She reminded herself that Miss Froy was merely a stranger whom she had tried to help. To persist merely meant a double—and useless—sacrifice.

"Yes," she replied dully.

"You'll make no more scenes?" went on the professor.

"No."

"Good. . . . Now, will you admit to me that you invented Miss Froy?"

Iris felt plunged in the hell of Judas Iscariot and all traitors as she made her denial.

"Yes. I invented her. There's no Miss Froy."

CHAPTER THIRTY-ONE
A CUP OF SOUP

The doctor looked after the professor as he went from the dining-car.

"That is a very clever man," he said dryly. "He would cure illness by a scolding. Yet he may be right. Indeed, for the first time in my career, I hope I shall be proved wrong."

He watched Hare's frowning face closely and asked, "What is your opinion?"

"I know he's making a damnable blunder," growled the young man.

"'He that knows, and knows that he knows,'" quoted the doctor, "'he is wise.' . . . Well—what then?"

"Hanged if I know."

"Ah, you feel, perhaps, that the professor is cleverer than you?"

"I feel nothing of the kind. Our lines are different."

"Then probably you are not used to exert authority?"

"Oh, no. I've only got to control hundreds of toughs—and some of them ready on the draw."

"Then, frankly, I do not understand your hesitation. Unless, of course, you fear the young lady's anger when she discovers she has been tricked. She has what you call 'spirit,' and what I call 'temper,' since I have a very sweet wife myself. . . . Well, it is for you to decide whether you prefer the angry words of a sane woman to the gentle smile of an imbecile."

"Don't rub it in," muttered Hare. "I've got to *think.*"

"There is not much time left," the doctor reminded him.

"I know. But—it's the hell of a risk."

"Not at all. Here is my card. I will write a declaration on it that the drug is harmless, under penalty of heavy damages, should the lady be ill afterwards as a direct result. . . . I will do more. You shall have a sample to take back to England, so that you may have it analysed."

Hare pulled at his lip. He knew that the doctor's offer was fair, yet he could not shake off his distrust of the unknown.

The doctor seemed to read his thoughts.

"Perhaps," he said, "you hesitate because I am not Dr. Smith, of London, England. Yet, if you were in a strange city and had a raging toothache, you would seek relief from the first dentist. Remember, a man's name on a brass plate, with certain letters after it, is a profession's guarantee of good faith to the public."

He let the argument sink in while Hare continued to maltreat his face and hair. Presently he glanced at his watch, and then thrust his wrist before the young man's eyes.

"See the time. I must go back to my patient."

Hare sprang up as though galvanised.

"One minute, doctor. How could we give the stuff?"

The doctor knew that the bridge had been crossed as he hastened to explain.

"That poor young lady has had no dinner," he said reproachfully. "Surely you will bring her a small cup of soup, since there will be no opportunities on the Italian train, until they couple the breakfast-car."

"Chump," exclaimed Hare, hitting his head. "I never thought that she'd be hungry. . . . But if she is asleep, how will I manage changing trains at Trieste?"

"Ah, my dear sir, you must not expect miracles. You are too impatient. The drug will not take full effect until she is in the Italian train. Then, she will sleep and sleep. But at Trieste she will merely be very dull, very heavy, very docile. And"—the doctor's eyes narrowed—"she will be far too torpid to worry about any phantom lady."

"Suits me all right. . . . I'll take a chance."

The doctor accompanied him to the kitchen-car and fought a battle with the protesting chef. In the end medical authority won the day. Not long afterwards, Hare, with anxious eyes and tightly compressed lips, began his fateful journey along the corridors, holding a half-filled bowl.

But he carried so much more than soup. Within the narrow circle of the cup lay the destiny of a woman.

As he staggered on his way—by a coincidence due to the time, in a small stone house in England, Mrs. Froy's thoughts turned to nourishment.

"I do hope Winnie will eat something before she gets to Trieste," she said to Mr. Froy. "Her dinner won't stand by her all through the night. Besides she is always too excited to eat on a journey. She merely pecks her first supper at home."

Her husband gave a guilty smile, for he knew the reason for Winnie's lack of appetite.

Meanwhile, Hare was still scared by the responsibility of his step. While he assured himself that he was actually carrying a gift of sanity to Iris, he could not rid himself of apprehension. Tormented by indecision, he proposed a foolish test for himself.

"If I don't spill any it's going to be O.K. But if I do, I'll cry off."

He crabbed slowly along, with utmost care and caution while the train seemed to put on an extra spurt of speed. The soup splashed furiously against the rim of the cup—for ever on the point of brimming over. Yet, in some extraordinary manner, it always whirled within its confines.

Hare was reminded of a simple circus trick he used to practise—as a boy—with a hoop and a glass of water. Apparently the same principle operated now, and the soup could not be spilt from sheer velocity of motion.

But just before he reached the reserved portion of the train he came to grief completely. As he was crossing the connecting passage, a small boy—rushing from the pursuit of a smaller girl—charged into him and received a baptism of soup, together with an undesirable name.

Hare broke off in his malediction to wipe his fingers.

"That's torn it," he muttered. "Well, it's out of my hands now."

Meanwhile Iris was actually in the grip of a brainstorm. When the professor left her she was numb with fear. Some vital mainspring in her brain seemed to have snapped, reducing her mind to a limp tangle. Miss Froy was a lost cause—so she denied her. But nothing was left but a void, without aim or hope or self-respect.

"I was her only chance," she told herself. "And now I've crashed too."

The knowledge was torture which she tried vainly to forget. But vivid little thumbnail pictures persisted in flashing before

her closed eyes. Two bent old people, huddled in a lighted doorway—waiting. Sock—
a woolly blunderbuss—rushing off to meet
a mistress who would never come home.

She was most affected by the thought of
the dog, for she assumed the senility of the
aged parents. She told herself that the
shock would probably kill them both, since
they would be too devoted—or too used to
each other—to survive singly. And then—
what would become of the dog, stranded
and hungry in a country cottage?

She worked herself into a positive fever
about him. As her temperature rose, her
head began to ache so furiously that it
seemed to bang in a series of small explo-
sions which kept time with the frantic revolutions of the wheels.

"You're get-ting near. You're get-ting
near."

And then the rhythm changed and began to chop out a devil's tattoo. "Nearer—
nearer—nearer—*nearer*—NEARER."

Nearer to Trieste. The express was in the
relentless grip of the schedule. The pulsa-
tions of the engine throbbed through Iris
like the shaking arteries of an overdriven

heart. It rocked and roared over the rails—
a metal monster racing an invisible rival.

It had to beat Time.

When Hare came into her carriage she
hardly raised her eyes, and did not speak
to him.

"Still hating me?" he asked.

"I only hate myself," she said dully.

He looked furtively at her twitching face
and burning cheeks, which, to his mind,
confirmed the doctor's diagnosis of dangerously overstrung nerves, while he assured himself that—since he could not give
her that essential sock on the jaw—he was
rendering her a real service.

"I've brought you some soup," he said
guiltily.

She shrank from it even while she thanked
him.

"Sweet of you—but I couldn't touch it."

"Try. It'll make a new man of you."

"All right, then. Leave it, will you?"

"No, that's too old a dodge. The instant
I go you'll chuck it out of the window.
Well—I'm not going."

Iris clutched her head.

"I feel so sick," she pleaded.

"Lack of nourishment. Listen, my child,

there's a history of the try-try-again kind connected with that simple bowl of soup. I slaughtered the chef to get it in the first place. Then, on my way here, some wretched kid bowled the whole lot over. . . . I said, 'Kismet.' And then I said, 'She's had nothing all day and she'll have nothing until to-morrow's breakfast.'

"And I went all the way back and slaughtered another chef, all to bring you a second cup."

"Oh, well—" sighed Iris helplessly. "But have I got to be grateful?"

She swallowed the first spoonful with reluctance, grimacing as though it were a nauseous draught; then she paused, while Hare waited in acute suspense.

"What is it?" she asked. "It's got a horribly druggy taste."

"It's the same soup I wolfed down at dinner. That's all I know," lied Hare.

"Well, I'd better get it over."

Raising the cup to her lips, she gulped it down with a shudder.

"You'll feel better soon," Hare assured her as he took the empty bowl from her nerveless hands.

For some time they sat in silence, while

he watched her stealthily, hoping to detect the first sign of drowsiness. He knew that drugs affect people differently, and that it was difficult to gauge the right dose for Iris, because of her abnormal condition.

"If anything goes wrong," he thought desperately, "I'll have to take the rap."

At intervals he heard the whine of the professor's voice, as he strained it in an effort to be audible above the uproar of the train. He was in the next compartment, improving an acquaintance with the Misses Flood-Porter, which he hoped to authorise with the discovery of a third-party link.

"You live in Somersetshire," he remarked. "It is a county where I have stayed often. I wonder if we know any mutual friends."

"I hate every single person living there," said Miss Rose vehemently, sweeping away any claimants to friendship.

"Stag-hunting," supplemented Miss Flood-Porter.

Relieved by the explanation the professor began gently and skilfully to extricate a few worthy persons from under the wholesale ban. He was rewarded when the ladies recognised a name.

"Oh, yes. Charming people. Great friends of ours."

The contact was complete and they all shouted against each other.

Iris recognised the voices for, after a time, she spoke to Hare.

"That's the professor, isn't it? I wish you'd tell him I want to sleep, but can't, because he's making too much noise. And slip in something about him being a public nuisance, will you? He'd appreciate it. Because that's what he called me."

The speech was so unexpectedly jaunty, that Hare stared her in surprise. He did not know whether he were imagining changes, but her eyes were less strained, while her face seemed to have lost the glazed flush of fever.

"That doctor's sold me a pup," he thought wrathfully. "She is not settling down. She's gingering up. At this rate she'll be fighting-mad at Trieste."

As a matter of fact their little conspiracy was hampered by their ignorance of working conditions. On the rare occasions when Iris was unwell, her response to treatment was almost immediate. In her abnormal state she was now beating her own speed record. Although its effects were bound to be short-lived, she was feeling miraculously restored by the nourishment, while the drug was beginning imperceptibly to soothe her brain-storm, like the first film of oil spreading over a rough sea.

She was conscious of a glow of spurious strength, followed by a rush of confidence, as she climbed out of the traitor's hell into which she had hurled herself.

"Lost causes are the only causes worth fighting for," she told herself.

In her relief at her own restoration, she smiled at Hare, who grinned back at her.

"Didn't I tell you you'd feel better after that nice strong good nourishing soup?" he asked.

"It tasted as though it was made from a mummy—but it has picked me up," she admitted. "My head's clearer. I realise now that the professor was right. I've made an awful fool of myself."

Hare chalked up a good mark to the properties of the drug.

"You mean—you've chucked Miss Froy off the train?" he asked incredulously.

"Please, don't bring her up again. Of

course, there's no such person. I told the professor so."

Iris felt a momentary pang as she looked into his guileless eyes.

"It's a shame to trick him," she thought.

She had resolved on a policy of stratagem. She would sham docility, to avert suspicion. When Trieste was reached, she would contrive to give them the slip and hire a taxi, in which to follow the ambulance. They would not suspect any outside interest in their movements, since she was definitely out of the running.

Having warned the taxi-driver in advance to memorise the address to which Miss Froy was taken, he would drive furiously back to the British Embassy. She had always found Italians gallant and susceptible, so she was sure of enlisting their sympathies and getting immediate action.

Her jammed brain was now clicking on with amazing speed. She told herself that the success of her plan depended on whether she could fool them all. She must return to her own carriage, which was full of the doctor's spies, and sham the requisite limp submission.

"I mustn't overdo it," she thought. "They

might want to fuss over me if they thought I was ill."

She counted on the confusion when the passengers, with their luggage, changed trains at the terminus. Hare must be sent off on some errand, since he was her only obstacle. The rest of the travellers would remain true to type and look after their own interests.

She raised her eyes and met Hare's earnest gaze. He was thinking of the nice long sleep which awaited her in the Italian train.

"It's a shame to trick her," he thought.

CHAPTER THIRTY-TWO
THE DREAM

Although it was still some distance from Trieste, the train was already astir with the projected bustle of its arrival. Passengers were beginning to lock opened suitcases and to pull on their coats and hats. Infected by the unrest, the leisurely professor left the Misses Flood-Porter and entered his own coupé.

"I don't want to disturb you," he hinted to Iris. "But we shall soon reach Trieste."

Iris showed none of her former morbid reluctance to return to her own carriage.

"I must get my suitcase," she said, eager to impress the professor with her obedience.

He rewarded her with an approving smile. For the last time she made the shaky journey along the train. Nobody laughed at her or took any notice of her, for every one was too pre-occupied with affairs. Suitcases and bags had already been lifted down from racks and stacked outside the carriages, increasing the congestion. Mothers screamed to collect those children who were still chasing each other in the corridors.

They washed their chocolate-grimed mouths with corners of moistened handkerchiefs. Banana skins were thrown out of the windows—newspapers bundled under the seats.

The heat and the jam were so oppressive that Iris was actually glad to reach her own compartment. But before she could enter, she shrank back as the doctor came out of the invalid's carriage. His face looked dry and white as the pith of willow above the black blotch of his spade-beard, and his eyes—magnified by his glasses—were dark turgid pools.

As he looked at her, she felt that it was useless to try to deceive him. Like an expert chess player he would have forseen any possible move of her own and would be prepared with a counter stroke.

"Is madame better?" he asked.

"Oh, yes. I'm merely slack. Everything seems an effort. And once I sit down I shan't want to move again."

Iris was encouraged by the success of her strategy when the two men exchanged a glance of understanding. She went inside her compartment, but no one appeared to take any interest in her return. The mother and child were reassembling the contents of the family suitcases, while the blonde made an elaborate toilet. The father had taken charge of the baroness' dressing-bag and was evidently prepared to act as temporary courier.

Iris sat and watched them until the spectacle of noses being powdered and waves reset reminded her of her own need to repair. It was essential to make a good impression at the Embassy. She opened her bag languidly and drew out her flapjack, yawning the while with sudden drowsiness. Blinking her eyes violently, she began to apply powder and lipstick.

But before she could finish, her lids were drooping so continuously that she could not see properly. To her dismay, she realised that she was being overwhelmed with waves of sleep.

They were too powerful to resist, although she struggled vainly to keep awake. One after another they swept over her, piling up in a ceaseless procession.

The other passengers began to waver like shadows. Outside, Trieste was visible as a quivering red glow on the night sky. The engine thundered and panted in a last stupendous effort to breast that invisible tape stretched in front of the buffers. Almost abreast, skimmed the vast shadow, with beating wings and swinging scythe.

There was exultation in the stokehold and driver's car, for they were actually ahead of the schedule. Time was beaten, so they relaxed their efforts and slackened speed gradually in readiness for their arrival at Trieste.

Iris' head had fallen forward and her eyes were closed. Then a dog barked in the distance, jerking her awake. As she stared out of the window with clouded gaze, a few scattered lights speckling the darkness told her that they were reaching the outskirts of Trieste.

In that moment she thought of Miss Froy.

"Trieste," she agonised. "I must keep awake."

Then, once again, everything grew blurred and she sank back in her corner.

When Hare returned to the carriage his jaw dropped at the sight of her huddled figure. He called to the doctor, who merely rubbed his bony hands with satisfaction.

"Excellent," he said. "She has responded with most extraordinary rapidity."

"But how will I get her out at Trieste?" demanded Hare.

"You will have no trouble. You can wake her at a touch. This is merely preliminary— what you call a cat's-sleep. She will be merely somewhat dazed."

The doctor turned away, but paused to give a word of advice.

"Better leave her alone until you have secured porters. If you wake her too soon she may sleep again. Each time it will be for longer."

Hare took the hint and stood in the corridor, staring out of the window. The reflection of the lighted train flowing over the masonry of roofs and walls transformed them to the semblance of quivering landscape and water. In every carriage luggage was being lowered. Voices shouted for service. The fleeting friendships of a railway journey were being at once sealed and broken in handshakes and farewells.

Iris slept. . . .

In the coupé of the bridal pair, the barrister—Todhunter, for a few minutes longer—was doing his utmost to reconcile a gesture of renunciation with a strategic retreat.

"Shall we say 'Good-bye' now?" he suggested. "Before we are surrounded with a cloud of witnesses."

Mrs. Laura ignored his overture.

" 'Good-bye,' " she said, carefully curling her lashes upwards. "Thanks for your hospitality. It's been a cheap holiday for me. Cheap in every sense."

In the next coupé the Misses Flood-Porter were facing a major tragedy. It was Miss Flood-Porter who threw the bombshell.

"Rose, did you see the brown suitcase put in the van?"

"No."

"Then I believe it's been left behind. It was pushed under the bed, if you remember."

Their faces were rigid with horror, for their purchases had been packed together for conscientious declaration.

"I was counting on Captain Parker to get them through the Customs for us," lamented Miss Rose. "But it may be in the van."

"It may. We can do nothing but hope for the best."

Iris slept on. . . .

When she was a child she suffered from an unsuspected inferiority complex, due to the difference between her lot and that of other children. Although pampered by adults she was exposed to the secret hostility of some of her companions. She was not equal to reprisals, but, at night, her inhibitions found expression in dreams of power, when she sacked the toy-stores and sweet-shops of London with glorious immunity.

Time brought its revenge and Iris got on top of her own little world. But now the professor's hostility, the antagonism of the doctor and baroness, together with the derision of the other passengers had combined with her sunstroke to make the old inferiority complex flare up again.

The result was that she passed from unconsciousness into one of her childish dreams of power.

She thought she was still on the express and on her way to rescue Miss Froy. The corridors were hundreds of miles long, so that it took her centuries to complete what passed within the limit of a minute. The doctor and a crowd of passengers kept trying to oppose her passages, but she had only to push back their faces, when they dissolved like smoke.

She was mowing them down in swathes when she was aroused by the scream of the engine. Shouts and sudden flashes of light told her that they were rushing into Trieste. Instantly she staggered to her feet—half-awake and half in a dream—and walked directly into the next compartment.

Her action took every one by surprise. No one expected it as it was believed that she was asleep. The doctor and the disguised chauffeur were looking out of the window, watching for the arrival of the ambulance. But Hare—who was chatting to the guard—saw her enter, and he made a frantic effort to stop her.

He was too late. Still under the influence

of her dream of power and secure in her knowledge of immunity which raised her high above the fear of consequences—Iris rushed towards the invalid and tore the plaster from her face.

The doctor had made the final mistake of an unlucky venture when he gave her the sleeping-draught. Had she carried out her threat to go to the Embassy, she might have encountered incredulity and delay. But the drug had given her the courage to do the impossible thing.

As the criss-cross of strips peeled off and dangled in her fingers like a star-fish, Hare held his breath with horror. Then the guard behind him gave a whistle of astonishment as, instead of spurting blood and raw mutilated flesh, the sound though reddened skin of a middle-aged woman was revealed. Iris gave a low cry of recognition.

"Miss Froy."

CHAPTER THIRTY-THREE
THE HERALD

Two days later Iris stood on the platform of Victoria Station, watching the dispersal of the passengers. Among the first to leave were the Misses Flood-Porter. Confident in their right to preferential treatment, they stood aloof with pleased expressions, while an influential gentleman, with an authoritative voice and an infallible method with officials, shouted and shepherded their luggage through the Customs.

Once, by mistake, they looked at Iris, but they were too preoccupied to bow. This was England, where she went out of their lives.

They were very gracious, however, to Mrs. Barnes, when she came to wish them "Good-bye." Her face was radiant with happiness born of a telegram which she had received at Calais.

"Gabriel's cold quite gone very well again."

In spite of her impatience to get home to him she lingered to listen to the last snatch of gossip from the sisters.

"Wasn't it *peculiar* about the honeymoon couple?" asked the elder Miss Flood-Porter. "I know he wasn't on the Venice train, because I looked. And she got off at Milan—alone."

"Yes," nodded Mrs. Barnes. "I know my husband wouldn't like me to say it—but it makes you wonder if they were really married."

"Of course they weren't," scoffed Miss Rose. "I'm precious glad we had nothing to do with them. If there had been a divorce action later on, *we* might have been subpœnaed as witnesses."

"Exactly," agreed her sister. "It just shows how careful one should be when one is abroad. We always keep to our rule *never* to get mixed up in other people's business."

Iris smiled rather bitterly at the conscious virtue in their voices. It reminded her of what she had suffered as a result of their policy of superb isolation. With a shrug she turned her back on the affectionate leave-taking to watch instead the long thin white beams—as of a myriad searchlights—thrown by the sun through the smoky glass roof.

Although she was still shaky she felt quick with fresh life—glad to be back—glad to be alive. While Hare was scouting round the piles of luggage, her thoughts slipped back journey. Her memories were dim, with many blanks.

There was a black-out at Trieste, when she crashed completely, and she did not realise her surroundings until she was rushing through the darkness in the Italian train. Some one with lustrous black eyes looked after her, while Hare came and went. She slept most of the time, but whenever she woke she was conscious of happiness.

The carriage was crowded with other passengers, all shouting, smoking and gesticulating. She could not understand a word, but she felt in perfect tune and sympathy with all of them. There was so much happiness in the world with the prospect of joyous reunions. The barriers of language were down, so that they were not alien nationalities but fellow-citizens of the world, united by the common touch.

In the morning she discovered another passenger in the carriage—a little drab, middle-aged woman, with a small lined face and vivid blue eyes.

Iris gave a cry of rapture as she hugged her.

"Miss Froy. You horrible little brute to give me all that trouble. . . . Oh, darling, darling."

In spite of the joy of reunion Miss Froy proved a bad exchange for the Italian stranger. Her fussy attentions, her high tinkling laugh, her incessant chatter, became such a strain that Hare had to scheme for intervals of release.

For all the drawbacks, however, there was a sense of great adventure and high hope about the journey. The wind seemed to blow them along when they travelled across the flat stretches of France. Everything moved with them—streaming smoke and fluttering clouds. The wide fields and white sky swam in light, so that they felt that they were sailing through a magic country.

Although she was better Hare refused to answer any of Iris' questions.

"Tell you in London," he always said.

She reminded him of his promise when he returned with her suitcase, duly chalked.

"I can't wait another minute," she told him.

"Righto," he agreed. "Take a pew."

Squatting together on a luggage truck and smoking cigarettes, she listened to his story.

"It was all very tame. No rough-house— no nothing. The guard was a hero. He knew just what to do, and the doctor and the two nurses went like lambs. You see, they'll probably only be charged with attempted abduction."

"What happened to the baroness?" asked Iris.

"Oh, she just sailed out, twice her natural size. No connection at all with the next carriage. . . . But she'll pull wires and wangle their discharge. Wheels within wheels, you know."

Iris felt indifferent to their fate.

"What did the others say when they

heard about Miss Froy?" she inquired eagerly. "After all, I was right—and every one was out of step but me."

"To be quite candid," said Hare, "it all went in one ear and out at the other. We had a close shave at Venice and some of the Miss Flood-Porters' luggage was missing. They were in such a panic about it that they were prostrate afterwards. And the parson's wife was very worried about her husband."

"But the professor?"

"Well, he's the sort that doesn't like to be proved wrong. When he saw Miss Froy running about like a two-year-old, he thought it was all exaggerated. I overheard him saying to Miss Flood-Porter, 'People generally get what they invite. I cannot imagine anything of the kind happening to Miss Rose.' "

"Neither can I. . . . Every one seems to be saying 'Good-bye.' Here's my Miss Froy."

Hare hurriedly made his escape just in time to avoid the little woman. She looked wonderfully fit and seemed actually rejuvenated by her terrible experience.

Although she had grown so irritated by

the touch of those hard, dry hands, Iris felt a pang of regret now that the parting was near.

"I'm stopping in London for a few hours," confided Miss Froy. "Selfridge's, my dear. Just wandering. Topping."

She looked after Hare as he chased a taxi, and lowered her voice.

"I'm just making up my story to tell them at home. Mater will be *thrilled.*"

"But do you think it wise to tell her?" objected Iris. "At her age it might prove a shock."

"Oh, you mean about me." Miss Froy shook her head and gave Iris the conspiratorial wink of one schoolgirl to another. "I'm going to keep mum about *that.* She'd throw a fit and she wouldn't let me go back."

"Are you?" gasped Iris.

"Of course. I shall have to give evidence at the trial, very likely. Besides, all the exciting things seem to happen abroad."

"You're a marvel. . . . But what is the story you're making up?"

Miss Froy grew suddenly young.

"It's about you—and your romance. Is it true?"

Iris did not know herself until that minute.

"Yes," she replied. "I'm going with him on his next trip."

"Then I'm first to congratulate you. And, one day, perhaps you'll congratulate me. . . . And now I must fly to send off my wire."

Not long afterwards, a telegram was received at the little grey stone house. Mr. and Mrs. Froy read it together, and later each read it, privately, to Sock.

"Home 8.10 too topping Winnie."

That evening Mrs. Froy stood at the window of Winnie's bedroom. Although she could not see the railway station, she got a glimpse of one amber signal lamp through a gap in the trees.

Everything was ready for her daughter's return. The table was laid in the dining-room and decorated with vases of white dahlias and claret-tinted carrot-tops. The hot-water bottles had been removed from the bed. The rarely-used lamp had been lit in the hall, and the front door thrown open in readiness, so that a strip of light carpeted the mossy garden path.

The supper was keeping hot in the oven. Mrs. Froy always cooked sausages and mashed potatoes for the first meal, under the mistaken impression that it was Winnie's favourite dish. It had been, some thirty years ago—but Winnie never had the heart to undeceive her.

Outside the window was darkness and silence. The stars were frosty and the keen air held the odour of autumnal bonfires. Then, suddenly, the stillness was torn by the scream of the distant train.

Mrs. Froy could trace its approach by the red cloud, quivering about the belt of elms which hid the station. She knew when it stopped, because the engine panted and blew off some steam.

It rattled on again, leaving her guessing. She wondered whether it had brought Winnie. Perhaps she had lost her connection in London. She could see nothing—hear nothing—for she was growing deaf and her eyes were beginning to fail.

The surrounding darkness baffled her and cheated her with unredeemed promises. Figures advanced through the gloom, but—just as her heart leaped in welcome—they always changed back to trees. She strained vainly to catch the first sound of voices—her husband's deep tones and a girl's high-pitched treble.

As she held her breath in suspense, somewhere in the distance a dog barked. Again and again, in frantic excitement Then through the open gate and up the lighted path charged the clumsy shape of a big shaven dog—capering like an overgrown puppy—whirling round in circles—leaping at his shadow—falling over himself in his blundering haste.

It was the herald who had rushed on ahead, to tell her that the young mistress had come home.

THE END

LAURA

PART ONE

CHAPTER ONE

The city that Sunday morning was quiet. Those millions of New Yorkers who, by need or preference, remain in town over a summer week-end had been crushed spiritless by humidity. Over the island hung a fog that smelled and felt like water in which too many soda-water glasses have been washed. Sitting at my desk, pen in hand, I treasured the sense that, among those millions, only I, Waldo Lydecker, was up and doing. The day just past, devoted to shock and misery, had stripped me of sorrow. Now I had gathered strength for the writing of Laura's epitaph. My grief at her sudden and violent death found consolation in the thought that my friend, had she lived to a ripe old age, would have passed into oblivion, whereas the violence of her passing and the genius of her admirer gave her a fair chance at immortality.

My doorbell rang. Its electric vibrations had barely ceased when Roberto, my Filipino manservant, came to tell me that Mr. McPherson had asked to see me.

"Mark McPherson!" I exclaimed, and then, assuming the air of one who might meet Mussolini without trepidation, I bade Roberto ask Mr. McPherson to wait. Mahomet had not rushed out to meet the mountain.

This visit of a not unimportant member of the Police Department—although I am still uncertain of his title or office—conferred a certain honor. Lesser folk are unceremoniously questioned at Headquarters. But what had young McPherson to do with the murder? His triumphs were concerned with political rather than civil crime. In the case of The People of New York *vs*. Associated Dairymen his findings had been responsible—or so the editorial writers said—for bringing down the price of milk a penny a quart. A senatorial committee had borrowed him for an investigation of labor rackets, and only recently his name had been offered by a group of progressives as leader of a national inquiry into defense profits.

Screened by the half-open door of my study, I watched him move restlessly about my drawing-room. He was the sort of man, I saw at once, who affects to scorn affectation; a veritable Cassius who emphasized the lean and hungry look by clothing himself darkly in blue, double-breasted worsted, unadorned white shirt and dull tie. His hands were long and tense, his face slender, his eyes watchful, his nose a direct inheritance from those dour ancestors who had sniffed sin with such constancy that their very nostrils had become aggressive. He carried his shoulders high and walked with a taut erectness as if he were careful of being watched. My drawing-room irritated him; to a man of his fiercely virile temperament, the delicate perfection must be cloying. It was audacious, I admit, to expect appreciation. Was it not slightly optimistic of me to imagine that good taste was responsible for the concentration with which he studied my not unworthy collection of British and American glassware?

I noted that his scowl was fixed upon a shining object, one of my peculiar treasures. Habit, then, had made him alert to detail. On the mantel of Laura's living-room he had, no doubt, observed the partner to my globe-and-pedestal vase of mercury glass. He stretched his hand toward the shelf.

I leaped like a mother leopard.

"Careful, young man. That stuff's priceless."

He turned so sharply that the small rug slid along the polished floor. As he steadied himself against the cabinet, porcelain and glass danced upon the shelves.

"A bull in a china shop," I remarked. The pun restored my humor. I extended my hand.

He smiled mechanically. "I'm here to talk about the Laura Hunt case, Mr. Lydecker."

"Naturally. Have a seat."

He settled his long frame carefully upon a frail chair. I offered cigarettes from a Haviland casket, but he pulled out a pipe.

"You're supposed to be quite an authority on crime yourself, Mr. Lydecker. What do you think about this business?"

I warmed. No writer, however popular, disdains a reader, however humble. "I am honored to know that you read *And More Anon*."

"Only when my paper happens to open to the page."

The affront was not displeasing. In the world I frequent, where personality is generously exposed and friendship offered without reticence, his aloofness struck an uncommon note. I offered my charm. "You may not be a Lydecker fan, Mr. McPherson, but I confess that I've followed your career with breathless excitement."

"You ought to know enough not to believe everything you read in the papers," he said dryly.

I was not to be discouraged. "Isn't criminal investigation a bit out of your line? A trifle unimportant for a man of your achievements?"

"I've been assigned to the case."

"Office politics?"

Except for the purp-purp of his pipe, the room was silent.

"The month is August," I mused. "The Commissioner is off on his holiday, the Deputy Commissioner has always been resentful of your success, and since retail murder is somewhat out of fashion these days and usually, after the first sensation, relegated to Page Two or worse, he has found a convenient way of diminishing your importance."

"The plain truth, if you want to know it"—he was obviously annoyed with himself for bothering to give an excuse—"is that he knew I wanted to see the Dodgers play Boston yesterday afternoon."

I was enchanted. "From trifling enmities do great adventures grow."

"Great adventures! A two-timing dame gets murdered in her flat. So what? A man did it. Find the man. Believe me, Mr. Lydecker, I'm seeing the game this afternoon. The killer himself couldn't stop me."

Pained by his vulgar estimate of my beloved Laura, I spoke mockingly. "Baseball, eh? No wonder your profession has fallen upon evil days. The Great Detectives neither rested nor relaxed until they had relentlessly tracked down their quarry."

"I'm a workingman, I've got hours like everyone else. And if you expect me to work overtime on this third-class mystery, you're thinking of a couple of other fellows."

"Crime doesn't stop because it's Sunday."

"From what I've seen of your late girl friend, Mr. Lydecker, I'd bet my bottom dollar that whoever did that job takes his Sunday off like the rest of us. Probably sleeping until noon and waking himself up with three brandies. Besides, I've got a couple of men working on detail."

"To a man of your achievement, Mr. McPherson, the investigation of a simple murder is probably as interesting as a column of figures to a public accountant who started as a bookkeeper."

This time he laughed. The shell of toughness was wearing thin. He shifted in his chair.

"The sofa," I urged gently, "might be easier on that leg."

He scowled. "Observant, aren't you?"

"You walk carefully, McPherson. Most members of your profession tread like elephants. But since you're sensitive, let me assure you that it's not conspicuous. Extreme astigmatism gives me greater power in the observation of other people's handicaps."

"It's no handicap," he retorted.

"Souvenir of service?" I inquired.

He nodded. "Babylon."

I bounced out of my chair. "The Siege of Babylon, Long Island! Have you read my piece? Wait a minute . . . don't tell me you're the one with the silver fibula."

"Tibia."

"How magnificently exciting! Mattie Grayson! There was a man. Killers aren't what they used to be."

"That's okay with me."

"How many detectives did he get?"

"Three of us with the machine-gun at his mother-in-law's house. Then a couple of us went after him down the alley. Three died and another guy—he got it in the lungs—is still up in Saranac."

"Honorable wounds. You shouldn't be sensitive. How brave it was of you to go back!"

"I was lucky to get back. There was a time, Mr. Lydecker, when I saw a great future as a night watchman. Bravery's got nothing to do with it. A job's a job. Hell, I'm as gun-shy as a traveling salesman that's known too many farmers' daughters."

I laughed aloud. "For a few minutes there, McPherson, I was afraid you had all the Scotch virtues except humor and a taste for good whiskey. How about the whiskey, man?"

"Don't care if I do."

I poured him a stiff one. He took it like the pure waters of Loch Lomond and returned the empty glass for another.

"I hope you don't mind the crack I made about your column, Mr. Lydecker. To tell the truth, I do read it once in a while."

"Why don't you like it?"

Without hesitancy he answered, "You're smooth all right, but you've got nothing to say."

"McPherson, you're a snob. And what's worse, a Scotch snob, than which—as no less an authority than Thackeray has remarked—the world contains no more offensive creature."

He poured his own whiskey this time.

"What is your idea of good literature, Mr. McPherson?"

When he laughed he looked like a Scotch boy who has just learned to accept pleasure without fear of sin. "Yesterday morning, after the body was discovered and we learned that Laura Hunt had stood you up for dinner on Friday night, Sergeant

Schultz was sent up here to question you. So he asks you what you did all evening . . ."

"And I told him," I interrupted, "that I had eaten a lonely dinner, reviling the woman for her desertion, and read Gibbon in a tepid tub."

"Yeh, and you know what Schultz says? He says this writer guy, Gibbon, must be pretty hot for you to have to read him in a cold bath." After a brief pause, he continued, "I've read Gibbon myself, the whole set, and Prescott and Motley and Josephus' *History of the Jews*." There was exuberance in the fession.

"At college or *pour le sport?*" I asked.

"When does a dick get a chance to go to college? But being laid up in the hospital fourteen months, what can you do but read books?"

"That, I take it, is when you became interested in the social backgrounds of crime."

"Up to that time I was a cluck," he confessed modestly.

"Mattie Grayson's machine-gun wasn't such a tragedy, then. You'd probably still be a cluck on the Homicide Squad."

"You like a man better if he's not hundred per cent, don't you, Mr. Lydecker?"

"I've always doubted the sensibilities of Apollo Belvedere."

Roberto announced breakfast. With his natural good manners, he had set a second place at the table. Mark protested at my invitation since he had come here, not as a guest, but in the pursuit of duty which must be as onerous to me as to himself.

I laughed away his embarrassment. "This is in the line of duty. We haven't even started talking about the murder and I don't propose to starve while we do."

Twenty-four hours earlier a cynical but not unkindly police officer had come into my dining-room with the news that Laura's body had been discovered in her apartment. No morsel of food had passed my lips since that moment when Sergeant Schultz had interrupted a peaceful breakfast with the news that Laura Hunt, after failing to keep her dinner engagement with me, had been shot and killed. Now, in the attempt to restore my failing appetite, Roberto had stewed kidneys and mushrooms in claret. While we ate, Mark described the scene at the morgue where

Laura's body had been identified by Bessie, her maid, and her aunt, Susan Treadwell.

In spite of deep suffering, I could not but enjoy the contrast between the young man's appreciation of the meal and the morbid quality of his talk. "When they were shown the body"—he paused to lift a morsel on his fork—"both women collapsed. It was hard to take even if you didn't know her. A lot of blood"—he soaked a bit of toast in the sauce. "With BB shot . . . You can imagine . . ."

I closed my eyes as if she lay there on the Aubusson rug, as Bessie had discovered her, naked except for a blue silk taffeta robe and a pair of silver slippers.

"Fired at close range"—he spooned relish on his plate. "Mrs. Treadwell passed out, but the servant took it like a veteran. She's a queer duck, that Bessie."

"She's been more than maid to Laura. Guide, philosopher, and worst enemy of all of Laura's best friends. Cooks like an angel, but serves bitter herbs with the choicest roasts. No man that entered the apartment was, in Bessie's opinion, good enough for Laura."

"She was cool as a cucumber when the boys got there. Opened the door and pointed to the body so calmly you'd have thought it was an everyday thing for her to find her boss murdered."

"That's Bessie," I commented. "But wait till you get her roused."

Roberto brought in the coffee. Eighteen stories below a motorist blew his siren. Through open windows we heard the rhythms of a Sunday morning radio concert.

"No! No! No!" I cried as Roberto handed Mark my Napoleon cup. I reached across the table and took it myself, leaving the Empress Josephine for my guest.

He drank his coffee in silent disapproval, watching as I unscrewed the carnelian cap of the silver box in which I keep my saccharine tablets. Although I spread butter lavishly on my brioches, I cling religiously to the belief that the substitution of saccharine for sugar in coffee will make me slender and fascinating. His scorn robbed my attitudes of character.

"I must say you go about your work in a leisurely way," I remarked petulantly. "Why don't you go out and take some finger-prints?"

"There are times in the investigation of a crime when it's more important to look at faces."

I turned to the mirror. "How singularly innocent I seem this morning! Tell me, McPherson, have you ever seen such candid eyes?" I took off my glasses and presented my face, round and pink as a cherub's. "But speaking of faces, McPherson, have you met the bridegroom?"

"Shelby Carpenter. I'm seeing him at twelve. He's staying with Mrs. Treadwell."

I seized the fact avidly. "Shelby staying there! Wouldn't he just?"

"He finds the Hotel Framingham too public. Crowds wait in the lobby to see the fellow who was going to marry a murder victim."

"What do you think of Shelby's alibi?"

"What do I think of yours?" he retorted.

"But you've agreed that it's quite normal for a man to spend an evening at home with Gibbon."

"What's wrong about a man going to a Stadium concert?" Puritan nostrils quivered. "Among a lot of music-lovers and art collectors, that seems a pretty natural way to spend an evening."

"If you knew the bridegroom, you'd not think a twenty-five-cent seat normal. But he finds it a convenient way of not having been seen by any of his friends."

"I'm always grateful for information, Mr. Lydecker, but I prefer forming my own opinions."

"Neat, McPherson. Very neat."

"How long had you known her, Mr. Lydecker?"

"Seven, eight—yes, it was eight years," I told him. "We met in '34. Shall I tell you about it?"

Mark puffed at his pipe, the room was filled with its rancid sweet odor. Roberto entered noiselessly to refill the coffee-cups. The radio orchestra played a rhumba.

"She rang my doorbell, McPherson, much as you rang it this morning. I was working at my desk, writing, as I remember, a birthday piece about a certain eminent American, the Father of Our Country. I should never have committed such a cliché, but, as my editor had asked for it and as we were in the midst of some rather delicate financial rearrangements, I had de-

cided that I could not but gain by appeasement. Just as I was about to throw away a
substantial increase in earning power as
indulgence for my boredom, this lovely
child entered my life."

I should have been an actor. Had I been
physically better suited to the narcissistic
profession, I should probably have been
among the greatest of my time. Now, as
Mark let the second cup of coffee grow
cold, he saw me as I had been eight years
before, wrapped in the same style of Persian dressing-gown, padding on loose Jap-
anese clogs to answer the doorbell.

"Carlo, who was Roberto's predecessor,
had gone out to do the daily marketing. I
think she was surprised to see that I answered my own doorbell. She was a slender thing, timid as a fawn and fawn-like,
too, in her young uncertain grace. She had
a tiny head, delicate for even that thin
body, and the tilt of it along with the bright
shyness of her slightly oblique dark eyes
further contributed to the sense that
Bambi—or Bambi's doe—had escaped
from the forest and galloped up the eighteen flights to this apartment.

"When I asked why she had come, she

gave a little clucking sound. Fear had taken her voice. I was certain that she had walked around and around the building before daring to enter, and that she had stood in the corridor hearing her own heart pound before she dared touch a frightened finger to my doorbell.

" 'Well, out with it!' Unwilling to acknowledge that I had been touched by her pretty shyness, I spoke harshly. My temper was more choleric in those days, Mr. Mc-Pherson.

"She spoke softly and very rapidly. I remember it as all one sentence, beginning with a plea that I forgive her for disturbing me and then promising that I should receive huge publicity for reward if I would endorse a fountain pen her employers were advertising. It was called the Byron.

"I exploded. 'Give *me* publicity, my good girl! Your reasoning is sadly distorted. It's my name that will give distinction to your cheap fountain pen. And how dared you take the sacred name of Byron? Who gave you the right? I've a good mind to write the manufacturers a stiff letter.'

"I tried not to notice the brightness of her eyes, McPherson. I was not aware at this time that she had named the fountain pen herself and that she was proud of its literary sound. She persisted bravely, telling me about a fifty-thousand-dollar advertising campaign which could not fail to glorify my name.

"I felt it my duty to become apoplectic. 'Do you know how many dollars' worth of white space my syndicated columns now occupy? And do you realize that manufacturers of typewriters, toothpaste, and razors with fifty-thousand-dollar checks in their pockets are turned away from this door daily? You talk of giving me publicity!'

"Her embarrassment was painful. I asked if she would stay and have a glass of sherry. Doubtless she would have preferred flight, but she was too shy to refuse. While we drank the sherry, I made her tell me about herself. This was her first job and it represented the apex of her ambitions at the time. She had visited sixty-eight advertising agencies before she got the job. Buried beneath that air of timidity was a magnificent will. Laura knew she was clever, and she was willing to suffer endless rebuffs in order to prove her talents. When she had finished, I said, 'I suppose you think I'm moved by your story and that I'm going to break down and give you that endorsement.' "

"Did you?" Mark inquired.

"McPherson, I am the most mercenary man in America. I never take any action without computing the profit."

"You gave her the endorsement."

I bowed my head in shame. "For seven years Waldo Lydecker has enthusiastically acclaimed the Byron Pen. Without it, I am sure that my collected essays would never sell one hundred thousand copies."

"She must have been a terrific kid," he remarked.

"Only mildly terrific at that period. I recognized her possibilities, however. The next week I entertained her at dinner. That was the beginning. Under my tutelage she developed from a gauche child to a gracious New Yorker. After a year no one would have suspected that she came from Colorado Springs. And she remained loyal and appreciative, McPherson. Of all my friends she is the only one with whom I was willing to share my prestige. She became as well known at opening nights as Waldo

Lydecker's graying Van Dyke or his gold-banded stick."

My guest offered no comment. The saturnine mood had returned. Scotch piety and Brooklyn poverty had developed his resistance to chic women. "Was she ever in love with you?"

I recoiled. My answer came in a thick voice. "Laura was always fond of me. She rejected suitor after suitor during those eight years of loyalty."

The contradiction was named Shelby Carpenter. But explanation would come later. Mark knew the value of silence in dealing with such a voluble creature as myself.

"My *love* for Laura," I explained, "was not merely the desire of a mature man for a pretty young thing. There was a deeper basis of affection. Laura had made me a generous man. It's quite fallacious to believe that we grow fond of those whom we've hurt. Remorse cannot compensate. It's more human to shun those whose presence reminds us of a shoddy past. Generosity, not evil, flourishes like the green bay tree. Laura considered me the kindest man in the universe, hence I had to grow to that stature. For her I was always Jovian, in humanity as well as intelligence."

I suspected doubt behind his swift glance of appraisal. He rose. "It's getting late. I've got a date with Carpenter."

"Behold, the bridegroom waits!" As we walked to the door, I added, "I wonder how you're going to like Shelby."

"It's not my business to like or dislike anyone. I'm only interested in her friends . . ."

"As suspects?" I teased.

"For information. I shall probably call on you again, Mr. Lydecker."

"Whenever you like. I do indeed hope to aid, if I can, in the apprehension of the vile being—we can't call him human, can we?—who could have performed such a villainous and uselessly tragic deed. But in the meantime I shall be curious to know your opinion of Shelby."

"You don't think much of him yourself, do you?"

"Shelby was Laura's other life." I stood with my hand on the doorknob. "To my prejudiced way of thinking, the more commonplace and less distinguished side of her existence. But judge for yourself, young man."

We shook hands.

"To solve the puzzle of her death, you must first resolve the mystery of Laura's life. This is no simple task. She had no secret fortune, no hidden rubies. But, I warn you, McPherson, the activities of crooks and racketeers will seem simple in comparison with the motives of a modern woman."

He showed impatience.

"A complicated, cultivated modern woman. 'Concealment, like a worm i' the bud, fed on her damask cheek.' I shall be at your command whenever you call, McPherson. Au revoir."

I stood at the door until he had got into the elevator.

CHAPTER TWO

While a not inconsiderable share of my work has been devoted to the study of murder, I have never stooped to the narration of a mystery story. At the risk of seeming somewhat less than modest, I shall quote from my own works. The sentence, so often reprinted, that opens my essay "Of Sound and Fury,"[1] is pertinent here:

"When, during the 1936 campaign, I learned that the President was a devotee of mystery stories, I voted a straight Republican ticket."

My prejudices have not been shed. I still consider the conventional mystery story an excess of sound and fury, signifying, far worse than nothing, a barbaric need for vi-

---

[1]In the volume *Time, You Thief*, by Waldo Lydecker, 1938.

olence and revenge in that timid horde known as the reading public. The literature of murder investigation bores me as profoundly as its practice irritated Mark McPherson. Yet I am bound to tell this story, just as he was obliged to continue his searches, out of a deep emotional involvement in the case of Laura Hunt. I offer the narrative, not so much as a detective yarn as a love story.

I wish I were its hero. I fancy myself a pensive figure drawn, without conscious will, into a love that was born of violence and destined for tragedy. I am given to thinking of myself in the third person. Many a time, when I have suffered some clumsy misadventure, I am saved from remorse by the substitution for unsavory memory of another captivating installment in *The Life and Times of Waldo Lydecker*. Rare are the nights when I fail to lull myself to sleep without the sedative of some such heroic statement as "Waldo Lydecker stood, untroubled, at the edge of a cliff beneath which ten thousand angry lions roared."

I make this confession at the risk of exhibiting absurdity. My proportions are, if anything, too heroic. While I measure three inches above six feet, the magnificence of my skeleton is hidden by the weight of my flesh. My dreams dwindle in contrast. Yet I dare say that if the dreams of any so-called normal man were exposed, like Dali drawings, to the vulgar eyes of the masses, there would be no more gravity and dignity left for mankind. At certain times in history, flesh was considered a sign of good disposition, but we live in a tiresome era wherein exercise is held sacred and heroes are always slender. I have more than once endured the ordeal of reducing, but I always give it up when I reflect that no philosophy or fantasy dare enter a mind as usurious as Shylock's over each pound of flesh. So I have learned, at the age of fifty-two, to accept this burden with the same philosophical calm with which I endure such indecencies as hot weather and war news.

But it will not be possible to write of myself heroically in those chapters wherein Mark McPherson moves the story. I have long learned to uphold my ego in a world that also contains Shelby Carpenter, but the young detective is a more potent man. There is no wax in Mark; he is hard coin metal who impresses his own definite stamp upon those who seek to mould him.

He is definite but not simple. His complexities trouble him. Contemptuous of luxury, he is also charmed by it. He resents my collection of glass and porcelain, my Biedermeier and my library, but envies the culture which has developed appreciation of surface lustres. His remarking upon my preference for men who are less than hundred per cent exposed his own sensitivity. Reared in a world that honors only hundred per cents, he has learned in maturity what I knew as a miserable, obese adolescent, that the lame, the halt, and the blind have more malice in their souls, therefore more acumen. Cherishing secret hurt, they probe for the pains and weaknesses of others. And probing is the secret of finding. Through telescopic lenses I discerned in Mark the weakness that normal eyesight might never discover.

The hard coin metal of his character fails to arouse my envy. I am jealous of severed bone, of tortured muscle, of scars whose existence demands such firmness of footstep, such stern, military erectness. My own failings, obesity, astigmatism, the softness of pale flesh, can find no such heroic apology. But a silver shinbone, the legacy of a dying desperado! There is romance in the very anatomy of the man.

For an hour after he had gone, I sat upon the sofa, listless, toying with my envy. That hour exhausted me. I turned for solace to Laura's epitaph. Rhythms failed, words eluded me. Mark had observed that I wrote smoothly but said nothing. I have sometimes suspected this flaw in my talent, but have never faced myself with the admission of failure. Upon that Sunday noon I saw myself as a fat, fussy, and useless male of middle age and doubtful charm. By all that is logical I should have despised Mark McPherson. I could not. For all of his rough edges, he was the man I should have been, the hero of the story.

The hero, but not the interpreter. That is my omniscient rôle. As narrator and interpreter, I shall describe scenes which I never saw and record dialogues which I did not hear. For this impudence I offer no excuse. I am an artist, and it is my business to recreate movement precisely as I create mood. I know these people, their voices ring in my ears, and I need only close my eyes and see characteristic gestures. My written dialogue will have more clarity, compactness, and essence of character than their spoken lines, for I am able to edit while I write, whereas they carried on their conversations in a loose and pointless fashion with no sense of form or crisis in the building of their scenes. And when I write of myself as a character in the story, I shall endeavor to record my flaws with the same objectivity as if I were no more important than any other figure in this macabre romance.

CHAPTER THREE

Laura's Aunt Susan once sang in musical comedy. Then she became a widow. The period between—the hyphen of marriage—is best forgotten. Never in the years I have known her have I heard her lament the late Horace Q. Treadwell. The news of Laura's death had brought her hastily from her summer place on Long Island to the mausoleum on upper Fifth Avenue. One servant, a grim Finn, had accompanied her. It was Helga who opened the door for Mark and led him through a maze of dark canals into a vast uncarpeted chamber in which every piece of furniture, every picture and ornament, wore a shroud of pale, striped linen.

This was Mark's first visit to a private home on Fifth Avenue. As he waited, he paced the long room, accosting and retreating from his lean, dark-clad image in a full-length gold-framed mirror. His thoughts dwelt upon the meeting with the bereaved bridegroom. Laura was to have married Shelby Carpenter on the following Thursday. They had passed their blood tests and answered the questions on the application for a marriage license.

Mark knew these facts thoroughly. Shelby had been disarmingly frank with the police sergeant who asked the first questions. Folded in Mark's coat-pocket was a carbon record of the lovers' last meeting. The facts were commonplace but not conventional.

Laura had been infected with the week-end sickness. From the first of May until the last of September, she joined the fanatic mob in week-end pilgrimages to Connecticut. The mouldy house described in "The Fermenting of New England,"[1] was Laura's converted barn. Her garden suffered pernicious anaemia and the sums she spent to fertilize that rocky soil would have provided a purple orchid every day of

[1] In the volume *Time, You Thief,* by Waldo Lydecker, 1938.

the year with a corsage of *Odontoglossum grande* for Sundays. But she persisted in the belief that she saved a vast fortune because, for five months of the year, she had only to buy flowers once a week.

After my first visit, no amount of persuasion could induce me to step foot upon the Wilton train. Shelby, however, was a not unwilling victim. And sometimes she took the maid, Bessie, and thus relieved herself of household duties which she pretended to enjoy. On this Friday, she had decided to leave them both in town. She needed four or five days of loneliness, she told Shelby, to bridge the gap between a Lady Lilith Face Cream campaign and her honeymoon. It would never do to start as a nervous bride. This reasoning satisfied Shelby. It never occurred to him that she might have other plans. Nor did he question her farewell dinner with me. She had arranged, or so she told Shelby, to leave my house in time to catch the ten-twenty train.

She and Shelby had worked for the same advertising agency. At five o'clock on Friday afternoon, he went into her office. She gave her secretary a few final instructions, powdered her nose, reddened her lips, and rode down in the elevator with him. They stopped for Martinis at the Tropicale, a bar frequented by advertising and radio writers. Laura spoke of her plans for the week. She was not certain as to the hour of her return, but she did not expect Shelby to meet her train. The trip to and from Wilton was no more to her than a subway ride. She set Wednesday as the day of her return and promised to telephone him immediately upon her arrival.

As Mark pondered these facts, his eyes on the checkerboard of light and dark woods set into Mrs. Treadwell's floor, he became aware that his restlessness was the subject of nervous scrutiny. The long mirror framed his first impression of Shelby Carpenter. Against the shrouded furniture, Shelby was like a brightly lithographed figure on the gaudy motion-picture poster decorating the sombre granite of an ancient opera house. The dark suit chosen for this day of mourning could not dull his vivid grandeur. Male energy shone in his tanned skin, gleamed from his clear gray eyes, swelled powerful biceps. Later, as Mark told me of the meeting, he confessed that he was puzzled by an almost overwhelming sense of familiarity. Shelby spoke with the voice of a stranger but with lips whose considered smile seemed as familiar as Mark's own reflection. All through the interview and in several later meetings, Mark sought vainly to recall some earlier association. The enigma enraged him. Failure seemed to indicate a softening process within himself. Encounters with Shelby diminished his self-confidence.

They chose chairs at opposite ends of the long room. Shelby had offered, Mark accepted, a Turkish cigarette. Oppressed by Fifth Avenue magnificence, he had barely the courage to ask for an ashtray. And this a man who had faced machine-guns.

Shelby had borne up bravely during the ordeal at Headquarters. As his gentle Southern voice repeated the details of that tragic farewell, he showed clearly that he wished to spare his visitor the effort of sympathy.

"So I put her in the taxi and gave the driver Waldo Lydecker's address. Laura said, 'Good-bye until Wednesday,' and leaned out to kiss me. The next morning the police came to tell me that Bessie had found her body in the apartment. I wouldn't believe it. Laura was in the country. That's what she'd told me, and Laura had not lied to me before."

"We found the taxi-driver and checked with him," Mark informed him. "As soon as they'd turned the corner, she said that he was not to go to Mr. Lydecker's address, but to take her to Grand Central. She'd telephoned Mr. Lydecker earlier in the afternoon to break the dinner date. Have you any idea why she should have lied to you?"

Cigarette smoke curled in flawless circles from Shelby's flawless lips. "I don't like to believe she lied to me. Why should she tell me she was dining with Waldo if she wasn't?"

"She lied twice, first in regard to dining with Mr. Lydecker, and second about leaving town that night."

"I can't believe it. We were always so honest with each other."

Mark accepted the statement without comment. "We've interviewed the porters on duty Friday night at Grand Central and a couple remember her face."

"She always took the Friday night train."

"That's the catch. The only porter who

swears to a definite recollection of Laura on this particular night also asked if he'd have his picture in the newspapers. So we strike a dead-end there. She might have taken another taxi from the Forty-Second or Lexington Avenue exits."

"Why?" Shelby sighed. "Why should she have done such a ridiculous thing?"

"If we knew, we might have a reasonable clue. Now as to your alibi, Mr. Carpenter . . ."

Shelby groaned.

"I won't make you go through it again. I've got the details. You had dinner at the Myrtle Cafeteria on Forty-Second Street, you walked to Fifth Avenue, took a bus to a Hundred and Forty-Sixth Street, bought a twenty-five-cent seat for the concert . . ."

Shelby pouted like a hurt child. "I've had some bad times, you know. When I'm alone I try to save money. I'm just getting on my feet again."

"There's no shame in saving money," Mark reminded him. "That's the only reasonable explanation anyone's given for anything so far. You walked home after the concert, eh? Quite a distance."

"The poor man's exercise." Shelby grinned feebly.

Mark dropped the alibi, and with one of those characteristic swift thrusts, asked: "Why didn't you get married before this? Why did the engagement last so long?"

Shelby cleared his throat.

"Money, wasn't it?"

A schoolboy flush ripened Shelby's skin. He spoke bitterly. "When I went to work for Rose, Rowe and Sanders, I made thirty-five dollars a week. She was getting a hundred and seventy-five." He hesitated, the color of his cheeks brightened to the tones of an overripe peach. "Not that I resented her success. She was so clever that I was awed and respectful. And I wanted her to make as much as she could; believe that, Mr. McPherson. But it's hard on a man's pride. I was brought up to think of women . . . differently."

"And what made you decide to marry?"

Shelby brightened. "I've had a little success myself."

"But she was still holding a better job. What made you change your mind?"

"There wasn't so much discrepancy. My salary, if not munificent, was respectable.

And I felt that I was advancing. Besides, I'd been catching up with my debts. A man doesn't like to get married, you know, while he owes money."

"Except to the woman he's marrying," a shrill voice added.

In the mirror's gilt frame Mark saw the reflection of an advancing figure. She was small, robed in deepest mourning and carrying under her right arm a Pomeranian whose auburn coat matched her own bright hair. As she paused in the door with the marble statues and bronze figurines behind her, the gold frame giving margins to the portrait, she was like a picture done by one of Sargent's imitators who had failed to carry over to the twentieth century the dignity of the nineteenth. Mark had seen her briefly at the inquest and had thought her young to be Laura's aunt. Now he saw that she was well over fifty. The rigid perfection of her face was almost artificial, as if flesh-pink velvet were drawn over an iron frame.

Shelby leaped. "Darling! You remarkable creature! How you've recovered! How can you be so beautiful, darling, when you've gone through such intolerable agonies?"

He led her to the room's most important chair.

"I hope you find the fiend"—she addressed Mark but gave attention to her chiffon. "I hope you find him and scrouge his eyes out and drive hot nails through his body and boil him in oil." Her vehemence spent, she tossed Mark her most enchanting smile.

"Comfortable, darling?" Shelby inquired. "How about your fan? Would you like a cool drink?"

Had the dog's affection begun to bore her, she might have dismissed it with the same pretty indifference. To Mark she said: "Has Shelby told you the story of his romantic courtship? I hope he's not left out any of the thrilling episodes."

"Now, darling, what would Laura have said if she could hear you?"

"She'd say I was a jealous bitch. And she'd be right. Except that I'm not jealous. I wouldn't have you on a gold platter, darling."

"You mustn't mind Auntie Sue, Mr. McPherson. She's prejudiced because I'm poor."

"Isn't he cute?" cooed Auntie Sue, petting the dog.

"I never asked Laura for money"—Shelby might have been taking an oath at an altar. "If she were here, she'd swear it, too. I never asked. She knew I was having a hard time and insisted, simply insisted upon lending it to me. She always made money so easily, she said."

"She worked like a dog!" cried Laura's aunt.

The Pomeranian sniffed. Aunt Sue pressed its small nose to her cheek, then settled it upon her lap. Having achieved this enviable position, the Pomeranian looked upon the men smugly.

"Do you know, Mrs. Treadwell, if your niece had any—" Mark produced the word uneasily "—enemies?"

"Enemies!" the good lady shrieked. "Everyone adored her. Didn't everyone adore her, Shelby? She had more friends than money."

"That," Shelby added gravely, "was one of the finest things about her."

"Anyone who had troubles came to her," Aunt Sue declaimed, quite in the manner of the immortal Bernhardt. "I warned her more than once. It's when you put yourself out for people that you find yourself in trouble. Don't you think that's true, Mr. Mc-Pherson?"

"I don't know. I've probably not put myself out for enough people." The posturing offended him; he had become curt.

His annoyance failed to check the lady's histrionic aspirations. " 'The evil that men do lives after them; the good is oft buried with their bones,' " she misquoted, and giggling lightly, added, "although her poor bones aren't buried yet. But we must be truthful, even about the dead. It wasn't money principally with Laura, it was people, if you know what I mean. She was always running around, doing favors, wasting her time and strength on people she scarcely knew. Remember that model, Shelby, the girl with the fancy name? Laura got me to give her my leopard coat. It wasn't half worn out either. I could have got another winter out of it and spared my mink. Don't you remember, Shelby?"

Shelby had become infatuated with a bronze Diana who had been threatening for years to leap, with dog and stag, from her pedestal.

Auntie Sue continued naughtily: "And Shelby's job! Do you know how he got it, Mr. McPherson? He'd been selling washing machines—or was it casings for frankfurters, darling? Or was that the time when you earned thirty dollars a week writing letters for a school that taught people to be successful business executives?"

Shelby turned defiantly from Diana. "What's that to be ashamed of? When I met Laura, Mr. McPherson, I happened to be working as correspondent for the University of the Science of Finance. Laura saw some of my copy, realized that I was wasting a certain gift or flair, and with her usual generosity . . ."

"Generosity wasn't the half of it," Auntie Sue interrupted.

"She spoke to Mr. Rowe about me and a few months later, when there was a vacancy, he called me in. You can't say I've been ungrateful"—he forgave Mrs. Treadwell with his gentle smile. "It was she, not I, who suggested that you forget it."

"There were a number of other things, darling, that Laura asked me to forget."

"Mustn't be vicious, dear. You'll be giving Mr. McPherson a lot of misleading ideas." With the tenderness of a nurse Shelby rearranged Auntie Sue's cushions, smiling and treating her malice like some secret malady.

The scene took on a theatric quality. Mark saw Shelby through the woman's eyes, clothed in the charm he had donned, like a bright domino, for the woman's pleasure. The ripe color, the chiseled features, the clear, long-lashed eyes had been created, his manner said, for her particular enjoyment. Through it all Mark felt that this was not a new exhibition. He had seen it somewhere before. So irritated by faltering memory that he had to strain harshness from his voice, he told them he was through with them for the day, and rose to go.

Shelby rose, too. "I'll go out for a bit of air. If you think you can get along without me for a while."

"Of course, darling. It's been wicked of me to take up so much of your time." Shelby's feeble sarcasm had softened the lady. White, faded, ruby-tipped hands rested on his dark sleeve. "I'll never forget how kind you've been."

Shelby forgave magnanimously. He put

himself at her disposal as if he were already Laura's husband, the man of the family whose duty it was to serve a sorrowing woman in this hour of grief.

Like a penitent mistress returning to her lover, she cooed at Shelby. "With all your faults, you've got manners, darling. That's more than most men have nowadays. I'm sorry I've been so bad-tempered."

He kissed her forehead.

As they left the house, Shelby turned to Mark. "Don't take Mrs. Treadwell too seriously. Her bark is worse than her bite. It's only that she'd disapproved of my marrying her niece, and now she's got to stand by her opinions."

"What she disapproved of," Mark observed, "was Laura's marrying you."

Shelby smiled ruefully. "We ought all to be a little more decent now, oughtn't we? After all! Probably Auntie Sue is sorry she hurt poor Laura by constantly criticizing me, and now she's too proud to say so. That's why she had to take it out on me this morning."

They stood in the burning sunlight. Both were anxious to get away, yet both hesitated. The scene was unfinished. Mark had not learned enough, Shelby had not told all he wanted Mark to know.

When, after a brief pause devoted to a final struggle with his limping memory, Mark cleared his throat, Shelby started as if he had been roused from the remoteness of a dream. Both smiled mechanically.

"Tell me," Mark commanded, "where have I seen you before?"

Shelby couldn't imagine. "But I've been around. Parties and all that. One sees people at bars and restaurants. Sometimes a stranger's face is more familiar than your best friend's."

Mark shook his head. "Cocktail bars aren't in my line."

"You'll remember when you're thinking of something else. That's how it always is." Then, without changing his tone, Shelby added, "You know, Mr. McPherson, that I was beneficiary of Laura's insurance, don't you?"

Mark nodded.

"I wanted to tell you myself. Otherwise you might think . . . well . . . it's only natural in your work to—" Shelby chose the word tactfully "—suspect every motive. Laura carried an annuity, you know, and there was a twenty-five-thousand-dollar death benefit. She'd had it in her sister's name, but after we decided to get married she insisted upon making it out to me."

"I'll remember that you told me," Mark promised.

Shelby offered his hand. Mark took it. They hesitated while the sun smote their uncovered heads.

"I hope you don't think I'm completely a heel, Mr. McPherson," Shelby said ruefully. "I never liked borrowing from a woman."

CHAPTER FOUR

When, at precisely twelve minutes past four by the ormolu clock on my mantel, the telephone interrupted, I was deep in the Sunday papers. Laura had become a Manhattan legend. Scarlet-minded headline artists had named her tragedy THE BACHELOR GIRL MURDER and one example of Sunday edition belles-lettres was tantalizingly titled SEEK ROMEO IN EAST SIDE LOVE-KILLING. By the necromancy of modern journalism, a gracious young woman had been transformed into a dangerous siren who practiced her wiles in that fascinating neighborhood where Park Avenue meets Bohemia. Her generous way of life had become an uninterrupted orgy of drunkenness, lust, and deceit, as titivating to the masses as it was profitable to the publishers. At this very hour, I reflected as I lumbered to the telephone, men were bandying her name in pool parlors and women shouting her secrets from tenement windows.

I heard Mark McPherson's voice on the wire. "Mr. Lydecker, I was just wondering if you could help me. There are several questions I'd like to ask you."

"And what of the baseball game?" I inquired.

Self-conscious laughter vibrated the diaphragm and tickled my ear. "It was too late. I'd have missed the first couple of innings. Can you come over?"

"Where?"

"The apartment. Miss Hunt's place."

"I don't want to come up there. It's cruel of you to ask me."

"Sorry," he said after a moment of cold silence. "Perhaps Shelby Carpenter can help me. I'll try to get in touch with him."

"Never mind. I'll come."

Ten minutes later I stood beside him in the bay window of Laura's living-room. East Sixty-Second Street had yielded to the spirit of carnival. Popcorn vendors and pushcart peddlers, sensing the profit in disaster, offered ice-cream sandwiches, pickles, and nickel franks to buzzards who battened on excitement. Sunday's sweethearts had deserted the green pastures of Central Park to stroll arm-in-arm past her house, gaping at daisies which had been watered by the hands of a murder victim. Fathers pushed perambulators and mothers scolded the brats who tortured the cops who guarded the door of a house in which a bachelor girl had been slain.

"Coney Island moved to the Platinum Belt," I observed.

Mark nodded. "Murder is the city's best free entertainment. I hope it doesn't bother you, Mr. Lydecker."

"Quite the contrary. It's the odor of tuberoses and the timbre of organ music that depress me. Public festivity gives death a classic importance. No one would have enjoyed the spectacle more than Laura."

He sighed.

"If she were here now, she'd open the windows, pluck daisies out of her window-boxes and strew the sidewalks. Then she'd send me down the stairs for a penny pickle."

Mark plucked a daisy and tore off the petals.

"Laura loved dancing in the streets. She gave dollar bills to organ-grinders."

He shook his head. "You'd never think it, judging from the neighborhood."

"She also had a taste for privacy."

The house was one of a row of converted mansions, preserved in such fashion that Victorian architecture sacrificed none of its substantial elegance to twentieth-century chic. High stoops had given way to lacquered doors three steps down; scrofulous daisies and rachitic geraniums bloomed in extraordinarily bright blue and green window-boxes; rents were exorbitant. Laura had lived here, she told me, because she enjoyed snubbing Park Avenue's pretentious foyers. After a trying day in the office, she could neither face a superman in gilt braid nor discuss the weather with politely indifferent elevator boys. She had enjoyed opening the street door with a key and climbing the stairs to her remodeled third floor. It was this taste for privacy that led to her death, for there had been no one to ask at the door if Miss

Hunt expected a visitor on the night the murderer came.

"The doorbell rang," Mark announced suddenly.

"What?"

"That's how it must have happened. The doorbell rang. She was in the bedroom without clothes on. By the time she'd put on that silk thing and her slippers, he'd probably rung a second time. She went to the door and as she opened it, the shot was fired!"

"How do you know all this?" I demanded.

"She fell backward. The body lay there."

We both stared at the bare, polished floor. He had seen the body, the pale blue garment blood-stained and the blood running in rivulets to the edge of the green carpet.

"The door downstairs had evidently been left unlocked. It was unlocked when Bessie came to work yesterday morning. Before she came upstairs, Bessie looked for the superintendent to bawl him out for his carelessness, but he'd taken his family down to Manhattan Beach for the weekend. The tenants of the first and second floors are away for the summer and there was no one else in the house. The houses on both sides are empty, too, at this time of year."

"Probably the murderer thought of that," I observed.

"The door might have been left open for him. She might have been expecting a caller."

"Do you think so?"

"You knew her, Mr. Lydecker. Tell me, what kind of a dame was she anyway?"

"She was not the sort of woman you call a dame," I retorted.

"Okay. But what was she like?"

"Look at this room. Does it reveal nothing of the person who planned and decorated it? Does it contain, for your eyes, the vulgar memories of a bachelor girl? Does it seem to you the home of a young woman who would lie to her fiancé, deceive her oldest friend, and sneak off to a rendezvous with a murderer?"

I awaited his answer like a touchy Jehovah. If he failed to appreciate the quality of the woman who had adorned this room, I should know that his interest in literature was but the priggish aspiration of a seeker after self-improvement, his sensitivity no more than proletarian prudery. For me the room still shone with Laura's lustre. Perhaps it was in the crowding memories of firelit conversations, of laughing dinners at the candle-bright refectory table, of midnight confidences fattened by spicy snacks and endless cups of steaming coffee. But even as it stood for him, mysterious and bare of memory, it must have represented, in the deepest sense of the words, a *living room*.

For answer he chose the long green chair, stretched his legs on the ottoman, and pulled out his pipe. His eyes traveled from the black marble fireplace in which the logs were piled, ready for the first cool evening, to softly faded chintz whose deep folds shut out the glare of the hot twilight.

After a time he burst out: "I wish to Christ my sister could see this place. Since she married and went to live in Kew Gardens, she won't have kitchen matches in the parlor. This place has—" he hesitated "—it's very comfortable."

I think the word in his mind had been *class*, but he kept it from me, knowing that intellectual snobbism is nourished by such trivial crudities. His attention wandered to the bookshelves.

"She had a lot of books. Did she ever read them?"

"What do you think?"

He shrugged. "You never know about women."

"Don't tell me you're a misogynist."

He clamped his teeth hard upon his pipestem and glanced at me with an air of urchin defiance.

"Come, now, what of the girl friend?" I pleaded.

He answered dryly: "I've had plenty in my life. I'm no angel."

"Ever loved one?"

"A doll in Washington Heights got a fox fur out of me. And I'm a Scotchman, Mr. Lydecker. So make what you want of it."

"Ever know one who wasn't a doll? Or a dame?"

He went to the bookshelves. While he talked, his hands and eyes were concerned with a certain small volume bound in red morocco. "Sometimes I used to take my sisters' girl friends out. They never talked about anything except going steady and getting married. Always wanted to take you

VERA CASPARY

past furniture stores to show you the parlor suites. One of them almost hooked me."

"And what saved you?"

"Mattie Grayson's machine-gun. You were right. It was no tragedy."

"Didn't she wait?"

"Hell, yes. The day they discharged me, there she was at the hospital door. Full of love and plans; her old man had plenty of dough, owned a fish store, and was ready to furnish the flat, first payment down. I was still using crutches so I told her I wouldn't let her sacrifice herself." He laughed aloud. "After the months I'd put in reading and thinking, I couldn't go for a parlor suite. She's married now, got a couple of kids, lives in Jersey."

"Never read any books, eh?"

"Oh, she's probably bought a couple of sets for the bookcase. Keeps them dusted and never reads them."

He snapped the cover on the red morocco volume. The shrill blast of the popcorn whistle insulted our ears and the voices of children rose to remind us of the carnival of death in the street below. Bessie Clary, Laura's maid, had told the police that her first glimpse of the body had been a distorted reflection in the mercury-glass globe on Laura's mantel. That tarnished bubble caught and held our eyes, and we saw in it fleetingly, as in a crystal ball, a vision of the inert body in the blue robe, dark blood matted in the dark hair.

"What did you want to ask me, McPherson? Why did you bring me up here?"

His face had the watchfulness that comes after generations to a conquered people. The Avenger, when he comes, will wear that proud, guarded look. For a moment I glimpsed enmity. My fingers beat a tattoo on the arm of my chair. Strangely, the padded rhythms seemed to reach him, for he turned, staring as if my face were a memory from some fugitive reverie. Another thirty seconds had passed, I dare say, before he took from her desk a spherical object covered in soiled leather.

"What's this, Mr. Lydecker?"

"Surely a man of your sporting tastes is familiar with that ecstatic toy, McPherson."

"But why did *she* keep a baseball on her desk?" He emphasized the pronoun. *She* had begun to live. Then, examining the tattered leather and loosened bindings, he asked, "Has she had it since '38?"

"I'm sure I didn't notice the precise date when this *objet d'art* was introduced into the household."

"It's autographed by Cookie Lavagetto. That was his big year. Was she *a* Dodgers fan?"

"There were many facets to her character."

"Was Shelby a fan, too?"

"Will the answer to that question help you solve the murder, my dear fellow?"

He set the baseball down so that it should lie precisely where Laura had left it. "I just wanted to know. If it bothers you to answer the question, Mr. Lydecker . . ."

"There's no reason to get sullen about it," I snapped. "As a matter of fact, Shelby wasn't a fan. He preferred . . . why do I speak of him in the past tense? He prefers the more aristocratic sports, tennis, riding, hunting, you know."

"Yep," he said.

Near the door, a few feet from the spot where the body had fallen, hung Stuart Jacoby's portrait of Laura. Jacoby, one of the imitators of Eugene Speicher, had produced a flattened version of a face that was anything but flat. The best feature of

the painting, as they had been her best feature, were the eyes. The oblique tendency, emphasized by the sharp tilt of dark brows, gave her face that shy, fawn-like quality which had so enchanted me the day I opened the door to a slender child who had asked me to endorse a fountain pen. Jacoby had caught the fluid sense of restlessness in the position of her body, perched on the arm of a chair, a pair of yellow gloves in one hand, a green hunter's hat in the other. The portrait was a trifle unreal, however, a trifle studied, too much Jacoby and not enough Laura.

"She wasn't a bad-looking da—" He hesitated, smiled ruefully, "—girl, was she, Mr. Lydecker?"

"That's a sentimental portrait. Jacoby was in love with her at the time."

"She had a lot of men in love with her, didn't she?"

"She was a very kind woman. Kind and generous."

"That's not what men fall for."

"She had delicacy. If she was aware of a man's shortcomings, she never showed it."

"Full of bull?"

"No, extremely honest. Her flattery was

never shallow. She found the real qualities and made them important. Surface faults and affectations fell away like false friends at the approach of adversity."

He studied the portrait. "Why didn't she get married, then? Earlier, I mean?"

"She was disappointed when she was very young."

"Most people are disappointed when they're young. That doesn't keep them from finding someone else. Particularly women."

"She wasn't like your erstwhile fiancé, McPherson. Laura had no need for a parlor suite. Marriage wasn't her career. She had her career, she made plenty of money, and there were always men to squire and admire her. Marriage could give her only one sort of completion, and she was keeping herself for that."

"Keeping herself busy," he added dryly.

"Would you have prescribed a nunnery for a woman of her temperament? She had a man's job and a man's worries. Knitting wasn't one of her talents. Who are you to judge her?"

"Keep your shirt on," Mark said. "I didn't make any comments."

I had gone to the bookshelves and removed the volume to which he had given such careful scrutiny. He gave no sign that he had noticed, but fixed his fury upon an enlarged snapshot of Shelby looking uncommonly handsome in tennis flannels.

Dusk had descended. I switched on the lamp. In that swift transition from dusk to illumination, I caught a glimpse of darker, more impenetrable mystery. Here was no simple Police Department investigation. In such inconsistent trifles as an ancient baseball, a worn *Gulliver*, a treasured snapshot, he sought clues, not to the passing riddle of a murder, but to the eternally enigmatic nature of woman. This was a search no man could make with his eyes alone; the heart must also be engaged. He, stern fellow, would have been the first to deny such implication, but I, through these prognostic lenses, perceived the true cause of his resentment against Shelby. His private enigma, so much deeper than the professional solution of the crime, concerned the answer to a question which has ever baffled the lover, "What did she see in that other fellow?" As he glowered at the snapshot I knew that he was pondering on the quality of Laura's affection for Shelby, wondering whether a woman of her sensitivity and intelligence could be satisfied merely with the perfect mould of a man.

"Too late, my friend," I said jocosely. "The final suitor has rung her doorbell."

With a gesture whose fierceness betrayed the zeal with which his heart was guarded, he snatched up some odds and ends piled on Laura's desk, her address and engagement book, letters and bills bound by a rubber band, unopened bank statements, checkbooks, an old diary, and a photograph album.

"Come on," he snapped. "I'm hungry. Let's get out of this dump."

CHAPTER FIVE

"We've discovered certain clues, but we are not ready to make a statement."

The reporters found McPherson dignified, formal, and somewhat aloof that Monday morning. He felt a new importance in himself as if his life had taken on new meaning. The pursuit of individual crime had ceased to be trivial. A girl reporter, using female tricks to win information denied her trousered competitors, exclaimed, "I shouldn't mind being murdered half so much, Mr. McPherson, if you were the detective seeking clues to my private life."

His mouth twisted. The flattery was not delicate.

Her address and engagement books, bank statements, bills, check stubs, and correspondence filled his desk and his mind. Through them he had discovered the richness of her life, but also the profligacy. Too many guests and too many dinners, too many letters assuring her of undying devotion, too much of herself spent on the casual and petty, the transitory, the undeserving. Thus his Presbyterian virtue rejected the danger of covetousness. He had discovered the best of life in a gray-walled hospital room and had spent the years that followed asking himself timorously whether loneliness must be the inevitable companion of appreciation. This summing-up of Laura's life answered his question, but the answer failed to satisfy the demands of his stern upbringing. He learned, as he read her letters, balanced her unbalanced accounts, added the sums of unpaid bills, that while the connoisseur of living is not lonely, the price is high. To support the richness of life she had worked until she was too tired to approach her wedding day with joy or freedom.

The snapshot album was filled with portraits of Shelby Carpenter. In a single summer, Laura had fallen victim to his charms and the candid camera. She had caught him full face and profile, closeup and bust, on the tennis court, at the wheel of her roadster, in swimming trunks, in overalls, in hip boots with a basket slung over his shoulder, a fishing reel in his hand. Mark paused at the portrait of Shelby, the hunter, surrounded by dead ducks.

Surely the reader must, by this time, be questioning the impertinence of a reporter who records unseen actions as nonchalantly as if he had been hiding in Mark's office behind a framed photograph of the New York Police Department Baseball Team, 1912. But I would take oath, and in that very room where they keep the sphygmomanometer, that a good third of this was told me and a richer two-thirds intimated on that very Monday afternoon when, returning from a short journey to the barber's, I found Mark waiting in my apartment. And I would further swear, although I am sure the sensitive hand of the lie-detector would record an Alpine sweep at the satement, that he had yielded to the charm of old porcelain. For the second time I discovered him in my drawing-room, his hands stretched toward my favorite shelf. I cleared my throat before entering. He turned with a rueful smile.

"Don't look so sheepish," I admonished. "I'll never tell them at the Police Department that you're acquiring taste."

His eyes shot red sparks. "Do you know what Doctor Sigmund Freud said about collectors?"

"I know what Doctor Waldo Lydecker thinks of people who quote Freud." We sat down. "To what kind whim of Fate do I owe this unexpected visit?"

"I happened to be passing by."

My spirits rose. This casual visit was not without a certain warm note of flattery. Yesterday's disapproval had melted like an ice-cube surprised by a shower of hot coffee. But even as I hastened to fetch whiskey for my guest, I cautioned myself against an injudicious display of enthusiasm. Whereas a detective may be a unique and even trustworthy friend, one must always remember that he has made a profession of curiosity.

"I've been with Shelby Carpenter," he announced as we drank a small toast to the solution of the mystery.

"Indeed," said I, assuming the air of a cool but not ungracious citizen who cherishes a modicum of privacy.

"Does he know anything about music?"

"He talks a music-lover's patter, but his information is shallow. You'll probably find him raising ecstatic eyes to heaven at the name of Beethoven and shuddering piously if someone should be so indiscreet as to mention Ethelbert Nevin."

"Would he know the difference—" Mark consulted his notebook "—between 'Finlandia' by Si-bee-lee-us and 'Toccata and Fugue' by Johann Sebastian Bach?"

"Anyone who can't distinguish between Sibelius and Bach, my dear fellow, is fit for treason, stratagem, and spoils."

"I'm a cluck when it comes to music. Duke Ellington's my soup." He offered a sheet from his notebook. "This is what Carpenter told me they were playing on Friday night. He didn't bother to check on the program. This is what they played."

I drew a sharp breath.

"It shoots his alibi as full of holes as a mosquito net. But it still doesn't prove he murdered her," Mark reminded me with righteous sharpness.

I poured him another drink. "Come, now, you haven't told me what you think of Shelby Carpenter."

"It's a shame he isn't a cop."

I cast discretion to the wind. Clapping him on the shoulder, I cried zestfully: "My dear lad, you are precious! A cop! The flower of old Kentucky! Mah deah suh, the ghosts of a legion of Confederate Colonels rise up to haunt you. Old Missy is whirling in her grave. Come, another drink on that, my astute young Hawkshaw. Properly we should be drinking mint juleps, but unfortunately Uncle Tom of Manila has lost the secret." And I went off into roars of unrestrained appreciation.

He regarded my mirth with some skepticism. "He's got all the physical requirements. And you wouldn't have to teach him to be polite."

"And fancy him in a uniform," I added, my imagination rollicking. "I can see him on the corner of Fifth Avenue where Art meets Bergdorf-Goodman. What a tangle of traffic at the hour when the cars roll in from Westchester to meet the husbands! There would be no less rioting in Wall Street, I can tell you, than on a certain historic day in '29."

"There are a lot of people who haven't got the brains for their college educations."

LAURA

The comment, while uttered honestly, was tinged faintly with the verdigris of envy. "The trouble is that they've been brought up with ideas of class and education so they can't relax and work in common jobs. There are plenty of fellows in these fancy offices who'd be a lot happier working in filling stations."

"I've seen many of them break under the strain of intelligence," I agreed. "Hundreds have been committed for life to the cocktail bars of Madison Avenue. There ought to be a special department in Washington to handle the problem of old Princeton men. I dare say Shelby looks down with no little condescension upon your profession."

A curt nod rewarded my astuteness. Mr. McPherson did not fancy Mr. Carpenter, but, as he had sternly reminded me on a former occasion, it was his business to observe rather than to judge the people encountered in professional adventure.

"The only thing that worries me, Mr. Lydecker, is that I can't place the guy. I've seen that face before. But where and when? Usually I'm a fool for faces. I can give you names and dates and the places I've seen them." His jaw shot forward and his lips pressed themselves into the tight mould of determination.

I laughed with secret tolerance as he gave me what he considered an objective picture of his visit to the offices of Rose, Rowe and Sanders, Advertising Counsellors. In that hot-air-conditioned atmosphere he must have seemed as alien as a share-cropper in a night club. He tried hard not to show disapproval, but opinion was as natural to him as appetite. There was fine juicy prejudice in his portrait of three advertising executives pretending to be dismayed by the notoriety of a front-page murder. While they mourned her death, Laura's bosses were not unaware of the publicity value of a crime which cast no shadow upon their own respectability.

"I bet they had a conference and decided that a high-class murder wouldn't lose any business."

"And considered the titillating confidences they could whisper to prospective clients at lunch," I added.

Mark's malice was impudent. Bosses aroused no respect in his savage breast. His proletarian prejudices were as rigid as any you will find in the upper reaches of so-called Society. It pleased him more to discover sincere praise and mourning among her fellow-workers than to hear her employers' high estimate of Laura's character and talents. Anyone who was smart, he opined, could please the boss, but it took the real stuff for a girl in a high-class job to be popular with her fellow-employees.

"So you think Laura had the real stuff?"

He affected deafness. I studied his face, but caught no shadow of conflict. It was not until several hours later that I reviewed the conversation and reflected upon the fact that he was shaping Laura's character to fit his attitudes as a young man might when enamored of a living woman. My mind was clear and penetrating at the time, for it was midnight, the hour at which I am most brave and most free. Since I learned some years ago that the terrors of insomnia could be overcome by a half-hour's brisk walk, I have not once allowed lassitude, weather, nor the sorry events of a disappointing day to interfere with this nocturnal practice. By habit I chose a street which had become important to me since Laura moved into that apartment.

Naturally I was shocked to see a light

burning in the house of the dead; but after a moment's reflection, I knew that a young man who had once scorned overtime had given his heart to a job.

CHAPTER SIX

Two rituals on Tuesday marked the passing of Laura Hunt. The first, a command performance in the coroner's office, gathered together that small and none too congenial group who had been concerned in the activities of her last day of life. Because she had failed me in that final moment, I was honored with an invitation. I shall not attempt to report the unimaginative proceedings which went to hideous lengths to prove a fact that everyone had known from the start—that Laura Hunt was dead; the cause, murder by the hand of an unknown assailant.

The second ritual, her funeral, took place that afternoon in the chapel of W. W. Heatherstone and Son. Old Heatherstone, long experienced in the interment of movie

stars, ward leaders, and successful gangsters, supervised the arrangements so that
there might be a semblance of order among
the morbid who started their clamor at his
doors at eight o'clock in the morning.

Mark had asked me to meet him on the
balcony that overlooked the chapel.

"But I don't attend funerals."

"She was your friend."

"Laura was far too considerate to demand that anyone venture out at such a
barbaric hour and to exhibit emotions
which, if earnest, are far too personal for
scrutiny."

"But I wanted you to help me identify
some of the people whose names are in
her address book."

"Do you think the murderer will be
there?"

"It's possible."

"How'd we know him? Do you think he
might swoon at the bier?"

"Will you come?"

"No," I said firmly, and added, "Let Shelby
help you this time."

"He's chief mourner. You must come. No
one will see you. Use the side entrance and

tell them you're meeting me. I'll be on the balcony."

Her friends had loved Laura and been desolate at her passing, but they would not have been human if they had failed to enjoy the excitement. Like Mark, they hoped for some crisis of discovery. Eyes that should have been downcast in grief and piety were sliding this way and that in the hope of perceiving the flushed countenance, the guilty gesture that would enable lips, later, to boast, "I knew it the moment I saw that sly face and noted the way he rubbed his hands together during the Twenty-Third Psalm."

She lay in a coffin covered in white silk. Pale ringless hands had been folded against the lavender-tinted white moiré of her favorite evening gown. An arrangement of gardenias, draped like a confirmation veil, covered the ruined face. The only mourners deserving seats in the section reserved for deepest suffering were Auntie Sue and Shelby Carpenter. Her sister, brother-in-law, and some far-western cousins had been unwilling or unable to make the long journey for the sake of this hour in the mortuary. After the service was read,

the organ pealed and Heatherstone atten-
dants wheeled the casket into a private
chamber from which it was later trans-
ferred to the crematorium.

It is from the lush sentimentality of the
newspaper versions that I prune this brief
account of the obsequies. I did not attend.
Mark waited in vain.

As he descended from the balcony and
joined the slowly moving mass, he noted
a hand, gloved in black, signalling him.
Bessie Clary pushed her way through the
crowd.

"I got something to tell you, Mr. Mc-
Pherson."

He took her arm. "Shall we go upstairs
where it's quiet or does this place depress
you?"

"If you wouldn't mind, we could go back
to the flat," Bessie suggested. "It's up
there, what I got to show you."

Mark had his car. Bessie sat beside him
primly, black gloved hands folded in the lap
of her black silk dress.

"It's hot enough to kill a cat," she said by
way of making conversation.

"What have you got to tell me?"

"You needn't to yell at me. I ain't afraid of

cops, or dicks either." She drew out her best handkerchief and blew such a clarion note that her nose seemed an instrument fashioned for the purpose of sounding defiance. "I was brought up to spit whenever I saw one."

"I was brought up to hate the Irish," Mark observed, "but I'm a grown man now. I haven't asked for love, Miss Clary. What is it you want to tell me?"

"You won't get on my good side by that Miss Clary stuff either. Bessie's my name, I'm domestic and I got nothing to be ashamed of."

They drove across the Park in silence. When they passed the policeman who stood guard at the door of Laura's house, Bessie smiled down upon him with virtuous hauteur. Once in the apartment, she assumed the airs of ownership, raised windows, adjusted curtains, emptied trays filled with ashes from Mark's pipe.

"Cops, brought up in barns," she sniffed as she drew hatpins from out of the structure that rode high on her head. "Don't know how to act when they get in a decent house." When she had drawn off black gloves, folded them and stored them in her bag, settled herself on the straightest chair, and fixed a glassy stare upon his face, she asked, "What do they do to people that hide something from the cops?"

The question, so humble in contrast with her belligerence, provided him with a weapon. "So you've been trying to shield the murderer? That's dangerous, Bessie!"

Her knotted hands unfolded. "What makes you think I know the murderer?"

"By hiding evidence, you have become an accessory after the fact. What is the evidence, and what was your purpose in concealing it?"

Bessie turned her eyes ceilingward as though she expected help from heaven. "If I'd hold out on you, you'd never know nothing about it. And if they hadn't played that music at the funeral, I'd never've told you. Church music makes me soft."

"Whom were you shielding, Bessie?"

"Her."

"Miss Hunt?"

Bessie nodded grimly.

"Why, Bessie? She's dead."

"Her reputation ain't," Bessie observed righteously and went to the corner cabinet, in which Laura had always kept a small stock of liquor. "Just look at this."

Mark leaped. "Hey, be careful. There may be fingerprints."

Bessie laughed. "Maybe there was a lot of fingerprints around here! But the cops never seen them."

"You wiped them off, Bessie? For God's sakes!"

"That ain't all I wiped off," Bessie chuckled. "I cleaned off the bed and table in there and the bathroom before the cops come."

Mark seized bony wrists. "I've a good mind to take you into custody."

She pulled her hands away. "I don't believe in fingerprints anyway. All Saturday afternoon the cops was sprinkling white powder around my clean flat. Didn't do them no good because I polished all the furniture on Friday after she'd went to the office. If they found any fingerprints, they was mine."

"If you don't believe in fingerprints, why were you so anxious to get rid of those in the bedroom?"

"Cops got dirty minds. I don't want the whole world thinking she was the kind that got drunk with a fellow in her bedroom, God rest her soul."

"Drunk in her bedroom? Bessie, what does this mean?"

"So help me," Bessie swore, "there was two glasses."

He seized her wrists again. "Why are you making up this story, Bessie? What have you to gain by it?"

Hers was the hauteur of an enraged duchess. "What right you got to yell at me? You don't believe me, huh? Say, I was the one that cared about her reputation. You never even knew her. What are you getting so mad about?"

Mark retreated, the sudden display of temper puzzling and shaming him. His fury had grown out of all proportions to its cause.

Bessie drew out a bottle. "Where do you think I found this? Right there." She pointed through the open door to the bed-room. "On the table by the bed. With two dirty glasses."

Laura's bedroom was as chaste and peaceful as the chamber of a young girl whose experience of love has been con-fined to sonnets, dreams, and a diary. The white Swiss spread lay smooth and starched, the pillow rounded neatly at the polished pine headboard, a white-and-blue knitted afghan folded at the foot.

"I cleaned up the room and washed the glasses before the first cop got here. Lucky I come to my senses in time," Bessie sniffed. "The bottle I put in the cabinet so's no one would notice. It wasn't her kind of liquor. I can tell you this much, Mr. McPherson, this here bottle was brought in after I left on Friday."

Mark examined the bottle. It was Three Horses Bourbon, a brand favored by frugal tipplers. "Are you sure, Bessie? How do you know? You must keep close watch on the liquor that's used in this place."

Bessie's iron jaw shot forward; cords stiffened in her bony neck. "If you don't believe me, ask Mr. Mosconi, the liquor fellow over on Third Avenue. We always got ours from Mosconi, better stuff than this, I'm telling you. She always left me the list and I ordered on the phone. This here's the brand we use." She swung the doors wider and revealed, among the neatly arranged bottles, four unopened fifths of J and D

Blue Grass Bourbon, the brand which I had taught her to buy.

Such unexpected evidence, throwing unmistakable light on the last moments of the murdered, should have gladdened the detective heart. Contrarily, Mark found himself loath to accept the facts. This was not because he had reason to disbelieve Bessie's story, but because the sordid character of her revelations had dis-arranged the pattern of his thinking. Last night, alone in the apartment, he had made unscientific investigation of Laura's clos-ets, chests of drawers, dressing-table, and bathroom. He knew Laura, not only with his intelligence, but with his senses. His fin-gers had touched fabrics that had known her body, his ears had heard the rustle of her silks, his nostrils sniffed at the varied, heady fragrances of her perfumes. Never before had the stern young Scot known a woman in this fashion. Just as her library had revealed the quality of her mind, the boudoir had yielded the secrets of feminine personality.

He did not like to think of her drinking with a man in her bedroom like a cutie in a hotel.

In his coldest, most official voice he said, "If there was someone in the bedroom with her, we have a completely new picture of the crime."

"You mean it wasn't like you said in the paper, that it must have happened when the doorbell rang and she went to open it?"

"I accepted that as the most probable explanation, considering the body's position." He crossed from the bedroom slowly, his eyes upon the arrangement of carpets on the polished floor. "If a man had been in the bedroom with her, he might have been on the point of leaving. She went to the door with him, perhaps." He stood rigid at the spot where the river of dark blood had been dammed by the thick pile of the carpet. "Perhaps they were quarreling and, just as he reached the door, he turned and shot her."

"Gosh," said Bessie, blowing her nose weakly, "it gives you the creeps, don't it?"

From the wall Stuart Jacoby's portrait smiled down.

CHAPTER SEVEN

On Wednesday afternoon, twenty-four hours after the funeral, Lancaster Corey came to see me. I found him contemplating my porcelains lustfully.

"Corey, my good fellow, to what do I owe this dispensation?"

We wrung each other's hands like long-lost brothers.

"I'll not mince words, Waldo. I've come on business."

"I smelled sulphur and brimstone. Have a drink before you reveal your diabolical schemes."

He twisted the end of his white, crisp mustache. "I've got a great opportunity for you, my good friend. You know Jacoby's work. Getting more valuable every day."

I made a sound with my lips.

"It's not that I'm trying to sell you a picture. As a matter of fact, I've already got a buyer. You know Jacoby's portrait of Laura Hunt . . . several of the papers carried reproductions after the murder. Tragic, wasn't it? Since you were so attached to the lady, I thought you'd want to bid before . . ."

"I knew there was something divine about your visit, Corey. Now I see that it's your insolence."

He shrugged off the insult. "Merely a courtesy."

"How dare you?" I shouted. "How dare you come to my house and coolly offer me that worthless canvas? In the first place, I consider it a bad imitation of Speicher. In the second place, I deplore Speicher. And in the third, I loathe portraits in oil."

"Very well. I shall feel free to sell it to my other buyer." He snatched up his Fedora.

"Wait a minute," I commanded. "How can you offer what you don't own? That picture is hanging on the wall of her apartment now. She died without a will, the lawyers will have to fight it out."

"I believe that Mrs. Treadwell, her aunt, is assuming responsibility for the family. You might communicate with her or with

Salsbury, Haskins, Warder, and Bone, her attorneys. The landlord, I heard this morning, had released the estate from its obligation to fulfill the lease on condition that the apartment is vacated by the first of the month. They're going to make a special effort to hurry the proceedings . . ."

His knowledge infuriated me. "The vultures gather!" I shouted, smacking my forehead with an anguished palm. And a moment later cried out in alarm: "Do you know what arrangements have been made for her other things? Whether there's to be a sale?"

"This bid came through a private channel. Someone who had seen the portrait in her apartment, no doubt, made inquiries of several dealers. He hadn't known that we were Jacoby's agents . . ."

"His taste makes it clear that he knows very little about painting."

Corey made a purse of his lips. "Everyone is not as prejudiced as you are, Waldo. I prophesy the day when Jacoby will be worth real money."

"Comfort yourself, my sweet buzzard. Both you and I shall be dead by that time. But tell me," I continued mockingly, "is your prospective sucker some connoisseur who saw the picture in the Sunday tabloids and wants to own the portrait of a murder victim?"

"I do not believe that it would be strictly ethical to give my customer's name."

"Your pardon, Corey. My question must have shocked your delicate sensibilities of a business man. Unfortunately I shall have to write the story without using names."

Lancaster Corey responded like a hunting dog to the smell of rabbit. "What story?"

"You have just given me material for a magnificent piece!" I cried, simulating creative excitement. "An ironic small story about the struggling young painter whose genius goes unrecognized until one of his sitters is violently murdered. And suddenly he, because he had done her portrait, becomes the painter of the year. His name is not only on the lips of collectors, but the public, the public, Corey, know him as they know Mickey Rooney. His prices skyrocket, fashionable women beg to sit for him, he is reproduced in *Life, Vogue, Town and Country* . . ."

My fantasy so titivated his greed that he

could no longer show pride. "You've got to mention Jacoby's name. The story would be meaningless without it."

"And a footnote, no doubt, explaining that his works are on view in the galleries of Lancaster Corey."

"That wouldn't hurt."

I spoke bitterly. "Your point of view is painfully commercial. Such considerations never enter my mind. Art, Corey, endures. All else passes. My piece would be as vivid and original as a Jacoby portrait."

"Just include his name. One mention of it," Corey pleaded.

"That inclusion would remove my story from the realms of literature and place it in the category of journalism. In that case, I'd have to know the facts, even if I did not include all of them. To protect my reputation for veracity, you understand."

"You've won," Corey admitted and whispered the art-lover's name.

I sank upon the Biedermeier, laughing as I had not laughed since Laura had been here to share such merry secrets of human frailty.

Along with this genial and amusing tidbit, Corey had, however, brought some distressing information. As soon as I had got rid of him, I changed my clothes, seized hat and stick, and bade Roberto summon a taxi.

Hence to Laura's apartment, where I found not only Mrs. Treadwell, whom I had expected to find there, but Shelby and the Pomeranian. Laura's aunt was musing on the value of the few genuinely antique pieces, Shelby taking inventory, and the dog sniffing chair legs.

"To what do we owe this unexpected pleasure?" cried Mrs. Treadwell, who, in spite of expressing open disapproval of my friendship with her niece, had always fluttered before my fame.

"To cupidity, dear lady. I have come to share the booty."

"This is a painful task." She sank back into an upholstered chair watching, through heavily blackened lashes, my every movement and glance. "But my lawyer simply insists."

"How generous of you!" I chattered. "You spare yourself no pains. In spite of grief and sentiment, you carry on bravely. I dare say you'll account for every button in poor Laura's wardrobe."

A key turned in the lock. We assumed postures of piety as Mark entered.

"Your men let us in, Mr. McPherson," explained Mrs. Treadwell. "I called your office, but you weren't in. I hope there's nothing wrong about our . . . our attempt to bring order. Poor Laura was so careless, she never knew what she owned."

"I gave orders to let you in if you came," Mark told her. "I hope you've found everything as it should be."

"Someone has been in the closet. One of the dresses has fallen off the hook and perfume was spilled."

"The police are heavy-handed," was my innocent observation.

Mark, I thought, took extra pains to appear nonchalant.

"There's nothing of great value," Mrs. Treadwell remarked. "Laura would never put her money into things that lasted. But there are certain trinkets, souvenirs that people might appropriate for sentimental reasons." She smiled so sweetly in my direction that I knew she suspected the reason for my presence.

I took direct action. "Perhaps you know, Mrs. Treadwell, that this vase did not belong to Laura." I nodded toward the mercury glass globe upon the mantel. "I'd merely lent it to her."

"Now, Waldo, don't be naughty. I saw you bring that vase on Christmas, all tied up in red ribbons. You must remember, Shelby."

Shelby looked up as if he had not heard the argument. The rôle of innocence, he knew by experience, would protect him equally from my wit and her revenge. "Sorry, darling, I didn't hear what you were saying." He returned to his inventories.

"Not ribbons, dear lady. There was a string tied to my Christmas package. Laura wasn't to give it away. You know that Spanish prodigality of hers, handing things to anyone who admired them. This vase is part of my collection and I intend to take it now. That's quite in order, don't you think, McPherson?"

"You'd better leave it. You might find yourself in trouble," Mark said.

"How petty-official of you! You're acting like a detective."

He shrugged as if my good opinion were of no importance. I laughed and turned the talk to inquiry about the progress of his work. Had he found any clues that might lead to the murderer's house?

"Plenty," he taunted.

"Oh, do tell us," Mrs. Treadwell begged, sliding forward in her chair and clasping her hands together in a gesture of rapturous attention. Shelby had climbed upon a chair so that he might record the titles of volumes on the topmost bookshelf. From this vantage-point, he glanced down at Mark with fearless curiosity. The Pomeranian sniffed at the detective's trousers. All awaited revelation. All Mark said was, "I hope you don't mind," and took out his pipe. The snub was meant to arouse fear and bid us mind the majesty of the law.

I seized the moment for my own. "It might interest you to know that I've got a clue." My eyes were fixed on Mrs. Treadwell, but beyond her floating veil the mirror showed me Mark's guarded countenance.

"Do you know there's an art-lover connected with this case? As probable heir, Mrs. Treadwell, you might be pleased to know that this little museum piece—" I directed her attention to the Jacoby portrait "—has already been bid for."

"Really! How much?"

"I'd keep the price up if I were you. The portrait may have a sentimental value for the buyer."

"Who is it?" asked Shelby.

"Someone with money? Could we ask a thousand?" demanded Mrs. Treadwell.

Mark used the pipe as a shield for self-consciousness. Behind his cupped hand, I noted rising color. A man girding himself for the torture chamber could not have shown greater dignity.

"Someone we know?"

"Do you think there might be a clue in it?" I asked mischievously. "If this is a *crime passionnel*, the killer might be a man of sentiment. Don't you think the lead's worth following, McPherson?"

His answer was something between a grunt and a sigh.

"It's terribly exciting," said Mrs. Treadwell. "You've got to tell me, Waldo, you've just got to."

I was never a child to torture butterflies. The death agonies of small fish have never been a sight that I witnessed with pleasure. I remember blanching with terror and scurrying across the lane when, during an ill-advised visit to a farm, I was forced to watch a decapitated chicken running around and around its astonished head. Even on the stage I prefer death to follow a swift, clean stroke of a sharp blade. To spare Mark's blushes I spoke hastily and with the air of gravity: "I cannot betray the confidence of Lancaster Corey. An art dealer is, after all, somewhat in the position of a doctor or lawyer. In matters of taste, discretion is the better part of profit."

I sought his eyes, but Mark turned away. His next move, I thought, was meant to divert conversation, but I learned later that he had had a definite purpose in meeting Shelby here this afternoon.

"I've been working and could use a drink," he announced. "As chief trustee, Mrs. Treadwell, would you mind if I took some of Miss Hunt's liquor?"

"How stingy you make me sound! Shelby, darling, be useful. I wonder if the icebox is turned on."

Shelby leaped from his perch and went into the kitchen. Mark opened the corner cabinet.

"He certainly knows his way about this apartment," I observed.

He paid no attention. "What do you drink,

Mrs. Treadwell? Yours is Scotch, isn't it, Lydecker?"

He waited until Shelby returned before he brought out the Bourbon. "I think I'll drink this today. What's yours, Carpenter?"

Shelby glanced at the bottle, decorated with the profiles of three noble steeds. His hands tensed, but he could not hold them steady enough to keep the glasses from rattling on the tray.

"None—for—me—thanks."

The softness had fled his voice. He was as harsh as metal, and his chiseled features, robbed of color, had the marble virtue of a statue erected to the honor of a dead Victorian.

CHAPTER EIGHT

Mark asked me to dine with him that night.

"But I thought you were displeased with me."

"Why?"

"I failed you at the funeral."

"I know how you felt." His hand lay for a moment upon my coat-sleeve.

"Then why didn't you help me get my vase away from that she-vulture?"

"I was being petty-official," he teased. "I'd like to take you to dinner, Mr. Lydecker. Will you come?"

He carried a book in his coat-pocket. I saw only the top inch of the binding, but unless I was mistaken, it was the work of a not unfamiliar author.

"I am flattered," I remarked with a jocular nod toward the bulging pocket.

He fingered the book, with some affection, I fancied.

"Have you read it yet, McPherson?" He nodded. "And do you still consider me smooth but trivial?"

"Sometimes you're not bad," he conceded.

"Your flattery overwhelms me," I retorted. "And where shall we dine?"

His car was open and he drove so wildly that I clung with one hand to the door, with the other to my black Homburg. I wondered why he chose the narrowest streets in the slums until I saw the red neon above Montagnino's door. Montagnino himself met us and to my surprise greeted Mark as an honored customer. I saw then that it would take little effort to guide him along the road of good taste. We passed through a corridor steamy with the odors of tomato paste, peppers, and oregano to the garden, which was, on this incredible night, only a few degrees cooler than the kitchen; with the air of a Caesar conferring honor upon pet commoners, Montagnino led us to a table beside a trellis twined with artificial lilac. Through the dusty wooden lattice and weary cotton vines we witnessed a battle between the hordes of angry clouds and a fierce copper moon. The leaves of the one living tree in the neighborhood, a skinny catalpa, hung like the black bones of skeleton hands, as dead as the cotton lilac. With the flavors of Montagnino's kitchen and the slum smells was mingled the sulphurous odor of the rising storm.

We dined on mussels cooked with mustard greens in Chianti and a chicken, fried in olive oil, laid upon a bed of yellow taglierini and garlanded with mushrooms and red peppers. At my suggestion we drank that pale still wine with the magic name, *Lacrymae Christi*. Mark had never tasted it, but once his tongue had tested and approved the golden flavor, he tossed it off like Scotch whiskey. He came of a race of drinkers who look contemptuously upon an alcoholic content of twelve per cent, unaware that the fermented grape works its enchantments more subtly than the distilled spirits of grain. I do not imply that he was drunk; let us say, rather, that the Tears of Christ opened his heart. He became less Scottish and more boyish; less the professional detective and more the youth in need of a confidant.

I remarked that I had dined here with Laura. We had eaten the same food at this very table. The same weary cotton leaves had hung above her head. The place had been one of her favorites. Had he guessed it when he planned the dinner?

He shrugged. A mechanical contrivance filled the restaurant with music and sent faint melody into the garden. Noel Coward wrote an unforgettable line (whose precise wording I have forgotten) upon the ineluctable charm of old popular songs. That is why, I venture to say, a nation sways to George Gershwin while the good works of Calvin Coolidge have become arid words in unread volumes. Old tunes had been as much a part of Laura as her laughter. Her mind had been a fulsome catalogue of musical trivia. A hearty and unashamed lowbrow, she had listened to Brahms but had heard Kern. Her one Great had been Bach, whom she learned to cherish, believe it or not, by listening to a Benny Goodman record.

When I mentioned this to Mark, he nodded gravely and said, "Yep, I know."

"What do you know and how do you know so much?" I demanded, suddenly outraged by his superior airs. "You act as though you'd been Laura's friend for years."

"I looked at her records," he said. "I even played some of them. Make what you want of that, Mr. Lydecker."

I poured him another glass of wine. His belligerency dwindled and it was not long afterward that he poured forth the revelations recorded in foregoing chapters: the scene with Bessie; his annoyance at the clumsy flattery of the girl reporter; the sudden interest in painting which had caused him to discover Lancaster Corey and ask the price of the Jacoby portrait; and finally, with the second bottle of wine, of Shelby Carpenter.

I confess that I was not without guilt in plying him with liquor and provocative questions. We discussed the insurance policy, the false alibi, and, at my subtle instigation, Shelby's familiarity with firearms.

"He's quite the sporting type, you know. Hunting, shooting, and all that. Once had a collection of guns, I believe."

Mark nodded knowingly.

"Have you checked on them? How do you go about getting all these items of information? Or did Shelby confess that, too?"

"I'm a detective. What do you think I do with my time? It was a simple matter of two and two on the guns. Photographs in her album and storage receipts in his room at the Framingham. He went up to the warehouse with me himself on Monday and we looked over the arsenal. His father used to hunt foxes in a red coat, he told me."

"Well?" I awaited revelation.

"According to the records in the warehouse, nothing had been touched for over a year. Most of the stuff showed rust and the dust was an inch thick."

"Of course a man might have guns that he didn't put into a warehouse for safekeeping."

"He's not the type to use a sawed-off shotgun."

"A sawed-off shotgun!" I exclaimed. "Do you know positively?"

"We know nothing *positively*." He underscored the adverb brusquely. "But where do you use BB shot?"

"I'm no sportsman," I confessed.

"Imagine anyone trying to carry a shotgun around the streets of this town. How could he get away with it?"

"Sawed-off shotguns are carried by gangsters," I observed. "At least according to the education I've received at that fount of popular learning, the movies."

"Did Laura know any gangsters?"

"In a way, McPherson, we're all gangsters. We all have our confederates and our sworn foes, our loyalties and our enmities. We have our pasts to shed and our futures to protect."

"In the advertising business they use different weapons," he observed.

"If a man were desperate, might he not sacrifice sportsmanship for the nonce and step out of his class? And tell me, McPherson, just how does one saw off a sawed-off shotgun?"

My plea for practical information was disregarded. Mark became guarded again. I spoke of the insurance policy.

"Shelby's eagerness to tell you about it was undoubtedly a device for disarming you with his charming frankness."

"I've thought of that."

The music changed. My hand, holding a wineglass, was stayed on its journey to my lips. My face was drained of color. In the bewildered countenance of my companion I caught a reflection of my pallor.

Yellow hands slid coffee-cups across the table. At the next table a woman laughed. The moon had lost its battle with the clouds and retreated, leaving no trace of copper brilliance in the ominous sky. The air had grown heavier. In the window of a tenement a slim girl stood, her angular dark silhouette sharpened by a naked electric bulb.

At the table on our left a woman was singing:

> So I smile and say,
> When a lovely flame dies,
> Smoke gets in your eyes.

Fixing offended eyes upon her face, I spoke in my courtliest tones. "Madame, if you would spare the eardrums of one who heard Tamara introduce that enchanting song, you will restrain your clumsy efforts at imitation."

She made a remark and gesture which, lest my readers be squeamish, I shall not describe. Mark's eyes were fixed on my face with the squinting attentiveness of a scientist at a microscope.

I laughed and said hastily: "That melody is significant. Common as it has become, it has never lost a peculiarly individual flavor. Jerry Kern has never surpassed it, you know."

"The first time you heard it you were with Laura," Mark said.

"How astute of you!"

"I'm getting used to your ways, Mr. Lydecker."

"You shall be rewarded," I promised, "by the story of that night."

"Go on."

"It was in the fall '33, you know, that Max Gordon put on the show, *Roberta*, book by Hammerstein Junior after a novel by Alice Duer Miller. Trivia, of course, but, as we know, there is no lack of sustenance in whipped cream. It was Laura's first opening night. She was no end excited, her eyes burning like a child's, her voice rising in adolescent squeaks as I pointed out this and that human creature who had been, until that night, magic names to the little girl from Colorado Springs. She wore a gown of champagne-colored chiffon and jade-colored slippers. Extraordinarily effective with her eyes and hair.

" 'Laura, my precious babe,' I said to her, 'we shall drink to your frock in champagne.' It was her first taste of it, Mc-Pherson. Her pleasure gave me the sensation that God must know when He transforms the blasts of March into the melting winds of April.

"Add to this mood a show which is all glitter and chic, and top it with the bittersweet froth of song, throatily sung by a Russian girl with a guitar. I felt a small warmth upon my hand, and then, as the song continued, a pressure that filled me with swelling ecstasy. Do you think this a shameful confession? A man of my sort has many easy emotions—I have been known to shout with equal fervor over the Beethoven Ninth or a penny lollypop—but few great moments. But I swear to you, McPherson, in this simple sharing of melody we had attained something which few achieve in the more conventional attitudes of affection.

"Her eyes were swimming. Later she told me that she had recently been rejected in love—imagine anyone rejecting Laura.

The fellow, I take it, was rather insensitive. She had, alas, a low taste in love. Through the confession I clung to her hand tightly, that small, tender hand which held such extraordinary firmness that she used to say it was slightly masculine. But the elements are so mixed in us, McPherson, that Nature must blush to quote Shakespeare when she stands and says to all the world, 'This was a man!' "

The music flowed between the white dusty boards of the trellis, through vines of artificial lilac. I had never before spoken aloud nor written of the reverie which had filled me since that night with Laura at the theatre, yet I felt certain security in entrusting it to a man whose nostalgia was concerned with a woman whose face he had never seen.

At long last the song ceased. Freed from pensive memories, I drained my glass and returned to the less oppressive topic of murder. I had by this time sufficient command of myself to speak of the scene we had witnessed in Laura's room and of Shelby's pallor at the sight of the Bourbon bottle. Mark said that the evidence gathered thus far was too circumstantial and frail to give substance to a case against the bridegroom.

"Do tell me this, McPherson. In your opinion is he guilty?"

I had given myself freely. In return I expected frankness. He answered with an insolent smile.

I set to work on his emotions. "Poor Laura," I sighed. "How ironic for her if it actually was Shelby! After having loved so generously, to discover treachery. Those last hideous moments before she died!"

"Death was almost instantaneous. Within a few seconds she was unconscious."

"You're pleased, Mark, aren't you? You're glad to know she had no time to regret the love she had given?"

He said icily, "I've expressed no such opinion."

"Don't be ashamed. Your heart's no softer than any other Scot's. Sir Walter and Sir James would have been delighted with you. A nature rocky as the hills, a tombstone and a wee bit o' heather."

"You rockbound Americans, you're sentimental like worms." Bony hands gripped the table. "Let's have another drink."

I suggested Courvoisier.

"You order. I can't pronounce it."

After a short pause, he said: "Listen, Mr. Lydecker, there's one thing I want to know. Why did she keep putting off the wedding? She was crazy about him, she had pictures of him all over the place, and still she kept postponing it. Why?"

"The familiar curse of gold."

He shook his head. "Carpenter and I have gone into that. The guy's fairly decent about it, if a man can be decent and take money from a woman. But this is what gets me. They're going together for a hell of a long time and at last they decide to break down and get married. So she plans a vacation and a honeymoon, and then has to have a week by herself before she goes through with it. What was holding her back?"

"She was tired. She wanted to rest."

"When everyone says the same thing and it's the easiest answer, you know damn well it's baloney."

"Are you suggesting that Laura might have been seeking excuses for postponing the wedding? That she wasn't awaiting the great day with the tremulous expectancy of a happy bride?"

"Could be."

"Strange," I sighed. "Incredibly strange and tragic for us to be sitting here, at this very table, under these same weary lilacs, listening to her favorite tunes and stewing over our jealousy. She's dead, man, dead!"

Nervous hands toyed with the stem of the brandy snifter. Then, with his dark eyes piercing the gossamer of my defenses, he asked, "If you were so crazy about her, why didn't you do something about Shelby?"

I met this scrutiny contemptuously.

"Why?"

"Laura was a grown woman. Her freedom was dear to her and jealously guarded. She knew her own heart. Or thought she did."

"If I had known her . . ." he began in a voice of masculine omnipotence, but paused, leaving the rest unsaid.

"What a contradictory person you are, McPherson!"

"Contradictory!" He tossed the word into the very centre of the garden. Several diners stared at us. "I'm contradictory. Well, what about the rest of you? And what about her? Wherever you turn, a contradiction."

"It's the contradictions that make her seem alive to you. Life itself is contradictory. Only death is consistent."

With a great sigh he unburdened himself of another weighty question. "Did she ever talk to you about *Gulliver*?"

My mind leaped nimbly in pursuit. "It's one of your favorites, too, I take it."

"How do you know that?" he challenged.

"Your boasted powers of observation are failing sadly, my dear fellow, if you failed to notice that I took care to see what volume it was that you examined so scrupulously in her apartment on Sunday afternoon. I knew that book well. It was an old copy and I had it rebound for her in red morocco."

He smiled shyly. "I knew you were spying on me."

"You said nothing, because you wished to let me think it was a murder clue you sought among the Lilliputians. If it gives you pleasure, young man, I'll confirm the hope that she shared your literary enthusiasms."

His gratitude was charming. I counted the days that had passed since he had spoken of Laura as a two-timing dame. Had I reminded him tonight, I dare say he would have punched my face.

The genial combination of good food, wine, music, brandy, and sympathy had corrupted his defenses. He spoke with touching frankness. "We lived within half a mile of each other for over three years. Must have taken the same bus, the same subway, passed each other on the street hundreds of times. She went to Schwartz's for her drugs, too."

"Remarkable coincidence," I said.

The irony was lost. He had surrendered.

"We must have passed each other on the street often."

It was a slender morsel of consolation he had found among all the grim facts. I resolved then and there to write about this frustrated romance, so fragile and so typical of New York. It was the perfect O. Henry story. I can hear old Sydney Porter coughing himself into a fever over it.

"Wonderful ankles," he muttered, half-aloud. "The first thing I look at is the ankles. Wonderful."

They had turned off the music and most of the diners had left the garden. A couple passed our table. The girl, I noted, had remarkable ankles. Mark did not turn his head. He dwelt, for that brief moment, in the fancy of a meeting at Schwartz's drugstore. He had been buying pipe tobacco and she had put a dime into the postage-stamp machine. She might have dropped her purse. Or perhaps there had been a cinder in her eye. She had uttered but a single word, "Thanks," but for him sweet bells jangled and the harps of heaven were joined in mighty paean. A glance at her ankles, a meeting of their eyes, and it was as simple as with Charles Boyer and Margaret Sullavan.

"Have you ever read my story of Conrad?"[1] I inquired.

My question interrupted the schoolboy reverie. He regarded me with a desolate glance.

"It is a legend told over port and cigars at Philadelphia dining-tables some seventy-five years ago, and whispered in softer tones over tapestry frames and macramé work. The story has of late been attributed to me, but I take no credit. What I am telling

---

[1]"Conrad of Lebanon," in the volume, *February, Which Alone*, by Waldo Lydecker, 1936.

is a tale whose only basis of truth lies in its power over stolid folk celebrated for their honesty and lack of imagination. I refer to the Amish of Pennsylvania.

"Conrad was one of these. A stalwart, earthy lad more given to the cultivation of rutabagas than to flights of superstitious fancy. One day as he worked in the field, he heard a great crash upon the road. Running, hoe in hand, he came upon the confusion attendant upon an accident. A vegetable cart had collided with a smart carriage. To his great surprise Conrad found a woman in his arms in the place of his hoe.

"Among the Amish, who boasted that they were known as *plain*, buttons were considered ungodly ornament. To this moment in his life Conrad had seen only girls in faded ginghams hooked tight across their chests and with hair stretched from their temples into wiry pigtails. He wore a blue work shirt fastened severely to the throat and upon his chin a fringe, like monkey fur, of thin whiskers affected by his people as a mark of piety.

"The injury to the lady's carriage was repaired sooner than the damage to Conrad's heart. Never could he close his eyes without beholding a vision of this creature with her powdered skin, her wanton lips, and mischievous eyes, as black as the ebony stick of her lilac-silk parasol. From that day on, Conrad was no longer content with his pig-tailed neighbors and his rutabagas. He must find Troy and seek Helen. He sold his farm, walked dusty roads to Philadelphia, and being canny as the pious always are, invested his small capital in a lucrative business whose proprietor was willing to teach him the trade.

"Without money, without access to the society frequented by the elegant creature, Conrad was actually no closer to her than he had been at Lebanon. Yet his faith never flagged. He believed, as he believed in evil and sin, that he would again hold her in his arms.

"And the miracle occurred. Before so many years had passed that he was too old to know the joy of fulfillment, he held her close to his breast, his heart pounding with such a savage beat that its vigor gave life to every inanimate thing around him. And once again, as on the hot noon when he first beheld her, the lids lifted like curtains over those dark eyes . . ."

"How did he make it?" Mark inquired. "How did he get to know her?"

I waved aside the interruption. "She had never seemed so lovely as now, and though he had heard her name whispered in the city and knew her reputation to be unsavory, he felt that his eyes had never met such purity as he saw in that marble brow, nor such chastity as was encased in those immobile lips. Let us forgive Conrad his confusion. At such moments a man's mind does not achieve its highest point of logic. Remember, the lady was clothed all in white from the tips of her satin slippers to the crown of blossoms in her dark hair. And the shadows, lilac-tinted, in the shroud . . ."

At the word Mark recoiled.

I fixed my eyes upon him innocently. "Shroud. In those days it was still the custom."

"Was she," he asked, biting down slowly as if each word were poisoned fruit, "dead?"

"Perhaps I neglected to mention that he

had become apprenticed to an undertaker. And while the surgeon had declared her dead before Conrad was called to the dwelling, he afterward . . ."

Mark's eyes were dark holes burning through the white fabric of a mask. His lips puckered as if the poisoned fruit were bitter.

"I cannot tell if the story is true," I said, sensing his unrest and hastening the moral, "but since Conrad came of a people who never encouraged fantasy, one cannot help but pay him the respect of credence. He returned to Lebanon, but the folk around reported that women were forevermore destroyed for him. Had he known and lost a living love, he would never have been so marked as by this short excursion into necrophilia."

Thunder rumbled closer. The sky had become sulphurous. As we left the garden, I touched his arm gently.

"Tell me, McPherson, how much were you prepared to pay for the portrait?"

He turned on me a look of dark malevolence. "Tell me, Lydecker, did you walk past Laura's apartment every night before she was killed, or is it a habit you've developed since her death?"

Thunder crashed above us. The storm was coming closer.

PART TWO

Part Two

CHAPTER ONE

When Waldo Lydecker learned what happened after our dinner at Montagnino's on Wednesday night, he could write no more about the Laura Hunt case. The prose style was knocked right out of him.

He had written the foregoing between ten o'clock on Wednesday night and four on Thursday afternoon with only five hours' sleep, a quart of black coffee, and three hearty meals to keep up his strength. I suppose he had intended to fit the story to one of those typical Lydecker last paragraphs where a brave smile always shows through the tears.

I am going on with the story. My writing won't have the smooth professional touch which, as he would say, distinguishes Waldo Lydecker's prose. God help any of us if we'd tried to write our reports with style. But for once in my life, since this is unofficial anyway, I am going to forget Detective Bureau shorthand and express a few personal opinions. This is my first experience with citizens who get their pictures into that part of the funny papers called the Society Section. Even professionally I've never been inside a night club with leopard-skin covers on the chairs. When these people want to insult each other, they say *darling*, and when they get affectionate they throw around words that a Jefferson Market bailiff wouldn't use to a pimp. Poor people brought up to hear their neighbors screaming filth every Saturday night are more careful of their language than well-bred smart-alecks. I know as many four-letter words as anybody in the business and use them when I feel like it. But not with ladies. Nor in writing. It takes a college education to teach a man that he can put on paper what he used to write on a fence.

I'm starting the story where Waldo ended . . . In Montagnino's back yard after the third brandy.

As we stepped out of the restaurant, the

heat hit us like a blast from a furnace. The air was dead. Not a shirt-tail moved on the washlines of McDougal Street. The town smelled like rotten eggs. A thunderstorm was rolling in.

"Can I drive you home?"

"No, thanks; I feel like walking."

"I'm not drunk. I can drive," I said.

"Have I implied that you're drunk? It's my whim to walk. I'm working tonight." He started off, pounding his stick against the pavement. "Thanks for the feast," he called as I drove off.

I took it slowly because my head was still heavy. I drove past the corner where I should have turned for the Athletic Club, and then I knew that I didn't want to go home. I didn't feel like bowling or pool, my mind wasn't sharp enough for poker, and I've never sat in the lounge in the two years I've lived there. The steel furniture in my bedroom reminded me of a dentist's office. There wasn't a comfortable chair in the room, and if you lay on the couch the cover wrinkled under you. These are all the excuses I can find for going to Laura's apartment that night. Maybe I was just drunk.

Before I went upstairs, I stopped to raise

the top of my car and shut the windows.
Later, when the thing that happened
caused me to question my sanity, I remembered that I had performed the acts of a
sober man. I had the key in my pocket and
I let myself in as coolly as if I'd been entering my own place. As I opened the door I
saw the first streaks of lightning through
the blinds. Thunder crashed. It was followed by the stillness that precedes heavy
rain. I was sweating and my head ached.
I got myself a drink of water from the
kitchen, took off my coat, opened my collar, and stretched in the long chair. The light
hurt my eyes and I turned it off. I fell asleep
before the storm broke.

Thunder sounded like a squadron of
bombers above the roof. Lightning did not
flash away immediately. After a few seconds I saw that it was not lightning at all,
but the lamp with the green shade. I had
not turned it on. I had not moved from the
long chair.

Thunder crashed again. Then I saw her.
She held a rain-streaked hat in one hand
and a pair of light gloves in the other.
Her rain-spattered silk dress was moulded
tight to her body. She was five-foot seven,

weighed about one-thirty, dark eyes slightly slanted, dark hair, and tanned skin. Nothing wrong about her ankles either.

"What are you doing here?" she said.

I couldn't answer.

"What are you doing here?"

I remembered the wine and looked around to see if she'd brought any pink elephants.

"If you don't get out this moment," she said, and her voice trembled, "I'll call the police."

"I am the police," I said.

My voice told me that I was alive. I jerked myself out of the chair. The girl backed away. The picture of Laura Hunt was just behind her.

I had a voice. I spoke with authority. "You're dead."

My wild stare and the strange accusation convinced her that she was facing a dangerous lunatic. She edged toward the door.

"Are you . . ." But I couldn't say the name. She had spoken, she was wet with rain, she had been frightened and had tried to escape. Were these real evidences of life just another set of contradictions?

I don't know how long we stood, facing each other and awaiting revelation. For a crazy half-second I remembered what my grandmother used to tell me about meeting in heaven those whom we had lost on earth. Peal after peal of thunder shook the house. Lightning flashed past the window. The ground seemed to be trembling below us and the skies splitting overhead. This was Laura Hunt's apartment; I felt in my pocket for my pipe.

I had bought a paper. As I unfolded it, I said: "Have you seen any newspapers lately? Don't you know what's happened?" The questions made me feel sane again.

She shrank away, clinging with both hands to the table.

I said: "Please don't be frightened; there must be an explanation. If you haven't seen the papers . . ."

"I haven't. I've been in the country. My radio's broken." And then slowly, as if she were fitting the pieces together, she said: "Why? Do the papers say I'm . . ."

I nodded. She took the paper. There was nothing on Page One. A new battle on the Eastern Front and a speech by Churchill had pushed her off the front pages. I turned to Page Four. There was her picture.

Wind howled through the narrow court between the houses. Rain spattered the window-panes. The only sound inside the house was the rhythm of her breathing. Then she looked over the paper into my face and her eyes were filled with tears.

"The poor thing," she said. "The poor, poor kid."

"Who?"

"Diane Redfern. A girl I knew. I'd lent her the apartment."

CHAPTER TWO

We sat on the couch while I told her about the discovery of the body, the destruction of the face by BB shot, and the identification at the morgue by her aunt and Bessie Clary.

She said: "Yes, of course. We were about the same size and she had my robe on. We wore the same size; I'd given her a few of my dresses. Her hair was a little lighter, but if there was a lot of blood . . ."

She groped for her purse. I gave her my handkerchief.

After she had dried her eyes, she read the rest of the story in the paper. "Are you Mark McPherson?"

I nodded.

"You haven't found the murderer?"

"Nope."

"Did he want to murder her or me?"

"I don't know."

"What are you going to do now that I'm alive?"

"Find out who murdered the other girl."

She sighed and sank back against the cushions. "You'd better have a drink," I said, and went to the corner cabinet. "Scotch, gin, or Bourbon?"

There was the bottle of Three Horses. I should have asked her about it then, before she had time to think. But I was thinking less about the job than the girl, and still so dazed that I wasn't even sure that I was alive, awake and in my right mind.

"How do you know my house so well, Mr. McPherson?"

"There isn't much about you I don't know."

"Gosh," she said; and after a little while, she laughed and asked: "Do you realize that you're the only person in New York who knows I'm alive? The only one of six million people?"

Thunder and lightning had ceased, but rain beat on the windows. It made us feel separate from everyone else in the city, and important because we shared a secret.

She held up her glass. "To life!"

"To resurrection," I said.

We laughed.

"Go and change your dress," I said. "You'll catch cold."

"Oh," she said. "You're giving me orders."

"Change it. You'll catch cold."

"How masterful, Mr. McPherson!"

She went. I was too nervous to sit down. I was like a kid in a dark house on Hallowe'en; everything seemed mystic and supernatural, and I listened at the door so I should hear her moving about the bedroom, and know that she had not vanished again. My mind was filled with a miracle, life and resurrection, and I had to battle my way through clouds before I could think like a human being. Finally I managed to anchor myself to a chair and light my pipe.

There was, of course, no more Laura Hunt case. But what about the other girl? The body had been cremated. You've got to have a *corpus delicti* to prove murder.

This did not mean that my job was finished. Neither the Department nor the D.A.'s office would let a case slip through their hands so smoothly. Our job was to establish circumstantial evidence of the girl's disappearance, to discover where she had last been seen and by whom. Unless we had cogent evidence that the crime had been committed, the murderer might confess and still escape conviction.

"What do you know about this girl?" I called in to Laura. "What did you say her name was? Were you close friends?"

The bedroom door opened and there was Laura in a long, loose sort of gold-colored robe that made her look like a saint on the window of the Catholic Church. She carried the magazine that had been on the bed-table. On the back cover there was a photograph of a girl in evening clothes smiling at a fellow as he lit her cigarette. The advertisement said:

COMPANIONABLE!
THERE'S NOTHING AS COMPANIONABLE
AS A LANCASTER

"Oh, she was a model?"
"Wasn't she lovely?" Laura asked.
"She looks like a model," I said.
"She was beautiful," Laura insisted.
"What else?"

"What else what?"

"What was she like? How well did you know her? Where did she live? How much did she earn? Married, single, divorced? How old? Did she have a family? Who were her friends?"

"Please, Mr. McPherson. One question at a time. What was Diane like?" She hesitated. "I don't think a woman can answer that question quite honestly. You ought to ask a man."

"Your opinion would probably be safer."

"I might be prejudiced. Women with faces like mine can't be too objective about girls like Diane."

"I see nothing wrong with your face, Miss Hunt."

"Skip it. I've never tried to get by on my beauty. And if I should tell you that I considered Diane rather unintelligent and awfully shallow and quite a negative person, you might think I was jealous."

"If you felt that way about her, why did you let her have your apartment?"

"She lived in a hot little room in a boarding-house. And since nobody would have been using this place for a few days, I gave her the key."

"Why did you keep it so secret? Even Bessie didn't know."

"There was nothing secret about it. I had lunch with Diane on Friday. She told me how beastly hot it was in her room and I said she might come up here and live in comparative comfort. If I'd have come home on Friday afternoon or seen Bessie, I'd have mentioned it, but Bessie would have found it out anyway when she came to work on Saturday."

"Have you ever lent your apartment before?"

"Of course. Why not?"

"They said you were generous. Impulsive, too, aren't you?"

She laughed again. "My Aunt Susie says I'm a sucker for a hard-luck story, but I always tell her the sucker wins in the end. You don't get neuroses worrying over people's motives and wondering whether they're trying to use you."

"Sometimes you get shot by mistake," I said. "You happened to be lucky this time."

"Go on," she laughed. "You're not so hardboiled, McPherson. How many shirts have you given away in your life?"

"I'm a Scotchman," I said stiffly; I did not

want to show too much pleasure at the way she had read my character.

She laughed again. "Scotch thrift is vastly overrated. My granny Kirkland was the most liberal and open-handed woman in the world."

"You had a Scotch grandmother?"

"From a place called Pitlochry."

"Pitlochry! I've heard of Pitlochry. My father's people came from Blair-Atholl."

We shook hands.

"Were your people very religious?" Laura asked.

"Not my father. But original sin started in my mother's family."

"Ah-hah!" she said. "Dissension in the home. Don't tell me that your father read Darwin."

"Robert Ingersoll."

She clapped her hand to her head. "What a childhood you must have had!"

"Only when my old man took a drop too much. Otherwise Robert Ingersoll never even got to the Apostles' forty-yard line."

"But the name had a sort of magic and you read him secretly as you grew older."

"How did you know?"

"And you decided to learn everything in

the world so people couldn't push you around."

That started the life story. It must have sounded like a combination of Frank Merriwell and Superman in ninety-nine volumes, each worth a nickel. McPherson *vs.* Associated Dairymen. McPherson in Washington. McPherson's Big Night with the Hopheads. Down Among the Bucket Shops with Mark McPherson. Labor Spy Rackets as Seen by McPherson. Killers I Have Known. From there somehow we got back to Mark McPherson's Childhood Days. From Rags to Riches, or Barefoot Boy in Brooklyn. I guess I described every game I'd pitched for the Long Island Mohawks. And told her about the time I knocked out Rocco, the Wop Terror, and how Sparks Lampini, who had bet his paper route on Rocco, knocked me out for revenge. And about my folks, my mother, and my sister who had made up her mind to marry the boss, and what a heel she had turned out to be. I even told her about the time we all had diphtheria and Davey, the kid brother, died. It must have been ten years since I had mentioned Davey.

She sat with her hands folded against

the gold-colored cloth of her dress and a look on her face as if she were hearing the Commandments read by Moses himself. That's probably what Waldo meant by delicate flattery.

She said, "You don't seem at all like a detective."

"Have you ever known any detectives?"

"In detective stories there are two kinds, the hardboiled ones who are always drunk and talk out of the corners of their mouths and do it all by instinct; and the cold, dry, scientific kind who split hairs under a microscope."

"Which do you prefer?"

"Neither," she said. "I don't like people who make their livings out of spying and poking into people's lives. Detectives aren't heroes to me, they're detestable."

"Thanks," I said.

She smiled a little. "But you're different. The people you've gone after ought to be exposed. Your work is important. I hope you've got a million more stories to tell me."

"Sure," I said, swelling like a balloon. "I'm the Arabian Nights. Spend a thousand

and one evenings with me and you won't hear the half of my daring exploits."

"You don't talk like a detective, either."

"Neither hardboiled nor scientific?"

We laughed. A girl had died. Her body had lain on the floor of this room. That is how Laura and I met. And we couldn't stop laughing. We were like old friends, and later, at half-past three, when she said she was hungry, we went into the kitchen and opened some cans. We drank strong tea at the kitchen table like home-folks. Everything was just the way I had felt it would be with her there, alive and warm and interested in a fellow.

CHAPTER THREE

"Listen!" she said.

We heard the sound of rain and the crackling of wood in the fireplace and foghorns on the East River. "We're in the midst of Manhattan and this is our private world," she said.

I liked it. I didn't want the rain to stop or the sun to rise. For once in my life I had quit being restless.

She said, "I wonder what people are going to say when they hear I'm not dead."

I thought of the people whose names were in her address book and the stuffed shirts at her office. I thought of Shelby, but what I said was, "One thing I don't want to miss is Waldo when he finds out." I laughed.

She said: "Poor darling Waldo! Did he take it hard?"

"What do you think?"

"He loves me," she said.

I put another log on the fire. My back was turned so that I could not see her face when she asked about Shelby. This was Thursday, the twenty-eighth of August; it was to have been their wedding day.

I answered without turning around. "Shelby has been okay. He's been frank and cooperative, and kind to your aunt."

"Shelby has great self-control. You liked him, didn't you?"

I kept poking at the fire until I almost succeeded in smothering it. There had been the phoney alibi and the bottle of Three Horses Bourbon, the insurance money and the collection of unused shotguns. But now I had run into a new set of contradictions. Two and two no longer added up to four. The twenty-five-thousand-dollar insurance motive was definitely out.

It was hard for me to start asking her questions. She seemed tired. And Shelby was to have been today's bridegroom. I asked only one question:

"Did Shelby know this girl?"

She answered instantly. "Why, yes, of course. She modeled for several of the accounts in our office. All of us knew Diane." She yawned.

"You're tired, aren't you?"

"Would you mind very much if I tried to get some sleep? In the morning—later, I mean—I'll answer all the questions you want to ask."

I phoned the office and told them to send a man to watch her front door.

"Is that necessary?" she said.

"Someone tried to murder you before. I'm not going to take any chances."

"How thoughtful of you! Detectives are all right, I suppose, when they're on your side."

"Look here, Miss Hunt, will you promise me something?"

"You know me much too well to call me Miss Hunt, Mark."

My heart beat like the drum in a Harlem dance band.

"Laura," I said; she smiled at me. "You'll promise, Laura, not to leave this house until I give you permission. Or answer the phone."

"Who'd ring if everybody thinks I'm dead?"

"Promise me, just in case."

She sighed. "All right. I won't answer. And can't I phone anyone either?"

"No," I said.

"But people would be glad to know I'm alive. There are people I ought to tell right away."

"Look here, you're the one living person who can help solve this crime. Laura Hunt must find the person who tried to murder Laura Hunt. Are you game?"

She offered her hand.

The sucker took it and believed her.

CHAPTER FOUR

It was almost six when I checked in at the club. I decided that I'd need a clear head for the day's work and left a call for eight. I dreamed for two hours about Laura Hunt. The dream had five or six variations, but the meaning was always the same. She was just beyond my reach. As soon as I came close, she floated off into space. Or ran away. Or locked a door. Each time I came to, I cursed myself for letting a dream hold me in such horror. As time passed and I struggled from dream to dream, the real incidents of the night became less real than my nightmares. Each time I woke, cold and sweating, I believed more firmly that I had dreamed of finding her in the apartment and that Laura was still dead.

When the desk clerk called, I jumped as

if a bomb had gone off under my bed. Exhausted, my head aching, I swore never to drink Italian wine again. The return of Laura Hunt seemed so unreal that I wondered if I had ever actually considered reporting it to the Department. I stared hard at real things, the steel tubes of the chairs and writing desk, the brown curtains at the windows, the chimneys across the street. Then I saw, on the bureau with my wallet and keys, a spot of red. This brought me out of bed with a leap. It was the stain of lip rouge on my handkerchief which she had used. So I knew she was alive.

As I reached for the telephone, I remembered that I had told her not to answer it. She was probably sleeping anyway, and wouldn't have been pleased if a thoughtless mug called her at that hour.

I went down to the office, wrote out my report on the typewriter, sealed and filed all copies. Then I went in to see Deputy Commissioner Preble.

Every morning I had gone into his office to report on the Laura Hunt case and every day he had said the same thing.

"Stick to the case a little longer, my boy,

and maybe you'll find that murder's big enough for your talents."

His cheeks were like purple plums. I wanted to squash them with my fists. We represented opposing interests, I being one of the Commissioner's inside men, and more active than anyone in the Department on the progressive angle. Deputy Commissioner Preble was his party's front. Now that they were out of power, his was strictly an appeasement job.

As I walked into his office, he gave me the usual razzberry. Before I could say a word he started: "Do you know what this case is costing the Department? I've had a memo sent to your office. You'd better step on it or I'll have to assign someone to the case who knows how to handle homicide."

"You might have thought of that in the beginning," I said, because I wasn't going to let him know that I hadn't been on to his tactics. He had been waiting all along to show me up by letting me work until I'd hit a dead end and then handing the case to one of his favorites.

"What have you to say? Another of those minute-and-a-half reports, huh?"

"You needn't worry about our not getting

Laura Hunt's murderer," I said. "That part of the case is completed."

"What do you mean? You've got him?" He looked disappointed.

"Laura Hunt isn't dead."

His eyes popped like golf balls. "She's in her apartment now. I had Ryan on guard until eight this morning, then Behrens came on. No one knows of this yet."

He pointed at his head. "Perhaps I ought to get in touch with Bellevue, McPherson. Psychopathic Ward."

I told him briefly what had happened. Although the heat wave was over and there was a chill in the air, he fanned himself with both hands.

"Who murdered the other girl?"

"I don't know yet."

"What does Miss Hunt say about it?"

"I've reported everything that she told me."

"Do you think she knows anything she hasn't told you?"

I said: "Miss Hunt was suffering from shock after she heard that her friend had been killed. She wasn't able to talk a lot."

He snorted. "Is she pretty, McPherson?"

I said: "I'm going to question her this

morning. I also intend to surprise several people who think she is dead. It would be better if this were kept out of the newspapers until I've had time to work out my plans."

It was strictly Front Page even for the *Times*, and a coast-to-coast hook-up on the news broadcasts. I could tell by his face that he was working out an angle that would immortalize the name of Preble.

He said: "This changes the case, you know. There is no *corpus delicti*. We'll have to investigate the death of the other girl. I'm wondering, McPherson . . ."

"I wondered, too," I said. "You'll find it all in my report. A sealed copy has been sent to the Commissioner's office and you'll find yours on your secretary's desk. And I don't want to be relieved. You assigned me to the case in the beginning and I'm sticking until it's finished." I shouted and pounded on the desk, knowing that a man is most easily intimidated by his own methods. "And if one word of this gets into the papers before I've given the green light, there'll be hell to pay around here on Monday when the Commissioner gets back."

I told only one other person about

Laura's return. That was Jake Mooney. Jake is a tall, sad-faced Yankee from Providence, known among the boys as the Rhode Island Clam. Once a reporter wrote, "Mooney maintained a clam-like silence," and it got Jake so angry that he's lived up to the name ever since. By the time I came out of Preble's office, Jake had got a list of the photographers for whom Diane Redfern posed.

"Go and see these fellows," I said. "Get what you can on her. Look over her room. Don't tell anyone she's dead."

He nodded.

"I want all the papers and letters you find in her room. And be sure to ask the landlady what kind of men she knew. She might have picked up some boy friends who played with sawed-off shotguns."

The telephone rang. It was Mrs. Treadwell. She wanted me to come to her house right away.

"There's something I ought to tell you, Mr. McPherson. I'd intended going back to the country today; there was nothing more I could do for poor Laura, was there? My lawyers are going to take care of her things. But now something has happened . . ."

"All right, I'll be there, Mrs. Treadwell."

As I drove up Park Avenue, I decided to keep Mrs. Treadwell waiting while I saw Laura. She had promised to stay in the apartment and keep away from the telephone, and I knew there was no fresh food in the house. I drove around to Third Avenue, bought milk, cream, butter, eggs, and bread.

Behrens was on guard at the door. His eyes bulged at the sight of the groceries, but he evidently thought I'd set up housekeeping.

I had the key in my pocket. But before I entered, I called a warning.

She came out of the kitchen. "I'm glad you didn't ring the bell," she said. "Since you told me about the murder—" she shuddered and looked at the spot where the body had fallen "—I'm afraid of every stray sound."

"I'm sure you're the only detective in the world who'd think of *that*," she said when I gave her the groceries. "Have you eaten breakfast?"

"Now that you've reminded me, no."

It seemed natural for me to be carrying in the groceries and lounging in the kitchen while she cooked. I had thought of that kind of girl, with all those swell clothes and a servant to wait on her, as holding herself above housework. But not Laura.

"Should we be elegant and carry it to the other room or folksy and eat in the kitchen?"

"Until I was a grown man, I never ate in anything but a kitchen."

"Then it's the kitchen," she said. "There's no place like home."

While we were eating, I told her that I had informed the Deputy Commissioner of her return.

"Was he startled?"

"He threatened to commit me to the Psychopathic Ward. And then—" I looked straight into her eyes "—he asked if I thought you knew anything about that other girl's death."

"And what did you say?"

"Listen," I said, "there are going to be a lot of questions asked and you'll probably have to tell a lot more than you'd like about your private life. The more honest you are, the easier it will be for you in the end. I hope you don't mind my telling you this."

"Don't you trust me?"

I said, "It's my job to suspect everyone."

She looked at me over her coffee-cup. "And just what do you suspect me of?"

I tried to be impersonal. "Why did you lie to Shelby about going to Waldo Lydecker's for dinner on Friday night?"

"So that's what's bothering you?"

"You lied, Miss Hunt."

"Oh, I'm Miss Hunt to you now, Mister McPherson."

"Quit sparring," I said. "Why did you lie?"

"I'm afraid if I told you the truth, you might not understand."

"Okay," I said. "I'm dumb. I'm a detective. I don't speak English."

"I'm sorry if I've hurt your feelings, but—" she drew the knife along the checks in the red-and-white tablecloth "—it's hardly the sort of thing that one finds on a police blotter. Blotter, isn't that what you call it?"

"Go on," I said.

"You see," she said, "I've been a single woman for such a long time."

"It's as clear as mud," I said.

"Men have bachelor dinners," she said. "They get drunk. They go out for a last binge with chorus girls. That, I guess, is what freedom means to them. So they've got to make a splurge before they get married."

I laughed. "Poor Waldo! I bet he wouldn't care very much to be compared with a chorus girl."

She shook her head. "Freedom meant something quite different to me, Mark. Maybe you'll understand. It meant owning myself, possessing all my silly and useless routines, being the sole mistress of my habits. Do I make sense?"

"Is that why you kept putting off the wedding?"

She said: "Get me a cigarette, will you? They're in the living room."

I got her the cigarettes and lit my pipe.

She went on talking. "Freedom meant my privacy. It's not that I want to lead any sort of double life, it's simply that I resent intrusion. Perhaps because Mama always used to ask where I was going and what time I'd be home and always made me feel guilty if I changed my mind. I love doing things impulsively, and I resent it to a point where my spine stiffens and I get goose-flesh if people ask where and what and why." She was like a child, crying to be understood.

"On Friday I had a date with Waldo for a sort of bachelor dinner before I left for Wilton. It was to be my last night in town before my wedding . . ."

"Didn't Shelby resent it?"

"Naturally. Wouldn't you?" She laughed and showed the tip of her tongue between her lips. "Waldo resented Shelby. But I couldn't help it. I never flirted or urged them on. And I'm fond of Waldo; he's a fussy old maid, but he's been kind to me, very kind. Besides, we've been friends for years. Shelby just had to make the best of it. We're civilized people, we don't try to change each other."

"And Shelby, I suppose, had habits that weren't hundred per cent with you?"

She ignored the question. "On Friday I fully intended to dine with Waldo and take the ten-twenty train. But in the afternoon I changed my mind."

"Why?"

"Why?" she mocked. "That's precisely

why I didn't tell him. Because he'd ask why."

I got angry. "You can have your prejudices if you like, and God knows I don't care if you want to make your habits sacred, but this is a murder case. Murder! There must have been some reason why you changed your mind."

"I'm like that."

"Are you?" I asked. "They told me you were a kind woman who thought more of an old friend than to stand him up for the sake of a selfish whim. You're supposed to be generous and considerate. It sounds like a lot of bull to me!"

"Why, Mr. McPherson, you are a vehement person."

"Please tell me exactly why you changed your mind about having dinner at Waldo's."

"I had a headache."

"I know. That's what you told him."

"Don't you believe me?"

"Women always have headaches when they don't want to do something. Why did you come back from lunch with such a headache that you phoned Waldo before you took your hat off?"

"My secretary told you that, I suppose. How important trifles become when something violent happens!"

She walked over to the couch and sat down. I followed. Suddenly she touched my arm with her hand and looked up into my eyes so sweetly that I smiled. We both laughed and the trifles became less important.

She said: "So help me, Mark, I've told you the truth. I felt so wretched after lunch on Friday, I just couldn't face Waldo's chatter, and I couldn't sit through dinner with Shelby either because he'd have been too pleased at my breaking the date with Waldo. I just had to get away from everybody."

"Why?"

"What a persistent man you are!"

She shivered. The day was cold. Rain beat against the window. The sky was the color of lead.

"Should I make you a fire?"

"Don't bother." Her voice was cold, too.

I got logs out of the cabinet under the bookshelves and built her a fire. She sat at the end of the couch, her knees tucked up, her arms hugging her body. She seemed defenseless.

"There," I said. "You'll be warm soon."

"Please, please, Mark, believe me. There was no more to it than that. You're not just a detective who sees nothing but surface actions. You're a sensitive man, you react to nuances. So please try to understand, please."

The attack was well-aimed. A man is no stronger than his vanity. If I doubted her, I'd show myself to be nothing more than a crude detective.

"All right," I said, "we'll skip it now. Maybe you saw a ghost at lunch. Maybe your girl friend said something that reminded you of something else. Hell, everybody gets temperamental once in a while."

She slipped off the couch and ran toward me, her hands extended. "You're a darling, really. I knew last night that I'd never have to be afraid of you."

I took her hands. They were soft to touch, but strong underneath. Sucker, I said to myself, and decided to do something about it then and there. My self-respect was involved. I was a detective, a servant of the people, a representative of law and order.

I went to the liquor cabinet. "Ever seen this before?"

It was the bottle with the Three Horses on the label.

She answered without the slightest hesitation, "Of course; it's been in the house for weeks."

"This isn't the brand you usually buy, is it? Did you get this from Mosconi's, too?"

She answered in one long unpunctuated sentence. "No no I picked it up one night we were out of Bourbon I had company for dinner and stopped on the way home from the office it was on Lexington or maybe Third Avenue I don't remember."

She lied like a goon. I had checked with Mosconi and discovered that on Friday night, between seven and eight, Shelby Carpenter had stopped at the store, bought the bottle of Three Horses, and, instead of charging it to Miss Hunt's account, had paid cash.

CHAPTER FIVE

"What took you so long, Mr. McPherson? You should have come earlier. Maybe it's too late now, maybe he's gone forever."

In a pink bed, wearing a pink jacket with fur on the sleeves, lay Mrs. Susan Treadwell. I sat like the doctor on a straight chair.

"Shelby?"

She nodded. Her pink massaged skin looked dry and old, her eyes were swollen and the black stuff had matted under her lashes. The Pomeranian lay on the pink silk comfort, whimpering.

"Do make Wolf stop that sniffling," begged the lady. She dried her eyes with a paper handkerchief that she took from a silk box. "My nerves are completely gone. I can't bear it."

The dog went on whimpering. She sat up and spanked it feebly.

"He's gone?" I asked. "Where?"

"How do I know?" She looked at a diamond wristwatch. "He's been gone since six-thirty this morning."

I was not upset. One of our men had been following Shelby since I'd checked with Mosconi on the Bourbon bottle.

"You were awake when he left? You heard him go? Did he sneak out?"

"I lent him my car," she sniffled.

"Do you think he was trying to escape the law, Mrs. Treadwell?"

She blew her nose and dabbed at her eyes again. "Oh, I knew it was weak of me, Mr. McPherson. But you know Shelby, he has a way with him. He asks you for something and you can't resist him; and then you hate yourself for giving in. He said it was a matter of life and death, and if I ever discovered the reason, I'd always be grateful."

I let her cry for a few minutes before I asked, "Do you believe that he committed the murder . . . the murder of your niece, Mrs. Treadwell?"

"No! No! I don't, Mr. McPherson. He just

hasn't got the stomach. Criminals go after
what they want, but Shelby's just a big kid.
He's always being sorry for something. My
poor, poor Laura!"

I said nothing about Laura's return.

"You don't like Shelby very much, do
you, Mrs. Treadwell?"

"He's a darling boy," she said, "but not
for Laura. Laura couldn't afford him."

"Oh," I said.

She was afraid I had got the wrong impression and added quickly: "Not that he's
a gigolo. Shelby comes from a wonderful
family. But in some ways a gigolo's cheaper.
You know where you are. With a man like
Shelby you can't slip the money under the
table."

I decided that it was lucky that most of
my cases had not involved women. Their
logic confused me.

"She was always doing the most absurd
things about his pride. Like the cigarette
case. That was typical. And then he had to
go and lose it."

By this time I'd lost the scent.

"She couldn't afford it, of course; she
had to charge it on my account and pay me
back by the month. A solid gold cigarette

case, he had to have it, she said, so he'd feel equal to the men he lunched with at the club and the clients in their business. Does it make sense to you, Mr. McPherson?"

"No," I said honestly, "it doesn't."

"But it's just like Laura."

I could have agreed to that, too, but I controlled myself.

"And he lost it?" I asked, leading her back to the trail.

"Um-hum. In April, before she'd even finished paying for it. Can you imagine?" Suddenly, for no reason that I could understand, she took an atomizer from the bedtable and sprayed herself with perfume. Then she made up her lips and combed her hair. "I thought of the cigarette case as soon as he'd gone off with the keys to my car. Did I feel like a sucker!"

"I understand that," I said.

Her smile was a clue to the business with the perfume and lipstick. I was a man, she had to get around me.

"You're not going to blame me for giving him the car? Really, I didn't think of it at the time. He has a way with him, you know."

"You shouldn't have given it to him if you felt that way," said the stern detective.

She fell for it.

"It was weak, Mr. McPherson, I know how weak I was to have done it. I should have been more suspicious, I know I should, especially after that phone call."

"What phone call, Mrs. Treadwell?"

It was only by careful questioning that I got the story straight. If I told it her way, there would be no end to this chapter. The phone had wakened her at half-past five that morning. She lifted the receiver in time to hear Shelby, on the upstairs extension, talking to the night clerk at the Hotel Framingham. The clerk apologized for disturbing him at this hour, but said that someone wanted to get in touch with him on a life-and-death matter. That person was waiting on another wire. Should the clerk give that party Mr. Carpenter's number?

"I'll call back in ten minutes," Shelby had said. "Tell them to call you again."

He had dressed and tiptoed down the stairs.

"He was going out to phone," Mrs. Treadwell said. "He was afraid I'd listen on the extension."

At twenty minutes past six she had heard him coming up the stairs. He had knocked at her bedroom door, apologized for waking her, and asked for the use of the car.

"Does that make me an accessory or something, Mr. McPherson?" Tears rolled down her cheeks.

I phoned the office and asked if there had been any reports from the man who had been following Shelby Carpenter. Nothing had been heard since he went on duty at midnight, and the man who was to have relieved him at eight in the morning was still waiting.

As I put down the phone, the dog began to bark. Shelby walked in.

"Good morning." He went straight to the bed. "I'm glad you rested, darling. It was cruel of me to disturb you at that mad hour. But you don't show it at all. You're divine this morning." He kissed her forehead and then turned to welcome me.

"Where've you been?" she asked.

"Can't you guess, darling?"

He petted the dog. I sat back and watched. There was something familiar and unreal about Shelby. I was always uncomfortable

when he was in the room, and always struggling to remember where I had seen him.
The memory was like a dream, unsubstan-
tial and baffling.

"I can't imagine where anyone would go
at that wild hour, darling. You had me quite
alarmed."

If Shelby guessed that the lady's alarm
had caused her to summon the police, he
was too tactful to mention it.

"I went up to Laura's place," he said. "I
made a sentimental journey. This was to
have been our wedding day, you know."

"Oh, I'd forgotten." Mrs. Treadwell caught
his hand. He was sitting on the edge of the
bed, comfortable and sure of himself.

"I couldn't sleep. And when that absurd
phone call woke us, Auntie Sue, I was too
upset to stay in my room. I felt such a longing for Laura, I wanted to be close to
something she had loved. There was the
garden. She'd cared for it herself, Mr.
McPherson, with her own hands. It was
lovely in the gray morning light."

"I don't know whether I quite believe
you," Mrs. Treadwell said. "What's your
opinion, Mr. McPherson?"

"You're embarrassing him, darling. Remember, he's a detective," Shelby said as if she had been talking about leprosy in front of a leper.

"Why couldn't you take that telephone call in the house?" asked Mrs. Treadwell. "Did you think I'd stoop so low as to listen on the extension?"

"If you hadn't been listening on the extension, you'd not have known that I had to go out to a phone booth," he said, laughing.

"Why were you afraid to have me hear?"

Shelby offered me a cigarette. He carried the pack in his pocket without a case.

"Was it a girl?" asked Mrs. Treadwell.

"I don't know. He . . . she . . . whoever it was . . . refused to leave a number. I called the Framingham three times, but they hadn't called back." He blew smoke rings toward the ceiling. Then, smiling at me like the King of England in a newsreel showing their majesties' visit to coal miners' huts, he said: "A yellow cab followed me all the way to the cottage and back. On these country roads at that hour your man couldn't very well hide himself. Don't be angry with the poor chap because I spotted him."

LAURA   535

"He kept you covered. That was all he was told to do. Whether you knew or not makes no difference." I got up. "I'm going to be up at Miss Hunt's apartment at three o'clock. I want you to meet me there, Carpenter."

"Is it necessary? I rather dislike going up there today of all days. You know, we were to have been married . . ."

"Consider it a sentimental journey," I said.

Mrs. Treadwell barely noticed when I left. She was busy with her face.

At the office I learned that Shelby's sentimental journey had added a five-hour taxi bill to the cost of the Laura Hunt case. Nothing had been discovered. Shelby had not even entered the house, but had stood in the garden in the rain and blown his nose vigorously. He might also, it was hinted, have been crying.

CHAPTER SIX

Mooney was waiting in my office with his report on Diane Redfern.

She had not been seen since Friday. The landlady remembered because Diane had paid her room rent that day. She had come from work at five o'clock, stopped in the landlady's basement flat to hand her the money, gone to her room on the fourth floor, bathed, changed her clothes, and gone out again. The landlady had seen her hail a cab at the corner of Seventh Avenue and Christopher Street. She remembered because she considered taxis a sinful extravagance for girls like Diane.

The girl might have come in late on Friday night and gone out again on Saturday morning, but the landlady had not seen her. There were still boarders to be questioned, but the landlady had not known where they worked, and Mooney would have to go back at six o'clock to check with them.

"Did the landlady seem surprised that Diane hadn't been seen since Friday?"

"She says it doesn't matter to her whether the boarders use their rooms or not as long as they pay the rent. The girls that stay in places like that are often out all night."

"But it's five days," I said. "Was there nobody to bother about her disappearance?"

"You know how it is with those kind of girls, Mac. Here today, gone tomorrow. Who cares?"

"Hasn't she any friends? Didn't anyone come to see her or telephone?"

"There were some phone calls. Tuesday and Wednesday. I checked. Photographers calling her to come and work."

"Nothing personal?"

"There might have been a couple of other calls, but no messages. The landlady don't remember what she didn't write down on the pad."

I had known girls like that around New York. No home, no friends, not much

money. Diane had been a beauty, but
beauties are a dime a dozen on both sides
of Fifth Avenue between Eighth Street and
Ninety-Sixth. Mooney's report gave facts
and figures, showed an estimate of Diane's
earnings according to figures provided by
the Models' Guild. She could have supported a husband and kids on the money
she earned when she worked, but the work
was unsteady. And according to Mooney's
rough estimate, the clothes in her closet
had cost plenty. Twenty pairs of shoes.
There were no bills as there had been in
Laura's desk, for Diane came from the
lower classes, she paid cash. The sum of it
all was a shabby and shiftless life. Fancy
perfume bottles, Kewpie dolls, and toy animals were all she brought home from
expensive dinners and suppers in night
spots. The letters from her family, plain
working people who lived in Paterson, New
Jersey, were written in night-school English
and told about lay-offs and money troubles.

Her name had been Jennie Swobodo.

Mooney had taken nothing from the
room but the letters. He'd had a special
lock put on the door and threatened the

landlady with the clink if she opened her face.

He gave me a duplicate key. "You might want to look in yourself. I'll be back there at six to talk to the other tenants."

I had no time then to look into the life of Jennie Swobodo, alias Diane Redfern. But when I got up to Laura's apartment, I asked if there hadn't been any pocketbooks or clothes left there by the murdered model.

Laura said: "Yes, if Bessie had examined the clothes in the closet, she'd have found Diane's dress. And her purse was in my dresser drawer. She had put everything away neatly."

There was a dresser drawer filled with purses. Among them was the black silk bag that Diane had carried. There was eighteen dollars in it, the key to her room, lipstick, eyeshadow, powder, a little tin phial of perfume, and a straw cigarette case with a broken clasp.

Laura watched quietly while I examined Diane's belongings. When I went back to the living-room, she followed me like a child. She had changed into a tan dress and brown high-heeled slippers that set off her wonderful ankles. Her earrings were little gold bells.

"I've sent for Bessie."

"How thoughtful you are!"

I felt like a hypocrite. My reason for sending for Bessie had been purely selfish. I wanted to observe her reaction to Laura's return.

When I explained, Laura said, "But you don't suspect poor old Bessie?"

"I just want to see how a non-suspect takes it."

"As a basis for comparison?"

"Maybe."

"Then there's someone you do suspect?"

I said, "There are several lies which will have to be explained."

When she moved, the gold bells tinkled. Her face was like a mask.

"Mind a pipe?"

The bells tinkled again. I struck a match. It scraped like an emery wheel. I thought of Laura's lie and hated her because she was making a fool of herself for Shelby Carpenter. And trying to make a fool of me. I was glad when the doorbell rang. I told Laura to wait in the bedroom for my signal.

Bessie knew at once that something had happened. She looked around the room, she stared at the place where the body had fallen, she studied each ornament and every piece of furniture. I saw it with a housekeeper's eyes then, noticed that the newspaper had been folded carelessly and left on the big table, that Laura's lunch tray with an empty plate and coffee-cup remained on the coffee-table beside the couch, that a book lay open, that the fire burned behind the screen, and red-tipped cigarette stubs filled the ashtrays.

"Sit down," I told her. "Something's happened."

"What?"

"Sit down."

"I can take it standing."

"Someone has come to stay here," I said, and went to the bedroom door.

Laura came out.

I have heard women scream when their husbands beat them and mothers sobbing over dead and injured children, but I have never heard such eery shrieks as Bessie let out at the sight of Laura. She dropped her pocketbook. She crossed herself.

Then, very slowly, she backed toward a chair and sat down.

"Do you see what I see, Mr. McPherson?"

"It's all right, Bessie. She's alive."

Bessie called upon God, Jesus, Mary, and her patron saint Elizabeth to witness the miracle.

"Bessie, calm yourself. I'm all right; I just went to the country. Someone else was murdered."

It was easier to believe in miracles. Bessie insisted upon telling Laura that she had herself found the body, that she had identified it as Laura Hunt's, that it had worn Laura's best negligee and silver mules. And she was just as positive about her uncle's sister-in-law's cousin who had met her dead sweetheart in an orchard in County Galway.

None of our arguments convinced her until Laura said, "Well, what are we going to have for dinner, Bessie?"

"Blessed Mary, I never thought I'd be hearing you ask that no more, Miss Laura."

"I'm asking, Bessie. How about a steak and French fried and apple pie, Bessie?"

Bessie brightened. "Would a ghost be

asking for French fried and apple pie? Who was it got murdered, Miss Laura?"

"Miss Redfern, you remember . . . the girl who . . ."

"It's no more than she deserved," said Bessie, and went into the kitchen to change into her work clothes.

I told her to shop for dinner in stores where they did not know her as the servant of a murder victim, and warned her against mentioning the miracle of Laura's return.

"Evidently Bessie disapproved of Diane. Why?" I asked Laura when we were alone again.

"Bessie's opinionated," she said. "There was no particular reason."

"No?"

"No," said Laura firmly.

The doorbell rang again.

"Stay here this time," I whispered. "We'll try another kind of surprise."

She waited, sitting stiffly at the edge of the couch. I opened the door. I had expected to see Shelby, but it was Waldo Lydecker who walked in.

CHAPTER SEVEN

Self-centered people see only what they want to see. Astigmatism might have been his excuse for his failure to notice her at first, but I think it was covetousness. His gaze was so concentrated upon the antique glass vase that the rest of the room might have been sky or desert.

"Your office told me I'd find you here, McPherson. I've talked to my lawyer and he advises me to take my vase and let the bitch sue."

He had to pass the sofa on the way to the mantel. Laura turned her head, the gold bells tinkled. Waldo paused as if he had heard some ghostly warning. Then, like a man afraid of his imagination and determined to show himself above fear, he stretched his hands toward the shining globe. Laura turned to see how I was taking it. Her gold bells struck such a sharp note that Waldo whirled on his heels and faced her.

He was whiter than death. He did not stagger nor fall, but stood paralyzed, his arms raised toward the vase. He was like a caricature, pitiful and funny at the same time. The Van Dyke beard, the stick crooked over his arm, the well-cut suit, the flower in his buttonhole, were like decorations on the dead.

We were quiet. The clock ticked.

"Waldo," Laura said softly.

He seemed not to have heard.

She took hold of his rigid arms and led him to the couch. He moved like a mechanical doll. She urged him to a seat, gently pushed down his arms, handed me his hat and stick. "Waldo," she whispered in the voice of a mother to a hurt child. "Waldo, darling."

His neck turned like a mechanism on springs. His glazed eyes, empty of understanding, were fastened on her face.

"It's all right, Mr. Lydecker. She's alive and well. There's been a mistake."

My voice touched him, but not in the

right place. He swayed backward on the couch, then jerked forward with a mechanical rather than willful reaction. He trembled so violently that some inner force seemed to be shaking his body. Sweat rose in crystals on his forehead and upper lip.

"There's brandy in the cabinet. Get some, Mark. Quickly," Laura said.

I fetched the brandy. She lifted the glass to his lips. Most of the liquor trickled down his chin. After a while he lifted his right hand, looked at it, dropped it, and lifted the left. He seemed to be testing himself to see if he was capable of willing his muscles to action.

Laura kneeled beside him, her hands on his knees. Her voice was gentle as she explained that it was Diane Redfern who had died and been buried while Laura was staying at her little house in the country. I could not tell whether he heard or whether it was her voice that soothed him, but when she suggested that he rest on the bed, he rose obediently. Laura took him into the bedroom, helped him lie down, spread her blue-and-white cover over his legs. He let himself be led around like a child.

When she came back she asked if I thought we ought to call a doctor.

"I don't know," I said. "He's not young and he's fat. But it doesn't look like any stroke I've ever seen."

"It's happened before."

"Like this?"

She nodded. "In the theatre one night. He got angry that we'd called a doctor. Maybe we'd better let him rest."

We sat like people in a hospital corridor.

"I'm sorry," I said. "If I'd known it was Waldo, I'd have warned him."

"You're still planning to do it to Shelby, aren't you?"

"Shelby's nerves are stronger. He'll take it better."

Her eyes were narrow with anger.

I said: "Look here, you know that Shelby's lied. I'm not saying that he's committed murder, but I know he's hiding something. There are several things he's got to explain."

"He can, I'm sure he can. Shelby can explain everything."

She went into the bedroom to see how Waldo was getting on.

"He seems to be sleeping. He's breathing regularly. Maybe we'd better just leave him."

We sat without speaking until the doorbell rang again. "You'll have to see him first and tell him," Laura said. "I'm not going to let anyone else go through that shock." She disappeared behind the swinging door that led to the kitchen.

The bell rang again. When I opened the door, Shelby pushed past.

"Where is she?" he shouted.

"Oh, you know, then?"

I heard the back door open, and I knew that he had met Bessie on the stairs.

"God damn women," I said.

Then Laura came out of the kitchen. I saw at once that Bessie wasn't the woman who deserved my curses. The lovers' meeting was too perfect. They embraced, kissed, and clung. An actor after a dozen rehearsals would have groped for his handkerchief in that same dazed way. An actor would have held her at arm's length, staring at her with that choir-boy look on his face. There was something prearranged about the whole scene. His tenderness and her joy.

I turned my back.

Laura's voice was melted syrup. "Happy, darling?"

He answered in a whisper.

My pipe had gone out. If I turned and got a match from the table, they would think I was watching. I bit on the cold stem. The whispering and muttering went on. I watched the minute hand creep around the dial of my watch. I thought of the night I had waited for Pinky Moran to come out of his sweetheart's house. It had been four above at ten o'clock and by midnight it was below zero. I had waited in the snow and thought about the gangster lying warm in the arms of his fat slut. I turned and saw Shelby's hands feeling, touching, moving along the tan material of Laura's dress.

"How infinitely touching! What inexpressible tenderness! Juliet risen from the grave! Welcome, Romeo!"

It was, of course, Waldo. He had not only recovered his strength, but his bounce.

"Forgive me," he said, "for a wee touch of epilepsy. It's an old family custom." He jerked Laura away from Shelby, kissed both cheeks, whirled around with her as if they were waltzing. "Welcome, wench! Tell us how it feels to return from the grave."

"Be yourself, Waldo."

"More truly myself you have never seen me, you beautiful zombie. I, too, am resurrected. The news of your death had me at the brink of eternity. We are both reborn, we must celebrate the miracle of life, beloved. Let's have a drink."

She started toward the liquor cabinet, but Waldo barred her way. "No, darling, no whiskey tonight. We're drinking champagne." And he bustled to the kitchen, shouting that Bessie was to hurry over to Mosconi's and bring back some wine with a name that he had to write down on a piece of paper.

CHAPTER EIGHT

Laura sat with three men drinking champagne. It was a familiar scene to them, Old Home Week. Even Bessie took it like a veteran. They seemed ready to take up where they had left off last week, before someone rang the bell and blew a girl's face away with a charge of BB shot. That's why I was there, the third man.

When they drank a toast to Laura, I took a sip of the wine. The rest of it stayed in my glass until the bubbles died.

"Aren't you drinking?" Waldo asked me.

"I happen to be on a job," I said.

"He's a prig," said Waldo. "A proletarian snob with a Puritan conscience."

Because I was on a job and because Laura was there, I didn't use the only words I knew for describing him. They were short words and to the point.

"Don't be cross with us," Laura said. "These are my best friends in the whole world and naturally they want to celebrate my not being dead."

I reminded them that Diane Redfern's death was still a mystery.

"But I'm sure we know nothing about it," Shelby said.

"Ah-hah!" said Waldo. "The ghost at the feast. Shall we drink a respectful toast?"

Laura put down her glass and said, "Waldo, please."

"That's in questionable taste," said Shelby.

Waldo sighed. "How pious we've all grown! It's your influence, McPherson. As walking delegate for the Union of the Dead . . ."

"Please shut up!" said Laura.

She moved closer to Shelby. He took her hand. Waldo watched like a cat with a family of mice.

"Well, McPherson, since you insist upon casting the shadow of sobriety upon our sunny reunion, tell us how you're proceeding with the investigation. Have you cleared the confusion surrounding that bottle of Bourbon?"

Laura said quietly: "It was I who bought that bottle of Three Horses, Waldo. I know it's not as good as the stuff you taught me to buy, but one night I was in a hurry and brought it home. Don't you remember, Shelby?"

"I do indeed." Shelby pressed her hand.

They seemed to be getting closer together and shoving Waldo out into the cold. He poured himself another glass of champagne.

"Tell us, McPherson, were there any mysteries in the life of the little model? Have you discovered any evil companions? Do you know the secrets of her gay life in Greenwich Village?"

Waldo was using me as a weapon against Shelby. It was clear as water out of the old oaken bucket. Here he was, a man who had read practically all that was great in English literature, and a mug could have taught him the alphabet. I felt fine. He was shooting right up my alley.

"My assistant," I said with an official roll in my voice, "is on the trail of her enemies."

Waldo choked on his wine.

"Enemies," said Laura. "She?"

"There might have been things about her life that you didn't know," said Shelby.

"Pooh!"

"Most of those girls live very questionable lives," Shelby said firmly. "For all we know, the poor girl might have got herself mixed up with all sorts of people. Men she'd met in night clubs."

"How do you know so much about her?" Waldo asked.

"I don't know. I'm merely mentioning possibilities," Shelby said. He turned to me and asked, "These models, they're often friendly with underworld characters, aren't they?"

"Poor Diane," Laura said. "She wasn't the sort of person anyone could hate. I mean . . . she didn't have much . . . well, passion. Just beauty and vague dreams. I can't imagine anyone hating a kid like that. She was so . . . I mean . . . you wanted to help her."

"Was that Shelby's explanation?" Waldo asked. "His was a purely philanthropic interest, I take it."

Bright spots burned on Laura's cheeks.

"Yes, it was!" she said hotly. "I'd asked him to be kind to her, hadn't I, Shelby?"

Shelby went to the cupboard for a log. He was glad for the excuse to move around. Laura's eyes followed his movements.

"Had you asked him to be particularly kind to her last Wednesday, darling?" Waldo pretended to ask the question innocently, but he was slanting curious glances at me.

"Wednesday?" she said with an effort to appear absent-minded.

"Last Wednesday. Or was it Tuesday? The night they did the Toccata and Fugue at the Stadium, wasn't that Wednesday?" He rolled his eyes toward the fireplace and Shelby. "When was your cocktail party, Laura?"

"Oh, that," she said. "On Wednesday."

"You should have been here, McPherson," Waldo said. "It was too, too jolly."

Laura said, "You're being silly, Waldo."

But Waldo wanted to put on a show and nothing could stop him. He got up with the champagne glass in his hand and gave an imitation of Laura as hostess to a lot of cocktail-drinkers. He did not merely speak in a falsetto voice and swing his hips the way most men do when they imitate women. He had a real talent for acting. He was the hostess, he moved from guest to guest, he introduced strangers, he saw that the glasses were filled, he carried a tray of sandwiches.

"Hello, darling, I'm so glad you could come . . . you must meet . . . I know you'll simply adore . . . Don't tell me you're not drinking . . . Not eating! . . . Come now, this tiny caviar sandwich wouldn't put weight on a sturgeon . . . You haven't met . . . but how incredible, everyone knows Waldo Lydecker, he's the heavyweight Noel Coward . . . Waldo darling, one of your most loyal admirers . . ."

It was a good show. You could see the stuffed shirts and the highbrow women, and all the time that he moved around the room, imitating Laura and carrying that imaginary tray, you knew she had been watching something that was going on at the bay window.

Now Waldo skipped to the bay window. He changed his movements and his gestures became manly. He was Shelby being gallant and cautious. And he was a girl, looking up at Shelby, blinking her eyes and tugging at his lapels. He caught Shelby's voice perfectly, and while I had never heard her voice, I'd known plenty of dolls who talked as he had Diane talking.

"Oh, but darling, you are the best-looking man in the room . . . Can't I even say so?" "You're drunk, baby, don't talk so loud." "What harm can there be, Shelby, if I just quietly worship you?" "Quietly, for God's sakes, kid. Remember where we are." "Shelby, please, I'm not tight, I never get tight, I'm not talking loud." "Sh-sh, honey, everyone's looking at you." "Let 'em look, you think I care?" The doll-voice became shrill and angry. Drunken young girls in bars always scream like that.

Shelby had left the fire. His fists were clenched, his jaw pushed forward, his skin green.

Laura was trembling.

Waldo walked to the middle of the room, said in his own voice: "There was a terrible hush. Everyone looked at Laura. She was carrying that tray of hors d'oeuvres."

Everyone in the room must have felt

sorry for Laura. Her wedding was to have taken place in a week and a day.

Waldo crossed toward the bay window with catlike, female steps. I watched as if Diane were there with Shelby.

"Diane had taken hold of his lapels . . ."

Laura, the real one, the girl on the couch in the tan dress, said: "I'm sorry. For God's sakes, how often do I have to say I'm sorry?"

Shelby raised his clenched fists and said: "Yes, Lydecker, we've had enough. Enough of your clowning."

Waldo looked at me. "What a shame, McPherson! You've missed the best part of the scene."

"What did she do?" I asked.

"May I tell him?" said Waldo.

"You'd better," said Shelby, "or he'll imagine something far worse."

Laura began to laugh. "I conked her with a tray of hors d'oeuvres. I conked her!"

We waited until her hysteria had died down. She was crying and laughing at the same time. Shelby tried to take her hand, but she pulled away. Then she looked at me with shame on her face and said: "I'd

never done anything like that before. I
didn't dream I could do such a thing. I
wanted to die."

"Is that all?" I asked.

"All!" said Shelby.

"In my own house," Laura said.

"What happened afterward?"

"I went into my bedroom. I wouldn't let
anyone come in and talk to me. I was so
ashamed. Then after a while Shelby did
come in and he told me Diane had left and
that I'd simply have to come out and face
my guests."

"After all," said Shelby.

"Everyone was tactful, but that made me
feel worse. But Shelby was darling, he insisted that we go out and get a little tight
so I wouldn't think about it and keep re-
proaching myself."

"How kind of him!" I couldn't help saying.

"Shelby's broad-minded, he forgives
easily," added Waldo.

"Shelby couldn't help it if Diane fell in
love with him." Laura ignored the other
two; she was explaining it to me. "He'd
been kind and polite and thoughtful as he

always is. Diane was a poor kid who'd come from the sort of home where they beat up women. She'd never met a . . . a gentleman before."

"Oddzooks!" Waldo said.

"She wanted something better than she'd had at home. Her life had been terribly sordid. Even her name, silly as it sounded, showed that she wanted a better sort of life."

"You're breaking my heart," Waldo said.

Laura took a cigarette. Her hands were unsteady. "I'm not so different. I came to New York, too, a poor kid without friends or money. People were kind to me—" she pointed with the cigarette at Waldo "—and I felt almost an obligation toward kids like Diane. I was the only friend she had. And Shelby."

It sounded simple and human as she stood there, so close that I could smell her perfume. I backed away.

She said, "You believe me, don't you, Mark?"

"What was this lunch on Friday? An armistice?" I asked her.

She smiled. "Yes, yes, an armistice. I went around from Wednesday evening until Friday morning feeling like a heel. And I knew if I didn't see Diane and say I was sorry my whole vacation would be ruined. Do you think I'm very silly?"

"A soft-hearted slob," said Waldo.

Shelby picked up the poker, but it was only to stoke the fire. My nerves were on edge and I saw violence every time a cigarette was lighted. That was because I craved violence. My hands itched for a fat neck.

I took two steps forward and was close to Laura again. "Then it was at lunch that you smoked . . ."

I stopped right there. She was whiter than the white dress that Diane had been buried in.

"Smoked," she whispered the word.

"Smoked the pipe of peace," I said, "and offered her your apartment."

"Yes, the pipe of peace," Laura said. She had come to life again. Her eyes sparkled, her cheeks glowed with color. Her thin, strong fingers lay on my coat-sleeve. "You must believe me, Mark, you must believe that everything was all right when I offered her the apartment. Please, please believe me."

Shelby didn't say a word. But I think he was smiling. Waldo laughed aloud and said, "Careful, Laura, he's a detective."

Her hand slipped off my coat-sleeve.

CHAPTER NINE

I ate dinner again that night with Waldo.
Ask me why. I asked myself as I looked at
his fat face over a bowl of bird's-nest soup
at the Golden Lizard. It was raining. I was
lonely. I wanted to talk. I wanted to talk
about Laura. She was eating steak and
French fried with Shelby. I clung to Waldo.
I was afraid of losing him. I despised the
guy and he fascinated me. The deeper I got
into this case, the less I seemed like myself
and the more I felt like a green-horn in a
new world.

My mind was foggy. I was going somewhere, but I'd lost the road. I remember
asking myself about clues. What were
clues, what had I looked for in other cases?
A smile couldn't be brought into court as
evidence. You couldn't arrest a man be-

cause he had trembled. Brown eyes had stolen a peep at gray eyes, so what? The tone of a voice was something that died with a word.

The Chinese waiter brought a platter of eggroll. Waldo reached for it like a man on the breadline.

"Well," he said, "what do you think of her now that you've met her?"

I helped myself to eggroll. "It's my job . . ."

He finished for me. ". . . to look at facts and hold no opinions. Where have I heard that before?"

The waiter brought a trayful of covered dishes. Waldo had to have his plate arranged just so, pork on this side, duck over there, noodles under the chicken-almond, sweet and pungent spareribs next to the lobster, Chinese ravioli on a separate plate because there might be a conflict in the sauces. Until he had tried each dish with and without beetle juice, there was no more talk at our table.

At last he stopped for breath, and said: "I remember something you said when you first came to see me on Sunday morning. Do you remember?"

"We said a lot of things on Sunday morning. Both of us."

"You said that it wasn't fingerprints you'd want to study in this case, but faces. That was very dull of you, I thought."

"Then why did you remember it?"

"Because I was moved by the sorry spectacle of a conventional young man thinking that he had become radically unconventional."

"So what?" I said.

He snapped his fingers. Two waiters came running. It seems they had forgotten the fried rice. There was more talk than necessary, and he had to rearrange his plate. Between giving orders to the Chinese and moaning because the ritual (his word) of his dinner was upset, he talked about Elwell and Dot King and Starr Faithful and several other well-known murder cases.

"And you think this is going to be the unsolved Diane Redfern case?" I asked.

"Not the Redfern case, my friend. In the public mind and in the newspapers, it will be the Laura Hunt case forevermore. Laura will go through life a marked woman, the living victim of unsolved murder."

He was trying to get me angry. There were no direct hits, only darts and pin-pricks. I tried to avoid his face, but I could not escape that doughy smirk. If I turned around, he moved too, his fat head rolling like a ball-bearing in his starched collar.

"You'd die before you'd let that happen, my gallant Hawkshaw? You'd risk your precious hide before you'd let that poor innocent girl suffer such lifelong indignity, eh?" He laughed aloud. Two waiters poked their heads out of the kitchen.

"Your jokes aren't so funny," I said.

"Woof! Woof! How savage our bark is tonight. What's tormenting you? Is it fear of failure or the ominous competition with Apollo Belvedere?"

I could feel my face getting red. "Look here," I said.

Again he interrupted. "Look here, my dear lad, at the risk of losing your esteemed friendship . . . and the friendship of such an estimable character as yourself I do value, whether you believe me or not . . . at the risk, I say of losing . . ."

"Get to the point," I said.

"Advice to a young man: Don't lose your head. She's not for you."

"Mind your god-damned business," I said.

"Some day you will thank me for this. Unless you fail to heed my advice, of course. Didn't you hear her describing Diane's infatuation for Shelby? A gentleman, oddzooks! Do you think that Diane has died so completely that chivalry must die, too? If you were more astute, my friend, you would see that Laura is Diane and Diane was Laura . . ."

"Her real name was Jennie Swobodo. She used to work in a mill in Jersey."

"It's like a bad novel."

"But Laura's no dope. She must have known he was a heel."

"Long after the core of gentility is gone, the husks remain. The educated woman, no less than the poor mill girl, is bound by the shackles of romance. The aristocratic tradition, my dear good friend, with its faint sweet odor of corruption. Romantics are children, they never grow up." He helped himself to another round of chicken, pork, duck, and rice. "Didn't I tell you the day we met that Shelby was Laura's softer, less distinguished side? Do you see it now, the answer to that longing for perfection? Pass the soy sauce, please."

Romance was something for crooners, for the movies. The only person I ever heard use the word in common life was my kid sister, and she'd raised herself by romance, married the boss.

"I was hopeful once that Laura'd grow up, get over Shelby. She'd have been a great woman if she had, you know. But the dream still held her, the hero she could love forever immaturely, the mould of perfection whose flawlessness made no demands upon her sympathies or her intelligence."

I was tired of his talk. "Come on, let's get out of this dump," I said. He made me feel that everything was hopeless.

While we were waiting for change, I picked up his cane.

"What do you carry this for?" I said.

"Don't you like it?"

"It's an affectation."

"You're a prig," he said.

"Just the same," I said, "I think it's a phoney."

"Everyone in New York knows Waldo Lydecker's walking-stick. It gives me importance."

I was willing to let the subject drop, but he liked to brag about his possessions. "I picked it up in Dublin. The dealer told me that it had been carried by an Irish baronet whose lofty and furious temper became a legend in the country."

"Probably used it for beating up the poor devils who dug peat on his lands," I said, not being very sympathetic to hot-blooded noblemen, my grandmother's stories having given me the other side of the picture. The cane was one of the heaviest I have ever handled, weighing at least one pound, twelve ounces. Below the crook, the stick was encircled by two gold bands set about three inches apart.

He snatched it out of my hands. "Give it back to me."

"What's eating you? Nobody wants your damn cane."

The Chinese brought change. Waldo watched out of the corner of his eye, and I added a quarter to the tip, hating myself but too weak to give him a reason to sneer.

"Don't sulk," he said. "If you need a cane, I'll buy you one. With a rubber tip."

I felt like picking up that big hunk of blubber and bouncing him like a ball. But I couldn't take any chances of losing his friendship. Not now. He asked where I was going, and when I said downtown, asked me to drop him at the Lafayette.

"Don't be so ungracious," he said. "I should think you'd be glad for an extra quarter-hour of my admirable discourse."

While we were driving along Fourth Avenue, he grabbed my arm. The car almost skidded.

"What's the idea?" I said.

"You must stop! Please, you must. Be generous for once in your life."

I was curious to know the cause of his excitement, so I stopped the car. He hurried back along the block to Mr. Claudius' antique shop.

Mr. Claudius' last name was Cohen. He was more like a Yankee than a Jew. He was about five-foot eleven, weighed no more than a hundred and fifty, had light eyes and a bald head that rose to a point like a pear. I knew him because he had once had a partner who was a fence. Claudius was an innocent guy, absent-minded and so crazy about antiques that he had no idea of his partner's double-crossing. I had been able to keep him out of court, and in gratitude he had given me a set of the Encyclopaedia Britannica.

It was natural that he and Waldo should know each other. They could both go into a trance over an old teapot.

What Waldo had seen in Claudius' window was a duplicate of the vase he had given Laura. It was made like a globe set upon a pedestal. To me it looked like one of those silver balls that hang on Christmas trees, strictly Woolworth. And I understand that it is not so rare and costly as many of the pieces that cause collectors to swoon. Waldo valued it because he had started the craze for mercury glass among certain high-class antique snobs. In his piece, "Distortion and Refraction,"[1] he had written:

Glass, blown bubble thin, is coated on the inner surface with a layer of quicksilver so that it shines like a mirror. And just as the mercury in a thermometer reveals the body's temperature, so do the refractions in that discerning globe discover the fevers of tempera-

[1] In the volume, *February, Which Alone,* by Waldo Lydecker, 1936.

ment in those unfortunate visitors who, upon entering my drawing-room, are first glimpsed in its globular surfaces as deformed dwarfs.

"Claudius, you dolt, why in the sacred name of Josiah Wedgwood have you been keeping this from me?"

Claudius took it out of the window. While Waldo made love to the vase, I looked at some old pistols. The conversation went on behind my back.

"Where did you get it?" Waldo asked.

"From a house in Beacon."

"How much are you going to soak me for it, you old horsethief?"

"It's not for sale."

"Not for sale! But my good man . . ."

"It's sold," Claudius said.

Waldo pounded his stick against the skinny legs of an old table. "What right have you to sell it without offering it to me first? You know my needs."

"I found it for a customer. He'd commissioned me to buy any mercury glass I found at any price I thought was right."

"You had it in your window. That means you're offering it for sale."

"It don't mean that at all. It means I like to show the public something nice. I got a right to put things in my window, Mr. Lydecker."

"Did you buy it for Philip Anthony?"

There was a silence. Then Waldo shouted: "You knew I'd be interested in anything he'd want. You had no right not to offer it to me."

His voice was like an old woman's. I turned around and saw that his face had grown beet-red.

Claudius said: "The piece belongs to Anthony, there's nothing I can do about it now. If you want it, submit an offer to him."

"You know he won't sell it to me."

The argument went on like that. I was looking at an old muzzle-loader that must have been a relic when Abe Lincoln was a boy. I heard a crash. I looked around. Silver splinters shone on the floor.

Claudius was pale. Something human might have been killed.

"It was an accident, I assure you," Waldo said. Claudius moaned.

"Your shop is badly lighted, the aisles are crowded, I tripped," Waldo said.

"Poor Mr. Anthony."

"Don't make such a fuss. I'll pay whatever you ask."

From where I stood, the shop looked like a dark cavern. The antique furniture, the old clocks, vases, dishes, drinking-glasses, China dogs, and tarnished candlesticks were like a scavenger's storehouse. The two men whispered. Waldo, with his thick body, his black hat and heavy stick, Claudius with his pear-shaped head, reminded me of old women like witches on Hallowe'en. I walked out.

Waldo joined me at the car. He had his wallet in his hand. But his mood had improved. He stood in the rain, looking back at Claudius' shop and smiling. Almost as if he'd got the vase anyway.

CHAPTER TEN

Mooney's report on the murdered model hadn't satisfied me. I wanted to investigate for myself.

By the time I got to Christopher Street he had already interviewed the other tenants. No one had seen Miss Redfern since Friday.

The house was one of a row of shabby old places that carried signs: VACANCY, PERSIAN CATS, DRESSMAKING, OCCULT SCIENCE, FRENCH HOME COOKING. As I stood in the drizzle, I understood why a girl would hesitate to spend a hot weekend here.

The landlady was like an old flour-sack, bleached white and tied in the middle. She said that she was tired of cops and that if you asked her opinion, Diane was staying with a man somewhere. There were so many girls in the city and they were such loose creatures that it didn't make any difference whether one of them got misplaced once in a while. She wouldn't be a bit surprised if Diane turned up in the morning.

I left her chattering in the vestibule and climbed three flights of mouldy stairs. I knew the smells: sleep, dried soap, and shoe leather. After I left home I'd lived in several of these houses. I felt sorry for the kid, being young and expecting something of her beauty, and coming home to this suicide staircase. And I thought of Laura, offering her apartment because she had probably lived in these dumps, too, and remembered the smells on a summer night.

Even the wallpaper, brown and mustard yellow, was familiar. There was a single bed, a second-hand dresser, a sagging armchair, and a wardrobe with an oval glass set in the door. Diane had made enough to live in a better place, but she had been sending money to the family. And the upkeep of her beauty had evidently cost plenty. She'd been crazy about clothes; there were hats and gloves and shoes of every color.

There were stacks of movie magazines in the room. Pages had been turned down and paragraphs marked. You could tell that Diane had dreamed of Hollywood. Less beautiful girls had become stars, married stars, and owned swimming pools. There were some of those confession magazines, too, the sort that told stories of girls who had sinned, suffered, and been reclaimed by the love of good men. Poor Jennie Swobodo.

Her consolation must have been the photographs which she had thumb-tacked upon the ugly wallpaper. They were proofs and glossy prints showing her at work; Diane Redfern in Fifth Avenue furs; Diane at the opera; Diane pouring coffee from a silver pot; Diane in a satin nightgown with a satin quilt falling off the chaise-lounge in a way that showed a pretty leg.

It was hard to think of those legs dead and gone forever.

I sat on the edge of her bed and thought about the poor kid's life. Perhaps those photographs represented a real world to the young girl. All day while she worked, she lived in their expensive settings. And at night she came home to this cell. She must have been hurt by the contrast between those sleek studio interiors and the second-hand furniture of the boarding-house; between the silky models who posed with her and the poor slobs she met on the mouldy staircase.

Laura's apartment must have seemed like a studio setting to Jennie Swobodo, who hadn't been so long away from Paterson and the silk mills. Laura's Upper East Side friends must have been posing all the time in her eyes, like models before a camera. And Shelby . . .

I saw it all then.

I knew why Shelby was so familiar.

I'd never met him while I was pursuing crooks. He'd never mixed with the gents I'd encountered in my professional life. I'd seen him in the advertisements.

Maybe it wasn't Shelby himself. There was no record of his ever actually having been a photographer's model. But the young men who drove Packards and wore Arrow shirts, smoked Chesterfields, and paid their insurance premiums and clipped coupons were Shelby. What had Waldo said? *The hero she could love forever immaturely, the mould of perfection whose flawlessness made no demands upon her sympathies or her intelligence.*

I was sore. First, at myself for having believed that I'd find a real clue in a man who wasn't real. I'd been thinking of Shelby as I had always thought of common killers, shysters, finks, goons, and hopheads. The king of the artichoke racket had been real; the pinball gang had been flesh-and-blood men with hands that could pull triggers; even the Associated Dairymen had been living profiteers. But Shelby was a dream walking. He was God's gift to women. I hated him for it and I hated the women for falling for the romance racket. I didn't stop to think that men aren't much different, that I had wasted a lot of adult time on the strictly twelve-year-old dream of getting back to the old neighborhood with the world's championship and Hedy Lamarr beside me on the seat of a five-grand roadster.

But I had expected Laura to be above that sort of nonsense. I thought I had found a woman who would know a real man when she saw one; a woman whose bright eyes would go right through the mask and tell her that the man underneath was

Lincoln and Columbus and Thomas A. Edison. And Tarzan, too.

I felt cheated.

There was still a job to be done. Sitting on a bed and figuring out the philosophy of love was not solving a murder. I had discovered the dream world of Jennie-Swobodo-Diane-Redfern, and so what? Not a shred of evidence that she might also have been playing around with the kind of pals who used sawed-off shotguns.

The trail led back to Laura's apartment and Shelby. I found evidence in Diane's green pocketbook.

Before I left the house, I checked with the landlady, who told me that Diane had carried the green pocketbook on Friday. But I knew without being told. She had respected her clothes; she had put her dresses on hangers and stuffed shoe-trees into twenty pairs of slippers. Even at Laura's, she had hung her dress away and put her hat on the shelf and her pocketbook in the drawer. So I knew she had dressed in a hurry for her date on Friday night. Green hat, gloves, and pocketbook had been left on the bed. Her shoes had been kicked under a chair. I had seen the same thing happen at home. When my sister used to get ready for a date with her boss, she always left stockings curled over the backs of chairs and pink step-ins on the bathroom floor.

I picked up the green pocketbook. It was heavy. I knew it should have been empty because Laura had showed me the black purse she had found in her drawer, the purse into which Diane had put her compact, her lipstick, her keys, her money, and a torn straw cigarette case.

There was a cigarette case in the green pocketbook. It was made of gold and it was initialed with the letters S. J. C.

CHAPTER ELEVEN

Twenty minutes later I was sitting in Laura's living room. The cigarette case was in my pocket.

Laura and Shelby were together on the couch. She had been crying. They had been together since Waldo and I left them at five o'clock. It was about ten. Bessie had gone home.

I wondered what they had been talking about for five hours.

I was business-like. I was crisp and efficient. I sounded like a detective in a detective story. "I am going to be direct," I said. "There are several facts in this case which need explaining. If you two will help me clear away these contradictions, I'll know you're as anxious as I am to solve this murder. Otherwise I'll be forced to believe you have some private reason for not wanting the murderer to be found."

Laura sat with her hands folded in her lap like a schoolgirl in the principal's office. I was the principal. She was afraid of me. Shelby wore a death mask. The clock ticked like a man's heart beating. I took out the gold cigarette case.

The muscles tightened around Shelby's eyes. Nobody spoke.

I held it toward Laura. "You knew where this was, didn't you? She had the green pocketbook with her at lunch Friday, didn't she? Tell me, Laura, did you invite her to use your apartment before or after you discovered the cigarette case?"

The tears began to roll down Laura's cheeks.

Shelby said: "Why don't you tell him what you just told me, Laura. It was *before!*"

She nodded like a Sunday School kid. "Yes, it was before."

They didn't look at each other, but I felt a swift interchange of some sort. Shelby had begun to whistle out of tune. Laura took off her gold earrings and rested her head against the back of the couch.

I said: "Laura was feeling bad because she had been rude to Diane on Wednesday. So she invited her to lunch, and then, because Diane complained about her uncomfortable room, Laura offered her the use of this apartment. Later, probably when they were having coffee, Diane pulled out this cigarette case. Forgetting who she was with, maybe . . ."

Laura said, "How did you know?"

"Isn't that what you want me to know?" I asked her. "Isn't that the easiest way to explain the situation?"

"But it's true," she said. "It's . . ."

Shelby interrupted. "See here, McPherson, I won't have you talking to her like that." He didn't wear the death mask any longer. The plaster had cracked. His eyes were narrow and mean, his mouth a tight line.

"Shelby," said Laura. "Please, Shelby."

He stood in front of her. His legs were apart, his fists clenched as if I had been threatening her. "I refuse to let this go on, McPherson. These insinuations . . ."

"Shelby, Shelby darling," Laura said. She pulled at his hands.

"I don't know what you assume that I'm

insinuating, Carpenter," I said. "I asked Miss Hunt a question. Then I reconstructed a scene which she tells me is accurate. What's making you so nervous?"

The scene was unreal again. I was talking detective-story language. Shelby made it impossible for a person to be himself.

"You see, darling," Laura said. "You're only making it worse by getting so excited."

They sat down again, her hand resting on his coat-sleeve. You could see that he didn't want her to control him. He squirmed. He looked at her bitterly. Then he pulled his arm away and moved to the end of the couch.

He spoke like a man who wants to show authority. "Look here, if you insult Miss Hunt again, I'll have to lodge a complaint against you."

"Have I been insulting you, Miss Hunt?"

She started to speak, but he interrupted. "If she has anything to tell, her lawyer will make a statement."

Laura said: "You're making it worse, dear. There's no need to be so nervous."

It seemed to me that words were printed on a page or rolling off a sound-track. A gallant hero protecting a helpless female against a crude minion of the law. I lit my pipe, giving him time to recover from the attack of gallantry. Laura reached for a cigarette. He sprang to light it. She looked in the other direction.

"All I'm asking from you at this moment," I told him, "is the low-down on that bottle of Bourbon. Why have you told one story and Mosconi another?"

She slanted a look in his direction. Shelby gave no sign that he had noticed, but he could see her without moving his eyes. It struck me that these two were clinging together, not so much out of love as in desperation. But I couldn't trust my own judgment. Personal feelings were involved. I had got beyond the point where I cared to look at faces. Fact was all that I wanted now. It had to be black or white, direct question, simple answer. Yes or no, Mr. Carpenter, were you in the apartment with Diane Redfern on Wednesday night? Yes or no, Miss Hunt, did you know he was going to meet her in your house?

Laura began to speak. Shelby coughed. She glanced frankly in his direction, but she might have looked at a worm that way. "I'm going to tell the truth, Shelby."

He seized her hands. "Laura, you're crazy. Don't you see that he's trying to get a confession? Anything we say . . . will be . . . they'll misinterpret . . . don't talk unless you've consulted a lawyer . . . you can't hope . . ."

She said: "Don't be so frightened, Shelby. Since you didn't do it, you have nothing to fear." She looked up at me and said: "Shelby thinks I killed Diane. That's why he told those lies. He's been trying to protect me."

She might have been talking about the rain or a dress or a book she had read. Frankness was her rôle now. She put it on like a coat. "Mark," she said, in a gentle voice—"do you believe I killed her, Mark?"

There it lay in the lamplight, solid gold, fourteen-karat evidence of Shelby's treachery. Laura had bought it for him at Christmas, a gift she had to charge to her aunt's account. He had told her he lost it, and on Friday, when she was trying to make up for her rudeness to Diane, she had seen it in the green pocketbook.

She had got a sudden headache at

lunch that day. She hadn't waited to take off her hat to telephone Waldo and tell him she couldn't keep her dinner date. She hadn't mentioned her change of plans because she hated having people ask her questions.

It was still Thursday. Thursday, ten-fourteen P.M. They were to have been married by this time and on their way to Nova Scotia. This was the bridal night.

The lamp shone on her face. Her voice was gentle. "Do you believe I killed her, Mark? Do you believe it, too?"

PART THREE

A stenographic report of the statement made by Shelby J. Carpenter to Lieutenant McPherson on Friday at 3.45 P.M., August 27, 1941.

Present: Shelby J. Carpenter, Lieutenant McPherson, N. T. Salsbury, Jr.

Mr. Carpenter: I, Shelby John Carpenter, do hereby swear that the following is a true statement of the facts known to me concerning the death of Diane Redfern. At times this will contradict certain statements I've made before, but . . .

Mr. Salsbury: You are to take into consideration, Lieutenant McPherson, that any conflict between this and previous statements made by my client is due to the fact that he felt it his moral duty to protect another person.

Lieutenant McPherson: We've promised your client immunity.

Mr. Salsbury: Go on, tell me what happened, Carpenter.

Mr. Carpenter: As you know, Miss Hunt wished a few days' rest before the wedding. She had worked exceedingly hard on a campaign for the Lady Lilith cosmetic account, and I did not blame her for requesting that we postpone the wedding until she had time to recover from the strain. I have often protested at her arduous and unflagging devotion to her career, since I believe that women are highly strung and delicate, so that the burden of her position, in addition to her social duties and personal obligations, had a definite effect upon her nerves. For this reason I have always tried to understand and sympathize with her temperamental vagaries.

On that Friday morning, just a week ago, I went into her office to consult her about a piece of copy which I had written the day before. Although I had come into the business several years after she was established as an important copy-writer, she had great respect for my judgment. More than anyone knew, we depended upon each other. It was as usual for her to come to me for help in planning and presenting a campaign or merchandising idea as it was for me to seek her advice about the wording of a piece of copy. Since I was to take over the Lady Lilith account, I naturally asked her criticism. She was enthusiastic about my headline, which read, as I remember, "Is yours just another face in a crowd? Or is it the radiant, magnetic countenance that men admire and women envy?" She suggested the word "magnetic."

Lieutenant McPherson: Let's get down to facts. You can explain the advertising business later.

Mr. Carpenter: I just wanted you to understand our relationship.

Lieutenant McPherson: Did she tell you she was going to have lunch with Diane?

Mr. Carpenter: That was a subject we had agreed not to discuss.

Lieutenant McPherson: Lunch?

Mr. Carpenter: Diane Redfern. As a matter of fact, I did ask her if she'd lunch with me, but she told me she had some errands. Naturally I asked no questions. I went out with some men in the office, and later our chief, Mr. Rose, joined us for coffee. At about two-fifteen, we went back to the office and I worked steadily until about three-thirty, when the telephone rang. It was Diane.

Lieutenant McPherson: Did she tell you she'd had lunch with Laura?

Mr. Carpenter: The poor child was quite distraught. You didn't know her, McPherson, but she was one of the most feminine creatures I have ever met. Like my own mother, although she was a girl of very different background and breeding. Yet she always felt the need of turning to a man when anything distressed her. It was unfortunate that I happened to be the man of her choice. Women—I hope you don't mind my saying this, McPherson, but I'm trying to be as frank as possible—have more than once attached themselves to me quite without encouragement. As Miss Hunt herself remarked, Diane had not been bred among gentlefolk. What we considered merely good manners she took as evidence of . . . shall we call it love? Her emotions were wild and undisciplined. Although she knew that I was engaged to marry Miss Hunt, she declared herself madly in love with me and, I must say, often embarrassed me with her declarations. Perhaps you've known young girls like this, McPherson, who love so violently that nothing exists for them except their passion and the man upon whom it is fixed.

Lieutenant McPherson: You didn't exactly discourage her, did you?

Mr. Salsbury: The question is irrelevant. You needn't answer it, Mr. Carpenter.

Mr. Carpenter: I tried not to be unkind. She was young and very sensitive.

Lieutenant McPherson: Did she say anything to you about having had lunch with Laura?

Mr. Carpenter: She told me she was desperate. At first I thought her fears were nothing more than hysteria. "Don't dramatize yourself," I told her, but there was something about her voice, a wild, frightened tone, that distressed me. I knew her to be both impulsive and courageous. I was afraid she might . . . you know what I mean, McPherson. So I said I'd take her to dinner, as a sort of farewell, you understand. I meant to talk some sense into her. We agreed to meet at Montagnino's.

Lieutenant McPherson: Montagnino's.

Mr. Carpenter: I felt that Diane's morale needed a stimulant. And since Miss Hunt had often mentioned Montagnino's as a favorite restaurant, Diane considered the place quite glamorous. You have no idea of the child's devotion to Miss Hunt.

Lieutenant McPherson: You didn't mention this to Laura, did you?

Mr. Carpenter: It would only have distressed her. She had been quite unhappy about having been so rude to Diane, you know. Although I did intend to tell her about it later. And besides she was dining with Waldo Lydecker . . . or at least that's what I thought.

Lieutenant McPherson: When you had cocktails with Miss Hunt at the Tropicale Bar, what did you talk about?

Mr. Carpenter: What did we talk about? Oh . . . well . . . our plans, of course. She seemed cold and rather listless, but I attributed this to her nervous condition. I begged her to have a good rest and not to worry. Miss Hunt, you know, is a very intelligent young woman, but sometimes her emotions get the better of her, and she becomes almost hysterical about world conditions. She suffers a sort of guilt complex, and sometimes declares that we, innocent people of our sort, share the responsibility for the horror and suffering that one reads about in the newspapers. This, added to a certain cynicism about the work she does, gives her an emotional instability which, I thought, I might help to correct. And so I begged her not to read newspapers or listen to news broadcasts during this week of rest, and she was rather charming about it, unusually submissive and quiet. When we parted, she allowed me to kiss her, but there was little warmth in her response. I gave the taxi-driver Waldo Lydecker's address, since she had said nothing to me of a change in her plans. Then I went back to the hotel, changed my clothes, and went on down to Montagnino's. I must tell you that I was disappointed in the place.

Lieutenant McPherson: You'd never been there before?

Mr. Carpenter: Mr. Lydecker had always taken Miss Hunt there. They were quite exclusive about it. We'd only known it by hearsay.

Lieutenant McPherson: Did Diane tell

you about having had lunch with Laura and bringing out the cigarette case?

Mr. Carpenter: Yes, she did. And I was most unhappy.

Lieutenant McPherson: I suppose you and she tried to think of some excuse which you could give Laura.

Mr. Carpenter: I decided to tell my fiancé the truth.

Lieutenant McPherson: Before or after the wedding?

Mr. Salsbury: You needn't answer that, Mr. Carpenter.

Mr. Carpenter: You seem to think, McPherson, that there was something clandestine in my relationship with Diane.

Lieutenant McPherson: There were only two ways for her to have got hold of that cigarette case. Either she stole it or you gave it to her.

Mr. Carpenter: I admit that the incident looks very shabby, but if you knew the circumstances that brought about this . . . this . . . this gesture, I'm sure you'd understand.

Lieutenant McPherson: Diane was desperate, I suppose.

Mr. Carpenter: I don't like your tone,

McPherson. What you imply was not the situation.

Lieutenant McPherson: I didn't imply anything except that you had to be a big shot for Diane. Bigger than Laura. But if you want me to imply anything else, I can think of a couple of reasons why you might have given her that gold cigarette case.

Mr. Salsbury: Personal and irrelevant detail, Lieutenant.

Mr. Carpenter: Thank you, Mr. Salsbury.

Lieutenant McPherson: Okay, go on.

Mr. Carpenter: At about ten o'clock we left the restaurant. I had expected her to have recovered by that time, but she was more nervous and upset than before. She seemed to be suffering some nameless terror, almost as if she were afraid of violence. Although she would not definitely name her fear, I could see that this hysteria was not entirely groundless. In the circumstances I couldn't leave her alone, and so I promised to come up with her for a little while.

Lieutenant McPherson: To Laura's apartment?

Mr. Carpenter: I confess that I didn't quite enjoy the prospect, but in the circumstances I couldn't talk to her in a public place. And since she obviously couldn't come to my room in a hotel for men, and male guests were not allowed upstairs in her boarding house, it seemed the only practical arrangement. So we drove uptown to the apartment . . .

Lieutenant McPherson: Where was she when you stopped in at Mosconi's to buy the Bourbon?

Mr. Carpenter: I ought to explain that, oughtn't I?

Lieutenant McPherson: It'd help.

Mr. Carpenter: Diane was distressed and needed a stimulant. We felt a little queer about taking Miss Hunt's liquor, and so I stopped at Mosconi's . . .

Lieutenant McPherson: Leaving Diane outside because Mosconi knew you as Laura's friend.

Mr. Carpenter: Not at all. Diane had to stop in the drugstore . . .

Mr. Salsbury: You went right on to Miss Hunt's apartment, didn't you?

Lieutenant McPherson: Where Diane took off her clothes and put on Laura's silk robe.

Mr. Carpenter: It was a very hot night, as you'll remember.

Lieutenant McPherson: There was a breeze in the bedroom, I suppose.

Mr. Carpenter: We talked for three hours. Then the doorbell rang and . . .

Lieutenant McPherson: Tell us exactly what happened. Don't skip anything.

Mr. Carpenter: We were both surprised, and Diane was frightened. But knowing Miss Hunt as I've known her, I've learned to be shocked at nothing. When her friends are upset about their marriages or love affairs or careers, they think nothing of disturbing her with their troubles. I told Diane to go to the door and explain that she was using the apartment while Laura was away.

Lieutenant McPherson: You stayed in the bedroom, huh?

Mr. Carpenter: Suppose one of Laura's friends had found me there? Better to avoid gossip, wasn't it?

Lieutenant McPherson: Go on.

Mr. Carpenter: The bell rang again. I heard Diane's mules clattering on the bare boards between the rugs. Then there was a moment of silence, and the shot. You can imagine how I felt. By the time I reached her, the door had closed and she lay there on the floor. The room was dark, I saw only a vague light shape, her silk robe. I asked if she had been hurt. There was no answer. Then I stooped down to feel her heart.

Lieutenant McPherson: Go on.

Mr. Carpenter: It's too hideous to talk about.

Lieutenant McPherson: And then what did you do?

Mr. Carpenter: My first instinct was to call the police.

Lieutenant McPherson: Why didn't you?

Mr. Carpenter: Just as I was about to lift the receiver, I was struck by a paralyzing thought. My hand fell at my side. I just stood there. You must remember, McPherson, that I loved Laura dearly.

Lieutenant McPherson: It wasn't Laura who was shot.

Mr. Carpenter: I owed her a certain loyalty. And in a way I felt some responsibility for this affair. I knew at once why Diane had been so terrified, after that display of bad manners Wednesday afternoon. As soon as I had put two and two together, I realized that I had one duty in regard to this tragedy. No matter how difficult it might be for me to control myself, I must keep out of it. My presence in this apartment would not only be extremely awkward, but would indubitably cast suspicion upon that one person whom I must protect. I can see now that it was extremely foolish for me to have acted upon this impulse, but there are times when a man is moved by something deeper than rational emotion.

Lieutenant McPherson: Did it occur to you that, by leaving the apartment and withholding the truth, you were obstructing the processes of law?

Mr. Carpenter: I had only one thought in mind: the safety of a person whose life was dearer to me than my own.

Lieutenant McPherson: On Saturday morning, when our men came to the Framingham to tell you that Laura was dead, you seemed sincerely shocked.

Mr. Carpenter: I must admit that I was not prepared for that interpretation.

Lieutenant McPherson: But you had your alibi ready, and no matter who was dead, you stuck to your story.

Mr. Carpenter: If I had become involved in the case, someone else would eventually have been suspected. This is what I hoped to avoid. But you must realize that my grief was real, both for Diane and the other person. I don't believe I've slept a full two hours since this thing happened. It's not like me to lie. I'm happiest when I can be completely frank with myself and the world.

Lieutenant McPherson: Although you knew Laura was not dead, you evidently made no effort to get in touch with her. Why not?

Mr. Carpenter: Wasn't it better to let her pursue her own course? I felt that if she wanted me, she'd call upon me, knowing that I'd stand by her to the bitter end.

Lieutenant McPherson: Why did you go and stay with Laura's aunt?

Mr. Carpenter: Since I was almost a member of the family, it was more or less my duty to attend to the unpleasant details. Mrs. Treadwell was very gracious, I must say, in suggesting that public curiosity made it uncomfortable for me at the hotel. After all, I was in mourning.

Lieutenant McPherson: And you allowed Diane to be buried—or cremated—as Laura Hunt.

Mr. Carpenter: I can't tell you what I suffered during those terrible four days.

Lieutenant McPherson: On the night that

Laura came back, she phoned you at the Framingham, didn't she? And you'd given instructions that they weren't to give out your number . . .

Mr. Carpenter: The reporters were making me quite uncomfortable, McPherson. I thought it best anyway not to have her telephoning her aunt's house. When they phoned me on Wednesday night—or Thursday morning, it was—I knew at once. And although I don't wish to seem ungrateful to my hostess, I knew Mrs. Treadwell to be an inquisitive woman. And since it would have been a shock for her to hear the voice of a person whose funeral she had just attended, I went out to a pay booth to telephone Miss Hunt.

Lieutenant McPherson: Repeat that conversation as fully as you remember it.

Mr. Carpenter: She said, "Shelby?" and I said, "Hello, my darling," and she said, "Did you think I was dead, Shelby?" I asked her if she was all right.

Lieutenant McPherson: Did you say you thought she had died?

Mr. Carpenter: I asked if she was all right. She said that she felt terribly about poor Diane, and asked if I knew anyone who might have wished her to die. I knew then that Miss Hunt did not intend to give me her full confidence. Nor could I talk to her frankly on the telephone. But I knew there was one detail which might prove embarrassing—or downright dangerous— and I made up my mind to save her, if I could.

Lieutenant McPherson: What was that detail?

Mr. Carpenter: It's right there on your desk, McPherson.

Lieutenant McPherson: You knew she had the shotgun?

Mr. Carpenter: I had given it to her. She frequently stayed alone in her country house. Those initials are my mother's— Delilah Shelby Carpenter.

Lieutenant McPherson: And that's why you borrowed Mrs. Treadwell's car and drove up to Wilton?

Mr. Carpenter: Yes, that's right. But when your man followed me in the cab, I didn't dare go into the house. I stood in the garden for a while and I was considerably overcome because I couldn't help remembering what that little cottage and garden had meant to us. When I returned to town and found you with Mrs. Treadwell, I was not completely untruthful in saying that it had been a sentimental pilgrimage. Later in the day you asked me to come up to the apartment. I was to be surprised at finding Miss Hunt alive and as you were going to study my reactions, McPherson, I decided to give you the show that you expected, for I still believed that there was a chance to save the situation.

Lieutenant McPherson: But after I left, you talked it over with Laura. You told her exactly what you thought.

Mr. Carpenter: Miss Hunt has admitted nothing.

Mr. Salsbury: Lieutenant McPherson, my client has gone to considerable trouble and risked his personal safety in order to protect another person. He is not obliged to answer any question which might incriminate that person.

Lieutenant McPherson: Okay, I've got it straight. I'll get in touch with you if I need you, Carpenter. But don't leave the city.

Mr. Carpenter: Thank you so much for your understanding attitude, McPherson.

Part Four

CHAPTER ONE

Last week, when I thought I was to be married, I burned my girlhood behind me. And vowed never to keep another diary. The other night, when I came home and found Mark McPherson in my apartment, more intimate than my oldest friend, my first thought was gratitude for the destruction of those shameful pages. How inconsistent he would have thought me if he had read them! I can never keep a proper diary, simmer my life down to a line a day, nor make breakfast on the sixteenth of the month as important as falling in love on the seventeenth. It's always when I start on a long journey or meet an exciting man or take a new job that I must sit for hours in a frenzy of recapitulation. The idea that I am an intelligent woman is pure myth. I can never grasp an abstraction except through emotion, and before I can begin to think with my head about any fact, I must see it as a solid thing on paper.

At work, when I plan a campaign for Lady Lilith Face Powder or Jix Soap Flakes, my mind is orderly. I write dramatic headlines and follow them with sales arguments that have unity, coherence, and emphasis. But when I think about myself, my mind whirls like a merry-go-round. All the horses, the bright and the drab, dance around a shining, mirrored centre whose dazzling rays and frivolous music make concentration impossible. I am trying to think clearly of all that has happened in the last few days, to remember the facts and set them upon the horses and send them out in neat parade like sales arguments for Jix or Lady Lilith. They disobey, they whirl and dance to the music, and all I remember is that a man who had heard me accused of murder was concerned about my getting enough sleep.

"Sleep," he said to me, "get some sleep." As if sleep were something you could buy at the Five-and-Ten. After he'd been gone for a little while, he came back with a package from Schwartz's drugstore. They were pills to make me sleep, but he would only leave me two because he knew how sick I was with fear and worry.

"Do you believe I killed Diane?" I asked him again.

"It doesn't matter what I think." His voice grated. "It isn't my business to think; it's only facts I want, facts."

Shelby watched. He looked more than ever like a beautiful tomcat, ready to leap. Shelby said: "Be careful, Laura. Don't trust him."

"Yes," he said, "I'm a cop, you mustn't trust me. Anything you say might be used against you." His lips were drawn hard over his teeth; he spoke without opening his mouth.

"Are you going to arrest me?" I said.

Shelby became very man-of-the-house, protector of frail womanhood. It was all pretense, his courage was as thin as tissue paper, he trembled inwardly. Shelby used phrases like "false arrest" and "circumstantial evidence"; you could tell he was proud of displaying technical knowledge like when he could explain to people about the rules of fencing or backgammon.

Auntie Sue once told me I'd grow tired of a six-foot child. Auntie Sue said that when a woman feels the need for a man that way, she ought to have a baby. I kept thinking of Auntie Sue's remarks while Shelby talked about circumstantial evidence and Mark walked around and around the room, looking at things, at my autographed baseball and my Mexican tray and the shelf where I keep my very favorite books.

"She'll get in touch with her lawyer," Shelby said. "That's what she'll do."

Mark came back to me. "You mustn't try to leave here, Laura."

"No, I won't leave."

"He's got a man outside. You couldn't leave anyway," Shelby said. "He's having you watched."

Mark left without another word, without telling me to sleep again or good-bye.

"I don't like that fellow. He's a sly one," Shelby said as soon as the door had closed.

"You said that before."

"You're gullible, Laura. You trust people too easily."

I stood with my back to Shelby, looking at the shelf with all my favorite books.

"He's been very kind," I said—"consider-ing. I think he's nice. You'd never think of a detective being like that."

I felt Shelby's hands stretching toward me and I moved away. He was quiet. I knew, without turning, how his face would look.

He picked up the two pills that Mark had left on the table. "Do you think you ought to take these, Laura?"

I whirled around. "Great God, you don't think he's trying to give me poison!"

"He ought to be hardboiled. You'd ex-pect him to be tougher. I don't like his try-ing to act like a gentleman."

"Oh, pooh!" I said.

"You don't see it. The man's trying to make you like him so you'll break down and confess. That's what he's been work-ing for all along, a confession. Damned caddish, I'd say."

I sat down on the sofa and pounded my fists against a pillow. "I hate that word. Caddish! I've begged you a million times to quit using it."

Shelby said, "It's a good English word."

"It's old-fashioned. It's out of date. People don't talk about cads any more. It's Victorian."

"A cad is a cad, whether the word is obsolete or not."

"Quit being so Southern. Quit being so righteous. You and your damn gallantry." I was crying. The tears ran down my cheeks and dripped off my jaws. My tan dress was all wet with tears.

"You're nervous, sweet," Shelby said. "That damned cad has been working on you subtly, he's been trying to wear you down."

"I told you," I screamed, "that I wish you'd stop using that word."

"It's a perfectly good English word," he said.

"You said that before. You've said it a million times."

"You'll find it in Webster," he said. "And in Funk and Wagnalls."

"I'm so tired," I said. I rubbed my eyes with my fists because I'm never able to find a handkerchief in a crisis.

"It's a perfectly good English word," Shelby said again.

I jumped up, the pillow in my arms like a

shield against him. "A fine one you are to talk about cads, Shelby Carpenter."

"I've been trying to protect you!"

When he spoke like that, his voice deep with reproach, I felt as if I had hurt a helpless child. Shelby knew how his voice worked on me; he could color his voice with the precise shade of reproach so that I would hate that heartless bitch, Laura Hunt, and forgive his faults. He remembered as well as I the day we went duck hunting and he bragged and I said I despised him, and he won me again with the tones of his voice; he remembered the fight we had at the office party and the time he kept me waiting two hours in the Paramount lobby, and our terrible quarrel the night he gave me the gun. All of those quarrels rose in our minds now; there were almost two years of quarrels and reproach between us, and two years of love and forgiveness and the little jokes that neither could forget. I hated his voice for reminding me, and I was afraid because I had always been weak with a thirty-two-year-old baby.

"I've been trying to protect you," Shelby said.

"Great God, Shelby, we're right back

where we started from. We've been saying the same thing over and over again since five o'clock this afternoon."

"You're getting bitter," he said, "terribly bitter, Laura. Of course, after what's happened, one can't completely blame you."

"Oh, go away," I said. "Go home and let me sleep."

I took the two white pills and went into the bedroom. I slammed the door hard. After a while I heard Shelby leave. I went to the window. There were two men on the steps. After Shelby had gone a little way, one followed him. The other lit a cigarette. I saw the match flame and die in the misty darkness. The houses opposite mine are rich people's private houses. Not one of my neighbors stays in town during the summer. There was only a cat, the thin yellow homeless cat that nuzzles against my legs when I come from work at night. The cat crossed the street daintily, pointing his feet like a ballet dancer, lifting them high as if his feet were too good for the pavement. On Friday night when Diane was killed, the street was quiet, too.

CHAPTER TWO

Sleep he had said, try to get some sleep. Two pills weren't enough. When I turned out the lights, the darkness whined around me. The old dead tenants came creeping up the stairs, their footsteps cautious on the tired boards. They sighed and whispered behind doors, they rattled the old latches, they plotted conspiracies. I saw Diane, too, in my aquamarine house coat; I saw her with dark hair flowing about her shoulders, running to answer the doorbell.

The doorbell had rung, Shelby told me, and he stayed in the bedroom while she ran to answer it. As soon as she had opened the front door, he heard the shot. Then the door snapped shut. After a time that might have been thirty seconds or thirty years, Shelby said, he had left the bedroom. He tried to speak to her, his lips framed her name, but his voice was dead. The room was dark, the light came in from the street lamp in stripes through the Venetian blinds. He saw the pale silk of my robe spread about her on the floor, but he could not see her face. It seemed gone. When his blood had thawed, Shelby said, he had stooped to feel for the place where her heart should have been. His hand was paralyzed, he felt nothing, he knew she was dead. He went to the telephone, meaning to call the police. When Shelby told me about that part of it, he stretched out his hand as he had stretched it toward the telephone, and then he pulled his hand back quickly just as he had done that night. If the police had known he was there in my apartment with Diane, they would have known, too, who had killed her, Shelby said.

"That was your guilty conscience," I told him. "Guilty because you were here. In my own house with her. You wanted to believe *that*, because you were ashamed."

"I was trying to protect you," Shelby said.

This was early in the evening, after Mark

had gone off for dinner with Waldo, and before Mark came back with the cigarette case.

Auntie Sue told me I was a fool when I bought that cigarette case. I am so gullible that I trust a detective, but Auntie Sue didn't even trust Uncle Horace to make his will; she sat behind the curtains while he and the lawyer figured out the bequests. Auntie Sue said I'd always regret the cigarette case. I gave it to Shelby because he needed grandeur when he talked to prospective clients or had drinks with men he'd known at college. Shelby had his airs and graces, manner and a name that made him feel superior, but these were things that mattered in Covington, Kentucky, not in New York. Ten years in and out of precarious jobs hadn't taught him that gestures and phrases were of less importance in our world than aggressiveness and self-interest; and that the gentlemanly arts were not nearly so useful as proficiency in double-dealing, bootlicking, and pushing yourself ahead of the other fellow.

The tea was pale, pale green with one dark leaf curled in it, when I saw the cigarette case in Diane's hand. I saw Diane's pointed magenta nails curving over the edge of the gold case, but I could not look at her face. The tea had a delicate Chinese smell. I did not feel pain or anger, I felt giddy. I said to Diane, "Please, dear, I have a headache, do you mind if I leave now?" It was not like me to be calm. I tell the truth shrilly and then I am sorry. But this was deeper, so deep that I could only watch the leaf floating in the teacup.

Shelby had given her the cigarette case so that he might feel rich and generous, too. Like a gigolo seeking revenge against a fat old dowager with a jet band binding the wattles under her chin. It was all clear then, as if the tea leaf had been my fortune in the cup, for I knew why Shelby and I had quarreled so that we could go on pretending to love. He not sure of himself; he still needed the help I could give him; but he hated himself for clinging to me, and hated me because I let him cling.

They had been lovers since April eighteenth. I remember the date because it was Paul Revere's ride and Auntie Sue's birthday. The date smells of cleaning fluid. We were in a taxi on the way to the Coq d'Or where Auntie Sue was having her birthday party. I wore my sixteen-button fawn gloves; they had just come from the cleaner and the smell was stronger than the odor of taxi-leather and tobacco and the Tabu with which I had scented my handkerchief and my hair. That was when Shelby told me about losing the cigarette case. He used the hurt voice and his remorse was so real that I begged him not to feel it too deeply. Shelby said I was a wonderful woman, tolerant and forgiving. Damned patronizing bitch, he must have been thinking as we sat in the taxi, holding hands.

Lovers since April eighteenth. And this was almost the end of August. Diane and Shelby had been holding hands, too, and laughing behind my back.

When I walked through the office after lunch, I wondered if all the faces knew and were hiding themselves from my humiliation. My friends said they could understand my having fallen in love impulsively with Shelby, but they did not see how I could go on caring. This would make me angry; I would say they judged unfairly because Shelby was too handsome. It was almost as if Shelby's looks were a handicap, a sort of deformity that had to be protected.

Usually I anger quickly. I flame and burn with shrill vehemence and suffer remorse at the spectacle of my petty female spleen. This time my fury had a new pattern. I can feel that frigid fury now as I remember how I counted the months, the weeks, the days since the eighteenth of April. I tried to remember when I had seen Diane alone and what she had said to me; and I thought of the three of us together with Diane humbly acknowledging Shelby my lover; and I tried to count the evenings that I had spent alone or with other friends, giving Shelby to her on those evenings. How tolerant we were, how modern, how ridiculous and pitiful! But I had always told Shelby about dining with Waldo and he had never told me that he was seeing Diane.

Desperate, my mother used to say, I'm desperate, when she locked herself in her bedroom with a sick headache. I always envied her; I wanted to grow up and be desperate too. On Friday afternoon, as I walked up and down my office, I whispered it over and over. Desperate, desperate, at last I'm desperate, I said, as if the word were consummation. I can see the office now, the desk and filing-case and a proof of a Lady Lilith color ad with Diane lying backward on a couch, head thrown back, breasts pointed upward like small hills. I feel, rather than smell, the arid, air-conditioned atmosphere, and I tense my right hand as if the letter-opener were still cutting a ridge across my palm. I was sick, I was desperate, I was afraid. I hid my face in my hands, my forehead against the wood of my desk.

I telephoned Waldo and told him I had a headache.

"Don't be difficult, wench," Waldo said. "Roberto has scoured the markets for our bachelor dinner."

"I'm desperate," I said.

Waldo laughed. "Put your headache off until tomorrow. The country is a good place for headaches, that's all it's fit for; have your headache among the beetles. What time shall I expect you, angel?"

I knew that if I dined with Waldo, I should tell him about the cigarette case. He would have been glad to hear that I was done with Shelby, but he would have wrapped his satisfaction elegantly in sympathy. Waldo would never have said, I told you so, Laura, I told you at the start. Not Waldo. He would have opened his best champagne and, holding up his glass, would have said, "And now, Laura, you've grown up, let us drink to your coming of age."

No, thank you, no urbanity for me tonight, Waldo. I am drunk already.

When Shelby came to my office at five o'clock, I rode down in the elevator with him, I drank two dry Martinis with him, I let him put me into the cab and give Waldo's address to the driver just as if I had never seen the cigarette case.

CHAPTER THREE

On Saturday I thinned my sedum, transplanted primroses, and started a new iris bed near the brook. On Sunday I moved the peony plants. They were heavy, the roots so long that I had to dig deep holes in the ground. I had to keep myself occupied with hard physical work; the work soothed me and emptied my mind of Friday's terror.

When the gardener came on Monday, he said that I had moved the peonies too early, they would surely die now. Twenty times that day I went to look at them. I watered them gently with thin streams of tepid water, but they drooped, and I felt ashamed before the victims of my impatience.

Before the gardener left on Monday, I

told him not to tell Shelby that I had killed the peony plants by moving them too early. Shelby would never have mourned the peonies, but he would have had cause to reproach me for doing a man's work in the garden instead of waiting until he came. It was curious that I should say this to the gardener because I knew that Shelby would never dig and mow and water my garden again. I was still defiant of Shelby; I was trying to irritate him by absent treatment, and provoke imaginary argument so that I could hurt him with sharp answers. Challenging Shelby, I worked in my house, washing and polishing and scrubbing on my hands and knees. He always said that I shouldn't do menial work, I could afford to hire servants; he could never know the fulfillment of working with your hands in your own house. My people were plain folk; the women went West with their men and none of them found gold. But Shelby came from "gentle" people; they had slaves to comb their hair and put on their shoes. A gentleman cannot see a lady work like a nigger; a gentleman opens the door and pulls out a lady's chair and brings a whore into her bedroom.

I saw then, working on my knees, the pattern our marriage would have taken, shoddy and deceitful, taut emotion woven with slack threads of pretense.

The fault was mine more than Shelby's. I had used him as women use men to complete the design of a full life, playing at love for the gratification of my vanity, wearing him proudly as a successful prostitute wears her silver foxes to tell the world she owns a man. Going on thirty and unmarried, I had become alarmed. Pretending to love him and playing the mother game, I bought him an extravagant cigarette case, fourteen-karat gold, as a man might buy his wife an orchid or a diamond to expiate infidelity.

And now that tragedy has wiped away all the glib excuses, I see that our love was as bare of real passion as the mating of two choice vegetables which are to be combined for the purpose of producing a profitable new item for the markets. It was like love in the movies, contrived and opportune. And now it was over.

Two strangers sat at opposite ends of the couch. We tried to find words that had the same meaning for both of us. It was still

Thursday evening, before dinner, after Mark and Waldo had left. We spoke softly because Bessie was in the kitchen.

"This will all blow over in a few days," Shelby said. "If we sit tight and match our stories properly. Who'll know? That detective is an ass."

"Why must you keep on calling him *that detective?* You know his name."

"Let's not be bitter," Shelby said. "It'll only make it more difficult for us to go on."

"What makes you think I want to go on? I don't hate you and I'm not bitter, but I couldn't go on. Not now."

"I tell you, Laura, I only came because she begged me so. She begged me to come and say good-bye to her. She was in love with me; I didn't care two hoots about her, honestly, but she threatened to do something desperate unless I came up here on Friday night."

I turned my head away.

"We've got to stick together now, Laura. We're in this thing too deeply to fight each other. And I know you love me. If you hadn't loved me, you couldn't have come back here on Friday night and . . ."

"Shut up! Shut up!" I said.

"If you weren't here on Friday night, if you are innocent, then how could you have known about the Bourbon bottle, how could you have responded so instinctively to the need to protect me?"

"Must we go over it all again, Shelby? Again and again and again?"

"You lied to protect me just as I lied to protect you."

It was all so dreary and so useless. Three Horses had been Shelby's brand of Bourbon, he had been buying it for himself when he started coming to my house, and then I began buying it so he'd always find a drink when he came. But one day Waldo laughed because I kept such cheap whiskey on my shelves and named a better brand, and I tried to please Shelby with expensive Bourbon. His buying the bottle of Three Horses that night, like his giving Diane the cigarette case, was defiance, Shelby's defiance of my patronage.

Bessie announced dinner. We washed our hands, we sat at the table, we spread napkins in our laps, we touched water to our lips, we held knives and forks in our hands for Bessie's sake. With her coming and going, we couldn't talk. We sat behind steak and French fried, we dipped our spoons ceremoniously into the rum pudding which Bessie had made, good soul, to celebrate my return from death. After she had brought the coffee to the table before the fire and we had the length of the room between us and the kitchen door, Shelby asked where I had hidden the gun.

"Gun!"

"Don't talk so loud!" He nodded toward the kitchen door. "My mother's gun; why do you suppose I drove up there last night?"

"Your mother's gun is in the walnut chest, just where you saw me put it, Shelby, after we had the fight."

The fight had started because I refused the gun. I was not nearly so afraid of staying alone in my little house as of having a gun there. But Shelby had called me a coward and insisted upon my keeping it for protection, had laughed me into learning to use it.

"The first fight or the second fight?" he asked.

The second fight had been about his shooting rabbits. I had complained about their eating the iris bulbs and the gladiolus corms, and Shelby had shot a couple of them.

"Why do you lie to me, darling? You know that I'll stick with you to the end."

I picked up a cigarette. He hurried to light it. "Don't do that," I said.

"Why not?"

"You can't call me a murderer and light my cigarette."

Now that I had said the word aloud, I felt freer. I stood up, stretched my legs, blew smoke at the ceiling. I felt that I belonged to myself and could fight my own battles.

"Don't be so childish," Shelby said. "Can't you see that you're in a tight spot and that I'm trying to help you? Don't you realize the chances I've taken, the lies I've told to protect you, and last night, driving up there? That makes me an accomplice; I'm in a rather bad spot myself, and for your sake."

"I wish I hadn't phoned you last night," I said.

"Don't be petty, Laura. Your instinct was sound. You knew as well as I that they'd go up and search your place as soon as they discovered that you were back."

"That's not why I called you."

Bessie came in to say good night and
tell me again that she was happy that I had
not died. Tears burned the edges of my
eyes.

When the door had closed behind her,
Shelby said: "I'd rest easier if I had that gun
in my possession now. But how can we get
it with detectives on our trail? I tried to
shake the fellow, I took the back road, but
the cab followed me all the way. If I'd as
much as searched the place, I'd have given
it away instantly. So I kept up the pretense
of sorrow; I stood in the garden and wept
for you; I called it a sentimental journey
when that detective . . ."

"His name is McPherson," I said.

"You're so bitter," Shelby said. "You'll
have to get over that bitterness, Laura, or
you'll never be able to fight it out. Now, if
we stand together, my sweet . . ."

Mark returned. I gave Shelby my hand
and we sat on the couch, side by side, like
lovers. Mark turned on the light; he looked
into my face; he said he was going to
speak the truth directly. That was when he
brought out the cigarette case and Shelby
lost his nerve and Mark's face became the
face of a stranger. It's hard to deceive

Mark; he looks at you as if he wants you to be honest. Shelby was afraid of honesty; he kept losing his temper like a schoolboy, and it was, in the end, Shelby's fear that told Mark that Shelby believed me guilty.

"Are you going to arrest me?" I asked Mark. But he went to Schwartz's and got me the sleeping pills, and when he left, although I did not say so to Shelby, I knew he was going to Wilton to search my house.

CHAPTER FOUR

Salsbury, Haskins, Warder, and Bone. Every little movement has a meaning all its own, Salsbury, Haskins, Warder, and Bone. A small black mustache parted in the middle, a voice, the smell of mint, and all of this an enigma, a rush of words and sense memories as I woke after a hard sleep and two small white pills. Salsbury, Haskins, Warder, and Bone . . . I attached the words to a melody . . . I heard music beyond my door and the words were Salsbury, Haskins, Warder, and Bone.

The music was the vacuum cleaner outside my bedroom door. Bessie brought coffee and orange juice. The glass was beaded with ice, and as my hand chilled, grasping it, I remembered a dewy silvered vessel, the smell of mint, and the small black mustache crowning a toothpaste smile. It was on the lawn of Auntie Sue's place at Sands Point; the black mustache had asked if I liked mint juleps and explained that he was young Salsbury of Salsbury, Haskins, Warder, and Bone.

Bessie breathed heavily, adjusted her jaw, asked if I would eat a nice poached egg.

"A lawyer," I said, aloud. "He told me that if I ever needed a lawyer, they're a very old firm."

Having worried enough over my failure to settle the poached egg question, Bessie sighed and departed while I, remembering Shelby's advice, heard myself telling it all to the black mustache.

"And your alibi, Laura? What is your alibi for Friday night, August twentieth?" young Salsbury would ask, tweaking the end, which might or might not be waxed. Then I should have to repeat for the mustache what I had told Mark about Friday night after I left Shelby waving after my taxi on Lexington Avenue.

Mark had asked me while we were having breakfast together—it seems a thousand breakfasts ago—to tell him precisely how I had spent every minute of that Friday night. He had known, of course, that I had let Shelby give the taxi-driver Waldo's address and that I had then instructed the man to take me to Grand Central.

"And after that?" Mark had said.

"I took the train."

"It was crowded?"

"Terribly."

"Did you see anyone you know? Or anyone who might be able to identify you?"

"Why do you ask me these questions?"

"Routine," he said, and handed me his empty cup. "You make excellent coffee, Laura."

"You ought to come up sometime when I bake a cake."

We laughed. The kitchen was cozy with the checked cloth and my blue Danish cups. I poured cream and put two lumps of sugar into his coffee.

"How did you know?" he said.

"I watched you before. Now when you come here, you will get so much cream and two lumps."

"I'll come often," he said.

He asked about my arrival in Wilton, and I told him about getting off the train at

South Norwalk and of walking quickly alone down that deserted street to the garage back of Andrew Frost's house for my car. Mark wanted to know if there weren't any public garages near the station, and I said I saved two dollars a month this way. That made him laugh again. "So you do have some thrift in you." There was little of the detective in him and much of the admiring male, so that I laughed, throwing back my head and searching his eyes. He asked if Andrew Frost or any of his family had seen me, and when I told him that Mr. Frost is a misogynist of seventy-four who sees me only the first Saturday of the month when I give him two dollars, Mark laughed uproariously and said, "That's a hell of an alibi."

I told him about driving to Norwalk on Saturday for my groceries, and he asked if anyone there would remember. But I told him I had saved money again, going to the Super-Market and trundling a basket through aisles filled with the working people of Norwalk and the summer crowd from the surrounding countryside. I could not remember whether it had been the red-headed cashier who took my money or the man with the cast in his eye. After I left the market, I told him, I had driven home, worked in the garden again, cooked myself a light dinner, and read until bedtime.

He said, "Is that all, Laura?"

Safe and friendly in my warm kitchen, I shuddered. Mark's eyes were fixed on my face. I seized the coffee pot and ran with it to the stove, turning my back to him and chattering swiftly of irrelevant things, wanting to cleanse my mind. There, at the stove, the coffee pot in my hand, I felt his eyes burning through me, piercing flesh and bone, seeing me as he had seen Diane's face, with all the paint and prettiness gone and only blood and membrane and hideous shattered bone.

He said: "And you stayed alone for the rest of the time you were there, Laura? You didn't see anyone who might have heard the radio or read the newspaper and come to tell you that you were dead?"

I repeated what I had told him the night before, that my radio was broken, and that the only people I had seen were the gardener and the Polish farmer from whom I had bought some corn and lettuce and fresh eggs.

Mark shook his head.

"You don't believe me," I said.

"It doesn't sound like . . . like your sort of woman."

"What do you mean, my sort of woman?"

"You have so many friends, your life is so full, you're always surrounded by people."

"It's when you have friends that you can afford to be lonely. When you know a lot of people, loneliness becomes a luxury. It's only when you're forced to be lonely that it's bad," I said.

Thin fingers drummed the table. I set the coffee pot upon the blue tile and my hand ached to stretch out and touch the wrist that protruded bonily from his white cuff. Mark's loneliness had not been luxury. He did not say this aloud, for he was a strong man and would never be wistful.

As I thought about this, lying in bed with the breakfast tray balanced on my legs, I knew I could never speak so easily to the black mustache of young Salsbury. A hell of an alibi, he would say, too, but it would be without the humor or tolerance that were in Mark's eyes and his voice.

Bessie brought the poached egg. "He's

a man," Bessie said abruptly. Bessie's attitudes are high Tenth Avenue; she is off the sidewalks of New York and as unrelenting as any snob that came out of Murray Hill's stone mansions. I had met her brothers, outspoken and opinionated workingmen whose black-and-white rules of virtue my intellectuals and advertising executives could never satisfy.

"A man," Bessie said. "Most of them that comes here are big babies or old women. For once, even if he's a dick, you've met a man." And then, completely in the groove of man-worship, added, "Guess I'll bake a chocolate cake."

I bathed and dressed slowly, and said to Bessie, "I'll wear my new suit on account of claustrophobia." In spite of the rain, I had decided to leave the house, looking so calmly adjusted to my own importance—like a model in *Vogue*—that the officer at the door would never dare question my leaving. I pulled on my best gloves and tucked my alligator bag under my arm. At the door, my courage failed. So long as I made no move that showed the desire to leave, this was my home; but it needed only a word from the man at the door to make it a prison.

This is a fear which has always lived in me. I leave my doors open because I am not so frightened of intruders as of being locked in. I thought of a movie I had once seen with Sylvia Sidney's pale, frightened face behind bars. "Bessie," I said, "I'd better stay home today. After all, the world still thinks I am dead."

My name was at that moment being shouted by hundreds of newsboys. When Bessie came from the market, she brought the papers. LAURA HUNT ALIVE! streamed across all the front pages. On one tabloid my face was blown up to page proportions and looked like a relief map of Asia Minor. What, I asked myself, would tomorrow's pages scream?

LAURA HUNT GUILTY?

I read that I was staying at an unnamed hotel. This was to fool the newspapermen and my friends and keep me safe from intrusion, Aunt Sue said when she came with red roses in her hands. She had not learned about me from the newspapers, but from Mark, who had awakened her that morning to bring the news.

"How thoughtful he is!" said Aunt Sue.

She had brought the roses to show that she was glad that I had not died, but she could do nothing except condemn me for having lent Diane my apartment. "I always said you'd get into trouble, being so easy with people."

Mark had not told her of the later developments. She knew nothing of the cigarette case nor of Shelby's suspicions. Shelby, who had been staying at her house, had not come home last night.

We talked about my funeral. "It was lovely," Aunt Sue said. "You couldn't expect a great attendance at this time of the year, too many people out of town, but most of them wired flowers. I was just about to write the thank-you notes. Now you can do it yourself."

"I wish I had seen the flowers," I said.

"You'll have to outlive them all. Nobody could take a second funeral seriously."

Bessie said there were people coming to the door in spite of the fact that I was supposed to be hidden in an unnamed hotel. But there were now two detectives on my doorstep and the bell did not ring. I kept looking at the clock, wondering why I had not heard from Mark.

"I'm sure he can't make more than eighteen hundred a year, two thousand at the most," Auntie Sue said suddenly.

I laughed. It was psychic, like Bessie's suddenly saying, "He's a man."

"Some men," said Auntie Sue, "are bigger than their incomes. It's not often that you find one like that."

"From you, Auntie Sue, that's heresy."

"Once I was crazy about a grip," she said. "Of course it was impossible. I had become a star and I was young. How would it have looked to the chorus girls? Natural selection is the bunk, darling, except in jungles."

Auntie Sue is always nicer when there are no men around. She is one of those women who must flirt with every taxi-driver and waiter. And then she is horrid because she must punish men for not desiring her. I love Auntie Sue, but when I am with her I am glad that I was never a famous beauty.

She said, "Are you in love with him, Laura?"

"Don't be silly," I said. "I've only known him . . ."

I couldn't count the hours.

She said: "You've been watching the clock and cocking your ear toward the door ever since I came. You don't hear half that I say . . ."

"There may be other things on my mind, Auntie Sue. Certain things about this murder," I said, knowing I should have asked about Salsbury, Haskins, Warder, and Bone.

"You're preoccupied, Laura. Your mind is filled with the man." She came across the room; she touched me with her soft, boneless hand. Through the varnish, I saw a young girl's face. "Don't fight yourself too hard, Laura. Not this time. I've seen you give yourself too easily to all the wrong people; don't hold out against the right one."

That was strange advice from Auntie Sue, but in it I saw the design of her discontent. After she had gone, I sat for a long time uncomfortably on the arm of a chair, thinking.

I thought of my mother and how she had talked of a girl's giving herself too easily. Never give yourself, Laura, she'd say, never give yourself to a man. I must have been very young when she first said it to me, for the phrase had become deeply part of my nature, like rhymes and songs I heard when I was too small to fasten my own buttons. That is why I have given so much of everything else; myself I have always withheld. A woman may yield without giving, as Auntie Sue had yielded to Uncle Horace when she had wanted to give herself to a grip in the theatre.

I was ashamed; I kept thinking of my own life that had seemed so honest; I hid my face from daylight; I thought of the way we proud moderns have twisted and perverted love, making arguments for this and that substitute, just as I make arguments for Jix and Lady Lilith when I write advertisements. Natural selection, Auntie Sue had said, was the bunk, except in jungles.

Someone had passed the detectives at the threshold. Feet ascended to my door. I hurried to open it.

And there was Waldo.

CHAPTER FIVE

"Millions of people in the city and environs," Waldo said, with envy in his voice, "are talking about Laura Hunt. Your name, witch, is sizzling on all the wires in the country."

"Do stop being childish, Waldo. I need help. You're the only person in the world I can talk to. Will you be serious?"

His eyes were small islands beyond rippling light on thick lenses. "What of Shelby?" His voice rang richly with triumph. "Isn't it his place to be at your side in the hour of travail?"

"Waldo, darling, this is a terrible and serious moment. You mustn't torture me now with your jealousy."

"Jealousy!" He hurled the word like a

weapon. "Oughtn't you to be more tolerant of jealousy, my sweet?"

We were strangers. A wall had risen between us. Waldo's jealousy had been there long before Shelby's time; Waldo had been clever and cruel at the expense of other attractive men. I had been wickedly amused and proud that my charms had roused passion in this curiously unimpassioned creature. What a siren I had thought myself, Laura Hunt, to have won the love of a man born without the capacity for loving! People used to remark, to tease, to raise questioning eyebrows when they spoke of Waldo's devotion, but I had smugly enjoyed my position as companion and protégée of a distinguished man. The solid quality of our friendship had been, from my side, founded on respect for his learning and joy in the gay acrobatics of his mind. He had always insisted on the gestures of courtship; wooing had gone on for seven years with flattery and flowers, expensive gifts and oaths of undying affection. The lover rôle had been too unwavering for honesty, but Waldo would never relax it, never for a moment let either of us forget that he wore trousers and I skirts. But there had been a certain delicacy in our avoiding any implication that the wooing might have purpose beyond its charm. Auntie Sue had often said that she would shiver if Waldo kissed her; he had kissed me often; it was his habit to kiss when we met and when we parted, and often affectionately over some compliment. I felt nothing, neither shivering repulsion nor answering flame. A kitten nuzzled against my legs, a dog licked my hands, a child's moist lips touched my cheeks: these were like Waldo's kisses.

He caught my two hands, sought my eyes, said: "I love your jealousy, Laura. You were magnificent when you assaulted her."

I jerked my hands free. "Waldo, what would you think if I were accused of the murder?"

"My dear child!"

"I have no alibi, Waldo, and there's a gun up at my place in the country. He went there last night, I'm sure. I'm frightened, Waldo."

The color had left his face. He was waxen.

"What are you trying to tell me, Laura?"

I told him about the cigarette case, the Bourbon bottle, about my lies and Shelby's lies, and of Shelby's saying before Mark that he had lied to protect me. "Shelby was here with Diane that night, you know. He says he knew when the gun was fired that I had come back."

Sweat shone on Waldo's upper lip and on his forehead. He had taken off his glasses and was staring at me through pale, naked eyes.

"There is one thing you haven't told me, Laura."

"But Waldo, you don't believe . . ."

"Did you, Laura?"

Newsboys filled the streets with gutturals whose syllable formed my name. The colors of the day were fading. A phosphorescent green streaked the sky. The rain was thin and chill like summer sleet.

"Laura!"

His naked eyes, conical in shape and gleaming with white light, were hard upon my face. I shrank from that strained scrutiny, but his eyes hypnotized me so that I could neither turn away nor lower my eyelids.

A far-off church clock struck five. This is the way one waits, I thought, for the doctor when he is coming to say that the sickness is fatal.

"You're thinking of that detective, you're waiting for him to come and arrest you! You want him to come, don't you?"

I was caught by his hands, pinioned by his eyes.

"You're in love with him, Laura. I saw it yesterday. You looked away from us, you shrank from your old friends, Shelby and I, we had ceased to matter. Your eyes were on him all the time; you fluttered like a moth; you rolled your eyes and smirked like a schoolgirl before a matinée idol."

His damp hands increased their cold pressure.

My voice, small and weak, denied his charges. He laughed.

"Don't lie, woman. I've got the eye of a fluoroscope. I perceive now the strange quiverings of the female heart. How romantic!" He shouted the word hideously. "The detective and the lady. Have you given yourself yet; has he won your confession?"

I pulled away. "Please don't talk like that, Waldo. We've only known each other since Wednesday night."

"He works fast."

"Do, do be serious, Waldo. I need help so badly."

"This, my pet, is the most serious and important help that I can give you. To put you on your guard against the most dangerous man you've ever known."

"That's ridiculous. Mark's done nothing."

"Nothing, darling, except seduce you. Nothing but win your heart, my girl. He's engaged your warm and ready affection for the honor and glory of the Detective Bureau."

"That's what Shelby said. He said that Mark was trying to make me confess."

"For once Shelby and I agree."

I went to the couch and sat on the edge, hugging a pillow. Rough linen scratched my cheek. Waldo came toward me gently and offered his scented handkerchief. Then I giggled and said, "When there's a crisis, I can never find my handkerchief."

"Depend upon me, child, I shan't desert you. Let them accuse you; we'll fight them." He stood above me, his legs spread apart, his head high, his hand thrust in his coat like Napoleon in the picture. "I've every weapon, money, connections, prestige, my column, Laura. From this day forth, every day, eighty syndicated essays will be devoted to the cause of Laura Hunt."

"Please, Waldo," I begged. "Please tell me. Do you believe me guilty, too?"

He held my hand between cold, perspiring palms. Softly, as if I were a sick, fractious child, Waldo said, "Why should I care whether you're guilty or not guilty as long as I love you, my dear?"

It was unreal; it was a scene from a Victorian novel. I sat with my hand locked in his hands, a frail creature, possessed, like a gentle, fading, troubled woman of long ago. And he, by contrast, had become strong and masterful, the protector.

"Do you think I'd condemn you for it, Laura? Or even blame you? On the contrary—" he pressed my hand "—on the contrary, I adore you as I've never adored you before. You shall be my heroine, Laura, my greatest creation; millions will read about you, will love you. I'll make you greater—" the words rolled on his tongue "—than Lizzie Borden."

He said it mischievously as if he had been asked in some parlor game, "What would you do if Laura were accused of murder?"

"Please," I begged him, "please be serious."

"Serious!" He caught my word and tossed it back, mocking me. "You've read enough of Waldo Lydecker to know how seriously I regard murder. It is," he said, "my favorite crime."

I leaped up, jerked my hand away; I put the room between us.

"Come back, my precious. You must rest. You're very nervous. And no wonder, darling, with those vultures feeding on you. Shelby, with his precious gallantry; the other one, that detective fellow scheming to raise himself to front-page glory; they would destroy your self-esteem and corrupt the courage of your passion."

"Then you do believe me guilty."

Phosphorescent light gave green tints to Waldo's skin. I felt that my face, too, must reflect the sickly tint of fear. With an almost surreptitious movement, I pulled the cord of the lamp. Out of shadows my room grew real. I saw familiar shapes and the solidity of furniture. On the table, red against the pale wall, were Auntie Sue's roses. I pulled one from the vase, touched the cool petal to my cheek.

"Say it, Waldo. You believe me guilty."

"I adore you for it. I see before me a great woman. We live in an unreal, a castrate world, you and I. Among us, there are few souls strong enough for violence. Violence—" he spoke it like a love-word, his voice was the voice of a lover on a pillow "—violence gives conviction to passion, my loveliest love. You are not dead, Laura; you are a violent, living, bloodthirsty woman."

Red petals lay scattered at my feet on the figured rug. My hands, cold and nervous, pulled the last petal from the rose.

CHAPTER SIX

This is no way to write the story. I should be simple and coherent, listing fact after fact, giving order to the chaos of my mind. When they ask me, "Did you return on Friday night to kill her, Laura?" I shall answer, "He hasn't the face of a man who would lie and flirt to get a confession"; and when they ask me about ringing the bell and waiting at the door for her to come and be killed, I shall tell them that I wish, more than anything in the world, that I had met him before this happened.

That's how my mind is now. For two hours I've been shivering in my slip, unable to go through the movements of undressing. Once, long ago, when I was twenty and my heart was broken, I used to sit like this at night on the edge of the bed in a room with stained walls. I'd think of the novel I was writing about a young girl and a man. The novel was bad; I never finished it; but the writing cleansed all my dusty emotional corners. But tonight writing thickens the dust. Now that Shelby has turned against me and Mark shown the nature of his trickery, I am afraid of facts in orderly sequence.

Shelby's treachery was served to us with dinner, accompanied by the raspings and groanings of rainy-weather static. I could not pretend to eat; my leaden hands refused to lift the fork; but Waldo ate as greedily as he listened to every morsel of news.

Shelby had gone to the police and sworn to the truth of his having been in the apartment with Diane on Friday night. He had told them, as he told me, how the doorbell rang and how Diane had clattered across the room in my silver mules, and how she had been shot when she opened my front door. Shelby said that Diane had summoned him to the apartment because she was afraid of violence. Diane had been threatened, Shelby said, and although he had not liked the idea of seeing her in

Laura's house, she had begged so pitifully that he could not deny her.

Shelby's attorney was N. T. Salsbury, Jr. He explained that Shelby had not confessed earlier because he was shielding someone. The name of the suspect was not included in the broadcasts. Deputy Commissioner Preble had refused to tell reporters whether or not the police knew whom Shelby was shielding. Shelby's confession had turned him into a witness for the State.

In every broadcast Deputy Commissioner Preble's name was mentioned three times a minute. Mark's name was not used at all.

"Poor McPherson," Waldo said as he dropped two saccharine pills into his coffee cup; "between Shelby and the Deputy Commissioner, he's been crowded out of the limelight."

I left the table.

Waldo followed me to the couch again, the coffee cup in his hands.

"He's not that sort at all," I said. "Mark isn't like that, he'd never sacrifice anyone . . . anyone for the sake of notoriety and his own career."

"You poor dear child," Waldo said. The coffee cup rang against the wood of the table, and Waldo's free hands reached again for my hand.

"He's playing a game, Laura; the fellow's devilishly clever. Preble is enjoying his little victory now, but the plum in this pudding will be pulled out by our own little Jack Horner. Heed my warning, sweet, before you're lost. He's after you; he'll be here soon enough with some scheme to worm that confession out of you."

The shadow of hysteria returned. I pulled my hand away, stretched on the couch, closed my eyes and shivered.

"You're cold," Waldo said, and went into the bedroom to fetch my afghan. He spread it over my legs, smoothing out the wrinkled surface, tucking it under my feet, and then standing above the couch again, content and possessive.

"I must protect my sweet child."

"I can't believe he's only been trying to get a confession. Mark liked me. And he's sincere," I said.

"I know him better than you do, Laura."

"That's what you think," I said.

"I've dined with the fellow practically

every night since this affair began, Laura. He's courted me strangely, why I cannot say, but I've had a rare chance to observe his nature and his methods."

"Then he must be interesting," I said. "In all the years I've known you, I've never seen you dine with a dull person."

"My dear babe, you must always justify your bad taste, mustn't you?" Waldo laughed. "I spend a few hours with the fellow; *ergo*, he becomes a man of wit and profundity."

"He's a lot more intelligent than a lot of people who go around calling themselves intellectuals."

"What a die-hard you are, once you're interested in a man! Very well, if it will please you I'll plead guilty to a certain shabby interest in the fellow. I must confess, though, that my curiosity was roused by observation of the blossoming of his love for you."

"For me!"

"Don't sing so high, sweet canary. You were dead. There was dignity in that frustrate passion. He could make no use of you, he could destroy you no further, you

were unattainable and thus desirable beyond all desire."

"How you twist things, Waldo! You don't
understand Mark. There's something about
him," I insisted, "something that's alive. If
he'd been wallowing in frustrated romance,
he'd never have been so glad when I came
back."

"Trickery."

"You and your words," I said. "You always have words, but they don't always tell
meanings."

"The man's a Scot, child, as parsimo-
nious with emotion as with shillings. Have
you ever analyzed that particular form of
romanticism which burgeons on the dead,
the lost, the doomed? Mary of the Wild
Moor and Sweet Alice With Hair So Brown,
their heroines are always dead or tubercu-
lar, death is the leit-motif of all their love-
songs. A most convenient rationale for the
thriftiness of their passion toward living females. Mark's future unrolls as upon a
screen." Waldo's plump hand unrolled the
future. "I see him now, romanticizing frustration, asking poor cheated females to
sigh with him over the dead love."

"But he was glad, glad when I came

alive. There was a special quality about his gladness as if—" I flung the words bravely "—as if he'd been waiting for me."

"Ah!" said Waldo. "When you came alive!" His voice bubbled. "When Laura became reality within his grasp, the other side of sentiment was revealed. The basic parsimony, the need to make profit of the living Laura."

"You mean that all of his kindness and sincerity were tricks to get a confession? That's silly," I said.

"Had he merely been trying to get a confession, the thing would have been simple. But consider the contradiction in the case. Compensation as well as confession, Laura. You had become reality, you came within the man's reach, a woman of your sort, cultivated, fastidious, clearly his superior; he was seized with the need to possess you. Possess and revenge and destroy."

He had seated himself on the couch, balancing his fat buttocks on the edge, holding my hand for support!

"Do you know Mark's words for women? Dolls. Dames." His tongue clicked out the words like a telegraph instrument clattering out the dots and dashes of a code. "What further evidence do you need of a man's vulgarity and insolence? There's a doll in Washington Heights who got a fox fur out of him—got it out, my dear, his very words. And a dame in Long Island whom he boasted of deserting after she'd waited faithfully for years."

"I don't believe a word."

"Remember the catalogue of your suitors, darling. Consider the past," Waldo said. "Your defense is always so earnest, you blush in that same delightful way and rebuke me for intolerance."

I saw shadows on the carpet. A procession passed through my mind of those friends and lovers whose manliness had dwindled as Waldo's critical sense showed me their weaknesses. I remembered his laughter, fatherly and indulgent, the first time he had taken me to the theatre and I had admired a handsome actor's bad performance.

"I hope it's not too tactless of me to mention the name of Shelby Carpenter. How much abuse I've endured because I failed to discern the manliness, the integrity, the hidden strength of that gallant poop! I humored you, I allowed you to enjoy self-deceit because I knew you'd ultimately find out for yourself. And look, today." He spread his hands in a gesture that included the rueful present.

"Mark's a man," I said.

Waldo's pale eyes took color; on his forehead the veins rose fat and blue; the waxen color of the skin deepened to an umber flush. He tried to laugh. Each note was separate and painful. "Always the same pattern, isn't it? A lean, lithe body is the measure of masculinity. A chiseled profile indicates a delicate nature. Let a man be hard and spare and you clothe him in the garments of Romeo, Superman, and Jupiter disguised as a bull.

"To say nothing," he added after a moment's dreadful silence, "of the Marquis de Sade. That need is in your nature, too."

"You can't hurt me," I said. "No man's ever going to hurt me again."

"I'm not speaking of myself," Waldo said reproachfully. "We were discussing your frustrated friend."

"But you're mad," I said. "He's not frustrated. He's a strong man; he's not afraid."

Waldo smiled as if he were bestowing

some rare confidence. "That incurable female optimism has, I dare say, blinded you to the fellow's most distinguishing defect. He guards it zealously, my dear, but watch the next time you see him. When you observe that wary, tortured gait, you'll remember Waldo's warnings."

"I don't understand you," I said. "You're making things up." I heard my voice as something outside of me, shrill and ugly, the voice of a sullen schoolgirl. Auntie Sue's red roses threw purple shadows on the green wall. There were calla lilies and water lilies in the design of the chintz curtains. I thought of colors and fabrics and names because I was trying to turn my mind from Waldo and his warnings.

"A man who distrusts his body, my love, seeks weakness and impotence in every other living creature. Beware, my dear. He'll find your weakness and there plant his seeds of destruction."

I felt sorry for myself; I had become disappointed in people and in living. I closed my eyes, I sought darkness; I felt my blood chill and my bones soften.

"You'll be hurt, Laura, because the need for pain is part of your nature. You'll be hurt because you're a woman who's attracted by a man's strength and held by his weakness."

Whether he knew it or not, this was the very history of our relationship, mine and Waldo's. In the beginning it had been the steely strength of his mind, but the ripeness of my affection had grown with my knowledge of his childlike, uncertain heart. It was not a lover that Waldo needed, but love itself. With this great fat man I had learned to be patient and careful as a woman is patient and careful with a sickly, sensitive child.

"The mother," Waldo said slowly, "the mother is always destroyed by her young."

I pulled my hand away quickly. I rose, I put the room between us; I retreated from lamplight and stood shivering in shadows.

Waldo spoke softly, a man speaking to shadows. "A clean blow," Waldo said, "a clean blow destroys quickly and without pain." His hands, it seems as I grope for clear recollection, were showing the precise shape of destruction.

He came toward me and I shrank deeper into the corner. This was strange. I had never felt anything but respect and tender-

ness for this brilliant, unhappy friend. And I
made myself think of Waldo dutifully; I
thought of the years we had known each
other and of his kindness. I felt sick within
myself, ashamed of hysteria and weak
shrinking. I made myself stand firm; I did
not pull away; I accepted the embrace as
women accept the caresses of men they
dare not hurt. I did not yield, I submitted. I
did not soften, I endured.

"You are mine," he said. "My love and
my own."

Dimly, beyond his murmuring, I heard
footsteps. Waldo's lips were pressed
against my hair, his voice buzzed in my
ears. Then there were three raps at the
door, the grating of the key in the lock, and
his embrace relaxed.

Mark had climbed the stairs slowly,
he was slow to open the door. I backed
away from Waldo, I straightened my dress,
pulled at my sleeves, and as I sat down,
jerked my skirt over my knees.

"He enters with a latchkey," Waldo said.

"The doorbell was the murderer's signal," Mark said. "I don't like to remind her."

"The manners of the executioner are

known to be excellent," Waldo said. "It was thoughtful of you to knock."

Waldo's warning had posted signals in my mind. Seeing Mark with his eyes, I became aware of the taut, vigilant erectness of his shoulders, the careful balance, the wary gait. It was not so much the quality of movement as the look on his face that told me Waldo had been right in saying that Mark guarded himself. He caught my curiosity and threw back a challenge as if he were saying that he could match scrutiny with scrutiny and, as mercilessly, expose my most cherished weakness.

Seating himself in the long chair, his thin hands gripping the arms, he seemed to relax watchfulness. Tired, I thought, and noticed the hint of purple in the shadows of the deep-set eyes, the tension of flesh across narrow cheek-bones. Then, quickly, hailing into my mind the scarlet caution signal, I banished quick and foolish tenderness. Dolls and dames, I said to myself; we're all dolls and dames to him.

He said, "I want to talk to you, Laura," and looked at Waldo as if to say that I must get rid of the intruder.

Waldo had grown roots in the couch.

Mark settled himself in the long chair, took out his pipe, gave notice of endurance.

Bessie slammed the kitchen door and shouted good night. One of them in Washington Heights had got a fox fur out of him, I told myself, and I wondered how much it had cost him in pride and effort. Then I faced him boldly and asked, "Have you come to arrest me?"

Waldo swayed toward me. "Careful, Laura; anything you say to him can be used against you."

"How gallantly your friends protect you!" Mark said. "Didn't Shelby warn you of the same thing last night?"

I stiffened at the sound of Shelby's name. Mark might be laughing at me, too, for having trusted a weak man. I said boldly: "Well, what did you come here for? Have you been to Wilton? What did you find at my place?"

"Sh-sh," cautioned Waldo.

"I don't see how it can hurt if I ask where he's been."

"You told me that you knew nothing of the murder, that you bought no newspapers and that the radio at your cottage was out of order. Isn't that what you told me, Laura?"

"Yes," I said.

"The first thing I discovered is that your radio works perfectly."

My cheeks burned. "But it didn't work then. Honestly. They must have fixed it. I told the boys at the electric shop near the railroad station in Norwalk to go up there and fix it. Before I caught my train I stopped and told them. They've got my key, that will prove it."

I had become so nervous that I ached to tear, to break, to scream aloud. Mark's deliberate hesitancy was aimed, I felt, at torturing the scene to hysterical climax. He told of checking on my actions since my alleged (that was his word) arrival in Wilton on Friday night, and of finding nothing better than the flimsy alibi I had given.

I started to speak, but Waldo signaled with a finger on his lips.

"Nothing I discovered up there," Mark said, "mitigates the case against you."

Waldo said, "How pious! Quite as if he had gone to seek evidence of your innocence rather than proof of your guilt. Amazingly charitable for a member of the Detective Bureau, don't you think?"

"It's my job to uncover all evidence, whether it proves guilt or innocence," Mark said.

"Come, now, don't tell me that guilt isn't preferable. We're realists, McPherson. We know that notoriety will inevitably accompany your triumph in a case as startling as this. Don't tell me, my dear fellow, that you're going to let Preble take all the bows."

Mark's face darkened. His embarrassment pleased Waldo. "Why deny it, McPherson? Your career is nourished by notoriety. Laura and I were discussing it at dinner; quite interesting, wasn't it, pet?" He smiled toward me as if we shared opinions. "She's as well aware as you or I, McPherson, of the celebrity this case could give your name. Consider the mutations of this murder case, the fascinating facets of this contradictory crime. A murder victim arises from the grave and becomes the murderer! Every large daily will send its ace reporters, all the syndicates will fill the courtroom with lady novelists and psychic analysts. Radio networks will fight for the right to establish broadcast studios within the court building.

War will be relegated to Page Two. Here, my little dears, is what the public wants, twopenny lust, Sunday supplement passion, sin in the Park Avenue sector. Hour by hour, minute by minute, a nation will wait for dollar-a-word coverage on the trial of the decade. And the murderess"—he rolled his eyes. "You, yourself, McPherson paid tribute to her ankles."

The muscles tightened on Mark's cheeks.

"Who emerges as the hero of this plushy crime?" Waldo went on, enjoying his eloquence. "The hero of it all, that dauntless fellow who uncovers the secrets of a modern Lucretia is none other—" Waldo rose, bowed low "—none other than our gallant McPherson, the limping Hawkshaw."

Mark's hand, curved around his pipe, showed white at the knuckles.

The quiet and the dignity irked Waldo. He had expected his victim to squirm. "All right, go ahead with it. Arrest her if you think you've got sufficient proof. Bring her to trial on your flimsy evidence; it will be a triumph, I assure you."

"Waldo," I said, "let's quit this. I'm quite prepared for anything that may happen."

"Our hero," Waldo said, with swelling pride and power. "But wait, Laura, until he hears a nation's laughter. Let him try to prove you guilty, my love, let him swagger on the witness stand with his few poor shreds of evidence. What a jackanapes he'll be after I get through with him! Millions of Lydecker fans will roll with mirth at the crude antics of the silver-shinned bumpkin."

Waldo had taken hold of my hand again, displaying possession triumphantly.

Mark said, "You speak, Lydecker, as if you wanted to see her tried for this murder."

"We are not afraid," Waldo said. "Laura knows that I will use all of my power to help her."

Mark became official. "Very well, then, since you're assuming responsibility for Miss Hunt's welfare, there's no reason why you shouldn't know that the gun has been discovered. It was in the chest under the window of her bedroom in her cottage. It's a lady's hunting gun marked with the initials D. S. C. and was once owned by Mrs. John Carpenter. It is still in good condition, has been cleaned, oiled, and discharged recently. Shelby has identified it as the gun he gave Miss Hunt . . ."

It had been like waiting for the doctor and being relieved when the final word killed all hope.

I pulled away from Waldo and stood before Mark. "All right," I said. "All right, I've been expecting it. My attorneys are Salsbury, Haskins, Warder, and Bone. Do I get in touch with them now, or do you arrest me first?"

"Careful, Laura."

That was Waldo. I paid no attention. Mark had risen, too; Mark stood with his hands on my shoulders, his eyes looking into mine. The air shivered between us. Mark looked sorry. I was glad, I wanted Mark to be sorry; I was less afraid because there was a sorry look in Mark's eyes. It is hard to be coherent, to set this all down in words; I can't always remember the right words. I know that I was crying and that Mark's coat-sleeve was rough.

Waldo watched us. I was looking at Mark's face, but I felt Waldo watching as if his eyes were shooting arrows into my back.

Waldo's voice said, "Is this an act, Laura?" Mark's arm tightened.

Waldo said: "A classic precedent, you know; you're not the first woman who's given herself to the jailer. But you'll never buy your freedom that way, Laura . . ."

Mark had deserted me, he stood beside Waldo, fists aimed at Waldo's waxen face. Waldo's eyes bulged behind his glasses, but he stood straight, his arms folded on his breast.

I ran to Mark, I pulled at his arms. I said: "Mark, please. It won't do any good to get angry. If you've got to arrest me, it's all right. I'm not afraid."

Waldo was laughing at us. "You see, my noble lad, she spurns your gallantry."

"I'm not afraid," I said to Waldo's laughter.

"You ought to have learned by now, my dear, that gallantry is the last refuge of a scoundrel."

I was looking at Mark's face. He had gone without sleep, he'd spent the night driving to Wilton, he was a tired man. But a man, as Bessie had said, and Auntie Sue, when she had contradicted her whole way of life to tell me that some men were bigger than their incomes. I had been gay enough, I'd had plenty of fun, enjoyed men's companionship, but there had been too many fussy old maids and grown-up babies. I took hold of Mark's arm again, I looked at him, I smiled to give myself courage. Mark wasn't listening to Waldo either, he was looking at my face and smiling delicately. I was tired, too, longing to cling and feel his strength, to rest my head against his shoulder.

"Tough, Hawkshaw, to have to pull in a doll? Before you've had the chance to make the grade with her, eh, Hawkshaw?"

Waldo's voice was shrill, his words crude and out of character. The voice and words came between Mark and me, our moment was gone, and I was holding air in my closed fingers.

Waldo had taken off his glasses. He looked at me with naked eyes. "Laura, I'm an old friend. What I'm saying may be distasteful, but I beg you to remember that you've known this man for only forty-eight hours . . ."

"I don't care," I said. "I don't care about time. Time doesn't mean anything."

"He's a detective."

"I don't care, Waldo. Maybe he could scheme and lay traps for crooks and rack-eteers, but he couldn't be anything but honest with me, could you, Mark?"

For all Mark saw of me, I might have lived in another world. He was staring at the mercury-glass vase on my mantel, the gift Waldo had given me at Christmas. I looked at Waldo, then; I saw the working of his thick, sensitive lips and the creeping mist that rose over his pale conical eye-balls.

Waldo's voice taunted and tore at me. "It's always the same, isn't it, Laura. The same pattern over and over, the same trap, the same eagerness and defeat. The lean, the lithe, the obvious and muscular, and you fail to sense the sickness and decay and corruption underneath. Do you re-member a man named Shelby Carpenter? He used you, too . . ."

"Shut up! Shut up! Shut up!" I shouted at Waldo's swollen eyes. "You're right, Waldo, it's the same pattern, the same sickness and decay and corruption, only they're in you. You! You, Waldo. It's your malice; you've mocked and ridiculed and ruined every hope I've ever had, Waldo. You hate the men I like, you find their weak places, you make them weaker, you've teased and shamed them before my eyes until they've hated me!"

Bloodthirsty, Waldo had called me, and bloodthirsty I had become in the sudden fever of hating him. I had not seen it clearly with Shelby or the others, I had never smelled the malice until he tried to shame Mark before me. I shouted bravely; I spoke as if I had known before, but I had been too blind and obstinate to see how his sharp little knife-thrusts had hurt my friends and destroyed love for me. I saw it clearly now, as if I were a god upon a mountain, looking down at humans through a clear light. And I was glad for my anger; I exulted in hatred; I screamed for revenge; I was bloodthirsty.

"You're trying to destroy him, too. You hate him. You're jealous. He's a man. Mark's a man. That's why you've got to destroy him."

"Mark needs no help," Waldo said. "Mark seems quite capable of self-destruction."

Waldo could always do that to me, always diminish me in an argument, turning my just anger into a fish-wife's cheap frenzy. My face felt its ugliness and I turned so that Mark should not see me. But Mark was untouched, he held himself scornful. As I turned, Mark's arm caught me, pulled me close, and I stood beside Mark.

"So you've chosen?" Waldo said, his voice an echo of mockery. There was no more strength in the poison. Mark's hard, straight, unwavering gaze met Waldo's oblique, taunting glance and Waldo was left without defenses, except for the small shrill weapon of petulance.

"Blessings upon your self-destruction, my children," Waldo said, and settled his glasses on his nose.

He had lost the fight. He was trying to make a dignified retreat. I felt sorry. The anger was all drained out of me, and now that Mark had taken my fear, I had no wish to punish Waldo. We had quarreled, we had unclothed all the naked venom of our disappointments, we were finished with friendship; but I could not forget his kindness and generosity, the years behind us, the jokes and opinions we had shared. Christmas and birthdays, the intimacy of our little quarrels.

"Waldo," I said, and took a half-step toward him. Mark's arm tightened, he caught me, held me, and I forgot the old friend standing with his hat in his hand at my door. I forgot everything; I melted shamelessly, my mind clouded; I let go of all my taut fear; I lay back in his arms, a jade. I did not see Waldo leave nor hear the door close nor recollect the situation. What room was there in me for any sense of danger, any hint of trickery, any memory of warning? My mother had said, never give yourself, and I was giving myself with wayward delight, spending myself with such abandon that his lips must have known and his heart and muscles that he possessed me.

He let go so suddenly that I felt as if I'd been flung against a wall. He let go as if he had tried to conquer and had won, and were eager to be finished.

"Mark!" I cried. "Mark!"

He was gone.

That was three hours ago, three hours and eighteen minutes. I am still sitting on the edge of the bed, half-undressed. The night is damp and there is a dampness like dew on my flesh. I feel dull and dead; my hands are so cold that I can barely hold the pencil. But I must write; I have to keep on writing it down so I can clear my mind of confusion and think clearly. I have tried to remember every scene and incident and every word he said to me.

Waldo had warned me; and Shelby. He's a detective. But if he believed me guilty, why are there no more guards outside? Or had he grown fond of me and, believing me guilty, given me this chance to escape? Every excuse and every solace are crowded out of my mind by Waldo's warnings. I had tried to believe that these warnings were born of Waldo's jealousy; that Waldo had contrived with cruel cunning to equip Mark with a set of faults and sins that were Waldo's own disguised weaknesses.

The doorbell is ringing. Perhaps he has come back to arrest me. He will find me like a slut in a pink slip with a pink strap falling over my shoulder, my hair unfastened. Like a doll, like a dame, a woman to be used by a man and thrown aside.

The bell is still ringing. It's very late. The street has grown quiet. It must have been like this the night Diane opened the door for the murderer.

PART FIVE

PART FIVE

CHAPTER ONE

In the files of the Department you will find full reports on the Laura Hunt case. As officially recorded the case seems like hundreds of other successful investigations: Report of Lieutenant McPherson; Report of Sergeant Mooney; Report of Lieutenant McPherson; case closed, August 28th.

The most interesting developments of the case never got into the Department files. My report on that scene in Laura's living room, for instance, read like this:

At 8.15 found Lydecker in Hunt apartment with Laura. He was doing some fast talking to prove that I was plotting to get her to confess. Stayed until 9.40 (approx.), when he left; sent Behrens and Muzzio, who had been stationed at door, to trail him. I proceeded to Claudius Cohen's place . . ."

The story deserves more human treatment than police records allow.

I want to confess, before I write any more, that Waldo's unfinished story and Laura's manuscript were in my hands before I put a word on paper. In writing that section which comes between his document and Laura's, I have tried to tell what happened as it happened, without too much of my own opinion or prejudice. But I am human. I had seen what Waldo wrote about me and had read Laura's flattering comments. My opinions were naturally influenced.

I can't help wondering what would have happened if the Deputy Commissioner hadn't pulled the snide trick of assigning me to the case when he knew I was counting on a Saturday afternoon at Ebbetts Field. The murder might never have been uncovered. I say this without trying to take any bows for solving the mystery. I fell for a woman and she happened to like me. That circumstance furnished the key that unlocked the main door.

I knew from the start that Waldo was hiding something. I cannot honestly say that I suspected him of love or murder. That Sunday morning when he looked in the mirror and talked about his innocent face, I knew I was playing with a screwball. But it was not unpleasant; he was always good company. He had told me plainly that he had loved Laura, but I thought that he had become adjusted to the rôle of faithful friend.

I had to know what he was hiding, although I suspected the sort of game that would make an amateur feel superior to a professional detective. Waldo imagined himself a great authority on crime.

I played my own game. I flattered him, I sought his company, I laughed at his jokes; while I asked questions about Laura's habits, I studied his. What made a man collect old glassware and china? Why did he carry a stick and wear a beard? What caused him to scream when someone tried to drink out of his pet coffee cup? Clues to character are the only clues that add up to the solution of any but the crudest crime.

Before that night in Montagnino's back yard when he told me about the song,

Waldo's talk had made his *love* for Laura sound like a paternal and unromantic relationship. It was then that I began to see his midnight walks as something besides the affectation of a man who considered himself an heir to the literary tradition. Perhaps he had not spent all of Friday night reading Gibbon in a tepid bath.

Then Laura returned. When I discovered that it was Diane Redfern who had been murdered, I went completely off the track. There were so many crossed wires; Shelby, three unexplained lies, a gold cigarette case. During that stage of the investigation, I couldn't help looking in the mirror and asking myself if I looked like the kind of sucker who trusts a woman.

Shelby honestly believed that his fatal beauty had led Laura to murder. To relieve his two-timing conscience, Shelby protected her. If I ever saw gallantry in the reverse, that was it.

But Shelby was no coward. He risked his neck that night he went up to her cottage to get the gun. He failed because a yellow taxi was on his trail, and even Shelby was smart enough to know the Department wasn't spending money just to give one of its men a joy ride. When Shelby saw that shotgun for the first time after the murder, it lay on my desk.

The gun was a clue to Shelby. It was marked with his mother's initials. C stood for Carpenter, S for Shelby, and D for Delilah. I could see him as a kid in knee-pants and a Buster Brown collar reciting pieces for a mother named Delilah.

He told me the gun had been used a month before. He had shot a rabbit.

I said: "Look here, Carpenter, you can relax. If you tell the truth now, we might be able to overlook a few dozen lies that make you an accessory after the fact. Tomorrow may be too late."

He looked at me as though I'd said out loud what I thought about Delilah. He would never turn State's evidence, no suh, not a descendant of the Shelbys of Kentucky. That was an underworld trick which no gentleman could sanction.

It took three hours for me to make him understand the difference between a gentleman and an ordinary heel. Then he broke down and asked if he might send for his lawyer.

I let Preble give out the news of Shelby's

confession because I was playing a game with him, too. In world politics it's called appeasement. From Preble's point of view, the gun and Shelby's confession clinched the evidence against Laura. She looked as guilty as Ruth Snyder. We could have booked her then and there on suspicion of murder. A quick arrest, Preble thought, would bring a juicy confession. And orchids for the Department under the efficient administration of Deputy Commissioner Preble.

I could see his hand as clearly as though he'd shown me the cards. This was Friday, and on Monday the Commissioner would be back from his vacation. Preble had little time to garner his share of personal publicity. And this case, since Laura had come back alive, was strictly Front Page, and coast to coast on the networks. Preble's wife and kids were waiting at a summer hotel in the Thousand Islands to hear over the air waves that Papa had solved the murder mystery of the decade.

We had a knock-down and drag-out argument. I wanted time, he wanted action. I called him the worn-out wheelhorse of a political party that should have been buried years ago under a load of cow manure. He told the world that I was hanging on to the bandwagon of the party in power, a bunch of filthy Reds who'd sell the country short for thirty pieces of Moscow gold. I said he belonged back with the Indian chiefs who'd given their name to his stinking loyalties, and he said I'd send my old mother out on the Bowery if I thought it would further my career. I am not reporting our actual language because, as I mentioned before, I haven't had a college education and I keep my writing clean.

It ended in a draw.

"If you don't bring in the murderer, dead or alive, by tomorrow morning . . ."

"You're damned tooting," I said. "I'll have him stuffed and trussed and ready for your breakfast."

"Her," he said.

"Wait," I bluffed.

I hadn't a shred of evidence that wasn't against Laura. But even though my own hands had dragged that gun from the chest in her bedroom, I couldn't believe her guilty. She might conk a rival with a trayful of hors d'oeuvres, but she could no more plan a murder than I could go in for collecting antique glassware.

It was around eight o'clock. I had about twelve hours to clear Laura and prove that I wasn't one hundred per cent sucker.

I drove up to Sixty-Second Street. When I opened the door, I knew that I had burst in on a love-scene. It was the fat man's field day. Shelby had betrayed her and I seemed to be threatening her with arrest. He was the man in possession, and the deeper the spot she was in, the greater her need for him, the surer his hold. It would have been to his advantage in more ways than one to have her tried for murder.

My presence was poison to him. His face took on the color of cabbage and his fat flesh shook like cafeteria jello. He tried his best to make me look cheap, a cheap dick who'd try to make a woman fall for me so that I could advance myself. It was something like Preble's remark about my sending my mother out on the Bowery to help my career. Remarks like this are not so much accusations as revelations. Frightened people try to defend themselves by accusing others of their own motives. This was never so clear as when Waldo began to make cracks about my bad leg. When a man goes so far below the belt, you can be sure he's hiding his own weakness.

At that moment I quit thinking of Waldo as the faithful old friend. I understood why his manner toward me had changed after Laura came back. He had made a great romance of my interest in the dead girl; it gave him a companion in frustration. But with Laura alive, I had become a rival.

I sat back and listened while he called me names. The shabbier he tried to make me look, the more clearly I saw his motives. For eight years he had kept her for himself by the destruction of her suitors. Only Shelby had survived. Shelby might have been a weak man, but he was too stubborn to let himself be ousted. He had allowed Waldo to insult him again and again, but he had stuck, finding solace in playing big shot for Diane.

The pattern had straightened out, but evidence was lacking. I saw myself as the Deputy Commissioner might see me, a stubborn jackass working on instinct against known fact. Training and experience had taught me that instinct had no value in the courtroom. Your Honor, I know this man to have been bitterly jealous. Try that on the witness stand and see how far you get.

Under ordinary circumstances I do my love-making in private. But I had to turn the screws on Waldo's jealousy. When I took Laura in my arms, I was playing a scene. Her response almost ended my usefulness in the case. I knew she liked me, but I hadn't asked for heaven.

She believed that I was embracing her because she had been hurt and I, loving her, offered comfort and protection. That was the deeper truth. But I had Waldo on my mind, too. The love-scene was too strong for his sensitive nerves, and he slipped out.

I had no time to explain anything. It wasn't easy to break away, leaving Laura to think that Waldo had been right in accusing me of using her sincerity as a trap. But he was gone and I could take no chance of losing him.

I lost him.

Behrens and Muzzio let him pass. By my own instructions Waldo Lydecker had been allowed to come and go as he chose. The two cops had been lounging on the stoop, bragging about their kids probably, and not paying the slightest attention to his movements. It was my fault, not theirs.

There was no trace of his great bulk, his decorated chin, his thick cane, on Sixty-Second Street. Either he had turned the corner or he was hiding in some dark areaway. I sent Behrens toward Third Avenue and Muzzio to Lexington and ordered them to find and trail him. I jumped into my car.

It was just eighteen minutes of ten when I found Claudius putting up his shutters.

"Claudius," I said, "tell me something. Are people who collect antiques always screwy?"

He laughed.

"Claudius, when a man who's crazy about this old glassware finds a beautiful piece that he can't own, do you think he'd deliberately smash it so that no other man could ever enjoy it?"

Claudius licked his lips. "Guess I know what you're talking about, Mr. McPherson."

"Was it an accident last night?"

"I couldn't say yes and I couldn't say no. Mr. Lydecker was willing to pay and I took the money, but it could've been an accident. You see, I hadn't put any shot in . . ."

"Shot? What do you mean, shot?"

"Shot. We use it to weight down stuff when it's light and breakable."

"Not BB shot," I said.

"Yes," he said, "BB shot."

I had looked over Waldo's antiques once while I was waiting for him. There had been no BB shot weighing the old cups and vases down, but he was not such a cluck as to leave unmistakable evidence around for the first detective. I wanted to make a thorough examination this time, but I had no time to get a warrant. I entered the building through the basement and climbed eighteen flights to his apartment. This was to avoid the elevator man, who had begun to welcome me as Mr. Lydecker's best pal. If Waldo came home, he was not to have any suspicions that would cause him to leave hastily.

I let myself in with a passkey. The place was silent and dark.

There had been a murder. There had to be a gun. It wasn't a shotgun, whole or sawed-off. Waldo wasn't the type. If he owned a gun, it would look like another museum piece among the China dogs and shepherdesses and old bottles.

I made a search of cabinets and shelves in the living-room, then went into the bedroom and started on the dresser drawers. Everything he owned was special and rare. His favorite books had been bound in selected leathers, he kept his monogrammed handkerchiefs and shorts and pajamas in silk cases embroidered with his initials. Even his mouthwash and toothpaste had been made up from special prescriptions.

I heard the snap of the light switch in the next room. My hand went automatically to my hip pocket. But I had no gun. As I had once told Waldo, I carry weapons when I go out to look for trouble. I hadn't figured on violence as part of this evening's entertainment.

I turned quickly, put myself behind a chair, and saw Roberto in a black silk dressing-gown that looked as if he was paying the rent for this high-class apartment.

Before he had time to ask questions, I said: "What are you doing here? Don't you usually go home nights?"

"Mr. Lydecker need me tonight," he said.

"Why?"

"He not feel himself."

"Oh," I said, and took the cue. "That's why I'm here, Roberto. Mr. Lydecker didn't feel himself at dinner, so he gave me the key and asked me to come up and wait for him."

Roberto smiled.

"I was just going to the bathroom," I said. That seemed the simplest explanation of my being in the bedroom. I went to the bathroom. When I came out, Roberto was waiting in the parlor. He asked if I'd like a drink or a cup of coffee.

"No, thanks," I said. "You run along to bed. I'll see that Mr. Lydecker's okay." He started to leave, but I called him back. "What do you think's the matter with Mr. Lydecker, Roberto? He seems nervous, doesn't he?"

Roberto smiled.

I said, "It's this murder; it's been getting on his nerves, don't you think?"

His smile got me nervous. Even the Rhode Island clam was a big talker compared with this Filipino oyster.

I said, "Did you ever know Quentin Waco?"

That woke him up. There are only a few Filipinos in New York and they stick together like brothers. All the houseboys used to put their money on Quentin Waco, who was top lightweight until he got mixed up with the girls around the Sixty-Sixth Street dancehalls. He spent more than he made, and when young Kardansky knocked him out, they accused him of pulling the fight. One of Quentin's pals met him at the door of the Shamrock Ballroom one night and pulled a knife. For the honor of the Islands, he told the judge. A little later it came out that Quentin hadn't pulled the fight, and the boys made a martyr of him. The religious ones kept candles burning in a church on Ninth Avenue.

I happened to have been the man who got hold of the evidence that cleared Quentin's name and, without knowing it, restored the honor of the Islands. When I told this to Roberto, he stopped smiling and became human.

We talked about Mr. Lydecker's health. We talked about the murder and about Laura's return. Roberto's point of view was strictly out of the tabloids. Miss Hunt was a nice lady, always friendly to Roberto, but her treatment of Mr. Lydecker showed her to have been no better than a dance-hall hostess. According to Roberto all women were the same. They'd turn down a steady fellow every time for a big sport guy who knew all the latest steps.

I jerked the talk around to the dinner he had cooked on the night of the murder. It wasn't hard to get him going on that subject. He wanted to give me a mushroom by mushroom description of the menu. Every half-hour during the afternoon, Roberto said, Mr. Lydecker had quit his writing and come into the kitchen to taste, smell, and ask questions.

"We have champagne; six dollars a bottle," Roberto bragged.

"Oh, boy!" I said.

Roberto told me there had been more than food and wine prepared for that evening. Waldo had arranged the records on his automatic phonograph so that Laura should enjoy her favorite music with the meal.

"He certainly prepared. What a disappointment when Miss Hunt changed her mind!" I said. "What did he do, Roberto?"

"Not eat."

Waldo told us he had eaten a solitary meal and spent the evening reading Gibbon in the bathtub.

"He didn't eat, huh? Wouldn't go near the table?"

"He go table," Roberto said. "He have me bring food, he put on plate, not eat."

"I don't expect he played the phonograph either."

"No," said Roberto.

"He hasn't played it since, I suppose."

The phonograph was big and expensive. It played ten records, then turned them over and played the other side. I looked at them to see if any of the tunes checked with the music they had talked about. There was none of this Toccata and Fugue stuff, but a lot of old songs from shows. The last was "Smoke Gets in Your Eyes."

"Roberto," I said, "maybe I'll have a whiskey anyway."

I thought of that hot night in Montagnino's back yard. A storm had been rolling in and the lady at the next table sang with the music. Waldo had talked about hearing that song with Laura as if there had been a lot more to it than just listening to music with a woman.

"I think I'll have another, Roberto."

I needed Scotch less than I needed time to think it out. The pieces were beginning to fit together. The last dinner before her marriage. Champagne and her favorite songs. Memories of shows they had seen together, talk of the past. Old stories retold. And when the meal was over and they were drinking brandy, the last record would fall into place, the needle fit into the groove.

Roberto waited with a glass in his hand. I drank. I was cold and sweating.

Since that Sunday when I'd first walked into his apartment, I'd been reading the complete works of Waldo Lydecker. There is no better key to a man's character than his use of the written word. Read enough of any man's writing and you'll have his Number One Secret. There was a line that I remembered from one of his essays: "The high crisis of frustration."

He had planned so carefully that even the music was timed for it. And that night Laura had failed to show up.

I said: "Go to bed, Roberto. I'll wait up for Mr. Lydecker."

Roberto disappeared like a shadow.

I was alone in the room. Around me were his things, spindly overdecorated furniture, striped silks, books and music and antiques. There had to be a gun somewhere. When murder and suicide are planned like a seduction, a man must have his weapon handy.

CHAPTER TWO

While I waited in his parlor, Waldo was pounding his stick along the pavements. He dared not look backward. His pursuers might see him turn his head and know that he was frightened.

Muzzio caught sight of him almost a block ahead on Lexington. Waldo gave no sign that he observed Muzzio, but walked on quickly, turning east at Sixty-Fourth. At the end of the block, he saw Behrens, who had turned north on Third Avenue.

Waldo disappeared. The two men searched every areaway and vestibule on the block, but Waldo had evidently used the service tunnel of a big apartment house, gone through the basement to the rear of the building, and found another basement and service entrance on Seventy-Second.

He walked for three hours. He passed a lot of people on their way home from theatres and picture shows and bars. He met them in the light of arc lamps and under the lighted marquees of picture shows. We learned about it later the way we always do when an important case is finished and people phone in to make themselves important. Mary Lou Simmons, fifteen, of East Seventy-Sixth, had been frightened by a man who darted out of the vestibule as she came home from an evening at a girl chum's house. Gregory Finch and Enid Murphy thought it was Enid's father leaning over the banister in the dark hall where they were kissing. Mrs. Lea Kantor saw a giant ghost behind her newsstand. Several taxi-drivers had stopped in the hope of picking up a passenger. A couple of drivers had recognized Waldo Lydecker.

He walked until the streets were quiet. There were few taxis and hardly any pedestrians. He chose the darkest streets, hid in doorways, crouched on subway steps. It was almost two o'clock when he came back to Sixty-Second Street.

There was only one lighted window on

the block. According to Shelby, that light had been burning on Friday night, too.

Her door was not guarded. Muzzio was still waiting on Sixty-Fourth Street and Behrens had gone off duty. I had given no instructions for a man to replace him, for I had no idea, when I left Laura alone and sent the men to follow him, that he was carrying his weapon.

He climbed the steps and rang her doorbell.

She thought I had come back to arrest her. That seemed more reasonable than a return of the murderer. For a moment she thought of Shelby's description of Diane's death. Then she wrapped herself in a white bathrobe and went to the door.

By that time I knew Waldo's secret. I found no gun in his apartment; he was carrying the gun concealed on his person, loaded with the rest of the BB shot. What I found was a pile of unfinished and unpublished manuscript. I read it because I was planning to wait in the apartment, confront him, make the accusation, and see what happened. I found the following sentence in a piece called "The Porches of Thy Father's Ear":

In the cultivated individual, malice, a weapon darkly concealed, wears the garments of usefulness, flashes the disguise of wit or flaunts the ornaments of beauty.

The piece was about poisons hidden in antique rings, of swords in sticks, of firearms concealed in old prayer-books.

It took me about three minutes to realize that he was carrying a muzzle-loader. Last night, when we were leaving the Golden Lizard, I had tried to look at his stick. He had snatched it away with a crack about getting me a rubber-tipped cane. That crack was loaded. Resentment kept me from asking any more questions. Possessions were like people with Waldo. He wanted to protect his precious stick from my profane hands, so he brought out his malice without the garments of wit or beauty. I had thought that he was showing off another of his whims, like drinking his coffee from the Napoleon cup.

Now I knew why he had wanted to keep me from examining his cane. He carried it, he had told me, to give himself importance. There was the man's hidden power. He probably smiled as he stood before Laura's door, preparing to use his secret weapon. The second time was like the first. In his failing and disordered mind there was no original crime, no repetition.

When the doorknob turned, he aimed. He knew Laura's height and the place where her face would appear like an oval in the dark. As the door opened, he fired.

There was a shivering crash. Turning, Laura saw a thousand slivers of light. The shot, missing her by the fraction of an inch, had shattered the glass bowl. Its fragments shone on the dark carpet.

He had missed his aim because, as he fired, his legs were jerked out from under him. I had left his apartment as soon as I realized where the gun was hidden and re-membered that I had deliberately put on a scene to stir up his jealousy. He was on the third-floor landing, his finger on the bell, when I opened the door downstairs.

The old-fashioned hall was dimly lighted. On the landings pale bulbs glowed. Waldo was struggling for his life with an enemy whose face he couldn't see. I am a younger man, in better condition, and know how to handle myself in a fight. But he had the strength of desperation. And a gun in his hand.

When I jerked his legs out from under him, he rolled over on top of me. Laura came out of her door, looked down at us, straining to see our dark struggle on the staircase. We rolled down the steps.

Under the bulb of the second-floor landing I saw his face. He had lost his glasses, but his pale eyes seemed to see into the distance. He said, "While a whole city pursued the killer, Waldo Lydecker, with his usual urbanity, pursued the law."

He laughed. My spine chilled. I was fighting a madman. His face contorted, his lips writhed, pointed eyeballs seemed to jerk out of their sockets. He wrenched his arm loose, raised the gun, waved it like a baton.

"Get back! Get out of the way!" I shouted up at Laura.

His flesh had seemed flabby, but there were over two hundred and fifty pounds of it, and when I jerked his arm back, he rolled over on me. The light flashed in his eyes, he recognized me, sanity returned, and with it, hatred. White streaks of foam soaped his lips. Laura called out, warning me, but his groans were closer to my ears. I managed to shove my knees up under his fat belly and push him back toward the post of the banister. He waved his gun, then shot wild, firing without aim. Laura screamed.

With the firing of that shot, his strength was gone. His eyes froze, his limbs became rigid. But I was taking no chances. I knocked his head against the banister post. On the third-floor landing, Laura heard bone crack against wood.

In the ambulance and at the hospital he kept on talking. Always about himself, always in the third person. Waldo Lydecker was someone far away from the dying fat man on the stretcher, he was like a hero a boy has always worshiped. It was the same thing over and over again, never straight and connected, but telling as much as a sworn confession.

Ever the connoisseur who cunningly mates flavor with occasion, Waldo Lydecker selected the vintage of the year '14 . . .

As might Cesare Borgia have diverted himself on an afternoon pregnant with the infant of new infamy, so Waldo Ly-

decker passed the nervous hours in civilized diversion, reading and writing . . .

A man might sit thus, erect as a tombstone, while composing his will; so sat Waldo Lydecker at his rosewood desk writing the essay that was to have been his legacy . . .

The woman had failed him. Secret and alone, Waldo Lydecker celebrated death's impotence. Bitter herbs mingled their savor with the mushrooms. The soup was rue-scented . . .

Habit led Waldo Lydecker that night past windows illumined by her treachery . . .

Calm and untroubled, Waldo Lydecker stood, pressing an imperious finger against her doorbell . . .

When he died, the doctor had to unclasp the fingers that gripped Laura's hand.

"Poor, poor Waldo," she said.

"He tried to kill you twice," I reminded her.

"He wanted so desperately to believe I loved him."

I looked at her face. She was honestly mourning the death of an old friend. The malice had died with him and Laura remembered that he had been kind. It is generosity, Waldo said, not evil, that flourishes like the green bay tree.

He is dead now. Let him have the last word. Among the papers on his desk I found the unfinished piece, that final legacy which he had written while the records were waiting on the phonograph, the wine being chilled in the icebox, Roberto cooking the mushrooms.

He had written:

Then, as the final contradiction, there remains the truth that she made a man of him as fully as man could be made of that stubborn clay. And when that frail manhood is threatened, when her own womanliness demands more than he can give, his malice seeks her destruction. But she is carved from Adam's rib, indestructible as legend, and no man will ever aim his malice with sufficient accuracy to destroy her.

THE END